WILD ENOUGH

RIVER'S EDGE SERIES

BOOK ONE

BONNIE POIRIER

THINGS IN THIS BOOK

Welcome to the town of River's Edge, Alberta Canada.

This is a fictional town set where the foothills meet the Rocky Mountains.

This book is set in Canada and there for will have an added U in places. Words like colour, honour or neighbour. R's come after E's in words like metre.

Distance is measured in kilometres or drive time. It takes Wyatt two hours to get to Calgary. What's the distance? Who knows but it takes two hours.

So sit back and enjoy the read, I promise there's no Eh's in this book other than this sentence.

There's statements like "yeah, no" which means no. The last word's always your answer.

So grab your toques, and your 2-4, pull up a chair and enjoy the book!

B.

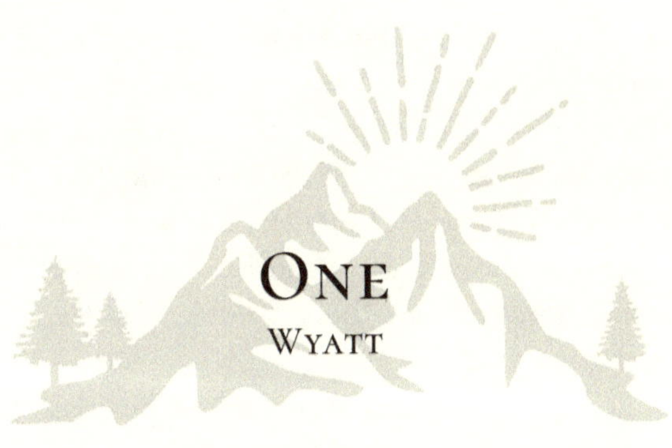

ONE
WYATT

Ray Callahan died the way he lived, stubborn as the devil and set on doing things the hard way. I could still hear his gravelly voice in my head, sharp as rusted barbed wire.

"You think I can't mend a simple goddamn fence, Wyatt? I was fixing this fence line before you were out of diapers."

He'd been leaning against the gate that morning with one elbow perched on the fence post and the other rubbing that stiff knee that had been giving him trouble as long as I'd known him. The sun was already high, the horses restless in the corral behind me, and dust rose off the dry ground like smoke. The faint, sweet scent of fermenting barley drifted over from Hargrove Brewing, three miles north of where we were standing. It was the smell of progress, a smell Ray hated. His attitude ran hotter than the August heat on our backs.

"Your heart's been acting up," I said flatly. It wasn't concern for the sake of it, though anyone with half a brain could see he needed watching. He asked me to look at the east fence the week before. I'd ridden the line, seen the rot, seen the wire splitting apart like frayed hair. It needed more than a hammer and a stubborn streak.

"Sell me your land, Ray, I'll take care of everything. You can stay in the house; I don't want or need it. Take a load off yourself and let me help." I pleaded. Ray was in trouble, and unless someone else with deeper pockets came along, I was the only one who could help him. I needed his land, and he needed to retire.

He hadn't liked hearing that. Ray stepped right into my space, his chin jutting like picking a fight might keep him upright. "I'm fine, and I'm not fucking selling you my land so you can destroy it. It's prime pasture land, not farmland," he shouted back at me.

It was true: the land was prime real estate, but it was being wasted on pasture. It was meant for farming, or that's what the soil testing I'd done said loud and clear. I needed it for the brewery. I'd wait him out and buy it at auction to clear his debt, or he would sell it to me at a value that he'd still be able to live. At this point, it was up to him; if I bought it now, at least he'd keep his dignity.

"You're not fine, Ray."

"Don't tell me what I am." He jabbed a gnarled, sun-leathered finger into my chest with all the brittle pride in the world, a finger that shook just enough to betray him. "I'll fix the fence myself. And when I'm done, I'm calling my niece. The one in Calgary."

I stared down at that finger and fought the urge to snap it off. "You'll fall over before you make it to the first post. And you only have one niece, Ray. I know where she lives." I resisted rolling my eyes at the old man.

He scoffed, pushed off the gate, and stomped up the path toward the house, muttering about young men who thought they knew everything. I let him go. Arguing with Ray was like arguing with a stubborn horse or with God. Pointless and loud. When he slammed the door behind him, I sighed, rolled my shoulders then sent two of my guys to fix the fence anyway. Not for Ray. For the cattle. Winter wasn't far off, and loose livestock in the foothills was every rancher's nightmare.

A few hours passed before I headed up to tell him the job was done. The house was quiet, a little too quiet. Inside, the air felt stale, heavy with old coffee and dust. The TV murmured, playing one of those cowboy shows Ray liked, where men solved their problems with silence and rifles.

"Ray?" I called. Nothing.

I stepped into the living room, boots thudding on the floorboards, and saw him slumped in his recliner like he drifted to sleep. His head tipped to the side, and the wrinkles at the corners of his eyes softened. One worn hand rested limply on his lap, fingers slack. A coffee cup sat half full on the table beside him, a faint brown ring marking where the liquid had cooled.

Something inside me dropped, flat and final. I crouched down beside him, my knees creaking in protest.

"God dammit, Ray," I muttered. I wasn't family. Half the time, I wouldn't have even called myself a friend. But Ray was Ray. A fixture. A thorn. A pain in my ass I'd grown used to sparring with. We fought because that was our way. Our language.

The man in the chair wasn't the one who yelled at me only a few hours before. That version was gone. Sunlight filtered through the window, catching dust that drifted lazily through the quiet, warm air. The mid-August light painted everything soft and reflective. It was everything Ray hadn't been.

I sat back on my heels and scrubbed a hand down my face. Grief wasn't unfamiliar. I'd buried enough people to know how it settled. But finding Ray like this carved something sharp across my chest. I reached over and switched off the TV. The sudden silence roared in my ears.

I stood slowly, heavy from the weight of it all, and crossed to the phone hanging on the kitchen wall. My thumb hovered over the keys a moment longer than necessary. Calling an ambulance felt pointless, but what else was I supposed to do? The dispatcher's voice was brisk, and she assured me help was on the way.

When I hung up, my gaze drifted to the counter where Ray kept his important things, unopened mail, and a half-used notebook. In the center sat the offer. The formal paperwork I'd brought over three weeks ago to buy the ranch and fold his operation into mine.

All he'd needed to do was sign it. My jaw tightened as I stared at the empty signature line. On the back, in his shaky, cramped handwriting, he'd started a list: Tessa's number.

Lawyer.

Don't let the vulture win.

The "vulture." That was me.

Things had just gotten complicated because the land didn't belong to me. Now, it belonged to her. Tessa Callahan..

"She's a city girl now, Wyatt," he grumbled once. "Doesn't know a damn thing about ranching."

"You raised her here, Ray. She'll remember," I said, because I thought he wanted reassurance.

"She won't." His frown had deepened. "She doesn't want this life."

That had been the end of it. Now I needed to call her. I pulled up the number he pressed into my hand months earlier, "In case I keel over," he'd said. I wished I'd laughed then. The call rolled to voicemail. "Hi, this is Tessa. I don't want to talk; text if it's important." The beep to leave a message sounded.

"Tessa, this is Wyatt Hargrove. I'm at your uncle's place. You need to call me back immediately."

I hung up, jaw tight. I hated leaving a message for someone who didn't know me and probably didn't care to. The last time I tried calling, nudging Ray toward the sale, she hadn't answered either.

Footsteps crunched outside. The paramedics arrived, working with calm, practiced efficiency. I followed them onto the porch as the screen door clapped shut. Outside, the heat wrapped around me like a heavy blanket. The sun hovered above the ridge, stretching long shadows across the valley.

The ambulance drove away slowly, with no flashing lights or blaring siren; the crunching of gravel and the engine were the only sounds. I stared out over the foothills and reached for my phone. I tried calling again.

My own ranch sprawled across the opposite rise, miles of fencing and irrigation pivots turning slow circles. North of town, the brewery sat with its steel tanks gleaming and barley silos lined up against the sky. Two lives that didn't make sense on paper, but I needed both. Between them, I'd built something that almost felt like enough.

I stood there for a long moment, breathing through the tightness in my chest. Grief. Frustration. I looked over the horizon at Ray's sagging buildings and peeling paint. The whole place was a storm waiting to break.

If Tessa didn't want to answer, if she didn't know what she just inherited, it didn't matter. Ray tied us together when he handed me that number. Whether she liked it or not, she was stepping into a life she wasn't prepared for.

I turned toward my truck, the gravel crunching under my boots, and felt the familiar pull of responsibility settle in, heavy and sure. I still had a ranch to run and a brewery full of people counting on me, but tonight, there was only one thing that mattered. Finding Tessa Callahan and telling her that the man who raised her was gone.

Two

Tessa

"Whatever this is, make it quick," I said. "I still need to catch the train," I said hastily as I glanced at my watch. I have so much to do tomorrow. I couldn't stay here all night, and Colin would never offer to drive me home.

Colin shut the patio door behind us, and the noise of his parents' dinner party dulled to a muffled, distant hum. It was as if someone threw a pillow over the entire house, muting every voice and smothering each burst of laughter until all that remained was the faint clink of cutlery and glassware.

"Tessa," he said, his voice low and careful. "I've been doing a lot of thinking."

A cold knot pulled tight behind my ribs. Not panic. Dread. Familiar, grainy dread that scraped my chest from the inside out.

"Colin," I whispered, which only made him smile, and that hadn't been my intention when I said it.

He reached into his pocket with practiced certainty, the kind of motion a man rehearsed in front of a mirror to make sure he looked perfect while doing this. The air around us thickened as if it knew what was coming.

"Don't," I said hastily, hoping that would be enough to stop this before he embarrassed himself. He froze for a moment, his hand still deep in his pocket, his eyes flicking to mine with a startled edge. Colin hated being off-balance.

He stood near the short steps that led to the paved path; the patio lights cast a dingy glow over him. His pale blue button-down clung damply to his back and underarms, the shirt he bragged about buying from some expensive menswear place.

Colin wasn't ugly, but he wasn't handsome either. His features never quite resolved into anything worth remembering. He was a man who looked better surrounded by wealth. Without props, the plainness showed.

His carefully styled hair wilted in the humidity, flattening against his head, and his clean-shaven jaw looked almost raw in the porch light, like he went over it twice for safety. His throat bobbed. That tiny swallow should have warned me. If he was nervous, it meant whatever he planned wasn't going the way he expected.

"Tessa," he said gently. "Just let me—"

He pulled his hand free, and the box caught the porch light. Small, dark, and velvet, the type used in commercials where beautiful couples made perfect life decisions. My stomach lurched. He cradled it in his palm like it was delicate instead of life-altering. Sweat ran down my spine as a shiver ran up.

"Colin," I said. "Put it away."

His expression tightened, though he tried for a smile that never reached his eyes. "Come on. Don't be like that."

"Like what?"

"Difficult." The word slid from him with a thin seam of

irritation beneath the practiced softness. "You're always difficult."

A car drove past the front of the house, headlights sweeping across the fence. Someone inside laughed. Life went on while the moment out on this patio turned into something sharp and wrong.

"You have to see the ring," he said, not reading the moment between us. The hinge squeaked softly. The ring inside glinted with cold, confident brightness, the diamond catching even the weak porch light. Of course, it was expensive. His family wouldn't allow anything less.

"Tessa," he said softly. "I love you. Even if you don't come from the right side of the tracks or have an illustrious career, which won't matter when we're married anyway. You're it for me."

Everything inside me recoiled. He didn't love me; he loved the image, the narrative, the way I looked sitting beside him at dinners. Over the years, he made no qualms about making sure people knew he'd been the one to sophisticate me. I could perform well enough in situations where his parents were pleased and overlooked my ranch upbringing, but it was made well known that I wasn't good enough.

"Say something," he said. "You're freaking me out."

"You should put that away," I told him.

His brows snapped together. "That's not funny."

"I'm not joking," I said as I shook my head, and the silence stretched, sticky and hot.

"You're serious," he said slowly. "You're actually serious."

"Yes."

He blinked as if trying to force the world back into the shape he preferred. "We've been together for years," he said. "This is what people do. You have a stable job. I'm moving up at the firm. My parents adore you; you belong here. This is the next step."

"Off and on for years," I said. "Mostly off. Your parents barely tolerate me, and we both know I don't belong here; this isn't the life I want."

He flinched. The word landed like a slap. "But it was real," he insisted. "We've put in the time. We've built something. You're part of this family." From inside the house, his mother's laugh floated out, polished and fake.

"It wasn't what you think it was," I said. He never knew about the mumbled comments at parties or the meetings I had with his mother, that she pretended were just a girl's lunch. In reality, they were subtle threats about behaviour over a too-expensive salad with water chestnuts. All the moments I hadn't been enough flashed through my head.

"I'm not marrying you, Colin."

For a moment, wounded shock flickered across his face. It looked almost genuine, but only almost. Then it vanished beneath something colder as he slid his mask back into place.

"You don't mean that," he said.

"I do," I whispered.

He shook his head in tight, jerky movements. "No. You're tired. You're overworked. You're stressed about money. Your judgement is—"

"My judgment is fine."

"You don't know what you're saying. How much have you had to drink tonight?" The words were snapped out. Always a projection because when Colin was drinking, I didn't. He wasn't predictable, and one of us needed to be fully capable of functioning.

"I haven't had anything to drink, and I do mean this, Colin." I looked down at the ground and hoped this would be enough for him to leave me alone on the porch.

He stepped toward me, each stride slow and deliberate, like he expected proximity to change my answer. The porch light cast shallow shadows across his face. Sweat glistened above his lip.

"I've been here. I've been patient and given you space when you asked for it. I've put up with your crazy schedule and your late shifts. Do you know what it does to a man when you aren't there for his needs?" His voice rose, and he tamped it back down.

Oh, I knew, I knew full well what it did for him. He'd cheat, we'd break up, and he'd always come crawling back, and like an idiot, I let him back in.

"I never asked you to do any of that. Especially the cheating," I added quickly.

His jaw twitched. "You owe me," he growled.

"I don't owe you anything." The silence that followed hit like a lid slamming shut. Something cracked across his expression. A subtle fracture, but enough to let something hard leak through.

"You're being irrational. You always do this when you're overwhelmed. You push people away and shut down. I know you'll regret this, Tessa."

"No," I said quietly. "I won't."

He stepped closer again, closing the last inches between us until his breath brushed my cheek. He smelled like aftershave and wine and something stale beneath both. His free hand lifted, hovering near my shoulder, fingers flexing.

"I've been the one who shows up," he said firmly. "Not your cowboy fantasies. Not whatever daydreams you chase. Me. I'm the one who gives you stability."

"I don't have any fantasies, Colin. I do know that I deserve better than what's in front of me."

His hand curled into a fist and dropped.

"We're good together. Everyone says so. My colleagues like you. You fit."

I thought of every dinner where I swallowed discomfort

and let myself fade into the wallpaper because it was easier than explaining why a comment stung. I thought of every time he said, Don't make a thing of it.

"Everything is ready. I'm ready. You just need to say yes."

"I'm saying no."

His eyes hardened. The ring box snapped shut with a sharp click. He slid it back into his pocket with careful precision, not like a man defeated but rather a man recalculating.

"This isn't the smart choice," he said calmly. "You won't find better than me."

"I'll take my chances." Turning, I wanted to run, but my purse was inside the house. I needed to get it, then I'd get far away from this place. His hand shot out. He grabbed my arm just above the elbow, squeezing hard enough to send pain up my shoulder. He yanked me closer, his breath hot on my cheek.

"Don't walk away from me." Resentment burned in his eyes. Entitlement. Not love. Never love.

"Let go of me," I pleaded, but he didn't. "I said let go." This time, my voice came from somewhere deep, scraped raw with fury. He hesitated, then released me. I jerked back so fast the railing bit into my spine. His fingers left a burning touch on my skin.

"You'll regret this," he whispered. "You'll see what you threw away."

It wasn't fear that settled in me. It was clarity. "I'm not the one who threw anything away. Your cheating, your demands, and now this," I said as I lifted my arm, "you threw it away."

Confusion flickered across his face, sharp and brief. "Where are you going?" he demanded.

"Away." I opened the door and stepped back inside. The noise of the dinner party crashed over me, voices, clinking glasses, a burst of laughter. The air smelled like roasted meat, rosemary, and money.

His mother spotted me, her eyes twinned briefly, like she knew what happened, but she took a step back as I frowned when I saw her. "Everything okay, dear?"

"Fine." I kept walking. The front door loomed ahead, and my purse sat on the table. My hand shook as I grabbed my bag and reached for the door. I didn't stop. Not for her. And certainly not for him.

Outside, the city air slapped me with humidity and exhaust. The sky was a bruised gold, the last light clinging to the clouds. Music thumped from an apartment window. A child laughed somewhere down the street. An ordinary life, one that was normal and unremarkable. For a moment, it made my eyes sting.

My phone buzzed in my purse. Twice. Then again. I ignored it until I couldn't, then pulled it out with unsteady fingers. Sixteen messages.

> Colin: Tessa, come back.
>
> Colin: You're not thinking straight.
>
> Colin: Don't embarrass me.
>
> Colin: We need to talk about this like adults.

Cold tightened low in my stomach. I clicked the screen off and kept walking. The station wasn't far. The streetlights flickered on as I reached the next block. My phone buzzed again, insistently, but I didn't look this time. I already knew. Colin never apologized. He never explained, only twisted the narrative to fit what made him look good.

But tonight, I didn't have to play his game.

The platform smelled like hot metal. A train screeched as it approached, headlights carving a bright path along the tracks. The doors opened with a sigh. I stepped inside, wrapped my fingers around the rail, and caught my reflection in the dark window.

Same hair. Same freckles. Same tired eyes. But the girl looking back at me wasn't pretending to be lucky anymore. My phone buzzed again.

Colin: Tessa, don't ignore me.

Colin: Bitch, this isn't over.

I locked the screen, slid the phone back into my purse, and held on as the train lurched forward. I'd blown up my life with one word. I couldn't tell the future, but I knew, with perfect certainty, that it wasn't with him.

THREE

TESSA

My roommate was already halfway through a bottle of her favourite rosé when I got home, which really meant two things: she had a long day and was coping the only way she knew how. And I was about to be violently mothered with carbs and alcohol, whether I consented or not.

"TessaaAAAAA!" Dani sing-songed from the living room, dragging out my name in a pitch that could shatter windows and attract distressed raccoons. She was perched cross-legged on the couch like the gremlin queen of our apartment, hair mussed, mascara slightly smeared, surrounded by open chip bags as if she were being worshipped by offerings.

The living room was a disaster in progress. A throw blanket was half on the floor, two half-eaten spring rolls were abandoned on the coffee table, and a mug that said Girlboss held three forks for no reason. It smelled like incense, takeout, and quite possibly weed. She was usually a gummy girl, but occasionally she'd switch it up.

Dani craned her neck back so she could look at me upside down, her hair dangling like a mop in a shampoo commercial gone horribly wrong. "You look like someone drop-kicked your soul," she said in a delightedly savage tone. "Tell Mommy everything." Switching to her concerned tone.

I closed the door behind me, dropped my purse, my keys, and whatever dignity I had left onto the kitchen counter, and felt the emotional exhaustion hit me. "Colin proposed," I said, my voice wooden, "and I said no."

Dani froze mid-crunch, the chip suspended millimetres from her mouth. Her whole body went still, like someone hit pause. She blinked once, then again, and then shrieked, launching herself upright with enough force to shake the couch. "He did it? He actually did it? I knew it. I told you. I smelled the desperation on him like too much Axe body spray."

I collapsed onto the couch, the cushions dipping under the weight of emotional damage. "It was so bad," I murmured, leaning my head back until I stared at the ceiling like it owed me answers.

"Start from the beginning." She shoved the wine bottle toward me with her foot, queen-like. "I'm invested. I deserve this tea."

I told her everything as I stared at the bottle of wine in my hand and waited for her to say something.

"That motherfucker." She shifted dramatically, her legs flopping across my lap like a Victorian heroine on her fainting chaise. "I told you he'd get twitchy. Men only ask for private conversations when they're about to confess their undying love, propose marriage, or ask if you'll donate a kidney."

"He grabbed my arm when I tried to leave."

Dani froze again, statue-still, serial-killer-in-the-room still. Her head snapped toward me, eyes widening. "He grabbed you?"

I swallowed. "Yeah." I brushed my fingers over my arm,

rubbing the ghost of his grip. The memory felt hot and humiliating.

Dani's jaw set. She rose like a woman preparing for war, set the wine down with surgical precision, cupped my cheeks, and stared directly into my soul. "We should buy shovels."

I choked. "No."

"Fine," she snapped, "if we can't bury him alive, we might as well get drunk." She marched to the kitchen with the chaos of a toddler in a toy store. "Tequila or vodka?"

"No tequila."

"Great, tequila it is." Something clattered in the kitchen, a cupboard door bounced open, and a string of curses filled the air like seasoning. "Okay," she announced triumphantly, returning with a tray of shot glasses, salt, lime slices, tequila, and a look that said we were destroying our livers on purpose tonight. "Let the ritual of forgetting commence."

I was more than ready to forget tonight even happened. Hell, I was more than ready to forget the week even happened. This disaster of this proposal, on top of losing my job because I argued with my boss about an equine treatment in front of a client, is something I would rather not remember.

I licked my hand, sprinkled the salt, and we clinked glasses. The tequila burned my throat, dissolving my sins in one messy gulp. By shot three, my shoulders slid down from my ears. By shot four, Dani tried to teach me a TikTok dance involving hip rolls and hand flicks, and I shoved her hands away because my coordination decided to be nonexistent.

"I hate men," she announced loudly, kicking her legs over the back of the couch like she was auditioning for an interpretive dance, "that hot firefighter on your FYP could stay though."

She flopped onto the couch next to me and rested her head on my shoulder. "I'm proud of you."

"For what?"

"For saying no and leaving. For not letting a man with zero upper lip convince you that marriage was the only way you could be happy."

"That was a lot of words."

She nodded solemnly. "What can I say, I'm a poet when drunk."

My phone buzzed again, then again, then again, six times in thirty minutes. Dani glared at it with venom. "Whoever that is needs to get a life."

"It's probably spam," I muttered, though something tightened in my stomach. The buzzing continued, and my pulse stuttered.

"Maybe you should answer," Dani said.

"Absolutely not. For all I know, Colin stole a stranger's phone and is trying to bait me."

We finished the tequila, then wine, and before I knew it, Dani opened the vodka, because sobriety was for people who hadn't been proposed to by their gaslighting ex that day. Eventually, we lay sprawled on the living room floor like two corpses who died of drama. The ceiling fan spun above us like a lazy helicopter blade.

"I'm never drinking again," I mumbled.

"You say that every weekend," Dani muttered.

A moment passed. Maybe three. The room swayed gently like a boat. Dani groaned beside me and flopped an arm across her forehead.

Then a knock sounded. Sharp. Firm. Authoritative.

Dani shot upright so fast she gasped for air. "Who the hell is knocking at what time even is it?"

I blinked at my phone. "Two in the morning." Another knock came, louder, and my heartbeat tripped.

"That's not Colin," I whispered. "He does that stupid song knock."

Dani crawled across the coffee table, sending the contents

flying, and moved toward the door like a woman with nothing left to lose.

"Dani, no," I scrambled after her, half running, half stumbling as the room wobbled. She flung the door open.

A man stood in the doorway. Not a boy. Not Colin. Not anything that belonged in this building or this hour. He was tall and broad, built like a brick shit house. Sun-worn skin, dark hair slightly mussed like he'd run a hand through it in frustration, his shoulders blocking out the hallway light. Cowboy boots, jeans that hugged his thighs, looked worked in hugged his thighs, and a pearl snap plaid shirt rolled up with strong forearms.

"Did we die and go to heaven?" Dani whispered as she stared at the man.

"No," he said in a deep, gravelly voice, steady and even, "I'm looking for Tessa Callahan."

Dani pointed at me instantly. "She's Tessa."

"Traitor," I mumbled under my breath.

He looked at me, really looked, and I felt it like heat under my ribs. His eyes swept over my messy hair, my flushed face, the emotional ruin of my night. He didn't blink.

"I'm Wyatt Hargrove," he said. His name sounded vaguely familiar, but there was no way I could unscramble my brain fast enough to figure out where I knew him from.

"I've been trying to contact you."

Dani whispered, "Why does he have to sound so sexy?"

Wyatt's jaw flexed as he turned his attention fully toward me with a gaze that pinned me to the spot. My throat dried instantly, and I wasn't sure my legs still worked. Wyatt Hargrove stood in my doorway, boots planted, hat in hand like he was attending a funeral, broad shoulders blocking the hallway light, eyes fixed on me with an intensity I wasn't built to handle, while my bloodstream consisted mostly of alcohol.

Everything about him was too much. Too tall. Too solid.

Too real. Not like Colin, with his curated cologne and catalog-ready smile. Wyatt looked carved from Rockies, a lifetime of labor, the kind of man who didn't complain about things, he'd just fix them.

I opened my mouth, but nothing came out. My tongue felt like carpet. Wyatt waited, not shifting or fidgeting, simply watching me with the steady patience of a man bracing for impact.

He slid his hat from one hand to the other, a quiet, unconscious adjustment. Not nerves. Something heavier.

"I've been trying to reach you," he repeated, his voice cutting through my drunken fog.

"My phone's somewhere." I gestured at the floor where it lay face down like a dead bug.

Wyatt glanced at it briefly, the judgment almost tangible, but he said nothing. His gaze returned to mine, steady and weighted. "Tessa. It's important."

My heartbeat tripped. "Important how?"

Silence stretched, thick and buzzing. I heard the fridge humming, the ceiling fan ticking, Dani breathing beside me.

"We should talk inside," he said.

Inside meant reality. Inside meant facing something I didn't want to face. "Just tell me."

"Tessa." He said my name in a way that under different circumstances would have made me drop my panties and drag him to my room. I swayed. Dani nudged me gently. I wasn't okay.

Wyatt watched me, something heavy in his expression; it was soft now, like he was trying to figure out the proper words he was going to use. He'd been so confident only a moment ago, but now I wasn't sure what I saw.

"It's about Ray," he said again, softer.

FOUR
WYATT

Wood met bone, paint dust jumped from the casing, and for a moment, the cheap light in the hallway buzzed like it was considering giving up.

"Dani, what the hell was that?" Tessa hissed.

"He looked like a murderer, Tess." The women's voices flowed through the door like there was no barrier between us.

"He knew my name," Tessa said. Her volume was too high; words blurred at the edges. She sounded drunk. Not tipsy, not warm and loose, but properly drunk. "Why does he know my name?"

"He probably searched you online before he came to cut you up," Dani said. "I bet Colin set him."

I closed my eyes and inhaled slowly. Of all the tasks I had expected to handle today, knocking on the door of a rundown city apartment to deliver a death notice to a drunk niece who wanted nothing to do with her family had not been on the list. Yet here I was.

I knocked again, and both of them screamed.

"Tessa, he is still there," Dani hissed.

"Oh my God, do you think he can hear us?" Tessa asked.

Her voice climbed higher with each word, like panic was driving it up by the inch.

"Yes," I said, pitching my voice low. "I can hear you." I let the irritation slide through me and settle into something colder. I spent all afternoon managing shocked neighbours and the logistics that came with a body. This was the last stop. I wasn't leaving without doing what needed to be done. I knocked again, slower, the sound echoing down the narrow hall.

On the other side, there was a flurry of movement. Something clattered to the floor. Someone cursed.

The lock slid, and the door opened the width of a finger. A single brown eye peered out at me. "Tessa," I said. Hearing her own name seemed to go through her like a jolt. Her gaze dragged over my face, my shoulders, the hat in my hand. Mascara smudged beneath her eyes, dark crescents against red blotches. Her cheeks were flushed from liquor. Her hair fell around her face in careless waves, half knotted, half smooth, as if she had run her hands through it too many times.

"What do you want?" she asked. Her voice landed somewhere near exhausted.

"I need to speak with you," I said, "in private."

"About what?"

"Open the door."

There was a pause long enough for me to see how her fingers trembled against the edge of the door. Behind her shoulder, Dani appeared. Pink hair, wild eyes, a pillow clutched to her chest as if that would help.

"Maybe we should let him in," Dani said.

"He is not coming in," Tessa muttered, but it was more to herself than to me.

I felt the muscle in my jaw tighten. I'd chased cattle through ice, pulled stuck calves in the dark, and squared off with bulls that hated me on principle. I wasn't about to stand in a hallway and argue with two drunk women who already decided I was the villain.

"Tessa," I said. "I wouldn't be here at this hour if this could wait until morning."

Her eyes flicked to mine. Something in what she saw there must have cut through the alcohol, because her shoulders sagged a fraction. She glanced back at Dani.

"You said something about Ray," she said quietly as she opened the door fully.

The apartment looked like an emotional storm went through it. There was an empty wine bottle tipped on its side, blankets in heaps, shoes in places shoes did not belong. A bra hung crookedly off a lamp, as if it surrendered mid-battle. I stepped inside and closed the door behind me.

"Tessa," I said, ignoring her. "Sit down."

She bristled immediately. I watched it roll through her, an instinctive push back against being told what to do. Under other circumstances, it might have amused me. Tonight it simply got in the way.

"Don't tell me to sit," she said, voice cracking. "You show up at my door in the middle of the night, and you expect me to just do what you say? Who even are you?"

I held her gaze. "Again, my name is Wyatt Hargrove. I live in River's Edge, your Uncle Ray is my neighbor. I am here because he can't be."

Her lips parted. Color rushed into her face, then drained just as fast. Dani made a small, wounded sound, sank down onto the arm of the couch, and hugged the pillow to her chest.

The moment stretched. I could feel Tessa struggling under the weight of it, trying to force the pieces into a shape that was not as obvious as it was.

"Say it," she whispered. "Don't make me ask."

There were a dozen ways people tried to soften this kind of

blow. I heard most of them. I did not use any. "Your uncle died yesterday afternoon," I said.

For a few seconds, nothing moved. The air felt thick, like the walls had crept closer. Then the meaning hit her all at once. Her knees buckled, and she reached blindly for the nearest surface. The edge of a stool caught the backs of her legs, and she folded onto it like someone cut her strings.

Dani slid off the couch and went to her, arms wrapping around her shoulders. She turned her face toward me with a glare that could have flayed a weaker man.

"What happened?" she demanded.

"His heart, I'm guessing," I said. "I found him when I went to let him know I'd fixed his fence."

Tessa stared at me like she was looking at a stranger speaking a language she didn't understand. Her eyes were too bright, glassy and wide, as if they were trying to hold back water that had already broken through.

"If this is some sort of sick joke, I swear to God I will…" Her voice broke. The last words never made it out.

"It isn't a joke," I said. There was no point trying to sugar-coat anything. "I've been trying to reach you for hours, and decided to come in person."

She sucked in a breath that shook. Dani tightened her hold and shot me another look, full of accusation. As if delivering the news made me responsible for the death. That was fine; people needed something to aim at. I had broad shoulders.

I stayed where I was, my hat still in my hand. The brim dug into my palm, and I focused on the pressure and not on the way Tessa's grief cut through the room. I had seen this before, more times than I cared to remember. Parents, siblings, friends. The first moment when reality slammed down, and they realized the world changed, and nobody asked their permission.

"I have to go," she said. "I have to get home. I shouldn't

have left; he needed me. I should've been there." She pushed off the stool too fast. Her legs wobbled. The room tilted for her. She staggered sideways toward the counter, reaching for balance.

I moved without thinking about it. My hand closed around her upper arm before she could hit the floor. Even through the thin cotton of her shirt, her skin was hot. Her muscles tensed beneath my fingers, electricity jolted through my hand. Annoying. Unwanted. I let go as soon as she was steady.

"Don't touch me," she snapped.

"You can barely stand on your own," I said.

"I'm fine," she insisted, although her voice slurred on the last word, and she had to curl her fingers into the counter behind her to stay upright. "I can pack a bag. I can call for a ride. I can get a flight. I can…"

"You're not going anywhere tonight," I said. Her eyes snapped to mine. There was fire there now, banked under the grief. The kind that burned and didn't know what to do with itself.

"You don't get to tell me what to do," she said. "You don't know me."

"I know you've had too much to drink," I said as I glanced over at the coffee table. "I can smell it from here, and I know you nearly fell on your face twice in the last ten seconds. And I know you would be a danger to yourself and anyone unlucky enough to share a road with you if you went anywhere right now."

"We can call a cab," Dani said from the stool, voice small but stubborn.

"You're not putting her in a car tonight either," I told her, not taking my eyes off Tessa. "You want her home in one piece, you wait until morning."

"You can't force me to stay here," Tessa said. Her hands

clenched into fists at her sides. She was shaking, whether from anger or shock, I wasn't sure. "You're not my father, you're not family, you're some ranch hand my uncle hired."

The corner of my mouth moved, but it was not a smile. "I'm the neighbor, not a ranch hand."

"Then get out of my way." She took a step toward me, chin lifted. The room was small enough that there was not much space to close before she was right in front of me. She had to tilt her head back to meet my eyes. Her pupils were still too large, breath still smelled like tequila and lime and something sweet. Her t-shirt hung off one shoulder, exposing the soft curve of her collarbone.

Attraction slid through me again, slow and unwelcome, wrapping itself around old resentment. I didn't like that combination. It felt unstable, like a spark in a dry field. So I held my ground.

"You're not driving," I said. I kept my voice low, not gentle. "If you push it, you'll make a bad night into something worse. If you want to honor Ray, you show up tomorrow with enough sense in your head to stand at his gate without collapsing." God, this woman was stubborn, just like her uncle.

"He wouldn't want you out on the highway," I said instead. "He'd want you alive. You can hate me all you like. You can call me every name in the book. But you're not leaving this apartment tonight."

She stared at me, chest heaving, eyes shining. For a second, I thought she might actually hit me. Part of me almost wanted her to, to bleed some of the pressure off.

Behind her, Dani whispered, not nearly as quietly as she thought, "Tess, I kind of hate that he is right. Also, he is terrifying. A hot, terrifying authority figure. Like a cowboy probation officer."

"Shut up," Tessa hissed without looking back.

Silence settled over the three of us. The fridge hummed.

Someone above us stomped across their floor. The city outside kept moving, unaware that one small world just cracked.

"I'm never going to be able to sleep," Tessa said finally, voice hoarse. "Not after this."

"You don't have to sleep," I said. "You just have to stay put."

Her shoulders slumped. The fight went out of her all at once, leaving her looking hollow. She leaned back against the counter and covered her face with both hands.

"What am I supposed to do until morning?" she asked, voice muffled. "Just sit here and think about him lying in some freezer while I wait to be *allowed* to go home?"

"You can sit," I said. "You can cry. Maybe drink water instead of whatever is still in that bottle. Pack a bag if you can manage it without falling over. Tomorrow you'll have enough to deal with. I'll stay in the city and take you home tomorrow." Where this idea had come from, I'll never know, and I was sure by morning I'd regret it, but I made the offer.

The resentment was still there, but so was something else, something like wary curiosity. She looked like she was trying to solve a puzzle, but the pieces weren't cooperating. Now, I didn't fit into the story she had clearly written about me when she first saw me at the door.

"You'll come back," she said, but it wasn't really a question.

"Yes," I said. "Eight in the morning. Be ready. I'll drive you to the ranch."

Dani scrubbed at her own face with the heel of her hand. "Eight is so early."

"You can sleep all the way there," I told her.

Tessa's gaze dropped to my hand on the doorknob, then lifted back to my face. For a moment there was naked fear there, not of me exactly, but of what was coming. The funeral.

The house. The memories. The debt she owed, and had no idea how to pay.

"Was Ray alone when it happened?" she said, voice so quiet I almost missed it.

"Yes," I said quietly. "I got there shortly after."

A single tear slid down her cheek. She didn't bother to wipe it away. "Fine. "I'll be ready."

I put my hat back on and opened the door.

Behind me, Dani said, in what she must have thought was a whisper, "He smells annoyingly good for someone I was ready to fight with a couch cushion."

I didn't dignify that with a reaction. "Get some water," I said over my shoulder without turning. "Try to lie down, even if you only stare at the ceiling. Morning'll come either way."

Tessa didn't answer, but I felt her eyes on my back.

Tomorrow I'd come back and take Tessa Callahan home. Whatever she thought was waiting for her at that ranch, she was wrong.

Five

Tessa

I woke up on the couch with my face stuck to a tortilla chip, which honestly summed up my life. A low groan rattled out of me as I peeled the chip off my cheek; it made a faint tearing sound, like it had fused to my skin through sheer force of tequila and sadness.

I blinked at the blurry room, my eyes protested the light; my brain protested existence. Two empty bottles sat on the coffee table. A bra hung off the lamp like a flag of surrender. Half a lime lay on the floor.

And then there was Dani, laying on the floor, cocooned in a blanket like a corpse that died sometime during the night. One foot was sticking out and twitching occasionally as if she were dreaming of running.

My head throbbed, my stomach churned, and my throat felt like I'd swallowed dust. I pressed a hand to my temple, groaned again, and slowly sat up.

That's when it hit me.

Ray.

The memory slammed into my chest. My breath caught

mid-inhale, sharp and painful. I froze, hands gripping my knees as my stomach dropped fast and hard.

"Oh God," I whispered. "Oh God. Oh no."

Last night rushed back in a fragmented montage, tequila shots, Dani's terrible dance moves, me crying, the knocking, the stranger at the door, the hat in his hands, the words he'd said.

Uncle Ray was gone. Really gone. The man who raised me, the man who'd taught me how to tie knots, how to sit a stubborn horse, to recognize a fever in a calf before it got dangerous. The man who'd never once made things easy on me.

"Hey," Dani croaked again, dragging herself upright like a resurrected corpse. Her hair was tangled, and her eyeliner smudged, making her look worse than I felt. "You okay?"

No. Not even close. But my throat was tight, so I nodded. She scooted closer, blanket still wrapped around her, and rested her head on my shoulder. She was warm and familiar and exactly what I needed, steady pressure in a world that was cracked open. We sat like that for a while, quiet and hungover and broken.

Then she whispered, voice hoarse, "Did we hallucinate the hot cowboy?"

I let out a weak sound, something between a sigh and a dying animal. "No. Wyatt's real. I didn't know him well when I was growing up, but he lived at the next ranch."

Her eyes widened. "Oh, thank God. I was scared we'd invented him. That man looked like a responsible older lumberjack with emotional trauma."

I groaned into my hands. "Please stop talking."

"No, seriously," she said, rubbing her face.

I grabbed a pillow and covered my entire head with it. "Oh my God."

She snorted. "I can't believe he said he'd come get you this morning after the things we said to him."

I froze under the pillow, my heartbeat thudding loud enough that I could hear it. Right. He was coming back to take me home. To whatever waited at the ranch that was now my responsibility.

My stomach twisted. Grief pulled tight in my chest. Underneath it, something else flickered, fear maybe, pressure, reality. Everything was going to change.

I forced myself off the couch. My body screamed with every shift; my hips were stiff, my neck tight, my stomach rolling in protest. I needed water, painkillers, a shower, a therapist, and possibly divine intervention.

My phone buzzed on the counter. Unknown number, and my pulse skittered.

Dani perked up like a meerkat sensing danger. "Is it him?"

I nodded.

"Answer it," she squealed as she held her head.

"I can't." I stared at the unknown number on the screen.

"Then let me."

"No," I shouted loud enough to make me groan.

The buzzing stopped. Then started again. My palms went sweaty. Irrational, but real. He wasn't scary, not objectively. He was stern and steady and completely out of place in my tequila-soaked disaster of a life. But still, the thought of answering made something inside me seize.

I forced myself to pick up. "Hello," I croaked.

"Morning, Miss Callahan." His voice was deep and sleep-rough, a low, steady sound that tugged at something low in my stomach I didn't want to examine. "I'm outside."

I swallowed. "I'll be down in a minute."

"Take your time," he said. "We're not in a rush."

We.

The word landed strangely in my chest, heavy and present and loaded with something unnamed. I hung up and turned slowly.

"Oh my God," she said, pressing a hand to her chest dramatically. "You have to shower. You look like a raccoon that got hit by a bus."

"Have you looked in a mirror lately?" I asked after her insult.

She waved me off and frowned. "Brush your teeth twice."

"I know."

"And whatever you do, don't cry on him again."

I paused halfway into the bathroom. "I didn't cry on him."

"You did everything but fall into his arms," she said.

I threw a dirty look her way, grabbed the hand towel beside the sink, and threw it at her. She dodged the flailing linen and pointed into the bathroom. "Go. I'll clean the explosion zone."

I showered. Scalding water hit my skin, and the room steamed up instantly. The heat didn't wash the grief away, but it softened the edges. My muscles loosened. My hands stopped shaking, and my heartbeat calmed a little. I stood too long with my forehead against the tile, breathing slowly and shakily.

When I got out, I wrapped myself in a towel and stared at the foggy mirror until my reflection appeared. I barely recognized the woman looking back, because everything in her life shifted in less than twelve hours.

I dressed in something simple, jeans that weren't stained, a clean white tank top, and a light cardigan. I braided my hair with trembling fingers, too tight, then loosening it until it didn't make my head hurt worse.

Quickly, I packed a bag. Not much, just what I knew I'd need. A toothbrush, deodorant, a pair of boots that hadn't touched ranch dirt in years, clean socks, a worn flannel shoved in the back of my closet, a hair tie, a notebook I didn't remember buying, my phone charger, a sweatshirt that smelled like home even if I didn't want it to.

I zipped the bag and slung it over my shoulder. The weight of it pulled at me in a way that felt symbolic and stupidly literal.

I stepped into the hallway. Dani stood there holding a garbage bag in one hand and a mop in the other. Her eyes softened instantly. "You good?"

No. But I nodded anyway.

"You'll call?" she asked.

"Yes."

She hugged me quickly, tighter than expected. "For the record," she said into my shoulder, "I know today is awful. But if it helps at all, Wyatt showing up last night was hot. So hot."

I groaned. "Dani."

"What? I cope with grief using humour."

"I have to go."

She squeezed me once more and stepped back. "You got this, Tess."

I doubted it, but I walked toward the elevator anyway. My boots echoed in the hallway. My breath trembled. My hands shook.

I pushed the lobby doors open.

And there he was.

Wyatt Hargrove stood just outside the building, tall and solid. His blue plaid shirt was rolled at the sleeves, hands resting at his hips like he'd been waiting a long time but wasn't impatient about it. His boots didn't belong anywhere near a city sidewalk; dust clung to the seams, and the sun glinted off the worn leather.

He lifted his head when he saw me. His eyes took me in slowly and steadily, not judgmental or prying, just present.

"Morning," he said. My mouth opened. Nothing came out. He nodded once, a small gesture of understanding. "Let's get you home."

Six

Wyatt

As I waited, the sun was already high over the rooftops, and the heat was already rising off the pavement in slow, shimmering waves. August in the city had a way of baking everything early in the day, locking the warmth in until long after sunset.

It wasn't like the foothills, where mornings stayed cool, and the heat came at noon. Here, warmth came from every direction: concrete radiating up, humidity pressing sideways, millions of bodies moving through the same space.

She approached in slow, deliberate steps, meaning every part of her body hurt. Up close, I could see everything the sunglasses tried to hide: shadows under her eyes, faint red at the corners, lips pressed too tight, skin pale. She was holding herself together with sheer willpower, and that willpower was threadbare.

She climbed in without another word.

I shut the door carefully, like the noise might hurt her, then rounded the hood and slid behind the wheel.

"Have you eaten anything?" I asked.

"No." Her voice was barely audible.

"Drink some water." I pointed at the bottle, and she looked at me.

She reached for the unopened bottle in the console. When she unscrewed the cap, her fingers trembled, just slightly, but enough that something tight lodged itself in my chest. She took a small sip, swallowing carefully, each movement slow like she had to remind her body how to function.

There was a coffee place on the corner with a drive-through; the drive wouldn't be so bad if we were both caffeinated. With coffee and bagels in our possession, I eased the truck back into traffic.

She stared straight ahead. Not blinking much. Not really seeing anything, either. Ten full minutes passed before she spoke. "You found him," she said quietly.

"Yes." My grip tightened on the wheel.

"What was it like?" Her question was a small reach for something she could hold on to.

"He was in his chair," I said softly. "It looked like he'd just nodded off. It was peaceful."

A soft, broken sound escaped her. She pressed a hand over her mouth and nodded, once, hard, like she had to physically keep the reaction from spilling out.

"He didn't call me," she whispered.

"He never wanted to bother people."

She laughed, a hollow sound, sharp and brittle. "He raised me when nobody else wanted me. There was no way he could've bothered me once." Her voice cracked. She stared out the windshield, jaw tight, her breath unsteady.

"I should've called more," she said, voice fraying. "I should've checked on him. I should've…"

I reached across the centre console and put my hand on hers. "People don't get to choose the time they go," I said. "And Ray wouldn't have wanted you to blame yourself."

She flinched at his name. Then she leaned her head back slowly, eyes hidden behind her sunglasses, her breath shaky.

Her phone buzzed, too loud in the quiet cab. She stiffened immediately. I glanced sideways.

"Do you need to answer that?" I asked.

"No."

"You can turn it off. Nobody needs access to you," I wasn't sure why I was suddenly feeling extra protective of this woman, but here we were. She hesitated. Then shut the ringer off. Her hands trembled again.

"You're safe," I said quietly, not pushing. "Whoever it is can wait."

She didn't look relieved. She looked unsure how to accept a stranger telling her she was safe.

Twenty minutes later, the city was fully behind us. High-rises fell behind us like dominoes, replaced by rows of strip malls, then scattered houses, then open fields. The world spread wide and flat, the sky opening above us in a way the city never allowed.

Tessa stared out the window, eyes hidden behind the glasses, jaw tense, lips parted slightly as if trying to remember how to breathe.

"How long's it been since you've been home?" I asked quietly.

She kept looking out the window. "Too long apparently." Silence hung in the air between us, but I didn't push for more.

"Did you call anyone? His friends? Anyone who needed to know?"

"I called the authorities," I said. "Everything else waits for next of kin."

She swallowed. "Right. That's me." She said it like it was a weight dropping onto her chest. Responsibility settling in.

"But don't forget River's Edge is a small town, and news

travels fast. So I'm sure most of the town knows by now." I hated reminding her how nosy the place was, but hoped it would make it a little easier for her.

Her phone buzzed again. She jumped at the sound, actually jumped in her seat.

"Are you alright?" I asked.

"Yeah," she lied.

The number flashed again, a number she absolutely recognized. The same damn one from last time it rang. I could tell from her reaction that it was persistent and unwelcome. She slapped her hand over her mouth, and my stomach dropped.

"You want me to answer it?" I asked hastily.

She shook her head, jaw tightening.

"Alright," I said softly. "Suit yourself."

She turned the phone face down. But tension stayed carved into her posture.

The prairie unfurled around us in long, sweeping stretches. Wheat fields shimmering pale gold under the rising sun. Cattle scattered across distant pastures like dark brush strokes. A hawk gliding overhead, shadow rippling across the earth.

"There's something you should know about the ranch."

Her head snapped toward me. "What is it?" she asked, voice suddenly taut. Scared. She had every right to be scared. I inhaled. I opened my mouth, and then I looked at her.

Her glasses hid her eyes, but everything else was exposed: her stiff posture, white-knuckled grip on her sleeve, the tremor in her breathing. Her skin pale beneath the flush of earlier crying. Her shoulders rose too fast with each breath. She was already drowning under the weight of the news of Ray.

Not today.

"Not now," I said.

She blinked hard. "Why not?"

"It's not important until we get there." Her chin trembled. She didn't seem to know how to take those words. Gratitude flickered across her face, then confusion, then something else.

The road cut a straight line through the land stretched out endlessly ahead, a dark ribbon in a sea of gold and green.

She tugged at the sleeve of her sweater, voice barely audible. "I'm not ready."

"You don't need to be."

She didn't reply. But her shoulders eased just slightly, the first sign of release since she walked out of her building.

Fifteen minutes later, her body gave up. Her head tilted, drooped. She jerked awake once, fighting it. Then she slumped softly toward the window, fatigue finally overpowering the adrenaline and grief. Her breathing deepened. She relaxed, losing the tension etched into her bones.

I slowed the truck without thinking, letting the road smooth beneath us. The engine's hum became steady white noise, something gentle. She murmured something unintelligible, shifting just enough that a strand of hair fell across her cheek. I resisted the impulse to reach out and move it.

Ray talked about her, more than he meant to, I was sure. He worried about her and was angry she left sometimes, but he loved her. And now he'd left her with a mess she didn't deserve and a ranch too big for one person to carry alone.

And I was the one driving her straight toward it.

The foothills grew clearer on the horizon, soft shapes rising out of the prairie like a promise and a warning. Home for me. Something else entirely for her.

The land waited, and the truth wasn't urgent. The problems Ray left would be there in an hour or a few days.

I steadied my grip on the wheel and kept driving.

Beside me, Tessa Callahan slept, small, fragile, strong, exhausted, stubborn.

She had no idea what she was returning to. No idea what was coming.

But when she woke, I'd be there. And when I hit her with the truth, I'd be the one holding the ground steady beneath her feet.

Even if she hated me for it.

# SEVEN

TESSA

I jerked upright, heart pounding, the seatbelt cut into my shoulder, glancing around at the unfamiliar surroundings.

"You're alright," Wyatt said, calm as ever. His voice grounded me faster than the scenery did.

I blinked against the light and pushed my sunglasses back up my nose.

"I fell asleep," I said, brilliant as ever.

"You needed it," he said.

I rubbed the side of my face where it had been pressed to the seat. "Did I snore?"

"Little bit."

"Oh God," I groaned.

His mouth twitched like he was fighting a smile. "I've heard worse."

I stared out the window instead of at his profile. The sky felt too big. The colours were too clear. The air through the cracked window smelled like dust and sun-warmed grass, a scent I'd spent years trying to forget and now wanted to bottle and keep in my hands.

"How long was I out?" I asked.

"About an hour."

"Seriously?" I swallowed hard as we turned off the highway onto a narrower road I recognized, and my stomach dipped. The truck rattled over a rough patch. Cattle grazed along a far fence line, dark shapes against the pale grass. A hawk rode the air in slow, lazy circles above a stand of poplars. The windmills on the horizon turned lazy arcs.

I hated this drive when I was a teenager. It felt like the road to nowhere. Like, once you came out here, the rest of the world shrank. "We're almost there," I whispered.

"Yeah," he replied quietly.

I clenched my hands together in my lap. My fingers were cold even though the cab was warm.

"Can we, uh, not just drive straight up?" The words came out before I could swallow them. "I need a second."

"We can pull off by the river," he said without hesitating. He turned onto the gravel road that led deeper into the valley. Dust rose in the truck's wake. On either side of us, pasture opened like pages. There were differences if you knew where to look. New fencing on one property. A metal equipment shed where I remembered an old slanting barn. But the bones were the same.

Wyatt eased the truck off onto a small turnout near a stand of willows I remembered from fishing trips with Ray. The river ran quietly behind them, water glinting through the leaves.

"I don't know how to walk in there," I admitted, staring straight ahead. "I keep thinking if I don't see it, it won't be real."

"That isn't how it works," he said. "But I won't rush you."

I risked a look at him. His hands rested on the steering wheel. Big hands. Calloused. Relaxed but ready. His profile was all hard lines and sun, and a day's worth of stubble.

"Thank you," I whispered, "for going to check." My voice wobbled on the last word. "For coming to get me. For all of it."

"That's what you do for people like Ray," he said simply. "Drive each other to town. Pull each other out of ditches. Make phone calls when it's time."

I bit my lip.

He shifted slightly, the leather creaking. "You want to see the place from here first?"

My heart lurched. "Can you see it?"

He nodded toward the windshield. "Look past that stand of poplars on the right."

I followed where he pointed, and at first, all I saw were trees and the curve of the valley. But then I found the house peeked over the hills, low and familiar, grey shingles darkened by time. I could see the weathered red of the old barn with the tin roof, and the windmill tower that had been broken my entire life, still stubbornly jutting into the sky.

My breath hitched. The image blurred. Tears slipped free before I could stop them. I swiped them away with the heel of my palm.

"I should've come sooner," I choked out. "I should've been here before this."

"He wouldn't have wanted that for you." He said it like he knew. It made something hot and sharp flare in my chest.

"What if I wanted it?" I snapped, anger lashing outward before I could catch it. "What if I wanted to be there instead of getting a visit from some stranger who knew him better than I did at the end?"

Silence slammed down.

I squeezed my eyes shut. "I'm sorry. That wasn't fair."

"Tessa, you're grieving," he said. "You get to be mad."

I gave a half-hearted laugh. "What's the acceptable behavior toward the man who drove hours to come collect your sorry ass? Because I don't think I've been all that pleasant."

"One or two swings," he said. "After that, I'll start swinging back."

I glanced at him. The corner of his mouth turned up slightly as he stared out the windshield. And somehow that helped.

"I'm still sorry," I muttered.

"Accepted."

We sat there a little longer. "Okay," I finally whispered. "I'm ready. Or as close as I'm going to get."

"You sure?" he asked.

"No," I admitted. "But if we sit here any longer, I'm going to run."

He nodded once. "Then we go."

He eased the truck back onto the road. Gravel crunched under the tires. Every metre closer made my skin crawl, not because I didn't want to be there, but because I did. Desperately. And it was too late.

When we turned into the lane, my breath stalled. The ranch came full into view. The front fence sagged more than I remembered. The green gate into the coral leaned crooked, one hinge rusted and half pulled from the post. And burdock and dandelions crowded the corners of the paddock.

"This looks," I let my voice trail off because I couldn't find the right word.

"Tired," Wyatt finished.

I swallowed. "Yeah."

He drove slowly up the lane. The house loomed closer. The white paint had gone chalky and thin, streaked with grey. The front steps were the same cracked concrete Ray always cursed but never fixed. One of the eavestroughs hung crooked near the corner, dripping rust stains down the siding.

Wyatt parked beside the house and shut off the engine.

The sudden quiet roared in my ears. No traffic. No neighbours yelling. Just the far-off sound of wind running through dry grass and a magpie arguing with itself on the fence.

I opened the door before I could think too long. My feet crunched on the gravel. The yard looked smaller than I remembered. The garden, overgrown with weeds, had once been my happy place. I didn't let myself look too close, one thing at a time.

Wyatt came around the truck. "You want to go in first?" he asked.

I stared at the front door. The screen still had the same tear in the corner, mended with duct tape. The welcome mat was the one I'd bought Ray as a joke that said Wipe Your Damn Feet. It had faded to a soft, stubborn ghost of letters.

"Yes," I said.

I pushed the door open like I'd done every day for most of my life. The house breathed out at us. Old air. Stale coffee. Dust. The faintest trace of him under it all, wrapped around the walls and floors and furniture in a way that made my vision blur.

I stepped over the threshold, and the grief hit hard and fast because there wasn't anyone yelling out asking who it was.

This was where he'd cooked me breakfasts and lectured me and tucked me in after movies. Where I'd slammed doors when I was sixteen, convinced he didn't understand anything. Where I'd made the decision to leave for school at eighteen and not come back, and he'd hugged me so hard my ribs ached even though his face stayed mostly dry.

I swallowed hard and forced my feet to move. The living room opened up to the right. Same worn couch with the ugly plaid blanket draped over the back. Same scuffed coffee table. Same sagging bookshelf stacked with Western paperbacks and old manuals.

And there, in the centre of it all, facing the television that probably never left the news channel, sat Ray's recliner.

Empty.

The air went out of my lungs.

I stepped closer. The dent in the cushion was deep, more so than when I'd left years ago. The blanket over the back of it had slid sideways. On the end table beside it, his coffee mug sat half full, ring of dried brown along the inside.

I grabbed the back of the chair. My knees finally gave out.

I didn't sob. It wasn't dramatic. It was worse. Silent, shaking breaths that tore through my chest while my fingers dug into the worn upholstery.

"He's gone," I whispered. "He's really gone."

Behind me, the floorboard creaked. Wyatt stayed inside the doorway. He didn't move toward me. He didn't look away.

"He loved that chair more than any person," I said, the words tumbling out because if I didn't talk, I'd scream. "He used to say if the world ended, he'd ride it out right there, beer in one hand, remote in the other."

"Sounds like him," Wyatt said.

I wiped my face with shaking hands and turned away from the chair before I tried to climb into it and never move again. The kitchen door stood open, the worn linoleum catching the light.

"I can make coffee," I said, because the alternative was curling into a ball. "He'd want that. Coffee first, I'll cry more later."

"You don't need to make me coffee," Wyatt said.

"It's not for you, it's for him."

He dipped his head, conceding the point. "Then I'll drink it," he said. "On his behalf."

Something about that steadied me. I walked into the kitchen on autopilot. The counters were cluttered, but in a way I understood. A plate left drying. A jar of instant coffee.

The sugar canister I'd painted as a kid, still chipped along the rim.

My hands found what they needed without me having to think. Filters. Mismatched mugs. The sound of water running into the carafe filled the silence.

Behind me, Wyatt moved through the house. His footfalls were slow and respectful. Not snooping. Just taking stock. He paused near the back door, probably looking out over the yard.

"How long have things been like this?" I asked, measuring coffee that had probably been sitting there for months.

"Depends what you mean by this," he said.

"The house. The yard. Him."

"A while," he admitted.

I shut my eyes. "And he didn't call me."

"He didn't ask for help from anyone." Wyatt leaned against the doorway and crossed his arms, watching my every movement around the room.

"It seems like you helped him."

"Sometimes," he said. "When he let me."

The coffee machine gurgled to life. The smell hit me hard. I leaned my palms into the counter to keep my legs under me.

"Are you going to tell me the rest now?" I asked quietly. "About the ranch."

Wyatt did not pretend to know what I meant. His boots shifted on the tile. When I turned, he was leaning against the doorframe, arms crossed over his chest. He looked too big for the small kitchen, like the room shrunk around him.

He held my gaze. "Are you sure you want it today?"

"No," I said. "But I'd rather not get knocked over by surprises on top of everything else."

He nodded once, something like respect in the gesture.

"Alright," he said. "Then we'll start with the truth."

EIGHT

WYATT

The old drip machine on Ray's counter gurgled and hissed like it was dying slowly, the glass carafe half full, dark liquid bubbling up in uneven bursts. The smell hit me first, bitter, strong, familiar.

I should have waited another day. Maybe two. Let her get through the funeral arrangements. Let her find her feet on this land again before I kick them out from under her.

But she asked. And if there was one thing I knew, it was that lies by omission cut deeper than blunt honesty. When she inevitably learned how bad things were, finding out I'd known and said nothing would feel like betrayal. Worse than telling her outright.

So I braced myself. Not for her feelings. For the fallout.

Her eyes were tired, rimmed faintly red, but there was steel under the exhaustion. Like she layered armour under the grief sometime between last night and now. She studied my face, gauging something, how bad it would be, maybe. How honest was I going to be? Whether I was about to dismantle what little stability she had left.

"The truth is, your uncle was struggling," I said. "More than he let on to anyone."

Her jaw tightened almost imperceptibly, but she didn't interrupt. "Tell me everything," she said.

I pushed off the doorframe and stepped into the kitchen fully. The floor creaked under my weight. "Fences are failing," I continued. "Some of the cattle wandered last month and haven't been found. Equipment's shot. The tractor needs work. The baler's on its last legs. The truck should've been retired five years ago." I let my voice trail off because what I had to say next would only make things worse.

She nodded slowly, absorbing the blows in quiet, controlled increments. "I figured it'd be bad," she said. "He always put repairs off. Said things still had life left in them even when they rattled across the yard."

The corner of my mouth twitched. That sounded like Ray.

"There's more," I said, exhaling. She went still. Spoon hovering over the mug. Shoulders squared. Waiting for the real damage.

"The taxes," I said. "He fell behind. The county sent notices. More than one."

Her jaw clenched hard enough I could see the muscle jump. One hand tightened around the rim of the mug. The other flattened on the counter like she needed to feel something solid under her palm.

"And there's a loan, or more than one," I added. No sense avoiding it. "A big one."

Her shoulders went rigid. Every line of her body sharpened. "What kind of loan?"

"One secured against the land."

She blinked. Once. Twice. Swallowed. The tendons in her neck stood out. "You mean a lien," she said.

"Yes."

She stared at the mug for a second like she'd forgotten what it was. Her fingers tightened around the handle until her knuckles paled.

"So he could lose it," she said.

"He would've," I answered. "It was a matter of time." Silence settled between us. Heavy. Thick.

She swallowed again, hard. "Okay," she said at last. "That's a lot. But I can deal with it. I can figure something out. I'll get a payment plan, I can sell things, like equipment, and some cattle. The debt should be wiped out with his passing, right?"

There it was. She is reaching for the thin ice of hope.

"Tessa," I said quietly. She looked at me then. Really looked. Those tired eyes sharpened, defences drawing tight. "The bank will still want to get their money," I said. "So it'll be auctioned off for them to recoup the costs. Unless you decide to assume the debt yourself."

Ray hadn't been a talker, but he'd let me know what was happening. What the numbers looked like. What would the bleak future be if nothing changed?

She went very, very still. Her fingers loosened on the mug just enough for her hand to tremble.

"There's something else," I said.

Her eyes narrowed. Suspicion sparked fast and sharp. "What?"

I hesitated just long enough for her to feel the shift. To sense there was something personal in what I was about to say. Something that mattered. Something that could change how she saw me.

"I've been trying to buy the ranch," I said, and everything in her stopped.

Her breath. Her expression. The faint pulsing of her hands on the coffee mug as she started to lift it. All of it froze.

"You what?" she whispered.

Confusion crossed her face like a cloud. Her eyes focused in a new way, as if she'd finally sobered up.

"I made Ray an offer last year," I said. "Above market value. I asked again in the spring. And right before he passed." The words landed like fist blows. I could see each one hit. "I'd like to make you the same offer."

The mug came down hard on the counter. Porcelain clacked against laminate. Coffee sloshed up the sides, but somehow didn't spill over. I saw it then. The exact moment the switch flipped, and she became the spitting image of her uncle.

"Oh, I see what this is," she said. Her voice changed. Sharp. Cutting. "How absolutely stupid do you think I am?" A deep crease formed between her brows, her eyes blazing.

"You drive to Calgary to tell me he's gone," she said. "Offer to give me a ride, hide behind the concerned gentleman cowboy act. When in reality you're plotting to take all this from me." Her finger flicked outward, toward the window, the yard, the ranch beyond. The life she once had here. The life she chose to leave.

"Let me guess," she went on. "I can go back to a normal life again if I let you take it off my hands, right?" She stood in front of me now, glaring up like I was something tracked in on the bottom of a boot. Her jaw was tight, shoulders up, chest heaving.

"I'm not trying to steal anything," I said. I kept my voice level.

"What did Ray say to your offer?" she demanded.

"No," I said. "Every time."

Her laugh cracked. Wild. Bitter. "So you thought you'd try me the day after he died, because you're so sure I want to dump this place as fast as I can?" Her voice rose. Heat poured out of her in waves.

"For fuck's sake," she shouted, "he's not even in the

ground yet." Her words hit hard, but she wasn't done. "A fucking vulture is what you are."

"That isn't what I'm doing," I said.

"Really," she snapped. "Could've fooled me." She was shouting now. Her voice bounced around the small kitchen, filling every corner. I wondered if she knew how much she sounded like him, like Ray when he was cornered and scared and pretending he was just angry.

"I was trying to help him," I said evenly. "He needed someone to take over. Someone with the resources."

"You mean you," she fired back. I didn't respond. Her eyes shone suddenly. Fury. Heartbreak. Betrayal all tangled together. She looked at me like she wanted to hit me. Or scream. Or shove me out the door and bar it behind me.

"You should've told me this yesterday," she said.

"You weren't ready," I answered.

"You don't get to decide that," she said. Her voice climbed again, sharp and shaking. "You don't get to waltz in here and act like you're some hero when you've been waiting for the perfect moment to take everything."

"That isn't the truth," I said, quieter than before.

"It's exactly the truth," she shot back. "I see it now. You didn't come because you cared about Ray. You came because you wanted his land." She was wrong. She was also hurting, and grief made enemies out of anything close enough to strike.

"Tessa," I said quietly. "I didn't come get you to start a fight."

"Well, congratulations," she said. "Because you just started a war." The words hung there. Final. Cold.

Silence rang through the kitchen, loud in its own way. The coffee machine ticked. A fly bumped against the ceiling, and outside, somewhere, a cow mooed.

She stepped back. Not far. Just enough. Like, even the air between us burned.

"I want you to leave," she said. I didn't move. "Wyatt, leave."

I set my jaw, reached for my hat on the counter, and slid it on. The brim brushed my forehead, familiar weight settling in place, the one thing that felt steady right now.

I moved toward the doorway, eyes on her as she wrapped her arms tighter around herself, like she was holding her own ribs together.

As I reached the threshold, she choked out, "I trusted you."

The words landed inside my chest like a kick.

For a second, something cracked hard enough to make me falter. A fissure down the middle of the control I lived by. I almost said something then. Almost reached for some explanation that would make it hurt less. But explanations don't mend fresh wounds. Time does. Perspective. Sometimes nothing.

"Lock the door," I said quietly. "I'm nearby if you need anything, and my number's on the fridge."

"I don't need anything from you, and I won't be using that number," she snapped.

I stepped out into the sunlight. The screen door clapped shut behind me, rattling in its frame like the house itself decided it wanted me gone, too.

The ranch sat tired but sturdy under the late morning sky, faded paint, sagging fences, weeds along the driveway, cattle specks in the back pasture, the old barn roof catching the light. Ray's legacy. Her inheritance. A place stitched from stubbornness and history.

I walked down the steps, boots crunching on gravel, jaw tight, heart heavier than I liked to admit. The morning air was cool still, but the sun was climbing. Heat would come. So would decisions, and more hard truths.

Enemies, it was then.

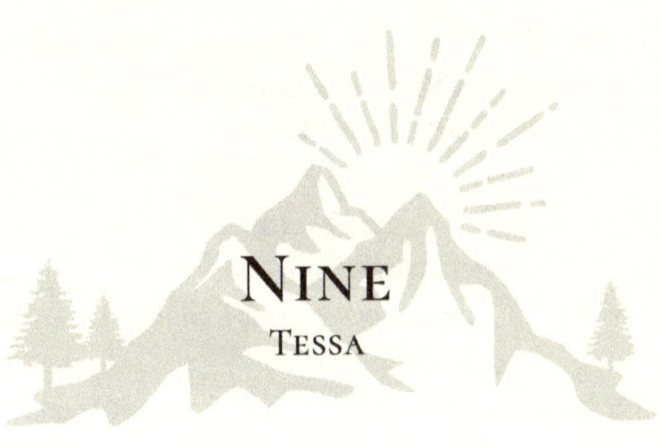

NINE

TESSA

I stood in Ray's kitchen in the silence left behind, hands braced on the counter, trying not to shake apart. The laminate edge dug into my palms, grounding me in a way the floor couldn't. My knees felt unreliable. My breath uneven. My whole body vibrated with leftover adrenaline, anger, and grief.

He'd tried to buy the ranch. He'd been trying for years. He'd shown up at my apartment. Driven me home. Stood here in this damn kitchen as silent support.

And I'd let him. "Fuck," I shouted, my voice reverberating off the appliances.

For a second, a single stupid second, I'd trusted him. He had been steady. Calm. A presence to lean toward when everything was unraveling. The kind of man who didn't flinch from chaos.

My phone buzzed in my pocket. I ignored it. Then it buzzed again. And again. And again. Repeated, insistent. Eventually, annoyance won over despair, and I dragged the phone out.

Colin's name flashed on the screen; there were a dozen

texts. Had he always been this annoying? No, he hadn't, it was only when he couldn't have me, he got like this.

The phone buzzed again, but this time it was Dani. I smiled as I answered.

"Oh my God," Dani breathed, her voice softening instantly. "I've been dying from worry." Her frantic voice should have made me feel better, but I couldn't even muster a laugh.

I sagged into one of the kitchen chairs. It creaked under me, and the sound nearly undid me. Ray's weight had made the same noise every morning while drinking coffee and complaining about the neighbours dog.

"He's trying to buy the ranch," I whispered.

Silence. Actual silence. No ranting. No threats. No immediate homicide.

Then Dani said, very calmly, "Which part of this sentence am I supposed to process first? The part where he tried to steal your family home or the part where he lied to you while being sexy and helpful?"

"This isn't funny."

"I'm not laughing," Dani snapped. "I'm homicidal." She meant it.

I pressed my fingers to my forehead. "He's been trying to buy it for years. Years. And Ray never told me. And now Wyatt just expects me to hand the place over to him."

"Okay." Dani took a breath so sharp I could hear the inhale. "Let me get this straight. Sexy rancher giant man shows up. Drives you across the prairies like some moody cowboy ride share. And then tells you he's been circling the property like a vulture?"

"That's exactly what I said," I muttered.

"I hate him," Dani declared. "I hope his sexy salt-and-pepper beard falls off."

"He doesn't have a beard." I hate that I knew that fact.

"Fine. I hope his jawline gets slightly less sharp."

"Do we have to go that far?"

"Yes," she hollered into the phone.

I stared at the kitchen table, the old place mats Ray never let anyone replace, still sitting where he'd left them.

"I can't do this," I whispered. "Dani, it's too much."

"Yes, you can," she said instantly. "I know you can because you're stubborn and angry and filled with rage right now, and that's basically rocket fuel."

"That's not helpful." My voice, oddly flat-sounding even to my ears.

"Actually, it is. You need to be pissed off, you need to fight. That ranch is rightfully yours."

I swallowed hard. "The debts are huge."

"Okay. And?"

"And the taxes are overdue," I answered, thinking that would be the end of the conversation.

"Alright."

"And there's a lien. A big one."

"Oh my God," she breathed. "Ray."

"I'm so mad at him." My voice cracked. "He didn't tell me anything. He left me with all of this."

"You're allowed to be furious at him," Dani said softly. "And sad. And confused. And overwhelmed. That doesn't make you ungrateful."

I put my head in my hands. Tears slid through my fingers. Too hot. Too fast. "I don't know where to start."

"You start by not trusting a tall, handsome, rugged man who hides financial betrayals."

"Dani," I sniffed.

"Fine. You start by breathing," her words soft and mildly reassuring. I inhaled. Slowly. Painfully. It didn't fix anything, but it stopped me from shaking.

"And then," she continued, voice sharpening with familiar

protective fire, "you're going to tell that man to stay off your property unless the house is literally on fire."

"I already did."

"Good. Tell him again."

"I don't want to fight with him forever," I admitted before I could stop myself.

"What did he do to your brain?" Dani demanded. "Did he hypnotize you with his forearms and cowboy hat?"

I frowned. "No."

"You paused."

I sighed. "Dani."

"No. This is important. Did he use the forearms?"

I stared at the ceiling. "Maybe."

She made a disgusted noise. "Ugh. Men."

I wiped my face. "I need to figure things out, okay? Without him. Without Colin. Without anyone."

Her voice softened. "You won't do it alone. You have me."

"You're in Calgary."

"I can be on your doorstep in two hours."

Despite everything, I laughed quietly. "Please don't drive here."

"Fine. But I'm on standby. And if you see Wyatt again, I want you to picture me beside you holding a frying pan. We'll go, Mary-Anne and Wanda, if we have to."

"Dani—"

"Nonnegotiable."

I let out a long breath and leaned back in the chair. The house hummed around me, the refrigerator still rattling, floorboards popping under temperature changes, dust drifting in the sun like tiny ghosts suspended in the air.

"Can you stay on the phone?" I whispered.

"As long as you need," she said instantly. "I'll even do my dramatic monologue voice if you want."

"No monologues."

"Fine. But I have them ready." She kept talking, ranting, occasionally dropping something I could hear crash in the background. She filled the silence with sarcasm and threats and wildly inappropriate jokes. She told me she'd hex Wyatt's truck. She told me the forearms were probably fake. She told me I was too smart to fall for cowboy sorcery.

It helped more than anything else could have.

When we finally hung up, I wasn't fixed. But I didn't feel as alone. And I wasn't about to roll over. I wiped my face, squared my shoulders, and pulled the first stack of overdue bills toward me. The envelopes felt heavy, the paper stiff. Debt. Taxes. Notices. Things left unopened, ignored, shoved in drawers.

Wyatt Hargrove might have plans for this ranch. But this land was Ray's. Ray was all I had aside from Dani. And I wasn't letting anyone, bank, buyer, or cowboy, take it without a fight.

I had just opened the first envelope when the knock came. Sharp. Three beats, and my entire body tensed. Not again. I was not doing Round Two with Wyatt.

I stomped to the door and flung it open, and stared right into the face of Marla Fincher.

"Oh, sweetheart," she gasped, hand flying to her chest in dramatic slow motion. "You look terrible."

I blinked. "Marla?" She was in her sixties. Floral dress. Pearls. Makeup done like she was attending church. She didn't wait for an invitation, just brushed past me, carrying a casserole so aggressively cheesy it could suffocate a grown man.

"I made a lasagna," she said. "Ray hated it, but grief makes people hungry for carbohydrates, dear." Marla set the casserole on the stove and turned to me with watery eyes. "I'm so sorry, darling."

Before I could respond, another knock came. I turned

slowly. I opened the door again, and Todd Halpern stood there. Wearing his feed store jacket and holding a pie tin.

"Your uncle always liked my wife's apple crumble," he said gruffly. "We figured you might need it." Behind him, Mrs. Kowalski from the quilting group peered past him like she was casing the joint.

I barely had time to register the sight before Todd shuffled inside, murmuring condolences while trying not to trip over his own oversized work boots.

"Oh," he added, "we told a few folks you were here."

"Why, why would you do that?"

Todd shrugged. "People want to help."

Another knock. This one is fast and urgent. I opened the door to find three more people: Jeanine, her husband, Mark, and someone carrying a crockpot the size of a toddler.

Jeanine brushed past me, sniffing loudly. "Tessa, sweetheart, why didn't you call us? We would have come sooner."

"I—"

Mark set the crockpot on the counter with a grunt. "Bison stew. Figured you'd be hungry."

"I'm... not," I stuttered.

"You will be. Grief is an appetite."

"What is wrong with all of you?" I whispered. But they weren't listening. People kept arriving. Knock after knock after knock. Condolences, casseroles, and unsolicited advice are pouring into the house like a flood.

Within fifteen minutes, Ray's kitchen was full. Three pies, four casseroles, a Tupperware container of muffins, a tray of Nanaimo bars, a crockpot full of soup, eight condolence cards, unsolicited hugs, and more busybodies than should legally be allowed on one property. It felt like a fucked up scene from the twelve days of Christmas.

Someone started making more coffee, and someone else reorganized the fridge. Then someone rearranged Ray's boots by the door "for tidiness." I stood in the middle of it all, dizzy from grief and noise and the scent of six different baked goods.

Jeanine squeezed my arm. "Do you need anything, dear?"

Yes. For all of you to leave. My brain screamed, but that's not what came out of my mouth. "Water," I croaked instead.

"Of course. Sit, sit." But I didn't sit. I started to move toward the back door, needing air, needing escape, and then I saw Wyatt's truck drive into the yard and park near the barn.

Inside the kitchen, Marla clapped loudly. "Everyone, let the girl breathe!"

The noise swelled, voices overlapping, plates clinking, casseroles warming, busybodies consoling each other about how devastated they were. I pressed my back to the wall and dragged a shaky breath into my lungs. This was too much.

All of it.

I pressed myself deeper into the wall, palms flat, breath thin and high in my chest. The kitchen had always been small, but now it felt microscopic.

Jeanine was telling me how Ray once fixed her fence for free. Todd was recounting a story from eight years ago that I wasn't even here for. Marla reorganized my entire spice cabinet in under two minutes.

The house felt crowded with strangers, ghosts, pity, and grief that wasn't theirs to share. I needed out.

Now.

I wove through the crowd, ignoring the "sweethearts" and "poor things" and "we're all here for you" voices clinging to me like static. The back door was ten feet away. Ten feet to freedom.

I grabbed the doorknob, but it clicked before I could turn it. The door swung inward, and Wyatt filled the frame. Cowboy hat low. Shoulders squared. Eyes sharp. But something in his face shifted when he saw the cluster of people behind me. A tightening of the jaw. A narrowing of his gaze. A silent *What in the hell?* I thought to myself as his gaze flicked down to me.

His eyes scanned my face, quick but thorough, taking in my pinched expression, my too-tight posture, the exhaustion hanging off me like a second skin. For a beat, we just stood there in the doorway. Close enough for the air between us to hum, close enough to feel the tension radiating off both our bodies.

Behind me, I could hear Jeanine gearing up for another condolence monologue. Wyatt's eyes flicked toward the sound. His jaw flexed once. Then he stepped inside.

A large, warm palm wrapped around my elbow, gentle but firm, and he pulled me to his side with a movement so smooth it stole my breath.

I should have yanked away or slapped his hand off me. I should have done anything except I didn't, I let him shift me to stand next to him.

And for the first time since the crowd arrived, I felt the faintest sense of air reaching my lungs.

The kitchen went quiet in stages, and voices petered out. People finally realized that something shifted.

Then Marla spoke, blinking rapidly. "Oh! Wyatt, dear, we didn't realize you were—"

"We're done here," Wyatt said, his tone wasn't sharp. It wasn't loud. But it carried across the kitchen. He released my elbow and stepped forward slightly, shoulders set like he'd just taken control of a barn full of wayward cattle.

"Folks," he said, nodding respectfully to the group, "I know you mean well. And Tess appreciates your concern."

I blinked. He'd called me Tess, and he said it without hesitation, as if he belonged here.

My stomach did a weird, traitorous flip.

"But this isn't helping her," he continued. "This house is full. And she needs a little space."

Todd cleared his throat. "We were just dropping food off."

"And you did," Wyatt said, calm but immovable. "Thank you, all of you. But it's time to give her some breathing room."

Jeanine's lips pursed. "We didn't mean to overwhelm her." Everyone was talking as if I wasn't even in the room.

"You didn't," Wyatt said. "But you all need to head out now."

A murmur rippled through the group. Offended. Confused. Uncertain who he thought he was. My heart pounded in my chest. I was supposed to tell him to back off, tell him he didn't get to speak for me.

But I didn't.

The truth settled like a stone in my chest. I wanted them out. And I didn't have the strength to do it alone.

Wyatt's presence filled the room, not loud, not aggressive. Just steady. Anchored. Like the only solid thing in a storm.

Marla stepped closer, frowning. "Well, if she needs anything, we're right up the road."

Wyatt's gaze flicked to me, asking without asking.

I nodded once.

He turned back to Marla. "She knows."

That was enough.

Slowly, grumbling, fussing, patting my arm too many times, people began drifting out, gathering their purses, their jackets, their condolences.

Todd placed a hand on my shoulder. "Call if you need an extra set of hands. Your uncle was a good man. You think about what you need. Don't let anyone rush you." His eyes cut pointedly to Wyatt.

"I will," I whispered, not trusting my voice to say more. Then he left, and Wyatt closed the door behind him. The house went still.

Wyatt exhaled. He glanced at the mountain of casseroles covering every surface. "They know how to feed a person."

I stared at him, but he didn't smile. Not really. But something warm flickered in the corner of his mouth.

I swallowed. My throat felt raw. "You didn't have to do that," I said quietly.

He shrugged lightly. "Seemed like you needed it."

"I could've handled it."

"No," he said, gentle but honest. "You couldn't." He took a step closer, but not too close. Just near enough, I could feel the warmth coming off him. "Tess—" he began.

"Don't," I said, too quickly. "Don't call me that."

His jaw twitched. "Alright."

Silence stretched between us. Not hostile. Not warm either. Just charged.

He gestured toward the table. "You should sit."

"I've been sitting."

"You should sit again."

My chest clenched. "Stop telling me what to do."

"Then sit because you want to. You're about to fall over."

I sank into the chair while Wyatt stayed standing. Solid. Unmoving. Hands braced against the back of the chair across from me, shoulders broad enough to block out half the kitchen light.

"You don't have to be strong every second," he said quietly.

My throat closed around the denial.

He watched me, not pitying, not pushing. Just watching. Like he was sorting through a dozen things he wanted to say but was waiting to see which ones wouldn't break me.

"You should eat something," he murmured.

I huffed. "You sound like Dani."

"I've been compared to worse." Wyatt shifted, leaning one hip against the counter. "They'll come back," he said. "The town. That's what they do, they care. Too much sometimes."

"I noticed."

"But it'll slow down. You'll get your space."

Outside, cattle bellowed in the distance. A raven cawed from the roof. The house creaked as it warmed under the rising sun.

"Thank you," I said, barely audible.

He nodded once. "You're welcome. I'll check the fences."

My voice trembled. "Do whatever you want."

He tipped his hat in a small, subtle motion that landed like a punch in my chest. Then he stepped back outside, pulling the door shut behind him. And for the first time since setting foot back on Callahan land, I exhaled without shaking.

TEN
TESSA

The funeral took place three days after the argument in the kitchen. They were the longest three days of my life. Every hour felt heavy. Every phone call felt like it took something from me. The paperwork, the condolences, the casseroles, the decisions, they all blurred together until I felt hollowed out.

When I arrived at the small white church in River's Edge, the parking lot was already full. Trucks and old sedans sat everywhere in crooked rows. People dressed in muted colours gathered on the steps, murmuring to each other with the soft, reverent tone small towns used when someone important passed.

Ray had been important here.

I stood on the bottom step for a long moment, clutching the hem of my black dress, trying to steady my breathing. The sky was pale, thin clouds drifting across the sun, softening the light. The air smelled faintly of wild sage. Somewhere nearby, cattle mooed, a reminder of the life outside this one moment.

When I finally walked inside, the sanctuary was already packed. Every pew was filled, and chairs lined along the back wall. People turned as I entered, familiar faces from childhood, neighbours, ranchers Ray argued with, old friends who loved him anyway.

And I wasn't ready to face any of them.

But I did.

I made my way down the centre aisle to the front row, the spot reserved for me, and sat alone for only a moment before I sensed him.

Turning around, I saw Wyatt step into the aisle. He wasn't wearing his hat. His hair was combed back, still damp, and he wore a black jacket that fit him too well. His gaze swept the room until it found me, and for a second, neither of us looked away.

He walked down the aisle with the other pallbearers, but when he reached the front, he sat beside me as Ray had explicitly written in his funeral instructions. The pew groaned slightly under his weight. His presence filled the small space between us. I stiffened, but I didn't move away.

The minister stepped up to the pulpit, smoothing the pages of his notes. "Good morning," he began gently. "We are here to honour the life of Raymond Callahan, a man who worked hard, argued harder, and loved in a way that wasn't always spoken aloud, but was always felt."

A soft ripple of warm laughter and murmurs of agreement moved through the crowd.

The minister continued. "Ray's life changed the day he became a father in the most unexpected way. Many of you know the story. One morning, more than twenty-three years ago, he opened his front door to find his two-year-old niece standing on his porch with a grocery bag of clothes and no explanation." My throat tightened, and my hands went cold.

"He never discovered who brought her to him," the minister said. "He only found a short note inside the bag telling him that he needed to look after Tessa. And from that moment on, she became his whole world."

My vision blurred. The room tilted. I felt Wyatt shift next to me, but he didn't touch me. He didn't speak. He just stayed exactly where he was.

"He raised Tessa as his own," the minister continued. "He taught her how to work the land, how to care for animals, how to be stubborn, how to be strong, and how to fight for the things that matter." I lifted the tissue to dab at the tears that came freely.

My jaw trembled. I pressed my fingers together so tightly my knuckles hurt. Wyatt shifted, and he put his arm over the back of the pew, gently wrapping his big hand around my shoulder.

"Ray wasn't perfect," the preacher said, smiling faintly, "but he was present. And that mattered. It mattered to the child he took in, and it mattered to this town."

Wyatt's breath slowed beside me. I could feel it even though he hadn't moved closer.

The minister opened the floor for memories. People stood and talked about Ray's kindness, his temper, the way he fixed fences for neighbours without being asked, and did not worry about his own work. The way he pretended it annoyed him when children offered to help, but secretly loved it.

When he gestured for me to speak, my chest tightened painfully. My throat closed. Words backed up behind my tongue, but none of them would come out.

Wyatt's shoulder brushed mine as he stood. A whisper of contact. But it steadied something inside me, and I hated that it did. He reached out his hand to help me stand, and I took it.

The church blurred around the edges as I moved toward the pulpit. My voice wavered at first, but I forced myself to speak.

"It's hard to believe after all these years, I still don't know who left me on Ray's doorstep. I don't even know if he is truly my uncle, but it never mattered," I said softly. "He took me in. He taught me how to be part of this town and gave me a home. And for every hard moment we had, and there were many, I knew he loved me. He loved me the best way he knew how. I will miss him terribly. Thank you, Uncle Ray, for making me the woman I am."

A few sniffles echoed across the room.

When I sat back down, my hands were shaking so badly I had to clasp them together again. Wyatt didn't look at me, but his jaw tightened in something like restraint or understanding. Maybe both.

Then it was time.

The six pallbearers, Wyatt included, stood and walked toward the casket. Wyatt took the front right position, closest to me. The wood looked heavy, carved from simple pine, exactly what Ray would have wanted.

They lifted it in one smooth motion.

My breath cracked.

Wyatt's fingers curled around the handle, and I watched his shoulders shift as he adjusted the weight. His face didn't move, but I could see the tightness behind his eyes.

They carried my uncle out of the church and into the sunlight.

I followed. My steps were unsteady, but I forced each one. People fell in behind us, their heads bowed, their hands folded.

The cemetery overlooked the open range, a rolling stretch of foothills, golden grass, and wide sky. It felt too big. Too quiet. Too permanent.

As the pallbearers set the casket down over the open grave, a breeze ran through the grass, whispering across the hillside. Birds circled overhead. The sun slid behind a thin cloud, dimming the light.

The minister spoke again, but the words washed over me. I

stared at the casket, willing myself not to fall apart in front of everyone.

When the time came to throw the first handful of soil, I stepped forward, but my knees nearly buckled. Wyatt moved before I could collapse.

He placed his hand gently, but firmly, around my waist. He didn't push; he didn't guide. He just kept me upright. His warmth anchored me in a way that made my throat burn.

"I've got you," he murmured quietly enough that only I could hear it.

I hated that I needed it. And I hated even more that I believed him. I hated him. Except I didn't, not really, at least not today.

I released the soil. It hit the wood with a soft thump that broke something inside me. When I stepped back, my breath hitched. Wyatt didn't touch me again, but he remained close, standing slightly behind me, like a wall between me and the rest of the world.

One by one, people followed. Soil. Flowers. Whispered goodbyes.

Eventually, the long walk back from the gravesite funneled everyone toward the parking lot. I expected people to drift to their trucks and head for the church, because that's what the minister announced, but instead the crowd was shifting north, chatting in small clusters, pointing toward the outskirts of town. I frowned and turned to my friend Brooke just as she looped her arm through mine like I was a toddler she wasn't confident would stay upright.

"Where is everyone going?" I asked.

"To the brewery," she said with a sympathetic little squeeze. "Wyatt closed the place for the afternoon. Said it was the only spot big enough to hold everyone."

I stopped walking, my boots sinking into the gravel. "The brewery?"

She blinked at me as if I'd asked what a cow was. "Hargrove Brewing. Didn't he tell you?"

Of course, he didn't. Why would he tell me anything he decided about my life?

Brooke mistook the shock tightening my throat for gratitude and patted my hand. "It was really generous of him. He told Natalie to cancel the lunch service, send the barflies home, and make Ray's family comfortable."

Family. The word scraped across something raw.

I followed the stream of mourners to the northern edge of town, where the brewery rose from the prairie like it had been built from the land itself. Timber beams, stone walls, wide windows catching every bit of late afternoon light. It was warm and alive and far larger than I remembered from childhood glimpses.

Inside, the shift in atmosphere hit immediately. Woodsmoke from the massive stone fireplace at the far end curled through the air. Glasses clinked. Voices murmured gently. Warm lighting spilled across comfortable chairs grouped around the fire, the way other restaurants used tables. People settled into them like they belonged there, like the space was designed to be a community hub.

My breath caught because it didn't look like a bar or a business. It looked like a haven.

And then I saw him.

Wyatt stood behind the long wooden bar, the black jacket gone, sleeves of his white button-down shirt rolled up to his elbows, showing off his forearms leading to it, tight over his shoulders. He was talking to a woman while pointing toward trays of food being laid out: beef sliders, roasted chicken, platters of vegetables, and dainties. As I watched him, he lifted a half keg and slid it into place while someone else steadied the tap line. His posture never faltered. His expression never wavered.

Commanding without raising his voice, calm without ever seeming soft, grounded in a way that made something in my stomach twist.

He glanced up.

Our eyes met across the space, sunlight washing in from the windows at my right. The room seemed to narrow around that single moment, the noise pulling back, a sharp and unwelcome heat tightening under my ribs. His expression didn't shift at all.

I tore my gaze away.

Mrs. Kowalski rested a warm hand on my shoulder. "Your uncle loved this place," she said gently. "Wyatt said he wanted folks to gather somewhere Ray loved, and this felt right."

My throat tightened. I didn't want it to feel right. I didn't want Wyatt to know anything about what Ray would've wanted. I didn't want the floor under my feet to steady just because Wyatt prepared it. But it did. And I hated that almost as much as I hated how much I needed it.

As I moved through the room, people hugged me, pressed plates into my hands, and offered condolences that blurred together.

The food disappeared quickly, trays emptied and refilled by staff moving with quiet efficiency. Laughter mixed with tears. Stories drifted like smoke up toward the vaulted wooden beams. It should've been comforting. It wasn't. It was too much. Too loud. Too kind. Too relentless.

I felt overwhelmed, untethered, as if the room kept shifting beneath my feet. Even with the fire glowing, none of the warmth seemed to reach my bones.

But every time I felt myself tipping toward the edge, I sensed Wyatt nearby. Never approaching. Never inserting himself. Just close enough to anchor.

I kept catching glimpses of him. Checking that the staff had enough trays prepared. Speaking quietly with older ranchers, steadying them when emotion caught them off guard. Adjusting a dimmer light so the room wasn't so harsh. Pouring coffee for a widow whose hands shook too much to lift the pot herself. Standing near the fireplace while talking with the minister, posture relaxed but controlled, as if the entire room ran on the same quiet pulse he carried.

Each moment tightened something deep inside my chest. I hated that he made this easier. I hated the strange, unwanted softening in me every time my eyes drifted in his direction.

By the time the room emptied, the tension I'd been gripping dropped all at once, leaving me hollow and shaking. I finally turned to where he stood watching me from a careful distance.

He didn't step forward or speak. He simply waited, steady and patient, like he understood something in me needed space to decide which emotion would surface first.

"You didn't have to help me today," I whispered.

"Yes, I did."

The simplicity of it landed like a hand pressed firm and warm against my sternum, steadying something I hadn't admitted was slipping.

"Do you want me to drive you home? " he asked.

I wanted to tell him no, I wanted to tell him to leave me alone. I wanted to walk all the way back to the ranch in these terrible shoes before I let him see me shake again. But I was so tired. My body ached from holding itself together.

"That would be great, thank you," I whispered. His jaw tightened like he hadn't expected me to say yes. He reached into the pocket of his suit coat and pulled out a phone.

"Holt's going to bring my truck; we can take yours. Then you don't have to worry about figuring out how to get it home."

He walked me to the truck without touching me. He

opened the passenger door. I climbed in. He shut it gently, then rounded the hood and slid behind the wheel.

When we reached the ranch, he pulled up to the house and put the truck in park. I stared at the front steps for a long minute before I had the strength to move to the door.

"Thank you. For everything," I said quietly.

Wyatt nodded once, expression unreadable. "Anytime."

I stepped out of the truck, closed the door behind me, and walked toward the house. The grief pressed down on me again, but something else lingered beneath it.

Something I didn't have the energy, or the courage, to name. I sank down the door once I made it inside, pulled my knees up to my chest, and sobbed.

ELEVEN
WYATT

My truck rolled into Ray's yard just as Tessa closed the front door behind her.

The house swallowed her up, the screen banging once and then settling. For a second, I just stood there in the gravel, staring at that closed door, my hands empty, my chest feeling like someone reached in and wrung it out.

Holt cut the engine, and the field settled into its usual sounds: a few heifers bawling in the back pasture, the faint rattle of the windmill that never quite spun right anymore. Holt climbed out, closed the door with a solid thunk, and squinted across the hood at me.

He glanced at the house, then back at me. "How's she doing?"

"There's no good way to bury the only parent you ever had," I said.

He nodded once, slowly. Holt was a big man, thicker through the shoulders than I, with dark hair going grey at the temples, lines around his eyes from years of squinting into the sun. He had been my ranch boss for more than a decade.

I cast one last look at the house. The curtains in the front room were drawn halfway. A sliver of movement passed behind them, just the flicker of a shadow. I didn't know if she was watching or not.

I climbed into the truck on the passenger side. He climbed back in, started the engine, and turned us around, heading out of the yard and back toward the gravel road. The ranch looked tired as we pulled away. The sagging fence. The chipped paint on the eaves. The barn roof needed more than a patch job. So much of it could have been avoided if Ray let someone in earlier.

"You carry him alright," Holt asked after a few miles, eyes still on the road.

"The casket was lighter than some of the bulls we shove onto trailers," I said.

"That's not what I asked."

"I know."

He waited.

"I did what he asked me to do," I said finally. "He wanted me there. He wanted me to walk him out, then bring her back. I did it."

"And she still thinks you want to pick his bones clean," Holt said.

"She has reason to," I said. "From where she is standing, I am the man who shows up and announces the place is drowning, that the bank will come, and the taxes are behind. That her uncle lied by keeping it from her."

"It's not your lie," Holt said.

"Doesn't matter. Truth hurts the same no matter who says it." I leaned my head back lightly against the seat and closed my eyes. "He talked about her more than he even realized."

"I know," Holt said. "I was there when he used to stand at the edge of his yard and stare up your way like you had his answers in your back pocket."

"He wanted to sell," I said. "Right up until he remembered she might come back one day. Then he wanted to hold it for her."

"And now she has it. Plus the mess that comes with it."

The truck hit a pothole, jostling us both. When we settled again, I opened my eyes. The land here rolled gently, not as dramatic as farther west, but still full of lines and curves that meant something. Fence lines marked the boundaries, and the cattle we passed were as familiar to me as neighbours.

"Did I ever tell you about the first time I saw him with her?" I asked.

Holt kept his eyes on the road. "No."

"She was little," I said. "Five, maybe six. He had her sitting on the fence rail down by the corrals. Big straw hat swallowing her head, boots that didn't fit, braids crooked as sin. He kept putting her back up every time she slipped. He complained the whole time. Said she was a handful, distracted, and had no sense of balance. Yet, he never once put her down."

"I was just a kid working whatever job that would get me out of my dad's place. But I knew he had something I didn't. Someone is waiting at the end of the day. Someone with his eyes and his features."

Holt flicked a glance at me. "You had that for a while, too."

I knew who he meant. Rena. My ex-wife. Dark hair, quick wit, a laugh that hooked into me before I could fight it. We built something once. A life. A routine. A future that seemed clear.

Then life changed. The ranch needed more, the brewery was a dream realized, and the markets tanked. Long days turned into longer nights. Rena got tired of talking to the back of my head. I hadn't seen it fast enough. Or maybe I had convinced myself that the land would be enough of an explanation.

"Yeah, well, that didn't work," I said.

"You've got Maddy, though," Holt said. "That counts for something."

"Yeah," I said quietly.

Fields flicked by outside, green giving way to golden patches. The sky was streaked with pink now. The long line of cottonwoods that hugged the creek glowed in the low light, their leaves shifting in a faint breeze.

"Are you going to give her time?" Holt asked, and I knew he was meaning Tessa.

"I have to," I said. "She is too raw to hear anything that sounds like sense. Every word out of my mouth sounds like a threat right now."

"You also can't let the bank call the note in," Holt reminded me. "And those notices are not going to stop."

"I know," I said. "One problem at a time."

He gave a small nod, as if that was all there was to say. When the lane to my house came into view, I turned my head and watched it approach. The house stood tall on the rise, lights now glowing in two front windows, the porch a long dark line against the sky.

Holt drove up to the gravel square and parked in front of the steps. He killed the engine and rested his hands on the wheel for a second.

"You want company?"

"No, I'm not really in the mood for it tonight. Go home."

"Call if you need something, Wyatt."

"Thanks."

He nodded once, then opened his door and climbed out. I did the same. The air felt cooler here, a faint breeze tugging at the front of my shirt.

When he disappeared past the tree line, the silence wrapped in.

The house loomed in front of me, dark wood and stone and glass. It had been my father's pride. Big porches, tall windows, heavy doors, rooms meant to fill with family and noise. I added new wings over the years, expanded the kitchen, redone the great room, and made sure the old beams stayed where they were, but reinforced where needed.

You could fit three of Ray Callahan's house inside mine and still have room for a barn.

From the outside, it looked like success. The kind people in town nodded at, the kind that made their voices shift when they said my name. Wyatt Hargrove, big operation, lots of land, successful brewery, and never stops to enjoy any of it.

I climbed the steps, opened the front door, and tossed my hat on the bench by the door, rubbing a hand over my face.

The great room stretched long and wide, anchored by the massive stone fireplace against the far wall. Above it hung a painting my mother had chosen, all sky and mountains and running horses. Leather couches framed a low table, a thick rug sprawled across the floor. One of the housekeepers arranged art books in a neat stack that had never once been opened. The place looked like a magazine spread. And I walked through it like a visitor.

The kitchen sat just beyond, separated by a long island with barstools. Six, to be exact. It was the kind of place meant for breakfasts with kids fighting over cereal and teenagers raiding the fridge late at night.

Only one mug sat in the drying rack. Mine from this morning. On the fridge, held in place by a magnet shaped like a boot, was a drawing my daughter made four summers ago. Bright crayons, a horse with legs too long, a sun that smiled in the corner, a stick figure man beside a shorter stick girl. She had written Dad in big letters.

My chest squeezed. I touched the corner of the paper with my fingertips, then dropped my hand.

Maddy lived in Calgary with her mother. They'd moved there after the divorce. It made sense for them. Rena's work was there, better schools, more friends, and better opportunities for Maddy to grow.

My life didn't allow me to drop it and follow her; what it gave me was weekend visits and phone calls. Almost every weekend, I'd meet Rena halfway and pick my daughter up, and life would be perfect for almost seventy-two hours.

She loved the ranch in the way children loved wild places; they didn't have to worry about anything but being free. The horses, the dogs, the big machines. Then she went back to the city where she had friends, show jumping practice, and a bedroom that didn't smell like leather and dust.

Standing at the counter, I could see the long line of buildings that made up the working part of the ranch. The calving barns, the machine shed, and the long structure that held the squeeze chutes and pens. Beyond them, the fields stretched, lit by the last light clinging to the sky. Somewhere out there, my men were finishing evening checks, setting things up for the night. Work didn't stop because a man got buried.

It hadn't stopped when my father died either. I'd been younger then, less worn in. I remembered standing at his grave with my hat in my hand and the blunt understanding that the cattle didn't care that I lost my father. They only cared whether the feed was ready for them and the water ran.

Ray had been the same kind of man. He worked until his body shut down. People like us didn't know how to stop. Only how to pause and then start again with more weight on our backs.

Now Tessa was in his home, dealing with his unpaid bills and his half-finished projects. I'd seen the strain in her face when I told her about the loan. The anger when I admitted I tried to buy the place. The way her hands shook when she told me to leave.

It was easier to be angry instead of admitting you were scared.

The phone in my pocket buzzed. I pulled it out and felt something in my chest loosen a fraction.

I answered on the next ring. "Hey, bug."

"Hi, Dad." Her voice was light and clear and warm, the way kids' voices were when they had not yet learned to weigh every word. "Mom said I should call you."

"Your mom is smart," I said. "How are you?"

"I'm okay. Mom told me about Mr. Callahan, are you sad?" she said quietly.

"Yeah," I said honestly. "I am."

There was a pause on the line. I could picture her, lying on her bed in her room in Calgary, feet in the air, phone to her ear, brow furrowed in the way she had when she thought hard.

"I'm sad too. He was always nice to me. Did his niece come home?"

"Yeah, Tessa's here. I was with her for a bit today." Maddy hadn't ever met Tessa, but over the years, Ray had been like a grandfather to my daughter, even if he grumbled about the inconvenience.

"I bet she's sad too," Maddy said softly as if she was trying to imagine what it would be like if roles were different and it was her mourning me.

"Yeah," I said. "She is having a really hard time."

Another pause.

"Did you give her a hug?" Maddy asked.

I exhaled, the corner of my mouth lifting. "She's not really in a hugging mood right now."

"Is she mad at you?" Maddy asked.

"You could say that."

"Why," my daughter asked, straightforward as only a child could be.

"Because she thinks I am the bad guy. And I didn't do a good enough job convincing her otherwise."

"Are you the bad guy?" She asked hesitantly.

I looked around the empty room. At the big house. At the land outside. At the life I had built with my hands. At the memory of Tessa's eyes when she had called me a vulture.

"No. But I did some things that are hard to explain when a person is hurting."

She made a small humming sound, the way she did when she was turning something over in her head. "Is it like when you told Mom it was okay if I stayed in Calgary for my birthday because we'd already made plans with my friends, and I got mad at you because I thought you didn't care, but you did, you just didn't want me to be disappointed?"

"That's not a bad example."

"You're not very good at feelings."

I laughed. The sound surprised me. "That's probably true."

"I'm good at feelings."

"I know. You got that from your mom."

"Maybe I can help. You should say sorry to Tessa. And maybe fix something for her. Without asking for anything. That is what Mom says makes a good man."

"That's what your mom says, huh?" I used to be the good man for her, but my focus shifted, and I hadn't realized until it was too late.

"Yep."

I leaned a shoulder against the doorframe and rubbed a thumb across the edge of my phone. "I have tried to fix some things. Sometimes you have to go slow. Pushing too hard makes it worse."

"Like when you tried to teach me to lope, and I cried."

"Exactly."

She giggled. That sound filled more of the room than all the furniture.

"I miss you," she said abruptly.

I closed my eyes for a moment. "I miss you too, bug."

"When can I come out again? Mom said we have to see what your schedule is and the cows' schedule and the weather and the moon and the economy."

"Really soon. I'll call your mom when the dust settles around here, but it should be better come Monday." I hated that she was missing this weekend, but there were things she didn't have control over with her show riding schedule.

"I have to go. We are having pasta. Dad, I love you."

"I love you, bug." The line clicked off. I lowered the phone slowly and stood there for a moment, letting the silence fold back in around me. It did not feel as heavy now. There was still weight in it, but there was also the echo of her voice.

I slipped the phone back into my pocket and walked to the large window that overlooked the yard. The last of the light was fading. The security lights near the barns flicked on, casting pale circles onto the packed dirt. A few of the men crossed between buildings, their shadows long and stretched.

From here, it was easy to imagine a different life. One where Rena stayed, where Maddy was in her bedroom, with her music too loud, or friends giggling with her about people they liked. One where the kitchen would be full instead of eerily quiet.

The house felt huge around me, all that wood and stone and space built for a family I didn't have. For a legacy that was more weight than comfort. It wasn't so different from Ray's place in the end. His smaller, older, rougher, but the shape of loneliness was the same.

TWELVE

TESSA

I wasn't looking for anything; I was just opening drawers, moving through the kitchen, because sitting still meant thinking, and thinking meant remembering the way dirt hit the top of Ray's coffin.

The kitchen felt wrong without him. His mug sat upside down on the drying rack. His notebook sat on the end of the table where he always wrote feed numbers, weather conditions, and things he meant to fix. The light over the sink hummed faintly. Late evening slid through the window, soft and gold, touching every surface that still smelled like him.

I pulled open the junk drawer near the phone. The same one that had been a disaster since I was ten. Batteries that might be dead. Twist ties, old receipts, a tangled extension cord. Two faded takeout menus from places that probably didn't even exist anymore. And tucked between them, like it had slid sideways and gotten buried, was a small spiral notebook.

I froze.

It was one of the cheap ones from the hardware store, with a bent cardboard cover and wire coils half crushed on one side.

I pulled it free, scattering rubber bands and a dead pen across the floor. For a second, I almost put it back. Then I saw the handwriting on the front page.

Ray's uneven scrawl looped across the paper, slanting downhill just a little, like it always had.

Ranch To Do List: Spring

I smoothed the page with my fingers, feeling every groove of pen pressure like it might be the last physical proof that he stood at this counter, in this house, making plans. I flipped to the next page.

Fix the south fence.
Patch the barn roof before storms.
Replace the tractor belt.
Call Tessa. Ask about her job. Tell her I'm proud of her.

The words blurred. I blinked hard, once, twice, but the sting behind my eyes only sharpened.

He had written it down like it was just another chore. Right there between fixing fences and changing belts, like it was something he could schedule for a rainy afternoon.

Call Tessa. Ask about her job. Tell her I'm proud.

He never had.

He never asked about my job. Not more than a short, gruff, are you eating and are you getting yourself killed with those city dogs. And he never said he was proud, never once uttered the words I wanted you or I'm glad you're mine or anything that even came close.

Now I was staring at proof that somewhere inside his stubborn, silent skull, he meant to.

I pressed my fingertips over the sentence, slow and careful, like the ink might smear if I touched it too hard.

I turned the page. The next sheet was messier. Less list, more thoughts crammed in around the margins.

She doesn't need my problems.
She has a life.
Be better. Be strong.
Just make it to winter.
Give her something worth coming back for.

I read it twice, the words sinking slowly under my ribs, heavy and hot. My hands weren't just shaking now. They were trembling hard enough that I could hear the paper rustle.

He had been trying to hold it together for me. To protect me from the truth, while the truth chewed through him. I hadn't known. I had been too busy surviving my own life to ask the right questions about his.

A sob broke out of me then. My knees went weak. I folded over the counter, clutching the notebook to my chest like it was a lifeline and not a catalogue of everything I lost.

Tears hit the laminate in small, scattered drops. They made tiny circles that spread and faded, just like everything else in this house. The refrigerator hummed. The clock ticked. Somewhere outside, a truck passed on the distant road.

Inside, all I could hear was that list in my head. Call Tessa. Ask about her job. Tell her I'm proud of her.

I didn't know how long I stood there, shoulders shaking, forehead nearly touching the counter, crying into a notebook like a child. Long enough that the sunlight outside shifted from gold to amber. Long enough that the shadows from the table legs stretched across the floor, reaching for the opposite wall. Long enough that my skin felt tight, my eyes ached, my nose was clogged, and my throat burned.

Grief didn't care about dignity.

Eventually, my legs started to go numb. I peeled myself upright and wiped my face with the back of my wrist. My reflection in the dark window looked wrecked. Swollen eyes. Red nose. Hair falling out of its braid in frizzy strands.

I grabbed my boots from beside the door, shoved my feet into them without bothering with socks, and snatched the notebook off the counter. I couldn't seem to leave it behind. It felt alive in my hand, like proof and apology and accusation all at once.

Outside, the yard glowed bronze under the last light of day. The air cooled enough to raise goosebumps on my arms when the breeze hit. The sky to the west was a smear of orange and violet, clouds catching the color like they didn't understand that today should've been grey.

Crickets were already singing in the grass near the house. The wind carried the dry, eerie chorus of coyotes floating up from somewhere deeper in the valley. That sound always unsettled me, even when I was little. It reminded me that there were things with teeth out there watching, waiting for weakness.

The fencing bucket waited on the porch, in its usual place, so I grabbed it mid-stride, tossed the notebook in it, and started walking toward the south pasture.

My footsteps crunched softly over the packed dirt and gravel. Each step steadied me a little more. Movement pulled the grief into something sharper, something that could be turned outward instead of letting it chew at me from the inside.

Ray's list echoed in my head.

Fix the south fence.

The farther I walked, the more obvious the neglect became. A leaning post here, a sagging wire there. Nothing catastrophic, but nothing good either. Ray would've torn into me for letting things slide like this, then cursed himself for not doing it sooner.

I saw the problem before I reached it.

The fence at the low point of the pasture had collapsed in a tired heap, like it finally given up and decided to lie down. Two posts leaned at odd angles, the wire hung slack and twisted, and the brace was mostly on the ground.

"Dammit," I muttered.

The nearest cattle were higher up on the slope, just dark shapes against the fading light, but if they wandered down at night and found this hole, they'd be through it before I could even get my boots laced. Then I'd be chasing them through Hargrove coulees and draws all over hell's half acre.

I didn't have the energy for that. I barely had energy to stand upright.

I swung my leg over the fallen portion of the fence and walked along the opposite side to inspect the damage. The ground dropped a little here, just enough to make my footing unstable. The last windstorm had probably done most of the work. Time and stress finished it.

"Of course," I said softly, voice dry.

I set the notebook on the nearest intact post, flipped it open to the page with the list, and weighed it down with a rock.

"Fine," I said to the invisible ghost of Ray hovering over my shoulder. "I'm fixing it."

I grabbed the top wire and pulled. It shifted under my hands, the barbs catching my palms as it slid, but with enough coaxing, it might untangle and flip back into place. I braced my feet, bent my knees, and pulled. The muscles in my shoulders protested. I let it drop before I lost my grip and cut up my palms.

Sweat slid down my spine again, this time from effort rather than heat. Coyotes called farther up the valley, their voices rising and falling in a strange, layered chorus. The sound crawled up the back of my neck.

"You're fine," I told myself. "You're not five years old anymore, you can do this."

I scanned the line until I spotted an old wire stretcher hung off a post like he'd always left it. Rust flecked the metal, but it still looked solid.

Boots slipping occasionally in the dirt, I wedged the stretcher in place and hooked the wire. My hands were already sore from the earlier battles, but I ratcheted it, and the wire tightened.

Reaching into the bucket, I grabbed a gleaming silver fencing staple, reached for the fencing pliers from my back pocket, and hammered it in.

I followed the line and fixed what I could. When I headed back to the other end, I spliced the barbed wire and wrapped it around itself so it would hold tightly.

One down, three more strands to go. The sound echoed across the quiet pasture as I hammered in staples, bouncing back from the hill like someone else was working with me.

Darkness thickened around the edges of my vision as the light drained out of the sky. The corners of the pasture fell into shadow. The notebook on the post became a pale square in the dim.

Coyotes cried again, closer now. Their calls layered over one another like a steady, hungry chorus. My chest tightened.

"Almost done. You're not bait. You're fine."

My hand slipped on the next swing. The pliers glanced off the staple and slammed into my knuckles. Pain exploded up my fingers and into my wrist. I cursed loudly, dropping the tool into the dirt as I clutched my hand.

Tears sprang to my eyes faster than I wanted to admit. This kind of pain was small compared to everything else, but it was fresh. Immediate. Sharp enough to crack something I'd been holding together all day.

"Mother fucker, son of a whore bitch, ass hole," I hissed, cradling my throbbing knuckles against my chest.

Blood already smeared across my skin, mixing with dirt as the coyotes called again. The sound seemed to come from behind and to the side now. They were moving. Or my imagination was easily spooked. Both were entirely possible.

I bent to pick up the pliers, stubbornness rising to meet the pain. I wasn't leaving this fence half-finished. I wasn't letting Ray's list beat me on the first task. That would've been too on the nose, even for my life.

I set my jaw and reached for the staple again, ready to hurt my hands worse if that was what it took.

The ground lit up.

A bright, focused beam swept across the sagging fence, the broken posts, my scraped knuckles, and the notebook perched on the post.

My heart jumped into my throat.

I spun around, pulse hammering so hard I could feel it in my bruised fingers.

A person on a horse was about ten feet away and getting closer. Based on the build, it was a man, and based on the broad shoulders of the man, it was Wyatt Hargrove.

He hopped off the horse with ease, shoulders squared, and a flashlight held in one hand. His hat brim cast half his face into shadow, but the light caught the angles of his jaw, the blue of his eyes, and the dust on his jeans. His shirt clung to his shoulders like he'd been working too. He looked out of place and entirely at home at the same time, like the land itself decided to grow a man and send him down here.

My whole body went rigid.

"What do you want?" I snapped. My voice came out higher and thinner than I wanted.

He didn't answer right away. His gaze moved from my face to my hand, to the broken fence, to the notebook on the post, then back again. He started walking toward me, slow and steady, the beam dipping with each step.

"Don't," I warned, backing up half a pace. "I don't need help."

He didn't stop, but he didn't crowd me either. He lowered himself into a crouch beside the broken post, turning the flashlight so it illuminated the damage instead of my face.

Heat flared under my skin. Anger, humiliation, and something else I refused to name tangled in my chest. "I don't need you," I said.

Still nothing. He shifted the flashlight, gripped it gently between his teeth, and reached into his back pocket. When his hand came out, he had his own fencing pliers and didn't listen to me at all. He reached over to the bucket and grabbed a staple.

"I can do it," I muttered.

He nodded once, slow, like he was agreeing with me. Then he stood, stepped to the far end of the wire, and lifted. He just raised the tight wire into place and held it there, steady and sure.

He was making it possible for me to work, and somehow that felt worse than him doing it for me.

"I said," I started.

"I heard you," he mumbled around the flashlight, the words slightly muffled. "You're hurt."

"I am not," I scoffed, and his eyes flicked to my hand, where blood smeared across my knuckles and dirt already packed itself into the scrapes. He looked at it for half a second, long enough for shame to burn hot under my skin, then he looked away like he didn't want to embarrass me further.

His jaw tightened. He wasn't pushing, he wasn't taking over, he was just there. Steady. Solid. Uninvited.

I snatched up a staple, set it against the cool metal of the wire, and swung the pliers. The impact jolted all the way up my arm, and we fell into a rhythm.

He set the stretcher in place with ease and spliced the line. I drove the staples in, one by one, the sound beating a rough cadence into the quiet field. My breathing turned ragged, more from everything in my head than from the work.

The night thickened. Sweat cooled on my back. My fingers ached. Somewhere along the way, the trembling in my hands eased. The shakes shifted into something like focus.

We didn't speak.

He didn't correct me or rush me. He didn't tell me I was doing it wrong. The only sounds were the hammering against the staples, our breathing, and the distant wild calls that reminded me there were always eyes in the dark.

When I drove in the last staple, my shoulders sagged in relief. I stepped back and let the pliers drop to my side.

"It'll hold," he said. The words were simple, but something about the way he said them landed deeper than they should have.

I swallowed and looked at the fence, then at him. The flashlight beam cut across the lower half of his face, catching the stubble along his jaw and the faint lines at the corners of his eyes.

"Thank you," I said, the words dragged out of me like they weighed something.

He didn't say you're welcome. He just shifted the flashlight, so it swept along the repaired section one last time, like he wanted to be sure. Then he turned and let the beam slide back to me.

It caught my cheek and the curve of my mouth. Then it hit my eyes.

Our gazes met in that narrow circle of light.

For one heartbeat, all the noise dropped away. The coyotes. The hum of insects. The ache in my knuckles. Even the simmering anger that usually rose the second I saw him.

"Lock your doors tonight," he said quietly.

The lingering edge in his voice slid under my skin. "Why," I asked.

His eyes flashed briefly in the dark. "There are coyotes working closer than usual. A calf got pulled on my side last week. They're testing fences. They always do it harder when something changes."

"Have they evolved to opening doors?" I asked, my voice more bitter than I'd meant it to be.

He studied me for a moment. I could barely see his face now, but I felt his attention like a warm hand on my shoulder.

"Just lock the doors," he repeated, and handed me the flashlight. "Take it, I'll get it back one of these days."

"Don't you need it to get home?" I asked as I stared at the light in my hand.

"Nope, Lady knows how to get home." Before I could decide whether I was about to thank him again or yell at him, he turned away. The soft thud of his footsteps as he walked back to his horse. The leather of his saddle groaned as he sat in the seat. He didn't look back when he trotted away.

The tan hide of the horse was visible for a few moments in the waning light, but soon I was alone again. The repaired fence gleamed in the beam, the fresh metal of the staples catching what little light remained. Ray's notebook sat where I'd left it, cover flapping slightly in the breeze, pages ruffling like it wanted to say something else.

I picked it up with both hands and held it against my chest.

I hated Wyatt for being here and for seeing me like this. To make it easier, I'd decided the hard way was what I deserved.

I also needed what he'd just given me.

The help. The steady silence. The way he stepped into the dark without demanding a thank you for anything.

I turned back toward the house, the night sounding louder than before. The coyotes had gone quiet for now, but I knew they were still out there, waiting at the edges, watching.

The notebook felt heavy under my arm.

When I reached the porch, I stepped inside, turned the deadbolt, and listened to the lock slide into place. The least I could do was listen to him about this.

Thirteen

Tessa

After the funeral, I pretended all weekend the world was paused, as if government offices were closed, then the problems were too. Ray's debts didn't matter, and the loneliness that seeped into my bones every time the house shifted was nothing.

I'd patched a fence. Cleaned the stalls in the barn. Swept the kitchen twice a day. Reorganized Ray's pantry. Counted the envelopes on his desk, but didn't open a single one.

But Monday didn't care that I wasn't ready.

By the time I pulled into the gravel lot of the local Credit Union, sweat slicked the back of my neck. My fingers left damp prints on the steering wheel.

I sat there for a long moment, forehead against the wheel, breathing like I was training for a panic attack marathon.

"You can do this," I whispered. "You survived worse." I wasn't sure that was true, but I walked in anyway.

The cool air inside the bank hit like a slap. A clerk behind the counter lifted her head and smiled politely. "Morning. What can I help you with?"

My throat felt tight. "I need to speak with whoever handles agricultural loans."

"Do you have an appointment?"

"No."

She hesitated for a moment but nodded. "Let me check."

She disappeared through a side door. I clasped my hands together so she wouldn't see them shake. My palms were cold even though my skin felt too hot. My chest buzzed like bees lived under my ribs.

After a minute, she returned. "Mrs. Carson can see you."

I followed her into a small office with framed photos of barley fields and a giant poster about smart retirement planning. A woman in her fifties stood behind the desk and shook my hand.

"You must be Ray's niece. I've been expecting you," she confirmed. "I'm sorry for your loss."

The words hit like someone pressed on a bruise. "Thank you," I managed.

"Have a seat. So," she said gently, "what can I help you with?"

It took everything to force the words out. "I need to know what's owed on my uncle's accounts."

"Your uncle was behind on both property tax and operating credit," she said. "The arrears are not small." She didn't even have to look at her computer. That wasn't a good sign at all.

My stomach tightened. "He never mentioned any of this."

"We also need to discuss the outstanding loan secured against the back acreage," she said gently.

My pulse skipped. "The back pasture?"

She nodded. "The land itself is the collateral."

I leaned back in the chair and pressed my palms to the armrests, trying to breathe through the sudden weight in my chest. "And now that he's gone?"

"The debt remains attached to the property. If the estate is unable to service it, the bank will proceed toward recovery through auction."

Auction. The word landed like a punch.

"How much?" I asked. She slid a thin folder across the desk. The number was written on a yellow sticky note, and it made my vision blur.

"There is one interested party already," she added carefully.

"I'm aware," I said flatly, knowing she meant Wyatt. My hands curled into fists in my lap. "So everyone expected him to fail?" I asked accusingly.

Her expression softened. "I wouldn't put it that way."

"I would," I said.

Outside, the wind pushed against the window. A truck drove past on Main Street. Somewhere beyond the town limits, cattle needed feeding. Fences were falling down. The ranch was barely holding its breath. And Wyatt Hargrove already positioned himself to take it.

"What's the timeline?" I asked, my voice oddly confident.

"If the arrears aren't addressed, the process will begin within the month. I suggest you find legal counsel for this process."

A month.

I nodded once. I wasn't sure what I looked like from the outside, but inside everything felt unmoored.

"Thank you," I said, even though nothing about this felt like it deserved gratitude.

She gave me the kind of smile people give when they know they're about to become the villain in your story.

Hargrove Brewing sat just inside the town limits, like it muscled its way out of the prairie on purpose. The restaurant side was already open for lunch, a few dusty pickups and half-ton trucks scattered through the gravel lot.

I needed to learn more about Wyatt Hargrove, and where better than his place of business? Sure, I'd been there for Ray's luncheon, but that didn't give me an accurate idea of what I was up against. A random noon on Monday might.

I parked farther from the door than I needed to and sat there for a beat, fingers locked on the steering wheel.

My phone rang, and I held my breath as I looked at the number. It wasn't one I recognized, but it was one from someone in town.

"Hello?" I tried to make my voice sound more cheerful than I felt.

"Oh, good, you answered. I wasn't sure if you would. It's Brooke."

"Hi," I said as I smiled, "what can I do for you?" Hopefully, she didn't need money, because I didn't have any.

Brooke's husband died two years ago in an accident, and they had a son, who should be about fourteen. Maybe he needed some work? I bet he could help me fix fences.

"A lot, I hope. I'm calling to ask if you want a job. My last vet tech just quit, and I'm so behind on everything I'd completely understand if you said no, but I had to ask." There was desperation in her voice, but she didn't know that this was the best call I received in days.

"Are you serious? Yes, I'll take it. When do you want me to start?" I blurted out without stopping to take a breath.

"How about next week? Gives you a bit more time to settle in, and Jackson will be with his grandparents, so I can help you without him hanging around." Her voice was lighter now.

"Perfect, I'll see you Monday, and Brooke, thank you."

I climbed out, locked the truck, and walked toward the front entrance with a little more pep in my step than when I left the bank.

Inside, the temperature dropped a few degrees, and the

world shifted. Warm, low light filtered through the room. The smell of woodsmoke from the massive stone fireplace at the far end. The clink of cutlery, the low murmur of conversation, the faint hiss of a tap being opened behind the bar. Comfortable chairs gathered around the fire instead of stiff rows of tables, people sinking into them like they belonged there.

A server in a Hargrove Brewing tee shirt and black jeans came over with a menu tucked against her hip.

"Hey, I'm Natalie. Are you here for lunch or just coffee?"

"Coffee for sure. Maybe food. I haven't decided yet."

She gave me a small, knowing smile and nodded toward a two-top near the windows. "That one's quieter. I'll grab your drink."

I slid into the corner table, dropped my phone beside the napkin, and stared out the window. My hands wouldn't stop shaking.

The server brought a mug, set down cream and sugar, and moved away again. I wrapped both hands around the ceramic like I could siphon stability out of it, then unlocked my phone.

Legal counsel.

I typed "agricultural lawyer near River's Edge" before I could talk myself out of it, picked the first name with anything about rural property, and hit call.

"Law office of Elle Keene," a receptionist answered.

"Hi," I said. My voice sounded like it belonged to someone who'd been screaming. "My name's Tessa Callahan. I just inherited a ranch, and there's a lien, taxes are overdue, and I don't understand any of it."

There was a beat of quiet, a rustle of paper.

"Right," she said. "One moment, I'll see if Ms. Keene can take your call."

I traced the rim of the mug with my thumb, breathing

shallow. A few seconds later, another voice came on, low and brisk.

"Ms. Callahan? This is Elle. I understand you're dealing with a lien on inherited agricultural land. I'm sorry. It's always complicated."

"How bad is this?"

"Well," she said, and I could hear her shifting into work mode, "a lien gives the holder a claim on the property if the debt isn't resolved. If taxes are in arrears as well, the county can push for an auction. If there are delinquent equipment loans, those lenders may move to reclaim assets. It all comes down to timing and who's in first position."

Auction. Reclaim. First position. Every word landed like another weight on my chest.

"I don't understand any of this."

"Where are you right now, Ms. Callahan?"

"In River's Edge. At Hargrove Brewing. I couldn't make myself go home yet."

"Hargrove's," she repeated, like she knew it. "Alright. I'm in town this morning. I just left the county office. If you're comfortable with it, I can meet you there. It's easier to explain this when I can sketch things out."

"In person?" "Yeah. You'll still need to gather all the documents from the ranch, but we can at least get a head start on what you're dealing with before you're knee deep in notices."

I stared into my coffee. "Okay. I'm here."

"I'll be there in about ten minutes. Navy blazer, too much paper in my bag. You won't miss me."

When the call ended, the room came back into focus. Soft music. Someone laughed near the fireplace. Cutlery scraping against plates.

Movement at the far side of the room snagged my attention before I could drag my eyes away.

Wyatt came in from a side door that led, if I remembered

right, toward the brewhouse. He wore a dark Hargrove Brewing tee shirt that pulled across his shoulders, jeans faded and stained like he'd actually been working, and a ball cap shoved low to keep his hair out of his face.

He crossed behind the bar without looking at the tables, dropped a clipboard beside the till, and leaned over to check a set of gauges under the taps. The bartender said something I couldn't catch. Wyatt tapped the face of one dial with a knuckle, adjusted a valve, then reached into the cooler and hauled out a half keg like it weighed nothing.

He set it in place, checked the line, and pulled a short sample pour into a glass. He lifted it to the light, assessing the colour, took one small sip, then nodded once. Not showy. Not performative. Just a man making sure what he'd built was doing what it was supposed to.

He said something to the bartender and pointed toward the dining room. The volume of the music shifted slightly, softer near the fireplace, brighter near the bar. A server stopped beside him, and he listened to whatever she said, then flicked his eyes toward a row of tickets clipped above the kitchen window. Another nod. Another small adjustment.

He turned, wiping his hands on a towel, and his gaze moved across the tables, quick and automatic. It hit me like a spotlight when it landed.

Our eyes locked for half a second across the room. Firelight to my left, tap handles behind him, the hum of a normal weekday pressing between us.

His expression didn't change. No surprise. Just that steady, unreadable assessment, like he was making sure I was upright and breathing and not about to slide under a tide no one else could see.

Heat crawled up my neck. I tore my gaze away and looked down at the table, suddenly fascinated by the sugar packets.

By the time I risked a glance back, he was already moving

again, disappearing through the doorway that led to the brew-house, shoulders brushing the frame, attention on a world that wasn't mine.

Natalie reappeared with a notepad. "Do you want to order anything to go with the caffeine?"

I cleared my throat. "Soup. Whatever's on. And a grilled cheese if that's a thing."

"That's a very real thing," she said with a smile. "I've got you."

She walked away. I took two absentminded sips of coffee but tasted none of it.

The door opened again about ten minutes later. A woman in a navy blazer stepped inside and scanned the room, eyes catching on my corner table quickly. Dark hair, sensible shoes, satchel strap digging into her shoulder like it had been carrying too much weight for too many years.

"Tessa Callahan?" she asked when she reached me.

I stood, almost knocking my knee on the underside of the table. "Yeah. Hi."

"Elle Keene." Her handshake was firm, her palm warm. Her gaze flicked over my face, taking in all the wreckage without pity. "Do you mind if I sit?"

"Please."

She settled in across from me, flipped open a legal pad, and pulled out a pen.

"Alright," she said. "Tell me what you know so far. Start with the bank."

I handed over the file and told her about the arrears, the operating credit, the loan hanging off the back acreage. And dropped the phrase "interested party" like there was already someone with a knife and fork waiting.

She wrote as I talked, head bent, expression tight.

"Okay," she said when I ran out of words. "Here's the short version from the phone calls I made on the way over.

The ranch is over-leveraged. The tax arrears mean the county has the upper hand to push this to auction if you don't move quickly. The lien on the back pasture gives that creditor the first right to the proceeds from a sale or forced auction on that piece. If there are any other secured loans, they're going to want their slice too."

"Is there any way to stop it?" I asked.

"Yes," she said. "But you can't do it by pretending it will just go away. You're going to need every document, every tax notice, every loan statement, every past-due bill. Once we know exactly who's owed what, we can talk about options."

"Options like?"

"Payment plans with the county if they're willing. Consolidating or refinancing, if a lender thinks you're a good risk. Selling equipment or cattle. Maybe a small parcel of land to protect the rest, depending on how the lien's written. I'm not going to promise you miracles, but there are steps between today and losing everything."

"And if I can't pay?" The question scraped out of my throat.

"You already know the answer," she said quietly, and she was right; I was just hoping for a different one. My eyes burned. I stared hard at the saltshaker so I wouldn't cry in Wyatt Hargrove's nice, fancy ass brewery.

"What do you need from me right now?"

"I need you to go home and make a pile. Anything with a logo, a stamp, or numbers that scare you. When you've got it gathered, call me. I'm in Maple Ridge, but I'm in River's Edge on Mondays and Fridays. We can meet here again, or do it at the house if you're more comfortable."

She slid a card across the table. "That's my direct line. If something shows up in red ink or a sheriff ever thinks about putting a notice on your gate, I want to know the second it happens."

"Okay, thank you."

"For what it's worth," she added, tucking her pen back into the pad, "this place you're sitting in now? Wyatt nearly lost it when his dad passed. Different structure, similar mess. He fought hard to keep it. That's why he's on every committee no one wants and why people listen when he talks. He's seen this side of things. He might be a good person to talk to."

Of course, he'd be the town golden boy, well, not boy, but man. Wyatt Hargrove would be the last person on earth I'd talk to about this. Not with him circling, waiting for me to fail.

"I'll call you."

She left with a half-smile, stopping at the bar to pay for her coffee. I saw Wyatt come out from the brewhouse again, say something to her, listen, nod. They knew each other. Of course they did.

He turned slightly as she headed for the door, his gaze following her for a moment, then skimming across the room.

It landed on me, just for a beat. I looked away first.

Natalie brought my bill and smiled as she took my empty plate and bowl. Reaching for the paper, I frowned when it showed nothing was owed.

"Not a chance, I'm not taking charity from you, Wyatt Hargrove," I mumbled under my breath and mentally figured out what the coffee, soup and sandwich should cost and leaving a generous tip hoping I'd covered it, I walked to the bar and slammed the bill and the cash on the counter, Wyatt's expression never changed but his eyes sparkling gave him away. He was amused, and that irritated me even more.

"Make sure Natalie gets this," I instructed before I turned on my heel and walked out.

Fourteen

Tessa

The day didn't get any better. I was behind on chores because I'd gone to town first thing this morning, but this felt normal. I knew what to do, and muscle memory took over.

My phone buzzed in my pocket as I grabbed the feed bucket for the horses. I cursed the sound and almost ignored it. But the name made my blood run cold.

Colin.

I stared at the screen. The ringing didn't stop, and all I wanted was for it to stop. I should have thrown the phone in the manure pile, but instead I answered.

"Tess," he breathed, soft, too soft. Like he'd been waiting. "Thank God. I've been worried sick."

My throat tightened. "What do you want?"

"I heard what happened with your uncle," he said gently. "I'm so sorry. I didn't think you were close." The fake concern in his voice was nauseating.

"We weren't," I answered flatly.

"You don't have to pretend with me," he murmured. "I know you."

A chill crept up my spine. "I'm fine," I lied, trying to sound more composed.

"You don't sound fine. You sound overwhelmed. Panicked. You should've come back, or I can come there. I just want to support you."

Anger flared hot. "You don't get it at all, do you?"

"I'm just being honest. You take on too much. You're stubborn. You shut people out."

My breath hitched. "Colin—"

"I could help you," he whispered. "If you'd let me."

"No," I said sharply. "Absolutely not."

He sighed like I was a disappointment. "You don't have to be scared, Tess. You just need someone who cares. Someone who actually knows how to handle things."

"I'm hanging up."

"Don't," he said quickly. "Not when you're upset. You make rash decisions when you're emotional."

Ice slid through my veins. "This is not your business. We're done. Don't call me again." And with that, I ended the call.

My hand shook so hard I almost dropped the phone.

I sat there breathing fast, trying to steady myself, when footsteps crunched on gravel outside the barn door.

My heart lurched. I wiped sweat off my face quickly.

Wyatt stepped inside. The dying light cut across his shoulders. His shadow spilled long behind him. Dust coated his boots and jeans. His hat was tipped back slightly, exposing the line of his brow. His eyes found mine instantly.

Concern flickered there.

He masked it fast.

"What are you doing here?" I managed, voice raw.

"Checking fence lines. You should have stayed after you ate. I could have given you a tour."

I stiffened. "A tour, right. You probably would have hit me

over the head and tossed me in one of those big vats of beer you've got in the back."

"They're called fermentation tanks, and ruining a good tank of beer isn't business savvy." The corner of his mouth turned up, and I wanted to throw something at him, but that would have used the last bit of energy I had, so I just stared at him.

His jaw worked once, slowly. "What's wrong?" His brow furrowed, and his eyes narrowed in on me as if he could see into my soul.

"I'm fine."

"You're not."

And that was it, the match strike. The last crack in the dam. Everything I'd been holding in erupted. The words exploded out of me before I could hold them back.

"You don't know a fucking thing about me," I shouted as I launched myself off the bale.

Wyatt didn't move. Didn't flinch. He stood there like a wall built of quiet and patience, and something about that made the fury in me snap even harder.

"What do you want? Are you obsessed with me, or do you think if you stalk me and wear me down, I'll sell to you?"

His voice stayed painfully calm. "I was just out checking fences and thought I'd see how you were doing after your meeting today." His voice was calm. He hadn't raised it or moved closer. Those were all things Colin did when I'd gotten mad at him. He had to prove his dominance over the situation. But Wyatt Hargrove, who quite possibly could pick me up and toss me over his shoulder as easily as picking up a feather, didn't move.

I hated that everything inside me felt like it was unraveling, and he was just standing there, steady and immovable, watching me fall apart. "You don't get to be here," I said, voice cracking. "Not today. Not with what I've learned."

His eyes narrowed. "What did you learn?"

"Don't do that. Don't use that tone like you're surprised about anything. You know exactly what I was told," I snapped.

"I'm asking so I know what *you're* up against."

Laughter burst out of me, jagged and wrong. "Everyone knows what the truth is, everyone but me."

He exhaled slowly, a sound that made my heart lurch. "Tessa." He said my name with so much care. It's all I'd ever wanted to hear. Someone who could stop me in my tracks by whispering my name. And now the one man who could do it wanted to see me fail.

"No. Don't say my name like you care what happens to me, or this place."

He stood a little straighter. "I do care."

"Well, stop. Stop caring. Stop showing up and watching me. Stop pretending like you're the solution to a problem you helped create." My voice shook on every word.

His jaw flexed like I'd swung something heavy and landed it.

"What did you find out?" he asked, quieter this time.

I threw my hands out, wild and useless. "Everything, Wyatt. Everything. The taxes. The liens. The overdue notices. The goddamn auction timelines. He was drowning, and he didn't tell me. And now it's all on me." My voice rose until it cracked. "It's all on me, and I can't do it." The last word came out of me with a sob.

Something flickered in his eyes. Something I didn't want to see or deal with.

"You're not alone."

My breath hitched. "Oh, like you're going to help me, you just want this all for yourself. So yeah, *Mr. Hargrove,* I am on my own."

"You aren't."

"I am," I shouted. "Ray's gone. My parents left without a

care in the world. I left all this behind years ago. I have no one except a best friend over two hours away and a man standing in my barn pretending to comfort me, while he plots how to get my land and home from me."

"I'm not pretending, and I don't want your house. It's of no use to me."

"Oh well, should I curtsy to the king for not wanting me to be homeless?" I said, taking a step toward him even though every instinct screamed to run the other way.

"I didn't come here to talk about this."

"Then why are you here? Why do you keep showing up every time I'm falling apart? Do you want something from me other than my land? Is that it?" I had my arms out, waiting for him to say something or do something. His eyes never left mine; they were locked on me, and he refused to break eye contact.

"Stop," he said quietly, but there was something strained under the word.

"No," I said, tears spilling over again, hot and humiliating. "I won't stop. You want me to say it. Fine. You're the last man on earth I should trust. You walked into my house and dropped every truth like a bomb, and then you expect me to come to you when I can't breathe."

His throat worked. "That isn't what I expect."

"You don't respect me. You don't believe I can do this alone."

"That's not what I think at all."

"Then what? Why are you here? Why do you keep finding me and stepping in like you have any right to stand between me and the mess Ray left me?"

He didn't answer. Not for what seemed like hours. Then he stepped closer. Just a fraction. Just enough that I could see a muscle jump in his jaw and the tight set of his shoulders.

"Because I promised him I would," he said. The words hit the barn like a gunshot, and I took a step back.

I stared at him. "What?"

He exhaled slowly. "I promised Ray I'd look out for you when you came back."

My heart lurched. "When?"

"Months ago," he said. "He was getting worse, and he knew it. He asked me to keep an eye on things when you came home."

My knees wobbled. The ground felt thin. Everything in me rebelled at the idea of Ray making that choice without telling me. Without asking me. Without trusting me to show up for him.

"You should've told me before," I whispered.

"It wasn't my place." He shook his head, "Tessa," he said again, gentler now. "You've had a hell of a few days."

I choked out a laugh that tasted like salt. "Wyatt, I'm living in a nightmare of debt and foreclosure papers, broken machinery, and now I have you standing here telling me you and Ray made choices for me like I'm some kind of child."

His face tightened.

"You're not a child," he said. "You're..." He cut himself off, and I watched his eyes shift just slightly as if he was trying not to look at my body. "You're overwhelmed. And you're hurting. And you're aiming all that hurt at the closest target."

"That target is you. Because you are a part of this. Whether you want to pretend otherwise or not."

He lowered his gaze for a moment before he looked back up at me with sadness in his eyes. "I know I am. And I'm sorry you're having to carry this alone."

"I can't do this. I can't have you here, seeing me like this. I can't handle your hands or your voice or your goddamn calmness that makes me want to scream."

His breath caught, but he didn't move. I pushed the heel of my palms into my eyes. I tried to breathe. Failed. Then it all spilled out.

"I can't save this ranch," I sobbed. "I can't save anything. I don't even know where to start. I'm drowning, Wyatt. I'm drowning, and Ray didn't trust me enough to tell me how to save myself."

The barn blurred. My lungs locked. I bent over at the waist, gulping for breath, my hands planted on my knees as if I could hold myself together through sheer force of will.

Wyatt took one step forward, then stopped, and he didn't cross that invisible line. He stood just close enough that I could feel the heat of him in the air. Close enough that the silence between us throbbed with everything we wouldn't say.

He didn't speak or offer comfort. He just stayed. Solid. Quiet. Unmoving. Letting me be broken without trying to fix it. And that wrecked me more than anything else.

Sinking down against one of the stalls, I covered my face and sobbed until my throat felt shredded, until my ribs ached from the force of it. Until there was nothing left in me but shaking breaths and the sound of the barn settling around us.

"I'm sorry," I whispered, because I didn't know what else to say.

"You don't need to be. Not for this."

I shook my head, wiping my cheeks. "Please leave."

For a moment, I thought he wouldn't. Something flickered in his face, something raw and dangerous and tender all at once, something that made my breath stall in my chest.

But then he nodded, stepped back, and turned. Wyatt walked toward the barn door, and when he reached it, he paused. His voice came low. Rough. "You're not drowning."

I almost broke again.

But then he walked out into the fading light, and I let my

head fall back against the stall, shaking and alone, feeling the truth of it. No, I wasn't drowning.

I was already underwater.

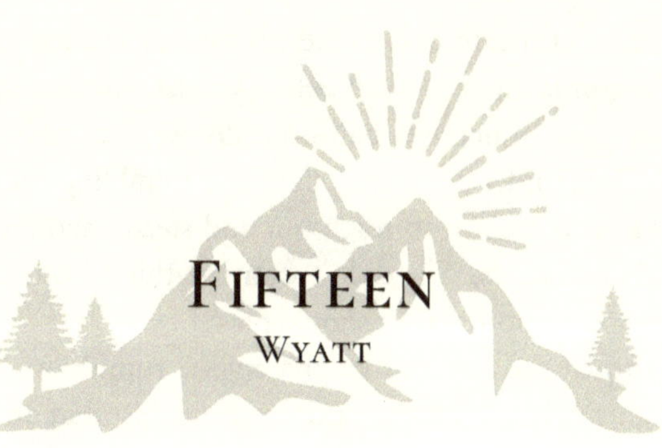

Fifteen
Wyatt

The barn door closed behind me with a soft thud that sounded too final. The sky outside dropped into that deep blue that comes right before full dark, and the first faint bit of night chill. I brushed the sweat off the back of my neck. I walked away from the barn slowly, giving her space even though every instinct I had told me not to leave her alone in that state.

The yard was quiet except for the low hum of insects rising out of the grass. The porch light blinked on as I passed. I didn't look back. If I did, I wasn't sure I'd be able to keep going.

I got in my truck and shut the door; my hands tightened on the steering wheel. I didn't start the engine right away. I just sat there, staring out at the darkening fields, feeling like someone hollowed out my chest with a rusted shovel.

I shouldn't have told her about the promise.

Not then.

Not like that.

But it had been the only truth I had left to give her, and she'd thrown it back like it burned her. .

"Tessa," I murmured to the empty cab, shaking my head. "You're gonna break yourself before you let anyone help."

The grief in her eyes had been deeper than anything she said. It lived under her words, tight and trembling, and it took everything in me not to reach out and steady her. She didn't want that from me. She didn't want anything from me. And that part hurt more than it should have.

I turned the key and let the engine rumble to life. The headlights swept across the yard, catching dust that drifted like tired ghosts in the air. I backed out slowly, gravel crunching under my tires, and made my way down the long drive that curved toward the main road.

Halfway down, movement caught my eye.

A flash of white in the field to my right. Not a deer. Not cattle. Something too still, too deliberate.

I slowed the truck, frowning, and grabbed my binoculars. There, parked at a crooked angle near the fence line, was a dark SUV. Blacked-out windows. Clean. No mud on the tires despite being halfway into a pasture. The kind of vehicle that didn't belong on gravel, let alone in a pasture.

My gut tightened; it wasn't there when I got to Tessa's.

I pulled to the side of the road, cut the engine, and stepped out. The wind picked up just enough to carry the dry smell of dust and sage. I could see a figure near the fence, crouched low with something in his hands.

A camera.

My jaw clenched.

I walked across the ditch, boots sinking into the soft dirt. When I was close enough, I spoke, my voice carrying low but steady.

"You're trespassing," I stated loudly, and calmly enough that he'd hear.

The man jerked upright, the camera swinging from a strap around his neck. He looked mid-forties, clean, with a pressed shirt and hair too perfect to survive ranch wind. His shoes were another giveaway. Polished leather loafers, already caked with dirt, he clearly hadn't expected.

He blinked at me. "Oh. Evening."

"Are you lost?"

He forced a smile that didn't come close to reaching his eyes. "Just taking some photos. Beautiful landscape. Didn't think it'd be a problem."

"It is when it's private property."

"Oh, this is the Callahan Ranch, right?"

I stepped closer. He shifted back.

"You got business here?" I asked without confirming.

"No. Just scenery." He lifted his camera, but that proved nothing. "I'm from Calgary. I freelance for outdoor magazines sometimes."

"Do you usually trespass onto private ranch land for that?"

He swallowed. "I didn't see a sign."

"There doesn't need to be a sign, and there's a gate at the road you had to drive around."

His gaze flickered toward his SUV, then back at me. He was calculating. Not apologetic. Not confused. Calculating.

"Look," he said with a shaky laugh, "I'm not hurting anything. Just got turned around."

"So, which is it, you're taking landscapes, or you got turned around?" The man's story wasn't adding up.

He hesitated, like he wanted to argue, then must've thought better of it. He nodded quickly, clutching his camera, and hurried toward the SUV.

I watched him climb in. The vehicle started with a smooth purr that told me it was new. Expensive. The kind of car belonging to someone who didn't come out here unless there was money involved. He drove off without another word, tires spinning a little too fast as if he expected me to follow.

I stood there long after the taillights disappeared, staring at the empty stretch of dirt he'd left behind. I looked around, and the grass was flattened in a circle from where he'd been standing. Moving over to it. I stood in the center and looked straight ahead of me. It was a direct view of Tessa's front door.

My gut churned, cold and tight.

I walked back to my truck, climbed in, and shut the door harder than I meant to. Anger simmered under my skin.

The road home stretched long and dark ahead of me, but I drove it fast, gravel popping under my tires like sparks. The closer I got to my place, the more that anger sharpened into purpose.

By the time the lights of my ranch appeared over the ridge, I'd already made up my mind.

I pulled up near the barn where Holt and two of the other hired men were gathered around the chute, dealing with porcupine quills in a curious cow's nose. They looked up as I approached. Holt straightened first, wiping his hands on a rag.

"You're back late," he said.

"Someone was out on Callahan land," I replied. "Trespassing. Taking pictures near the south fence."

Holt frowned. "Local?"

"No." The word came out rough. "He bolted when I confronted him."

"And you think he'll come back." The hands exchanged a look. Holt stepped forward. "What do you need?"

"I want more eyes out that way. Day and night. Anyone on that land that doesn't belong gets reported to me immediately."

Holt nodded once, firm. "You got it."

"Keep it quiet," I added. "I don't want her knowing."

Holt studied me for a long moment. "She won't like that."

"I know. But she's dealing with enough."

He held my gaze another moment, then nodded again. "We'll keep watch." The hands dispersed. Holt lingered.

"You planning on telling her what happened tonight?"

"Not until I have to."

Holt let out a slow breath. "You care about her more than you should."

I didn't answer. Couldn't. The truth was too raw and too close.

He didn't press. "I'll put the men on rotation."

"Good."

I walked toward the house, the night wind caught the edges of my shirt. Stars spread wide above the valley, clear and cold.

SIXTEEN
WYATT

The sun was barely up when my phone buzzed on the kitchen counter. I glanced at the screen, expecting a ranch alert or one of the crew asking about feed deliveries.

It was Maddy.

Something in my chest loosened.

I picked it up and leaned my hip against the counter. "Morning, sweetheart."

Her voice came through bright and still sleepy, full of a kind of energy I hadn't felt in days. "Dad. Guess what."

I smiled, slow and tired but real. "What's that?"

"I nailed my tryout," she said, pride ringing clear. "Coach says I'm basically a lock."

"That doesn't surprise me. You've been putting in the work."

She laughed. "You always say that."

"Because it's true."

I poured myself coffee while she talked, listening to the rustle of sheets on the other end of the line. Summer break meant she slept crooked and late unless someone forced her upright, and I pictured her sprawled across her bed in Calgary, hair probably sticking out in three directions.

"How's the rest of your day looking?"

"Mom's taking me shopping. Apparently, I've outgrown everything, like a beanpole.' Her words."

"You did grow. Last time I saw you, you were taller than Angie."

"I've been taller than Angie since grade four."

"Still counts."

She giggled, and the sound settled somewhere warm in my chest. Too warm. Too easy. Too far from the weight that'd been sitting there since Ray died.

"Hey," she said, quieter now. "You okay?"

I hesitated, just long enough for her to catch it.

"Yeah, just busy."

"Busy like ranch-and-brewery busy," she asked, "or busy like 'Dad's thinking too hard again' busy."

Kids noticed everything.

"Both," I admitted.

She hummed. "You're doing the thing where you pretend everything's fine, but your eyebrows look stressed."

"I don't have stressed eyebrows."

"You totally do."

I rubbed my face. "I'm alright. Just working through some stuff with a neighbor."

"A neighbor," she repeated. "Like land stuff or people stuff."

"Both."

There was a pause. "Is it bad?"

I thought of Tessa in the barn the night before, folded in on herself, fighting to breathe through grief she didn't know how to carry.

"It's complicated."

"Are you fighting with them?"

"Something like that."

She didn't miss a beat. "Well, you're stubborn and you always think you can fix everything alone. Maybe stop doing that."

A laugh slipped out of me before I could stop it. "Who taught you to talk like that?"

"You did."

Fair enough.

"I'll be out before school starts. I wanna see the horses. And help with the calves if you've still got any left."

"I'll make sure your mare's ready."

"You always do."

My chest tightened. "I'll see you soon, kiddo."

"Love you, Dad."

"Love you."

When the call ended, the kitchen went quiet again, the kind of quiet that pressed in instead of settling.

I finished my coffee, grabbed my keys, and headed out. Standing still wasn't doing me any favors, and I needed to put my hands on something solid before my head started spinning again.

The drive into town was short and familiar. Fields rolled past in long green and gold stretches, the early light softening everything it touched. By the time I pulled into the gravel lot north of town, the brewery was already awake. A delivery truck idled near the loading door, steam drifting from its exhaust, and the big glass windows reflected the pale sky like the place was breathing in daylight.

Inside, the air was warm and smelled faintly of grain and wood smoke. The kitchen crew was already moving, trays lined up along the prep tables, low voices cutting through the hum of refrigeration. Someone laughed near the back, the sound easy and familiar.

I rolled up my sleeves and got to work.

Mark was behind the bar checking inventory sheets, his pen tapping lightly against the clipboard. He looked up when he saw me, nodded once, and slid the papers across so I could scan them. I pointed out a miscount on one of the kegs, and he made a note without argument before heading toward the cold room to double-check.

I moved through the space after that, checking taps, fixing a handle that'd been sticking, adjusting a dimmer near the stone fireplace so the light wouldn't be too harsh once the lunch crowd rolled in. I stopped to talk with the head cook about the menu and the supplier delivery, making sure everything lined up with what we promised. Locally raised beef, roasted chicken, and fresh seafood that came in early that morning. It mattered to me that the place stayed honest, that it felt rooted in the land.

By midmorning, the doors opened, and people drifted in the way they always did. Ranchers grabbing coffee before heading back out. A couple of older locals settled into the chairs near the fireplace, talking low and slow like they had nowhere else they needed to be. The brewery wasn't just a business. It was an anchor. A place people came when they needed solid ground under their feet.

I stayed behind the bar longer than usual, pouring coffee, answering questions, lending a hand when needed. The rhythm steadied me. The work gave my hands something to do while my mind stayed half a step removed from everything.

Still, every so often, my thoughts drifted.

Not to the road. Not to the door.

To the knowledge that Tessa was out there, trying to hold together a ranch that was barely standing, carrying weight she hadn't asked for, and anger she didn't know where to put.

I figured she'd avoid town for a while. But the town would pull her in eventually. It always did. And when it happened, I wanted the Brewery to feel like solid ground, not another ambush.

Seventeen
Tessa

The morning sky hung low and pale, the light that made every window on Main Street glow. Trucks rolled past the four-way stop with that familiar small-town patience, tires whispering over pavement that had seen more gossip than traffic.

I drove in with both hands on the wheel and my shoulders tight, even though I knew this road like the back of my hand. Nothing much here changed, and I hadn't realized that over the last week I'd been here, because I hadn't left the ranch since Monday.

At the corner by the hardware store, two men leaned on a stack of feed bags, coffee cups in their hands. One lifted his chin as I passed, recognition sharpening his expression.

I pulled my truck into a spot in front of the clinic and forced my voice to sound normal.

"That you, Tessa?" A man called from the hardware store.

"Morning, Dale." Dale MacIntosh had been a fixture in this town since I was a child. And he was still sitting in the same place as always, whittling a piece of wood.

He smiled like he'd won something. "Are you back for

good?" The question wasn't casual. None of them were casual.

"For now," I said with a shrug, since I didn't really know what was happening with my life.

Dale nodded like that meant he could stop wondering. "Good. Town's been missing you."

"Town should get a hobby," I muttered under my breath and headed for the clinic door.

The white siding and big front windows, a little too clean for a building that saw blood and fear and fur on a daily basis, but it was the semblance of normal I was craving.

The bell rang above the door, and it took me back to my summer job working for Brooke's dad; he'd be barking orders and trying to fill his day with anything but yappy dogs and cats.

"About time," Brooke called from the back.

I shut the door behind me. "I'm ten minutes early."

"Yeah, but it's late for you," she yelled back. "I was expecting you here twenty minutes ago."

I smiled despite myself and walked toward the counter. That's one thing that hadn't changed: I was never late.

Brooke appeared from the hallway with a clipboard in one hand and a stethoscope slung loose around her neck. She had her hair twisted up, a pencil jammed through it like she'd done a hundred times. She looked the same, which in River's Edge counted as a miracle.

She stopped in front of me and didn't say anything for a second. Her eyes moved over my face, my shoulders, the way I was holding myself like my bones might crack if I relaxed.

"Are you ready for this? You don't have to start yet," she said, her eyes narrowing like she was trying to read my mind.

"I'm fine, and yes, I do need to start today. Sitting on the ranch isn't going to get the bills paid." Suddenly, the thought dawned on me that if Ray owed so many people money, there was a good chance he owed Brooke, too.

She stepped in and hugged me, quick and firm, her arms strong around my shoulders. She didn't do the soft friend hug; it was the kind to let you know she wasn't going to let you float away.

"He didn't owe me anything," she whispered before letting me go. "I'm glad you're here. I've missed you."

"Same," I managed.

"Good," she replied briskly, like she'd heard enough sentiment for one decade. She shoved the clipboard at me. "Mrs. Calder's the first appointment of the day. I have to get her done first, or she ruins everything I have planned. We'll put her in exam two.

Mrs. Calder sat on the bench in the waiting room, her spaniel Rosie panting on her lap like the world was ending.

"Mrs. Calder, let's get Rosie looked at," I said, and the older woman looked up and gave a slight frown. Rosie's tail thumped the bench when I approached, then she immediately tried to crawl into my arms.

"Hi, Rosie," I murmured, scratching behind her ears.

Mrs. Calder leaned forward, eyes shining. "Look at you. Back working. Back in town, how are you, dear?"

"I'm good," I said, snapping on gloves. Mrs. Calder patted my wrist anyway, like she didn't believe me and didn't want to embarrass me by saying so out loud.

"Your Uncle Ray always spoke so highly of you," she said.

My throat tightened. "Let's get Rosie's booster done."

Brooke tossed me a look that said, " thank you for steering," and we moved through the appointment. Rosie yelped like she'd been stabbed, then immediately tried to lick my face as if apologizing for the noise.

When Mrs. Calder left, the bell chimed again, and the

waiting room filled with a new set of voices. I heard my name in a murmur. Not loud. Not secret, either.

"Tessa Callahan's back."

"Brooke hired her."

"Good for her."

Good for her always sounded like a backhanded compliment.

Brooke shoved a new chart into my hand. "Next. Shepherd with a limp and an owner who's convinced it's cancer."

The owner was a man in his fifties with weathered hands and a cap pulled low. He didn't look at me at first. He watched Brooke like she was the only one who mattered, then his eyes flicked toward me and sharpened in recognition.

"You're Ray's niece," he said.

I kept my face still. "Yes."

He looked immediately regretful. "Sorry for your loss."

"Thank you," I said, because again, that was the line.

He shifted on his boots, clearing his throat. "Town's been wondering what you'll do next."

Brooke's pen paused over the chart. She didn't look up. "The town should mind its business."

He chuckled awkwardly. "That'd be a first."

As we examined the dog, he kept sneaking glances at me, like I was an exhibit at a museum. When I knelt to palpate the shepherd's leg, the dog leaned into me, trustful and heavy. I liked animals for that. They didn't ask for explanations. They just decided whether you were safe.

Brooke leaned close to my ear while the man talked about feed and fences. "You okay?" she murmured.

"I'm working," I whispered back.

"That's not an answer," Brooke said, but she didn't push further.

By midmorning, I'd already done more nails, vaccines, and restraining holds than I could count. The clinic felt like a world with rules that made sense. Injuries had causes. Symptoms had solutions. You did what you could. You didn't negotiate with the universe.

The bell chimed again, and I looked up automatically. For a second, my breath stopped. Across the street through the clinic window, a large, dark SUV was parked near the café. The glass reflected sky and movement, making it hard to see, but I felt eyes on me anyway.

Brooke noticed my freeze. "What is it?"

"Nothing," I said too fast.

Brooke turned and followed my gaze. Her posture shifted, subtle but immediate. Shoulders squaring. Jaw tightening.

"Do you know that vehicle?" "It just looks out of place here."

Brooke's eyes narrowed. "Maybe."

The bell chimed again as a patient entered, and when I looked back out the window a minute later, the SUV was gone.

Brooke watched me for a beat. "You want to tell me what's going on."

"It's nothing, really."

Brooke's expression didn't soften. "You're a terrible liar, Tessa."

"I'm going to get coffee, do you want anything?" I asked, grabbing my purse.

The café was warm and loud in that contained way small towns get, where everyone knew each other's names yet still talked like strangers might be listening.

The barista, Jenna, spotted me immediately. "Tessa," she called.

I moved toward the counter. "Hi, Jenna."

"Brooke finally got some help," she said, already reaching for a cup.

"Yeah."

Jenna slid the coffee across. "On the house. First day back deserves it."

"Thank you," I said.

Her smile faltered just a little, like she was deciding whether to speak. Her fingers tapped the counter once.

"Hey," she said. "Can I ask you something?"

"Sure," I replied, and my chest tightened anyway.

Jenna lowered her voice slightly, not enough to be secret but enough to feel personal. "Your boyfriend was in earlier."

The word boyfriend hit like a slap.

"My what?"

"Boyfriend," she repeated, eyebrows lifting. "Tall guy. Dark hair. Really polite. Asked where you'd be today."

"I don't have a boyfriend," I said, each word clipped.

Jenna's cheeks flushed. "Oh. Sorry, he just seemed concerned."

"Concerned," I echoed, and it came out sharp.

Jenna lifted her hands. "Not like, bad. Just like he was checking in."

"When," I asked, my pulse instantly racing.

"Half an hour ago," she said. "Maybe a bit more. He sat right there by the window." She pointed. "Watched the street. Then left."

"Did he say his name?" I asked.

Jenna shook her head. "No. Just smiled. Paid cash. Left a bigger tip than necessary."

My stomach turned over, cold.

"Did he ask anyone else about me?" I said.

Jenna's eyes widened. "Tessa..."

"Did he," I pressed.

Jenna nodded slowly. "He asked Kyle at the hardware store if he'd seen you. Kyle said you'd be at the clinic. That's how I knew. I thought... I thought he was with you."

River's Edge did what it always did. It filled in blanks. It assumed. It connected dots. It offered information like it was kindness.

My phone buzzed in my pocket before I could say anything else. I didn't need to look to know.

> Colin: Hope the first day's going well. Enjoy the coffee. I started a tab for you.

My skin prickled. I glanced up, scanning the café windows, the street outside, the reflections. People moved. A truck rolled by. A woman carried a bag of flour. Nothing obvious. Nothing provable.

Jenna watched my face. "Is everything okay?"

I slid the phone back into my pocket and forced my mouth into something resembling calm. "Yeah."

Jenna didn't believe me. She leaned forward, voice lower now. "Do you want me to call anyone? Wyatt?"

"No," I said too quickly.

Jenna's brows pinched. "Tessa, if someone's bothering you."

"It's nothing," I lied.

I picked up my coffee. My fingers shook just enough that the liquid rippled.

"Tell Kyle," I said, and my voice came out rougher than I wanted.

Jenna blinked. "Tell him what?"

"If anyone asks about me," I said, "tell him to stop answering." My voice was flat, and I hoped it got my point across.

Jenna's mouth tightened. "Okay."

Outside, the air felt colder. Or maybe it was me. I walked back to the clinic with our coffees held too tight, my gaze bouncing off windows and windshields, trying to catch something that wasn't there.

Brooke was at the counter. She looked up the second I walked in.

"You look like you swallowed a nail," she said.

"Jenna said my boyfriend was in earlier," I replied.

Brooke's pen stopped. "Your boyfriend? I didn't know you had one. Where was he when you laid Ray to rest?"

"I don't have one," I sighed, which made the look of concern change to confusion. Spilling all my personal secrets wasn't high on my list, but I told Brooke everything that had happened with Colin.

Brooke leaned forward slightly, voice low. "Tessa, if he walks in here, I'm throwing him out."

"I'm not asking you to do that," I said.

"I'm not asking you," Brooke snapped. "I'm telling you."

Brooke watched me like she was trying to read the parts of me I wasn't saying out loud. "How long has he been trying to contact you?"

I hesitated. That was an answer with too many edges.

"Since I left," I said.

Brooke's eyes narrowed. "Calls?"

"Texts."

"Threats?"

I shook my head. "Not direct."

"He knew enough to find me here. So really it's not shocking he did."

"But he knows exactly where you are, because this town can't keep its mouth shut," Brooke replied, eyes flashing.

"I can't control that," I said.

"No," Brooke agreed. "But you can control what happens next."

I met her gaze. "I'm not calling the cops."

Brooke's mouth tightened. "I didn't say cops."

"Then who?" I asked, crossing my arms and leaning up against the counter.

"Wyatt," She said, with a grimace.

"Not a chance," I spat at her with more force than I intended.

"Look, I'm just thinking about you being alone out on that ranch," Brooke said.

I forced myself to take a breath through my nose. "I'm fine, why does everyone think I need Wyatt Hargrove to babysit me?"

Brooke shook her head. "You're stubborn."

"I am not."

The rest of the afternoon passed with the kind of frantic normal that made your brain quiet. Animals didn't care about Colin. They didn't care about whispers. They cared about pain and comfort and hands that didn't shake.

But my phone buzzed twice more, and each time I felt it like a pressure point.

Colin: You always look prettier when you're mad.

When the last appointment left and Brooke flipped the sign to Closed, River's Edge exhaled its last bit of daylight.

The ranch should've felt like relief, instead, I felt exposed. When I pulled up, the gate wasn't latched. I stopped the truck so hard my seatbelt bit into my shoulder. For a second, I just stared at it, heart pounding, mouth dry.

"That's not possible," I said out loud, as I climbed out slowly, scanning the yard. The house sat dark. The barn loomed. Nothing moved except the wind pushing through dry grass.

I latched it hard enough to rattle the chain. Then I did it again, checking like repetition could make it true. My phone buzzed. I didn't look at it. I shoved it deeper into my pocket and headed for the barn.

Inside, the air was cooler, thick with hay and dust. The horses shifted in their stalls, quiet huffs and hoof scuffs. The mare in the corner stall lifted her head the moment I entered, ears flicking, restless.

"Hey," I murmured, moving toward her.

She tossed her head once, then pawed at the bedding. Not violent, not panicked, just wrong.

I checked her feed, and it was untouched, and she'd barely drank all day. My pulse tightened.

"Please be okay," I whispered, running a hand down her neck. Her skin twitched under my fingers. She swung her head toward her belly like something irritated her from the inside.

I stepped back, watching her posture, her breathing. She shifted her weight, then pawed again, sharper this time.

"No," I said, more firmly. I pulled my phone out, thumb hovering. Wyatt's name was there, right where it always was. A simple button. A simple call. I stared at it until my eyes burned.

Then I locked the screen and shoved the phone away.

"I can handle this," I said to the mare, like she understood pride.

She lowered her head and blew out a breath that sounded too heavy.

I went to the tack room for a lead rope. When I came back, the mare was down on her knees, trying to roll.

"Shit," I breathed, dropping the rope and rushing to her.

She heaved, legs scrabbling, eyes wild for the first time.

My hands went cold.

I grabbed her halter, my voice tight. "Up. Get up. Come on."

She surged, half rising, then tried to drop again.

I pulled, bracing my feet, trying to be stronger than panic.

My phone buzzed again in my pocket, like the world had a cruel sense of timing.

I fought with the mare, breath coming too fast, sweat already breaking on my skin. She lurched, and for a second I saw Ray's hands in my mind, steady and sure, and I hated that I didn't have them.

She tried to go down again.

I was alone.

The barn felt too big. The night felt too close. The gate clicking in my memory felt like a warning I'd ignored.

My hands started shaking, and I couldn't stop them.

That was when I yanked my phone out, thumb hitting Wyatt's name before I could talk myself out of it again. And when it rang, all I could think was that I waited too long.

Eighteen

Wyatt

It was early evening, I'd spent all day at the brewery, and now I was elbow deep in the engine of an old baler when Holt jogged across the yard toward me. He looked uneasy, and Holt never looked uneasy.

"She called."

My pulse snapped tight. "Tessa?"

He handed me my phone. "She's called three times."

I wiped my hands on a rag and hit callback. She answered on the first ring, breathless and shaking.

"Wyatt." Just my name, but said in a way that punched me straight in the sternum.

"What's wrong?"

"Ray's old cutting horse. She's down in her stall. Rolling. Sweating. You're closer than Brooke. I don't need her out, but I need help getting the horse up." Her words were fast, and while she was making sense, there was panic hiding in her voice.

Colic, shit.

"I'll be right there."

"I tried walking her. She keeps trying to throw herself

down. I don't know what's happening. I don't know how to stop it."

"You did the right thing calling me."

"I didn't want to."

"Oh, believe me, I know."

I hung up before I could say anything else stupid and grabbed Holt. "Bring the colic kit, a lead rope, and gloves." He didn't question it. We climbed into the truck and tore down the gravel road faster than was smart.

When we pulled into her yard, Tessa was already outside the barn, pacing like an animal that didn't know whether to run or fight. Her hair stuck to her forehead, her shirt was damp with sweat, and her hands were shaking hard enough that I could see it from the truck.

"She's in here," she said quietly, leading us inside.

The mare was down, flanks heaving, sides drenched with sweat as she rolled and kicked at her belly, eyes wild with pain. It was bad colic, the kind that didn't leave room for denial.

"What did you give her today?" I asked.

"Just her feed," Tessa said. "Not much. And she had plenty of water. She was fine this morning."

"It can come on fast."

"I know that, I'm not stupid," she snapped.

"I didn't say you were." I wasn't sure if I'd ever met a woman who was so maddening, but at least right now I could pinpoint the reason.

She rubbed her arms hard like she was trying to hold herself together. "I'm scared."

I knelt next to the mare and pressed my hand to her belly, checking for tension. Her gut was tight, too tight. Holt handed me the stethoscope, and I listened, already knowing what I was about to find. There was nothing. Not a single sound.

"Tessa," I said as I stood. "She needs to be walked hard. We can't let her go down again."

"I tried. I can't hold her alone. She's too strong." Tessa shook her head.

"That's why we're here."

"On your feet, girl," I murmured, guiding the mare up while Tessa pulled carefully at the halter. It took all three of us to get her standing, and when she swayed, Tessa let out a sharp, broken sound that twisted something low in my chest.

"We walk her. Don't let her stop."

We started moving the mare in slow circles through the barn aisle, Tessa on one side of her head, me on the other, Holt behind her, pushing gently when she tried to stall out. She kept stumbling, jerking sideways, trying to throw herself down.

Every time she lurched, Tessa panicked. "Stop. Don't fall. Please don't fall."

"Breathe."

"I am breathing."

"You're not."

"I am," she snapped, and her voice cracked on the last word.

The mare rolled her shoulder hard without warning and nearly crushed her. I grabbed Tessa around the waist and yanked her out of the way in one rough motion. She slammed into my chest, her hands fisting in my shirt, her breath hot against my throat as she dragged in air.

For one dangerous second, she stayed there before she shoved me away. "Don't touch me."

"If you want to stay alive, I'm going to touch you."

"That's not funny."

"It wasn't a joke."

We herded the mare through the barn, sweat dripping

from all of us, and out to the pasture. The immediate temperature change sent a shiver down my spine, but it was welcome.

"Keep her moving. She needs the pressure to shift."

Tessa shot me a look through hair plastered to her cheek. "I'm trying."

"You're doing good," I said softly.

"Don't patronize me." Tessa rolled her eyes, and I wanted to toss her over my knee. Good lord, this woman got on every nerve I possessed.

We walked until my shoulders burned and Holt's shirt was soaked through. The mare panted, foam streaking her neck, every part of her screaming distress. Tessa looked like she might break in two.

"Wyatt," she said suddenly. "Is she going to die?"

"No."

Her eyes flashed. "Stop lying to me."

"I'm not."

"You think I can't handle the truth. After everything else. After Ray. After the bank. After all of it."

I held her gaze. "I think you're exhausted, scared, and trying to carry this alone."

Her lip trembled. Her grip on the lead rope tightened like she was strangling it.

Then her phone rang. Tessa didn't look; she already knew.

The ringtone gave it away, the same ring as all the times in my truck on the way here.

She went pale. "Don't answer that."

"I have to."

"No, You don't." Before she could move, I grabbed the phone. "Wyatt," she hissed. "Give it back."

I lifted it to my ear. "What the hell do you want?"

"Who is this?" A man's voice asked

I smiled slowly and meanly. "Nobody that would mean anything to you."

"Put her on."

"No," I answered, my voice flat.

"Who the hell are you?" The fucker yelled.

"Someone who appreciates a beautiful woman far more than you ever could."

Tessa lunged for the phone. "Give it to me." I turned slightly so she couldn't reach it.

"Don't give Tessa another thought, she's got a real man to keep her company now." I winked at Tessa when I said it, and she threw her hands in the air.

"Fuck you, when I find out who you are, I'm going to…" he sputtered, and I cut him off.

"You're going to what? You don't even know who the fuck I am. If you ever come near my woman again, I will bury you so deep in the mountains that not even the coyotes will find your body to eat off your decaying flesh. I'm warning you now, you mother fucker, leave Tessa alone, because you're no match for me." I ended the call and handed the phone back.

"Your woman?" she asked, narrowing her pointed gaze at me.

"Little white lies never hurt." I shrugged and looked over at Holt, still walking the mare around the paddock.

"You're not my guard dog."

"Didn't claim to be."

"You're not anything to me."

That one landed harder than I liked. I nodded once. "Alright."

She looked startled that I didn't push back. The mare stumbled again, and Tessa caught the halter. We all pulled together.

"Easy," she whispered, her voice breaking as she pressed her forehead to the mare's neck.

Slowly, painfully, the mare loosened. Her breathing steadied. Her belly softened. Her ears flicked forward again. The worst passed.

Tessa sagged against the mare in relief. I let out the breath I'd been holding since the moment I walked in.

"She's okay," I said.

Tessa turned toward me. Her eyes were bright and wrecked, lashes damp with sweat and tears she hadn't bothered to wipe away. We were too close. Close enough that the heat between us was palpable. The barn dimmed around us, shadows pooling low, the world narrowing until it was just her and the space she was trying not to cross.

Her eyes tracked my mouth, lingered there for a heartbeat that dragged, like she was imagining something she was fighting to ignore.

Heat hit low and sharp, a sudden, vicious pull that tightened my hands at my sides.

I stepped closer before my thoughts could catch up, drawn in by the way she didn't move away. She stayed right there, breath shuddering, body pitched forward just enough to feel like permission.

I could see the exact second she realized it, too. Her breath stuttered. Her eyes darkened, panic and want collided hard enough to leave her shaken.

She blinked once, like she was forcing herself back into her body, then stepped away as if the space between us burned.

"This doesn't change anything," she said, voice thin, too fast. "You helped me, that's all. I still don't trust you."

My answer scraped out of me, rough and unfiltered. "Wasn't counting on it."

"Whatever that was, it won't happen again," she said, her words not convincing. The mare snorted behind me, sharp and impatient, and the sound cracked the moment open like a whip. I stepped back. "Keep her walking for ten more minutes, then water. Call me if the gut sounds drop again."

Tessa nodded, her hair falling into her face. I left the barn before instinct beat restraint. And before she realized how close she'd been to asking me to stay.

Nineteen

Tessa

The mare was finally quiet. I'd walked her until my knees shook, checked gut sounds twice an hour, forced water under her nose until she drank, and bedded her down with fresh straw. She breathed evenly now, sides still damp but no longer rigid with pain. I pressed my forehead to her shoulder, exhausted, and whispered for her not to scare me like that again.

But the truth was, it wasn't the mare that scared me. It was the man who'd shown up the moment I needed help. The way we'd moved together without thinking, like our bodies already knew the same rhythm. The way he'd pulled me out of the mare's path without hesitation.

The way he handled Colin was nothing short of a relief. Maybe it was enough to scare him off.

But it scared me how much trust I'd given him without thinking. It scared me most that for one breathless heartbeat, I'd almost kissed him.

I grabbed my phone without thinking, without breathing, and thumbed Dani's name. It rang once, twice.

"Tess?"

The sound of her voice cracked straight through the last thin wall I had left. I didn't say a word. I didn't need to.

"I'm coming," she said immediately.

"No, you can't, you've got a job," I sniffled.

"I can analyze data from anywhere, you know that."

"Okay," I whispered.

I sank down onto the couch with a long, shaking sigh. Everything would be fine, I told myself. I knew what I was doing with the animals. Other than needing Wyatt's help to get the mare on her feet, I could've handled it all alone. But as exhaustion dragged me toward sleep, the last thing I thought about was the man who'd wrapped his arm around my waist and held me so tightly against him that I could still feel the echo of it in my skin.

***

"Tess?" Dani shouted, already stomping through the kitchen. "Where are you?"

"Here," I said as I rubbed my eyes.

She took one look at me, sweaty, streaked with barn dirt, eyes swollen, and her entire face changed. "What happened to you?" Her arms were already open before she reached me, and the full-body smother hug hit a second later. I didn't exactly melt into her, but my knees did go weak in a way I wasn't proud of.

She pulled back just far enough to see my face. "Tell me what happened."

I swallowed hard. "The mare colicked."

Her hand flew to her mouth. "Is she—"

"She's okay. I think."

Dani blew out a sharp breath. "Good. Okay. That's good.

Now tell me why you sound like someone peeled your soul out through your ribs."

I tried, I really did, but when the words finally came, they came out jagged anyway. I told her how bad it was, how the mare thrashed, how I couldn't keep her on her feet alone and panicked. "I called Wyatt Hargrove for help."

"Oh shit."

"Don't," I warned.

"No, we are absolutely talking about this. You called the man you swore you hated?"

"He was the closest person," I snapped.

"That's not an answer. Try again."

"He knows horses better than I do. And I didn't have time to be picky."

Her expression softened in that maddening way only best friends manage. "Okay. Fair. But that still doesn't explain why you look like you got hit by a freight train."

I wrapped my arms around myself. "We worked well together."

Dani froze. Her eyes widened. "Oh no."

"Stop."

"Oh no no no."

"Dani," I whined because she could read me like a book.

"You didn't kiss him, did you?"

My face heated. "No. God no. Almost?"

She blinked slowly, knowingly, infuriatingly. "Oh my God. Did you want to kiss him?"

"No? No. No, I didn't want to kiss him." Even my own words sounded less than convincing. I groaned and paced the kitchen. "We were shoulder to shoulder, working together, and he looked at me like. I don't know, like he wanted me."

Dani's whole body softened. "Oh, honey."

"I don't want him to look at me like that," I said, my voice cracking. "I don't want him to be steady or kind or useful or close. Or tell Colin I was his woman." I knew I should have kept that to myself, but it just spilled out.

"Excuse me?" Dani's eyebrows lifted so high I wondered if they were going to stop.

"I need a drink for this explanation," I said as I walked over to the fridge and pulled out the alcohol I'd bought in town. "God, this is all a nightmare. The only good thing is I got a job, and you're here. Wait, how long are you here?" I asked as I slid a drink across the table.

"As long as you need, I can work from anywhere." She looked around the house. "As long as you've got wifi."

"It's probably the only bill that's paid up," I said with a laugh.

Then my phone buzzed on the counter, and both our heads snapped to it.

Colin.

The pit in my stomach dropped open. Dani grabbed the phone before I could.

"Absolutely not."

"He's probably livid, imagining me with Wyatt."

"Let him be mad, he's a fucking loser who fumbled everything about you." Dani took a sip of her drink. She frowned slightly. "Hargrove Brewing?"

"He owns a brewery too, how annoying is that?" I rolled my eyes as Dani took another sip of the fancy ass beer that Wyatt makes.

"I was kind of hoping Wyatt's talk with Colin would be the end of things, but I guess not," I said as I picked up the phone and looked at the text that just came through.

> Colin: If you're sleeping with someone else, there's going to be hell to pay.

Dani's voice dropped low. "Tessa. He's unhinged. Don't

respond, make him think that sexy cowboy is railing your brains out," she said again, smirking.

I pressed my hands to my forehead as Dani moved closer, gentler now. "Tell me the rest."

"There is no rest," I said hollowly. "I'm just tired. I'm terrified. And Wyatt..." I squeezed my eyes shut. "He's confusing."

"You like him."

"No."

"You're starting to trust him."

"Absolutely not."

"It's okay that you wanted him to stay."

I swallowed hard. "I wanted him to go," I whispered. "Because if he stayed, I didn't know what I was going to let happen."

"You're human, you're allowed to have those kinds of feelings," Dani said with a smile.

"I broke up with my long-term boyfriend two weeks ago, and I don't really think I should be jumping into anything else." I should have added the fact that I'd moved home at the drop of a hat, and the only parent I'd ever known was gone. This wasn't the time to jump into bed with some man I didn't even know.

"Live a little, Tess. We both know you've been mentally out of your relationship for over a year. Like, when was the last time you had lackluster sex with that asshole?" Dani reached for another can of beer and cracked it open.

"He lied to me. When he came to the city to get me, he lied to me," I said as I slumped back in the chair and crossed my arms. The light in the center of the room buzzed gently, and the refrigerator hummed in the silence.

"He omitted the truth to protect your emotions. Sounds pretty thoughtful to me." She shrugged.

"I can't believe you're on his side."

"I'm not on his side, but I am trying to get you to see that maybe he's not the big bad wolf you think he is."

"Go back to the city, you're not helping." I pointed to the door and glared at her.

"Sorry, bestie, you're stuck with me." Dani laughed as she grinned at me.

TWENTY
WYATT

I should've known the morning was going too damn smooth.

Kegs checked. Deliveries logged. Coffee is still hot. No calls from Holt. No suspicious vehicles. Just me and a quiet brewery before the doors officially opened.

Then the front door opened, and in walked trouble.

Pink-haired, five-foot-two, trouble in combat boots and eyeliner, scanning the room like she was casing the place. Dani, Tessa's roommate. The same woman who once slammed a door in my face, screamed-whispered at Tessa behind it, and called me a creep loud enough for the entire hallway to hear.

She spotted me instantly.

Her whole body stilled.

"Oh," she said, voice dropping with dramatic venom. "There you are, I thought you'd be harder to track down."

Fuck, I groaned to myself.

"Morning, Dani."

"You remember me, how nice," she said.

I took an involuntary step back as she stalked toward the

bar like a cat that had memorized every human pressure point. She hopped up on a barstool and slapped her hand on the wooden top. Her pink hair was bright enough to cause retinal damage against the warm wood and stone backdrop.

"Alright, Cowboy. Let's have a chat."

"I don't think we need to," I said as I shook my head.

"Oh, we need to. We absolutely need to. I have questions."

Of course she did.

"All right, I'm listening," I said, out of pure resignation, like I was in a hostage situation. She raised one perfectly sharp eyebrow.

"You answered her phone."

"Oh god," I muttered and rolled my eyes, wishing I'd stayed in bed this morning.

"Don't roll your eyes at me," she said, loud enough that the bartender polishing glasses at the far end suddenly found the ceiling fascinating. "You answered her phone and told that unhinged ex of hers, and I quote, *"If you ever come near my woman again, I will bury you so deep in the mountains not even the coyotes will find your body to eat off your decaying flesh."*

"That was situational."

"That was Cowboy Daddy energy," she countered.

I blinked. "Cowboy Daddy energy?" Not actually sure, I wanted to know what she meant.

"Yes. Alpha male, testosterone, cowboy toughness, territorial claiming. That whole vibe you have going on." She waved vaguely at all of me. "The boots. The shoulders. The broody, damaged, divorced man energy. It's sexy."

"I'm not broody." It was about the only thing I could argue about, because the rest was true.

She laughed. "Sweetie. I'm sure you brood in your sleep. In fact, I guarantee it."

I rubbed my jaw, trying very hard not to let this tiny pink menace get under my skin.

She leaned over the bar and narrowed her eyes at me. "Here's what we're not gonna do. We're not gonna pretend you didn't scare the shit out of Tessa by making her see you as someone she might not quite hate as much as she thought."

"I was just trying to help."

"She called me crying." Her face changed from fierce protector to concerned best friend.

My chest tightened. "Is she alright?"

"Oh, now you worry."

"From the moment I let her know about Ray, I worried about her." There was the revelation I'd tried to push down. I was worried about Tessa. There wasn't a reason for it. She was capable and smart, but she'd worked her way into my iron heart.

Dani froze. Her eyes softened in a way that made me deeply uncomfortable. "See," she said quietly. "That right there is the problem. You care about her."

"I don't see how that's a problem," I said as I turned to the beer tap and grabbed a mug. Having this conversation needed a drink.

I slid the beer toward her, and her brows furrowed slightly as she stared at it.

"On the house," I said as I poured one for myself. Having a beer at noon wasn't something I usually did, but this was an extenuating circumstance. "Follow me."

"Are you going to hit me over the head and toss me in one of those beer vats?" She asked as she trailed along behind me. I glanced over my shoulder and shook my head.

"You and Tessa lived together too long, she asked me the same thing, exactly."

"We like true crime," she said easily. Well, that explained it all then, didn't it?

"Why is it a problem that I care?" I asked as I sat in the oversized leather chair in front of the fireplace.

"Oh my GOD." She threw her hands in the air. "You giant prairie himbo. The problem is she doesn't know what to do with a good man who actually cares and doesn't manipulate her."

I stared. "A what?"

"Himbo," she repeated. "It means hot, incompetent, and emotionally stupid."

She shifted in her chair and tucked her feet up under her. "Why does Tessa attract men who can't give her what she needs emotionally? This is her curse. This is cosmic cruelty." Dani reached for her beer and took a sip. She frowned, looked at the mug, then took another sip. "This is good."

I went to say thank you, but she started talking again. "At least you look like you could pull down trees with your aura alone. That's better than the pipsqueak she was with. I think you have money too, maybe more money than she walked away from, but you don't flaunt it." She let her eyes gaze around the brewery.

She wasn't wrong, I did have money, and no, I didn't flaunt it all over creation. People around here know who I am; they don't need reminders every time they see me. I liked to live a quiet life, spoil Maddy at every opportunity, even when her mother says to stop.

"What are you getting at here, Dani?"

She shifted on the chair again, set down her beer on the coffee table in front of her, and planted her feet on the floor, resting her elbows on her knees. "Listen to me, Wyatt Hargrove. Tessa is fragile right now. She's mourning a man with whom she had a complicated relationship, extreme debt, and stupidity from every direction. She doesn't need a cowboy knight in shining emotional armour complicating her life."

"I'm not trying to complicate anything. I'm just trying to help." My voice dropped, and I suddenly felt exhausted. My life had been turned upside down by Tessa showing up, and part of me wasn't upset about it, but I needed to stop fighting with her at every turn.

Her eyes narrowed. "Do you like her?"

I didn't answer, just let my gaze drift to the windows.

Her jaw dropped. "OH MY GOD YOU DO." Her voice was far too loud for indoor use.

I cleared my throat and looked around to see who was in the bar and if they were listening to this conversation. Thankfully, at this moment, it was basically empty. "It doesn't matter what I feel. Tessa hates everything about me, and I won't add to her stress load or complicate her life."

"Oh, but it does. Because if you hurt her, I will destroy you."

"Destroy me?" I asked and arched my brow.

"Yes. Emotionally. Spiritually. Physically, if necessary. I will make your cattle turn against you, and figure out how to spoil every keg of beer you have in this place." She leaned back in her chair and stared me down, like she was offering a challenge to see how I was going to play this.

"That's not rational, or possible."

"And I will dye your horse's tails pink in retaliation," she added quickly. Now that she could do. I found her humorous, but I wasn't about to let her know that.

I blinked. "That seems extreme," I said flatly.

"Try me," she said, cocking her head slightly to the side, deadly serious. I stared at her. She stared right back. Then she broke into a feral grin.

"You're scared of me," she said, an evil grin spreading across her face.

"I'm not scared of you," I replied, unamused now.

"You are terrified."

"I could pick you up and throw you in a beer vat with one arm," I said, circling back to the earlier conversation.

"And I could ruin your entire life with one group chat."

That shut me right up, because it was probably true.

She smirked. "That's what I thought."

I exhaled slowly. "What do you want from me, Dani?" I asked and placed my elbows on knees and leaned forward slightly.

She softened again. "Take care of her. But don't let her know you are taking care of her. And don't make her feel like she owes you anything. That's the easiest way to get on Tessa's bad side."

The joke was on Dani, because I was already on Tessa's bad side, and I hadn't done either of those things. "I wasn't planning to."

"Good." She reached for her beer and took another sip. Maybe we were at the end of this conversation, but no, she took a deep breath again. "Also, if you decide to be Mr. overprotective, toxic masculinity, cowboy dude, can you please make sure Colin never bothers her again?"

I stared at her for a long moment.

Then, despite myself, I felt my mouth twitch.

She noticed.

"Oh lord," she gasped. "The cowboy actually smiles. What is happening?"

I shook my head. "You're something else."

She grinned triumphantly. "I know. Now I think you should buy me lunch, Cowboy Daddy."

I groaned. "Please don't call me that."

"Not a chance, it's your name now." Then she stood, turned on her heel, and headed toward the patio doors like she hadn't just verbally dismantled me in my own damn establishment.

And the worst part?

I liked her. She was a fierce friend and wasn't afraid to make sure everyone knew it. Dani was a person everyone needed in their corner. But I was never saying that out loud. I stood there for a solid thirty seconds after Dani left, staring at the fire like I'd just been hit by a pink-haired tornado with emotional brass knuckles.

"Cowboy Daddy, don't forget my lunch," she called out, and her voice carried easily from the patio into the main area.

"Jesus Christ," I huffed. Of all the things I'd been called in my life, boss, rancher, stubborn bastard, pain in the ass, this was a new one.

I muttered the words once under my breath, just to confirm they sounded as stupid as I thought. I punched in a burger and fries for the woman. Given my luck today, she'd be a vegetarian and offended I hadn't asked what she wanted.

"You alright, boss?"

I looked up. One of my bartenders stood there, eyebrows raised, pretending very hard she hadn't heard everything.

"Yep"

She hesitated. "You're kinda smiling."

"I am not."

"Okay," she shrugged and laughed quietly.

I turned toward the back hall, pushing through the swinging door and straight into Holt, who'd clearly been waiting and clearly had absolutely no business listening as hard as he had been.

He didn't say anything at first. He just stood there. I tried to walk past him, but he filled the doorway and smirked.

"Don't."

"Wouldn't dream of it," he said as he let me pass and followed me.

We took three steps. Three. Then he lost it.

"Cowboy Daddy," he wheezed, doubling over, laughing so hard he had to grab the wall. "She said it with her whole chest."

"She did not," I growled at him.

"Oh, she did. I've never seen a woman assign a grown man a porn name before lunch."

"I'll fire you," I muttered.

"No, you won't," he said cheerfully. "You're too busy here to run things at the ranch, too."

"Fuck off."

"Cowboy Daddy," he sang.

I closed my eyes and considered every poor decision that had led me to this moment. It wouldn't kill me. But it might shut him up.

"Why are you here anyway? I pay you to be at the ranch, not here." Pushing open the door to my office, I flopped into the chair and waited for him to talk.

Holt stepped inside and shut the door with his boot heel. The grin he'd been wearing died fast, replaced by something weightier. He hooked his thumbs into his back pockets, eyes cutting toward me in a way that told me I wasn't going to like what came next.

"Stopped at the feed store on my way in. Ran into Katherine Miller."

My jaw tightened. "From the county office."

"Yeah." He nodded once. "She pulled me aside. Didn't say much, she can't, but she said just enough. The bank's pushing Ray's file up the chain. 'Expedited review,' her words."

A slow, cold pressure tightened under my ribs. "Meaning?"

"Meaning they're looking at foreclosure timelines," he said quietly. "Soon. Sooner than Tessa's ready for."

The room went still around us. The hum of the walk-in fridge. The muffled clatter from the bar. All of it felt too far away.

"Katherine said a notice is probably being printed this

week," Holt added. "Thought you'd want the heads up before it hits her mailbox."

I blew out a breath that tasted like metal. Ray had run out of time. Tessa didn't have the luxury of any.

"Yeah," I murmured. "Thanks."

Twenty-One

Tessa

The day was flying by, Brooke had gone out to a ranch east of town to help with a cow that was having foot issues, and that left me here to man the clinic alone. Mostly, it was phone calls to rebook patients.

"Hey, roomie," Dani said as she waltzed into the clinic with two coffees in hand. "Do you know you've got a tab running at that coffee shop?"

"Yeah, Colin did that," I said flatly, and Dani stopped mid-sip. I was half expecting her to spit the coffee out, but she just shrugged. I couldn't blame her; it was good coffee. "I should refuse to use it, but I'm broke, and it's good coffee." I was a little too exhausted to worry about it at the moment.

"So. How's Cowboy Daddy?"

I choked hard. "How's who?"

Her grin widened. "Oh, good. He hasn't told you yet."

My stomach dropped. "What did you do?"

"I introduced myself properly."

"Dani."

She waved me off. "Relax. I told him to keep his distance.

Told him to behave. Told him if he hurt you, I'd burn his entire ranch to the ground, and ruin all his delicious beer."

"Dani," I said again, a little more exasperated.

"And," she added, clearly enjoying herself, "I gave him a nickname."

I dropped my forehead to the table. "I can't survive this."

"Oh, you can," she said cheerfully. "You're tougher than you think."

She sobered then, just a little, leaning forward with her elbows on her knees. "I did it because you're fragile right now, Tess. Not weak. Fragile. And you keep attracting men who think they get to decide what's best for you."

That hit a little harder than I wanted it to. I didn't argue, because underneath the embarrassment and irritation and the unwanted warmth curling low in my stomach, there was an uncomfortable truth pressing against my ribs.

Wyatt showed up when I needed him.

He knew exactly what to do.

He steadied me without taking over.

And he walked away before I realized how much I wanted him to stay.

That scared me more than the debt. More than the ranch. More than my grief.

I stood abruptly. "I need to go run a few errands for Brooke."

Dani raised a brow.

"I need to check on a feed order and talk to the local welding shop about looking at the cattle handling system in the back."

"Do you want company?"

"No," I said quickly. "You've done enough damage for one day."

She grinned. "You'll thank me later."

I grabbed my keys and left before she could say anything else that would lodge itself in my brain.

Downtown was busy in that deceptively cheerful way. Market umbrellas lined the sidewalks. Kids rode bikes between food trucks. Someone laughed too loudly near the bakery. Everything looked normal and bright and loud in a way that made me feel like I'd missed a step everyone else knew.

I parked near the co-op and stepped out.

At first, everything felt fine.

Then the prickling started at the back of my neck. The unmistakable awareness of being watched, not casually, not accidentally, but deliberately.

I turned my head just enough to see him.

A grey sedan sat across the street, engine running. Colin leaned against the hood with his arms folded, watching me like he had all the time in the world.

My stomach dropped straight to the pavement.

He didn't wave, or call out. He just smiled. That tight, controlled smile that made my skin crawl.

I looked away immediately and forced my feet to move. The co-op door jingled as I pulled it open, but my heart was already pounding hard enough to hurt.

Why was he here?

Why now?

Why like this?

I ordered mineral blocks and supplements like nothing was wrong, nodded at a man who used to know my uncle, signed the slip with a hand that shook no matter how hard I tried to steady it.

When I stepped back outside, Colin was gone.

The fear was not.

It stayed lodged in my chest, heavy and cold and certain, and suddenly I hated Dani's joke. Hated my attraction to Wyatt. Hated needing anyone at all.

Because when real trouble came knocking, I did not want to be someone's responsibility.

I ran the rest of my errands on sheer stubborn momentum. Feed store. Post office. Hardware store. I kept moving because stopping felt like surrender. If I stopped doing normal things, he won.

By the time I crossed back toward my truck, the late afternoon sun was low and sharp, throwing long shadows across the lot. I slowed.

Something was off.

The truck was locked, but the driver's window had smudges on the glass. Not mine. I always rolled it down by gripping the top. These prints were lower, angled differently.

Someone had leaned in close.

My breathing thinned. I scanned the lot. Nothing unusual. Just people. Just trucks. No grey sedan.

Then I saw it.

A small white envelope tucked under the driver's side wiper blade.

My name written across the front. Underlined twice.

No one in town would leave me a note like that. No one knew me well enough, or no one cared enough.

Except him.

My fingers felt disconnected as I reached for the envelope. It was thin. Too light. My mouth went dry as I opened it.

Inside were photos.

My barn, the door open, and Wyatt's truck parked in front. The night the horse colicked. Then there was another one of Wyatt's arms around my waist at Ray's funeral, Brooke and I laughing at something at the front desk. Then there was the front door of my home.

These were all recent. Intentional. Close. I didn't bother looking through the rest, my stomach was in knots, and I didn't want to know how truly close he'd gotten...

At the bottom, scrawled on a piece of paper, dark ink:

You're not safe out here alone.
Come home, Tess.
C.

I didn't realize I'd backed into the truck until the metal pressed into my spine.

This wasn't a phone call.

Wasn't a text.

Wasn't an angry ex.

This was a warning. A threat dressed up as concern.

I shoved the photo back into the envelope and scanned the lot again, panic licking up my spine. Every stranger looked wrong. Every car felt like it could be his.

I climbed into the truck and locked the doors immediately. My hands shook so badly I dropped the keys twice before managing to start the engine.

"Go," I whispered. "Just go."

As I pulled out of the lot, I kept checking the mirrors, searching for that grey sedan, those tinted windows, that smile.

All I saw was myself. And the envelope on the passenger seat stared back at me like a loaded gun.

I didn't want to call Wyatt.

I didn't want to need him.

I didn't want him to see me like this.

But as I drove home, one truth settled deep and cold in my bones. Colin wasn't just angry, he was escalating.

Twenty-Two

Wyatt

Holt and I were supposed to be fixing the bearings on the stock trailer. The morning air was crisp, tasting of mountain runoff and dry grass, but the sun was already starting to bake the grease into my skin.

Instead of working, I was staring at the same rusted bolt for five minutes, the wrench heavy and useless in my hand. Something had been crawling under my skin since yesterday, a prickly, restless feeling that usually preceded a summer storm or a predator in the brush.

"Tighten it or kiss it," Holt muttered from where he was hunkered down by the axle, his face streaked with oil. "Pick one, Wyatt. I'm losing circulation in my legs."

Before I could answer, he straightened, squinting past my shoulder toward the long, gravel drive. "Uh oh."

I turned, the wrench falling to the dirt with a dull thud.

A tiny, mud-splattered hatchback was rattling up the drive, its engine whining in protest. Dust boiled behind it like a smoke screen. It didn't slow down for the cattle guard, hitting the metal bars with a bone-jarring clatter.

Dani.

The car hadn't even fully stopped before the door swung open. She stepped out, her pink hair a shock of neon against the muted browns of the ranch. Her sunglasses were too big for her face, hiding her eyes, but the way she marched toward us, shoulders squared, chin tilted, radiated a kind of frantic determination.

"Did you invite her?" Holt asked, wiping his hands on a rag, his eyes fixed on Dani.

"Yeah, no," I said, my gut tightening. "And I don't like the look on her face."

"Looks like she's gonna set fire to something."

"Probably me."

She slammed the car door, a sound like a gunshot in the quiet valley, and marched over, pointing a finger at me like I'd committed a felony.

"We need to talk," she snapped. "Now."

Holt whistled low under his breath, leaning back against the trailer. "Someone woke up spicy."

Dani shot him a look sharp enough to cut tempered steel. Holt, a man who'd been stomped by rodeo bulls and broken wild colts without flinching, actually straightened his posture and took a half-step back.

Interesting. But I didn't have time to process it. I jerked my chin toward the heavy timber doors of the barn. "Inside."

I didn't wait to see if she followed. I led the way into the shadows of the barn, where the air was cooler and smelled of sweet alfalfa and leather. Dani stomped in behind me, her heels clicking on the hard-packed dirt. Holt trailed after us, his curiosity clearly overriding his concept of self-preservation.

Dani spun around, her shaky hands diving into the pockets of her denim jacket—another bad sign. She wasn't confident today. She was vibrating with a fear she was trying to mask with aggression.

"I don't know how to say this without breaking some kind

of girl code," she said, her voice cracking on the last word. "But Tessa is not okay, Wyatt."

My whole body went still. Every muscle, every nerve ending, went on high alert. "What happened?"

She swallowed hard, her throat working. With trembling fingers, she pulled a thick manila envelope from her purse and held it like it was radioactive.

I saw the name written on the front. Tessa. Underlined twice in a jagged, angry hand.

My chest tightened, a cold weight settling behind my ribs. "Dani."

"Don't freak out."

"I'm not prone to freaking out, Dani. Give me the envelope."

"No yeah you're totally mellow. Somehow I think that you might freak out now."

"Dani," I huffed, reaching out. She pressed the envelope into my hand.

I opened it carefully, my fingers clumsy. I pulled out the contents, and for a second, the breath left my lungs.

It wasn't one photo. It was a dozen. All glossy, high-resolution, and taken from a distance.

The first one hit me like a physical blow. Tessa was walking from the barn in the blue hour of early morning, her hair messy, a bucket in her hand. The next: Tessa unloading groceries with Dani, laughing at something. Then Tessa crouched by the broken fence line on the north ridge. Tessa was asleep in the porch chair, her head tipped back, vulnerable and completely unaware.

Every shot was telephoto. Every shot had been taken from the tree line or the roadside.

But the last one, the last one, made the blood in my veins turn to ice. It was Tessa with her hands on my chest, looking up at me in the yard two days ago. Looking at me like I was the only person in the world she could trust.

"He's been here," I said, my voice coming out low and dangerous. "He's been watching her on my land."

Holt stepped closer, looking over my shoulder. He swore, a vicious string of words. "Holy shit, Wyatt."

Dani's voice shook as she stepped into my line of sight. "Wyatt, these were all taken this week. Some of them are from yesterday."

I gripped the envelope so hard the paper crumpled. Every instinct in me—the man who'd promised Ray he'd watch over her, and the man who still hadn't figured out why his heart skipped when she walked into a room, went razor-sharp.

"Where did she find them?" I asked.

"On her truck," Dani whispered. "Tucked under the wiper. Yesterday, while she was at the co-op."

A hot, slow, deadly anger simmered through me. I hadn't felt this particular brand of rage in years, not since someone tried to cut my water rights. It was a cold, focused fire.

I forced myself to breathe, to keep my hands from shaking. "She didn't call me."

Dani laughed, a bitter, jagged sound. She wiped at her eyes, her sunglasses sliding down her nose. "Wyatt, she won't even tell me she's scared. She came home white as a ghost and made dinner like she was a Stepford wife. That's how I knew something was really, really wrong. She's acting like if she ignores it, it'll go away."

My jaw locked so tight it ached. "Why?"

"Because that's Tessa," Dani said, her eyes wet and furious. "She thinks being strong means being silent. She thinks if she asks for help, she's proving you right, that she can't handle this place."

Holt looked at me, his face grim. "We need to do something, Boss."

"We are," I said.

Dani pushed her pink hair back, her hands still trembling. "She didn't want me to tell you. She'd kill me if she knew I was here."

"She won't know."

"She'll know," Holt muttered, though he didn't disagree.

"She won't," I repeated, my gaze fixed on the photo of her sleeping. The sight of it made my stomach turn.

Dani's voice dropped to a whisper. "Wyatt, he's escalating. He followed her all the way from Calgary. She doesn't know what he wants."

I did. I'd seen men like this fucker before. It wasn't about love. It was about control. Possession. Fear. He didn't want her back; he wanted to own the fact that she was afraid of him.

I set the photos down on a hay bale with slow, lethal precision, as if I couldn't risk damaging the evidence. I went cold. Still. Focused.

Holt watched me, his own posture shifting. He knew this version of me. It was the version that didn't stop until the job was done.

"Boss?" he asked quietly.

"We're done playing nice," I said. I looked Dani dead in the eye. "You were right to come here."

She exhaled a shaky breath, her shoulders finally dropping a fraction. "Thank God. I thought you'd yell at me for interfering."

"I'm not mad at you, Dani," I said truthfully. "I'm pissed at him."

"Good," she said, wiping a stray tear. "Because I can't protect her from a man like this. I'm just a city girl with a loudmouth."

My stomach twisted at the raw honesty in her voice. "You shouldn't have to."

I turned back to Holt. "We watch the roads. We watch the

fence lines. Nobody—and I mean nobody—gets near that ranch without us knowing."

Holt nodded, his face hardening. "Done. I'll pull the night shift on the ridge."

"And Dani," I added, my voice softening but remaining firm. "She can't know about this. Not yet. If she finds out you broke her confidence, she'll shut us both out. Right now, she needs to feel like she has some ground under her feet."

Dani nodded reluctantly. "Okay. But Wyatt, she likes you. Even if she's too stubborn to admit it. Please don't let this scare you off."

I blinked, the comment catching me off guard. "This isn't about me."

Dani's lips twitched with a ghost of a smile. "That's exactly why I said it."

I ignored that, pushing the thought aside. "Go home. Stay inside. Don't travel alone for a few days."

She nodded and turned to leave, but stopped when Holt called out to her.

"Hey, Dani?"

She paused, looking back.

Holt rubbed the back of his neck, a rare flush creeping up his tan skin. "If you, uh, need someone to walk you to your car in town. Or whatever. My number's on the visor."

Dani raised an eyebrow, a bit of her usual spark returning. "Oh? Cowboy's got a soft spot?"

Holt scowled, looking at his boots. "Just bein' polite."

Dani smiled, a small, real one. "Thanks, Holt. I might take you up on it."

She walked back to her car, and we watched until the dust trail faded into the horizon. The silence in the barn was heavy, charged with the shift in the stakes.

I picked up the photos again, my thumb brushing over the one of Tessa on the porch. My hands curled into fists.

"What now?" Holt asked.

"Now," I said, folding the photo and tucking it into my pocket, "I find Colin Winters."

"And then?"

I met his eyes.

"Then I make sure he never looks at her again."

Twenty-Three

Tessa

The stock waterer sounded wrong before I even saw it. At first, it blended with the morning noise, cicadas, a distant cow bawling, the creak of the old wind vane, but underneath it was a low rushing sound that did not belong. A constant, pulsing roar that set my nerves on edge.

I stepped onto the porch with a mug of coffee warm in my palms and paused, a strange pressure settling in my chest as the heavy, overheated air pressed in around me like it was waiting for something to snap. I started toward the barn, every step tightening that feeling. The gravel under my boots felt softer than it should have. Darker. My stomach dipped hard as I rounded the corner.

A geyser of water blasted sideways out of the hydrant like someone had taken a bat to the metal. Water sprayed in vicious arcs, drenching the yard and turning the dirt into a churning swamp of dark mud. The mare in the nearest paddock was losing her mind, trotting the fence line, tossing her head, eyes white.

"Oh, come on," I muttered as I dropped my coffee straight into the mud and ran.

Cold water slammed into my legs and stole my breath as it soaked my jeans and pinned my shirt to my ribs. My boots sank deep as I reached the hydrant and fought with the valve, but the damn thing would not budge. I braced my shoulder against the post and hauled with everything I had, metal scraping under my hands as the water sprayed harder and slapped my face.

"Turn. Turn, you piece of shit," I screamed.

"Step back." His voice cut straight through the roar. Deep. Calm. Maddeningly steady.

I spun around and nearly lost my footing as Wyatt came through the spray like he owned the chaos. Black T-shirt, dark jeans, boots already coated in mud. His hat was pulled low, his eyes sharp and assessing, tracking every movement in the yard in a way that sent my pulse skidding.

"You scared me," I snapped.

"Didn't mean to," he said, already closing the distance. Water hammered into his chest and soaked him through, but he barely noticed.

"You don't get to just show up whenever something goes wrong."

"I wasn't planning to, but you can see this from the road," he shot back. "That is not a subtle malfunction."

"That's not helpful," I growled in frustration and shook the valve again like I could intimidate it into submission. "I've got it."

"You don't."

"I said I—"

He reached for me. His hand closed around my hip, firm and sure, and lifted me moving me to the side as if I weighed nothing. Heat shot through me, fast and dizzying, infuriating in how instinctive it felt.

He turned to the valve, planted both hands on the metal, and leaned into it. His back tightened. His arms flexed. Water poured over him. I tried very hard not to stare. I failed just as hard.

He shoved once with a low grunt. Metal shrieked. The valve finally gave, the geyser dropping to a violent sputter before cutting off completely.

Silence slammed down around us.

We stood there in the aftermath, both soaked through, chests rising and falling in uneven breaths. Wyatt pushed his hat back slightly, water streaming down his temples.

"You good?" he asked.

"I'm fine," I lied.

He stepped closer, close enough that I could feel the heat of him through our wet clothes. His gaze slid slowly over me, my hair glued to my face, my shirt clinging to my ribs, my scraped hands, my useless boots trapped in the mud.

"You're shaking."

"It's cold."

"It's not that cold."

"Maybe I'm pissed off," I spat as I glared at him. "I think someone did this on purpose."

"Yeah."

"That's all you've got? Yeah? Where's the man with the answers? God, you're impossible." I threw my hands in the air, then let them fall against my wet jeans with a slap.

He crouched and ran his fingers along the cracked metal instead of taking the bait. "Impact. Not a failure. Someone hit it."

Cold rolled through me. "So someone was here."

"Looks like it."

"Perfect. Just fucking perfect."

He stood again, his posture shifting in a way that made my skin prickle. Guarded. Ready.

"What else happened?"

"Nothing."

"Tessa."

"I said nothing."

"You're lying."

"Stop assuming you know everything."

"Then tell me."

My throat tightened as I looked away. "I didn't see anything last night."

"That's not what I asked."

I swallowed as he closed the last bit of space between us.

"I'm not here to fight you. I'm trying to keep you safe."

"I don't need—"

"You do," he cut.

My temper finally snapped. "I don't want you playing protector or sheriff or whatever the hell this is."

His jaw flexed. "What I'm doing is making sure you don't get hurt."

"That's not your job."

"Then whose is it?"

The question hit me hard enough to knock the air from my lungs. I turned away, blinking fast. "I can handle myself."

"Bullshit."

I spun back on him. "Excuse me?"

"You heard me," he said, his voice dropping rough and entirely too intimate. "You don't have to pretend with me."

"That's exactly what I have to do with you."

He lifted his hand slowly and brushed a streak of mud from my cheek. The moment his skin touched mine, heat exploded under my ribs. My breath hitched. His eyes dropped straight to my mouth.

"Wyatt," I whispered.

"Yeah?" he murmured.

"This is a bad idea."

"I know."

His fingers slid down the curve of my jaw, steady and

warm in a way the cold water was not. My pulse pounded where his thumb rested under my chin. He moved closer until his chest was almost touching mine, our wet clothes making every brush feel like skin.

"You're scared," he said quietly.

I did not argue. I could not.

He placed his other hand on my hip, slow and careful, giving me every chance to stop him. I did not. His touch spread warmth through the soaked fabric, fingers curving just enough to make my stomach clench.

"Tessa," he said, his voice rough now, "tell me you don't want me here."

I opened my mouth and found nothing there.

His forehead lowered toward mine. Our noses brushed. The shock of it shot straight through me. His breath was warm against my cheek. His lips hovered a breath from mine. I swayed, and his grip tightened just enough to steady me.

Then the gate slammed outside.

Metal rang. The mare squealed. Something thudded hard enough to rattle the walls.

We tore apart like lightning had struck between us.

Air crashed back into my lungs as Wyatt's hand dropped instantly, his fingers curling into a fist at his side as if he were physically holding himself back. For one raw second, he looked wrecked, wanting, and furious at himself all at once.

"We should check that," I said, my voice barely working.

"Yeah."

He turned first, movements sharp and controlled. I pressed my fingers to my neck where he touched me, my skin still humming with the heat from his touch...

By the time I reached the gate, he was already fixing it, jaw clenched tight enough to crack teeth. He glanced at me once.

"Change your clothes. You'll get sick."

"That's not how sickness works, and I'm fine."

"You're not."

"Wyatt."

"Don't," he said quietly, and the hurt threaded through it stopped me cold.

"Where's Dani?"

"She had to go back to Calgary for a meeting," I replied, and watched him look around.

"Keep the doors locked tonight."

Ice slid straight through my spine. "Why?"

"Just a feeling."

"Do you know something you're not telling me?"

His jaw flexed hard. "Just be careful. Please."

That single word hit me harder than everything else.

He got into his truck and drove off, gravel spitting under his tires. I stood there on the porch, dripping and shaking, my body still remembering his hands on my hips, his breath on my cheek, the phantom pressure of his mouth almost on mine.

I had wanted him. God help me, I wanted him. And wanting Wyatt Hargrove was dangerous in every possible way.

Because Colin was out there.

And Wyatt was getting close enough to see every crack inside me. I wasn't sure which one scared me more.

Twenty-Four
Wyatt

My shirt stuck to my back. My jeans clung to my legs. Water dripped off the brim of my hat every time I blinked, and the cold was setting deep in my bones. I should've gone home to change first. But Rena didn't give grace for delays, and Maddy didn't deserve to wait around for her dad to get his shit together.

I pulled into the grocery store parking lot and saw Rena immediately. Leaning against her shiny SUV, sunglasses on, arms crossed, impeccably polished and impatient as always.

But Maddy?

She sat on the curb, tapping her shoes on the asphalt like she was drumming out a song only she could hear. She spotted me before Rena did. Her face lit up, and my chest eased just seeing it.

I parked the truck and swung out, boots squishing.

Rena's mouth tightened instantly. "Wyatt. You're soaking wet."

"Stock water blew. Didn't have time to change."

"You couldn't even towel off?" she snapped. "You look like you came straight out of a cattle trough."

"Good morning to you, too."

"Honestly, Wyatt."

But Maddy was already running. "Dad!"

She barrelled into me with a hug like she was trying to tackle me. Her arms wrapped tight around my waist. She didn't care about the water, didn't care about the mud. She just clung.

The knot in my chest loosened.

"Hey, Mads," I said, smoothing a hand over the back of her head. "You doing okay?"

"I am now," she said, muffled against my shirt. Then she pulled back and scrunched her nose. "You smell like... a wet horse and old hay."

"That's accurate."

Rena stepped forward, visibly annoyed. "Please don't get her soaked. I just washed that hoodie."

"She hugged me," I said dryly. "And I also have laundry facilities out here in the back woods." I didn't usually get snappy with her; it wasn't fair to Maddy, but the amount of shits I had to give was at an all-time low.

Rena ignored that. "Her bag is packed. Practice clothes should actually be clean this time. Please don't let them sit for three days again."

Maddy groaned. "Mom, I washed them."

"And then left them in the washing machine until they smelled like feet."

Maddy grinned at me. "She exaggerates."

"*She* absolutely doesn't," Rena said, crossing her arms tighter. "Anyway, I'll text you, and we can figure out a pick-up arrangement. Maybe you can bring her to me, so I don't have to come *here*." It seemed to be lost on her that she grew up here. We grew up here together, and even though none of her family lived in River's Edge anymore, it didn't erase her past.

"That's fine," I said.

Rena adjusted her sunglasses. "At least try to make her look presentable when she comes home."

Maddy muttered, "I'm not livestock," under her breath.

Rena glared. "What did you say?"

"Nothing."

Rena sighed dramatically, like motherhood was an exhausting performance. "Goodbye, Maddy. Be good."

Maddy nodded, but she didn't look at her mother again.

Rena climbed into her SUV and drove off without a wave.

Maddy watched her go with a small frown she tried to hide. Then she sighed loudly. "She's in a mood."

"Seems like it," I replied, not wanting to speak poorly of her mom, but also not completely impressed with the situation.

"She gets weird every time she drops me off. Like she thinks I'm gonna turn feral the second I get to your ranch."

I snorted. "Too late, you're already feral."

"Facts," she said with a grin.

We loaded her bag into the truck. When she climbed in, she stuck her feet up on the dash like she owned the place. I got in on my side, water squishing from my jeans.

She studied me for a long second.

"You okay?" she asked quietly.

"Yeah."

"Liar."

I glanced over. She was watching me like she was trying to read the truth off my face.

"What happened?"

"My neighbours stock waterer blew."

"Those don't just blow. Not unless it's winter."

I tightened my grip on the wheel. "Sometimes they do."

"Dad."

The kid was too perceptive for her own good.

"It was just a long morning."

"Okay." She didn't believe me, but she didn't push—not yet. Instead, she squinted at my face. "You look stressed."

"I'm fine."

"Your eyebrow is doing the thing."

"What thing?"

"The thing it does when you're pretending you're fine."

Jesus.

"Want to get milkshakes?" I asked, desperate for a subject change.

Her whole face brightened. "Yes. Obviously. I'm practically wasting away."

I shook my head, fighting a smile. She always managed to drag me back to centre, even when the inside of my head was running like wildfire.

But even with her beside me, I couldn't shake the image of Tessa behind the barn. Water dripping down her neck. Her breath brushing my mouth. Her eyes blown wide with something that wasn't anger anymore. My chest tightened.

Maddy leaned back, stretching her legs. "So what're we doing while I'm here? Riding? Fishing? Avoiding the world?"

"A little of everything"

She hummed approvingly. "Love that for us. Two weeks, I can't believe it."

Milkshakes in hand, I took the highway out of town. The mountains rose in the distance. The air smelled like rain on dust. Maddy cracked the window and let the wind tangle her hair.

After a minute, she spoke again, quieter this time. "Dad?"

"Yeah?"

"You sure everything's okay out on the ranch?"

I paused.

She wasn't oblivious. She'd grown up with a father whose attention sharpened whenever danger lingered around the edges. She recognized the signs. I didn't want to lie. But I also

wasn't going to drag her into the mess swirling around Tessa
Callahan.

"We've taken some hits lately," I said slowly. "But it's
nothing big."

"You'll fix it."

I glanced at her, surprised.

She shrugged. "You always do."

I didn't feel like I could fix anything right now.

Not the stock waterer, or the fence she refused help with. I
had no idea what the hell was stalking Tessa's property lines.
And definitely not the way I'd almost kissed her in the barn
like a man who didn't know better.

Maddy rested her head against the window, eyes half
closed.

"I'm glad I'm here," she murmured.

That one sentence worked its way under every bruise
inside me.

"Me too."

Twenty-Five
Tessa

I was mucking out the stalls when I heard hoof beats coming up the drive.

I set down the pitchfork and stepped out of the barn, shading my eyes against the mid-morning sun. A chestnut mare was cantering up the driveway, and the rider, a teenage girl with dark hair pulled back in a ponytail, was sitting her horse with easy confidence.

I didn't recognize her.

The girl pulled her horse to a walk as she approached, and I could see her taking in the property, the barn that still needed paint, the fence line I'd been working on all week, the house that looked exactly like it had when Ray was alive because I hadn't had the heart to change much yet.

"Hi," she called out, bringing her horse to a stop near the paddock fence. "You must be Tessa."

I straightened, immediately wary. "I am. And you are?"

"Maddy Hargrove." She dismounted with practiced ease. "My dad told me about you. That you're Ray's niece, and you came back to take care of the place."

My entire body went rigid.

"You're Wyatt's daughter," I said, and it came out flat, almost accusatory.

Maddy blinked, clearly surprised by my tone. "Yeah. I'm guessing you know my dad?"

Know him? I wanted to laugh. *Your dad has made my life hell since I got back. Your dad thinks he has some claim to this land. Your dad looks at me like I'm an intruder, even though I grew up here.*

"Yeah, I know him," I said carefully.

"Oh." Maddy shifted her weight, picking up on the tension even if she didn't understand it. "Dad told me Ray passed away. I'm really sorry."

The genuine sympathy in her voice made some of my defensiveness crack. "Thank you. Did you know him?"

"Yeah." A sad smile crossed Maddy's face. "I used to visit him every time I came to stay with my dad. Usually in the summer or on long weekends. Ray was really cool. He let me ride his horses and taught me how to fix the fence line. He told the worst jokes."

My throat tightened unexpectedly. Ray had told terrible jokes. I'd grown up hearing them until I left at eighteen.

"He did tell terrible jokes," I agreed quietly.

"The worst," Maddy said, and for a second we just looked at each other, two people who'd both lost Ray, even if in very different ways.

"Your horse is beautiful," I said finally, gesturing to the chestnut mare who was now trying to reach the grass on the other side of the fence.

"Thanks. Her name's Cinnamon." Maddy ran a hand down the mare's neck. "Ray helped my dad pick her out for me, actually. When I was seven. He said she had good lines."

"That was nice of him," I managed.

Maddy studied me with those sharp grey eyes that were so

much like her father's. "Dad said you hadn't been back in a long time. Since you were like eighteen or something?"

"Yeah," I said shortly. "I left and didn't come back until he passed away."

"That's a long time to be away." There was no judgment in her voice, just curiosity.

"It is." I wasn't about to explain to Wyatt Hargrove's daughter why I'd stayed away, why I'd let anger and pain keep me from the man who'd raised me.

Maddy glanced at her horse, then back at me. "Look, I'm sorry for just showing up. I was riding, and I always used to stop by to see Ray, and I guess I just, I don't know. I wanted to see the place again. And Dad mentioned you were here, so I thought I'd say hi."

Part of me wanted to send her away. She was Wyatt's daughter, and Wyatt Hargrove was trying to claim grazing rights to land that belonged to Ray, to me now, even if the will was still in probate. Every interaction with anyone connected to him felt like a potential complication.

But another part of me, the part that loved Ray even when I was too stubborn and hurt to come back, the part that was drowning in guilt over the years I wasted, couldn't turn away a kid who missed him too.

"Your horse looks hot," I said finally. "You want to put her in the paddock for a bit? Let her cool down? I have water."

Maddy's face lit up. "Really? That'd be great. We've been riding for like an hour."

We got Cinnamon settled in the paddock with fresh water, and the mare immediately started rolling in the dirt with pure joy.

"She always does that," Maddy said, smiling as she watched. "No matter how clean I get her, she finds dirt immediately."

"Sounds like every horse I've ever known," I said, and was surprised to find myself almost smiling.

We walked toward the house, and I was hyperaware of how strange this was, offering hospitality to the daughter of a man I couldn't stand, a man who made it clear he thought I had no right to be here after abandoning Ray for so long.

I poured two glasses of iced tea, and we sat at the kitchen table. "So," Maddy said after a moment of uncomfortable silence. "You and my dad aren't getting along."

I nearly choked on my tea. "That obvious?"

"Kind of." She picked at the edge of her glass. "He gets tense when he talks about you. And you looked like you swallowed something sour when I said I was his daughter."

"I don't have a problem with you," I said quickly. "Your dad and I just disagree about some things."

"For what it's worth, my dad's not usually a jerk. He's actually pretty decent most of the time. But he gets really stubborn about stuff he thinks is important. And he's been stressed about the ranch lately."

"I've noticed the stubborn part," I said dryly.

Maddy grinned. "Ray used to say the same thing. Said my dad was stubborn as a mule but twice as useful."

That sounded exactly like something Ray would say, and despite everything, I felt my mouth curve into a reluctant smile.

We talked for another fifteen minutes, carefully avoiding the subject of her father, instead talking about horses and school and what it was like to be the new kid in town. Maddy was smart and funny and disarmingly honest, and I found myself wishing the circumstances were different. That her father and I weren't at odds. That this could be simple.

"I really should go," Maddy said eventually, checking her phone. "Dad doesn't know I came over here. He's probably going to freak out when he finds out."

"You're going to have to tell him," I offered.

"I know." She stood, carrying her glass to the sink. "Besides, maybe it'll help. You know, if he knows I like you, maybe he won't be so stubborn."

We walked back out to the paddock together. Cinnamon was still rolling, now completely covered in dust, and Maddy laughed as she called her over.

"You're a disaster," she told the mare affectionately. "Dad's going to make me bathe you before I put you away."

She tacked up quickly, and I watched, impressed by how efficient she was. When she was ready to mount, she hesitated.

"Would it be okay if I came back sometime? Not to spy for my dad or anything. Just being here makes me feel like Ray's not completely gone."

Something in my chest cracked open. "Yeah. You can come back."

"Cool." Maddy swung into the saddle, gathering her reins.

I watched her canter down the driveway and stood there for a long moment after she disappeared, trying to process what just happened.

Wyatt Hargrove had a daughter. A daughter who'd known Ray, who'd spent time here while I was gone, who'd been part of my uncle's life during the years I'd stayed away.

And somehow, despite everything, I just invited her to come back.

I went back to mucking stalls, my mind churning.

This didn't change anything between Wyatt and me. The land dispute was still there. His attitude was still infuriating. The way he looked at me like I had no right to be here after abandoning Ray for years, that still made my blood boil, even if part of me wondered if he was right.

But his daughter was a good kid who missed Ray.

And that made everything just a little bit more complicated.

I was working on the fence line before work when I heard a truck coming up the drive. I straightened, shading my eyes, and felt my stomach drop.

Wyatt's truck.

He parked near the barn and got out, and even from a distance, I could read the tension in his body. He walked toward me with purpose, and I set down my tools, bracing myself for whatever confrontation was coming.

"Maddy came to see you," he said when he was close enough. Not a question. A statement.

"Yeah," I said, lifting my chin. "She did."

Wyatt's jaw worked. "She told me about it. Said you gave her iced tea and talked about Ray."

"Yep."

"She also said you invited her to come back."

"Also accurate," I said, crossing my arms. "You have a problem with that?"

Wyatt stared at me, and I couldn't read his expression. Anger? Concern? Something else?

"I don't know yet, "Maddy liked you," Wyatt said, and his voice had lost some of its edge. "She came home and wouldn't stop talking about how you were honest with her and didn't treat her like a kid. That means something."

"She seemed like a good kid," I said carefully. "You should be proud."

"I am." Wyatt looked at me, really looked at me, and for the first time since I'd met him, I didn't see hostility in his gaze. Just weariness. "Look, I don't know how to do this. The property thing is still an issue we need to resolve. But if Maddy wants to come see you, and you're okay with it, I'm not going to stop her."

"Okay," I said, not sure what else to say.

Wyatt nodded once, then turned and walked back to his truck.

I watched him go, my anger draining away and leaving confusion and a dull ache in its wake.

That had not gone the way I'd expected.

Not at all.

Twenty-Six
Wyatt

Cleary's was loud enough that I could almost hear myself think.

Almost.

The lunch rush had hit full swing. Cutlery clinked, plates slid along rails, somebody laughed too hard at the far end of the room. The air smelled like coffee, grilled onions, and hot oil, the holy trinity of small-town diners. It was all familiar, easy, the kind of background noise I usually sank into without a second thought.

Today, it just made everything inside me feel louder.

Because Tessa Callahan was walking three steps behind me, and my daughter just invited her to lunch. Two days, Maddy had been home for two days, and decided she and Tessa were best friends.

"Come on," Maddy said, practically vibrating at my side. "The back booth is the best one; it has the least crying babies."

I grunted something that might have been an agreement and tried to look like my chest was not as tight as barbed wire.

Tessa followed us in with that slightly wary set to her shoulders like she was braced for impact. She still looked like she would rather be anywhere else than under anyone's scrutiny. A couple of people at the counter glanced our way. The hostess clocked us with a quick smile and grabbed three menus.

"Booth?" she asked.

"Yeah," Maddy answered before I could. "Corner, please."

Of course, she wanted a corner. Fewer escape routes.

The hostess led us toward the back. I felt Tessa behind me, every footstep an echo down my spine. I couldn't stop replaying the hydrant, her soaked shirt, the way her breath hitched when my hand held her steady in the barn. The way we hovered inches from one very bad idea.

Any sane man would have put distance between them after that. I didn't bring her to a diner. Don't let his kid sit there and get to know her. Apparently, I was not a sane man.

The corner booth was taken, so we got the one next to it. A table fixed to the floor, red vinyl that squeaked when you shifted. Maddy slid into the far side without hesitation and pointed to the empty bench across from her.

"You two can sit together," she said, all innocent brightness. "There's more room on that side."

There wasn't any more room on that side. I opened my mouth to tell her to knock it off. Tessa hesitated on the outside of the booth, clutching the strap of her bag, clearly expecting to be told to sit opposite.

For some reason, that made my chest tighten.

"It's fine," I said, and stepped in. The vinyl sighed under my weight. When she slid in beside me, her thigh brushed mine. That single point of contact sent a spark up my leg and lit up places I had no business paying attention to.

I shifted a fraction to the right. She shifted a fraction to the left at the same time, as if we shared one nervous system, and our knees bumped under the table.

She sucked in a little breath.

"Sorry," I muttered.

"No, that was me," she said quickly. "I moved."

We both went still. Maddy watched us with far too much interest for a kid who claimed to be bored by adults.

The hostess dropped menus in front of us and left us in the care of a young waitress who looked about sixteen and already exhausted.

"Be right back for drinks," the girl said.

Maddy leaned forward, chin in her hands, eyes bright. "This is so fun."

I let my head fall back against the booth for a second. "Define fun."

"You, out of the house, in public, with a person who is not Holt or one of the other guys," she said.

Tessa snorted softly beside me. She seemed to catch herself immediately and pressed her lips together, eyes down on the menu. Her shoulder still touched mine. She did not move away.

The waitress returned for drink orders. Maddy asked for a chocolate milkshake. I asked for coffee because I needed something to hold onto. Tessa hesitated.

"Vanilla milkshake, please," she said finally.

Maddy lit up like she had won a prize. "Excellent choice. Their shakes are life-changing. Dad pretends he only drinks coffee, but he likes them too."

"Keep talking, kid, see what happens," I said.

She grinned.

Once the waitress disappeared again, Maddy slid her menu aside and zeroed in on Tessa with laser focus. "So, you're Ray's niece? I sure am sorry he's gone; he was one of my favorite people."

Tessa tucked a stray piece of hair behind her ear, not quite looking at either of us. "Yes, I am, thank you for your kind words. He was pretty special."

"But you're out there all alone,' she said softly.

"My friend Dani is here for now. But I don't mind being there alone. I was raised in that home, so it's comfortable."

"That's kind of cool."

Tessa blinked, like it was the last word she expected. "Most people haven't used that term."

"What do they say?" Maddy asked.

The corner of Tessa's mouth turned up in something that was not quite a smile. "Mostly that I'm in over my head."

I watched her face as she said it. The way her throat moved when she swallowed. The quick flash of pain that she covered with dry humour. My jaw clenched.

"People talk a lot," I said.

"They do," Tessa murmured. "Small towns."

I knew she was talking to Maddy, but I felt the edge in it like it was aimed at me, too. I had good intentions, she knew that, but intentions did not always land the way you wanted.

"What do you do out there?" Maddy asked. "Like what's your day look like?"

"Fix everything that broke overnight," Tessa said. "Feed whoever is hungry enough to complain. Argue with my truck. Fill out paperwork I don't understand. And somewhere in that time, I go work my shift at the vet clinic."

"The paperwork sounds terrible," Maddy said cheerfully. "But everything else is kind of badass."

"I don't know about badass," she said. "Mostly just tired."

"I can tell," Maddy said, not unkind at all. Just honest.

I had the sudden urge to reach over and take her hand. To tell her she was not carrying this alone, no matter how much she fought it. But I kept my hands firmly where they were.

The waitress came back with our drinks, and we all ordered without much thought. Burgers and fries, the lunch default. I realized I hadn't stopped watching Tessa for the last ten minutes.

The food arrived, mercifully, right then. Burgers stacked high, fries spilling over like golden confetti. The waitress slid the plates in front of us, smiled, told us to holler if we needed anything.

We murmured thanks and dug in. The noise level around us swelled again. Someone dropped something behind the counter, and a burst of laughter followed. For a brief moment, it felt almost normal. Just a father, his kid, and a woman he happened to know. Nothing complicated. Nothing dangerous.

Then Tessa reached for the ketchup at the exact same time I did.

Our hands collided. Not a brush this time. Full palm to back of hand, warm and solid.

Her fingers flinched, then stilled.

So did mine.

I looked up. Her eyes met mine.

You should let go, my brain said.

I didn't. For a breath we stayed exactly like that. Neither of us moved. The rest of the diner faded into a dull hum.

Her lips parted, just a fraction. Her tongue flicked out to wet them, fast, automatic. I felt my stomach drop. Something in my chest shifted then, like a fence post giving way. I pulled my hand back, slowly, and let her take the bottle.

"Sorry," she said, voice a little rough.

"It's fine," I managed.

Under the table, my leg brushed hers again as I shifted. This time, I did not move away. Neither did she.

The spark that jumped through me before settled into a low-burning coil that did not go out.

Maddy, of course, saw all of it.

"So," she said, voice casual, "are you guys dating?"

Tessa inhaled milkshake down the wrong pipe. I swore

under my breath and thumped her gently between the shoulders until she stopped coughing.

"Mads," I said, sharper than I meant.

"What?" she asked, genuinely puzzled. "I'm just asking."

"We're not, no," Tessa said quickly. Too quickly. "We're just neighbors."

I felt that like a slap that I had no right to feel.

Maddy considered this, then looked at me. "You like her, though, Dad, I can tell."

I pinched the bridge of my nose. "Can we not have this conversation in public?"

"Why? Do you like to suffer in private?"

"Madelyn." The full name came out. It rarely did. She grinned, knowing she hit a nerve, and mercifully dropped it. For now.

The thing was, she was not wrong.

Liking Tessa was not the problem. Wanting her was not the problem. The problem was the timing. The weight of everything pressing on her shoulders. The fact that someone was messing with her land, and she did not want to admit it. The fact that I was already too invested, and getting more so by the hour.

The problem was sitting shoulder to shoulder with her while my kid tried to tug us closer with every question.

At some point while we were talking, I realized Tessa's hand ended up on the bench between us. Mine was resting near my thigh. Another crowd shifted past the end of the booth, and the table bumped slightly. Her fingers slid sideways on the vinyl, brushing my knuckles.

This time, her hand did not jump away.

It settled there. Barely touching. Fingers curled in, the lightest contact.

I told myself it was nothing.

I told myself to leave it alone.

Then her little finger twitched, just the smallest shift, like a hesitant knock.

I exhaled slowly and turned my hand over, palm up.

If she wanted to move away, she could. There was all the space in the world.

Instead, after one long second, I felt her fingertips stroke my palm, like she was tracing a line. Then she slid her hand into mine.

I kept my eyes firmly on my plate. The world narrowed to the feeling of her hand, cool and damp from condensation, sliding against my skin. My fingers closed around hers on instinct.

She laced hers with mine under the table and squeezed once. A quick, desperate little press, like she needed an anchor and hated that it was me.

I could not remember the last time anyone had taken my hand and meant it.

Heat rolled up my arm, into my chest, settled somewhere stubborn.

We sat like that, side by side, shoulders touching, eating fries with our free hands and pretending we were not holding on to each other like a lifeline under the table. Maddy was telling some story about her science teacher and an exploding experiment from last year. I couldn't have repeated a word of it if someone held a gun to my head.

All I knew was the pressure of Tessa's fingers curled with mine. The way she stroked her thumb over the side of my hand once, absent-mindedly, like she had forgotten she was doing it. The way my own thumb answered, sliding over the back of her knuckles in a slow, soothing circle.

If she'd pulled away then, I would have let her. I would have said nothing. Instead, she held on a little tighter.

The waitress came back to check on us. I managed to act normally. Barely. Maddy asked for a refill on her milkshake.

The girl smiled at us in that soft way people do when they are looking at something they think they understand.

"How are you all doing?" she asked. "Need anything else? Extra napkins, ketchup? This is so cute, out as a family for lunch." The waitress didn't read the awkwardness that overtook the booth, before she sighed and looked at the three of us again, before turning to leave.

"She must be new in town," Maddy said, a frown on her face.

"Kathleen must be hiring her winter staff already," I answered. Living in a tourist destination meant there were people coming and going all the time. Summer saw campers and hikers. In the winter, skiers, so there was always a revolving door of seasonal employees.

When she walked away, Tessa withdrew her hand from mine, ever so slowly, like she really was conflicted about letting me go.

She stared down at what was left of her burger, shoulders curling in. A flush crept up her neck. The real world came crashing back in. The word family lingered in the wake of the waitress's joke.

"This was," she started, then stopped. Her voice came out thin.

"Maddy talks too much," I said, because humor was easier than whatever was threatening to rise.

"Hey," my daughter protested.

Tessa shook her head. "She does not, take that back." Both Maddy and Tessa glared at me. Great, they were already ganging up on me.

"I should go," she said quietly. "I need to check in at the office, it's my day off, but since I'm here, I'll make sure Brooke's not swamped."

Maddy's face fell. "Already? But we just got here."

"Thank you for lunch," she said. "Thanks for getting me

out of the house." Tessa's smile was soft, and her attention was focused solely on my daughter.

Maddy nodded, recovering fast, determined to end this on her own terms. "You are absolutely invited to do it again."

Tessa gave a strangled little laugh. "Thanks."

Then she turned to me. Her gaze caught mine just long enough for me to see the storm still churning behind her eyes.

"Wyatt," she said with a slight nod. Just my name, packed with a thousand things neither of us were ready to say.

"Tessa," I answered.

That was all.

She hitched her bag higher on her shoulder and walked away, weaving through the maze of tables, shoulders stiff, head bent. I watched her until the door swung shut behind her.

I kept watching the door long after it settled.

"You really like her," Maddy said quietly.

I did not even pretend to misunderstand. I dragged a hand over my face and leaned back against the booth, feeling ten years older and also like my heart was beating too fast to belong to a man my age.

"It's complicated."

"It always is with you," she replied, not unkindly.

I huffed out a humourless breath. "Yeah. Seems that way."

Twenty-Seven

Tessa

The sunlight was too bright. The air was too warm. My chest felt too tight, like someone hooked fingers behind my ribs and pulled. It wasn't until I was in my truck, door shut, windows up, that the sound of my heartbeat softened enough for me to breathe.

I sat there a moment, hands on the wheel, head tipped back.

I could still feel him beside me. His thigh brushing mine under the table. His hand, God, his hand holding mine, warm and steady, like I could lean without falling. And for the first time in weeks, something in me unclenched and remembered what being wanted felt like.

I turned the key. The engine rumbled to life, grounding me but it wasn't enough.

Driving away from town, the image of the booth kept replaying.

Wyatt's profile in the soft light.

Maddy's eyes bright with curiosity.

His hand under the table, palm up, waiting without pressuring, letting me choose.

I'd chosen.

I didn't know what that said about me, except that maybe I'd been lonelier than I'd admitted. Try as I might to shove the feeling away, it stuck to me like dust on a wet boot.

Halfway down the long stretch toward the ranch, the unraveling shifted. The softness curdled.

No.

I didn't have time for this.

I had a ranch on the edge of collapse, a stack of debt so high I couldn't see over it, and a past relationship I hadn't fully escaped. Wanting someone, wanting him, was the last thing I should let myself do.

By the time I hit the gravel of my lane, the softness hardened into something sharper. Anger mostly. At myself. At him. At Ray for leaving me this mess. At the world for handing me everything at once.

I was still stewing in it when I noticed the gate latch hanging open.

Not loose-from-wind open, or something the livestock opened. It was deliberate.

I parked and stepped out slowly, eyes scanning the yard.

Another detail hit next, the barn door cracked wide, too wide for the breeze drifting across the foothills. The ground carried prints, boot treads I didn't recognize, edges sharp and fresh.

The unease slid from my stomach up into my chest.

Someone had been here.

Recently.

I walked toward the barn, drawn forward and repelled at the same time. Sunlight hit the dust motes floating in the doorway, and for a second, it felt like the world had gone too still, like even the air was holding its breath.

"Ray," I whispered, barely audible. "What did you leave behind?"

No answer came.

My own fear echoed back at me from the dim inside of the barn.

I stood there for a long moment, arms wrapped around myself, the afternoon heat pressing against my back, the cool of the barn brushing my face.

Everything felt wrong.

Everything felt unsettled.

And despite every part of me insisting I didn't need him—

The first name that rose in my throat was Wyatt.

I shoved it down, walked to the house, locked the door and closed the blinds.

And that night, when the house was quiet, and the fear finally dissolved into loneliness, I did the one thing I'd promised myself I wouldn't do.

I imagined him.

The bedroom felt too big that night.

Too quiet.

Too hollow around the edges.

I lay on my back in the dark, the sheet warm against my legs, the window cracked open enough for the breeze to carry in the smell of cut grass and the distant sound of cattle shifting somewhere beyond the tree line.

But all I could think about was the booth.

His thigh against mine.

His breath brushing the side of my cheek when he leaned in to pass me the salt.

Those long, roughened fingers curling slowly around my hand under the table.

My body remembered the moment before my brain did. Heat pooled low in my stomach, a slow, traitorous ache. I rolled onto my side, pulled the blankets up, pressed my knees together like that could smother the feeling.

It didn't.

It only made it worse.

I should've stopped myself. I should've shoved these thoughts down the way I always did. But the harder I tried, the clearer it became, I wanted the way he looked at me. I wanted the steadiness in his voice, the warmth of him beside me.

Slowly, almost reluctantly, my hand slid down my stomach beneath the sheet.

A soft exhale escaped my lips.

I closed my eyes and let the memory take shape.

Wyatt's hand finding mine first—firm, warm, certain.

His thumb brushing the inside of my wrist like he was memorizing my pulse.

That low breath I'd felt more than heard when I didn't pull away.

My fingers slipped lower, parting myself gently, the first touch sending a tightening shiver through me. A small, surprised sound escaped me, softer than a whisper.

I imagined him sitting beside me on the edge of the bed, the mattress dipping under his weight. Not touching yet—just close enough that I could feel the heat of him along my back. Close enough that the room itself felt smaller with him in it.

My breath hitched. My fingers moved again, slow circles, the kind that made my thighs tense.

I exhaled his name before I could stop it, barely audible in the dark.

My hips lifted slightly, chasing the pressure. I bit my bottom lip, trying to stay quiet, but it was impossible when the fantasy sharpened.

Wyatt leaning down behind me.

His breath warm against my shoulder.

His voice low in my ear, the way I imagined it would be when he was losing control.

"Tessa."

Just hearing it in my own mind made everything inside me tighten.

My fingers moved faster, small strokes that built heat with every breath. The tension coiled deep, the slow kind that spread upward, through my chest, into my throat.

I imagined his hand covering mine, guiding me.

The weight of it, the steadiness. The way he'd kiss the back of my shoulder first, not rushing, just learning me. How he'd murmur something quiet, something that made my whole body soften.

Another small sound slipped out of me, muffled by the pillow.

My breathing grew unsteady. My thighs shook faintly. The pleasure built quicker now, sharp and trembling around the edges, curling tight like a pulled thread.

"Wyatt..." Barely a breath.

The tension snapped.

Heat rushed through me, wave after wave, quiet but overwhelming. My body arched, my hand stilling against the ache as I came undone, soft and shaking, breath shuddering out of me into the dark.

When it passed, I lay still for a long moment, my heart slowing, the night air cooling the flush on my skin.

Shame didn't come. Only the surprising, painful truth, I wanted him.

Twenty-Eight
Wyatt

I knew I crossed a line the second I pulled into her driveway with the feed bags in the back of my truck. I knew it, and I did it anyway.

Tessa's barn door was open when I parked, and I could see her inside mucking stalls with the kind of aggressive focus that meant she was pissed off about something. The late afternoon sun cut through the doorway and caught the sweat on her neck, and I forced myself to look away before I started thinking about things I had no business thinking about.

I grabbed two feed bags and headed toward the barn before I could talk myself out of it.

She looked up when my shadow fell across the threshold, and the expression on her face went from surprised to wary in half a second.

"What are you doing here?" she asked, and there was no welcome in her voice.

"Brought you feed," I said, hefting the bags slightly. "John mentioned you were running low when I saw him at the co-op."

Tessa set down the pitchfork and wiped her hands on her jeans. "I didn't ask you to do that."

"I know."

"So why did you?"

Because I can't seem to stop myself from trying to take care of you, even when I know you don't want me to. Because watching you struggle with things I could easily fix makes my chest tight in ways I don't want to examine. Because every time I see you, I want to be closer to you, and bringing you feed was the only excuse I could think of that didn't involve admitting any of that.

"Because you needed it," I said instead.

Her jaw tightened. "I was going to pick it up tomorrow."

"Now you don't have to."

"Wyatt."

"Just let me help," I said, already walking past her toward the feed storage.

"I didn't ask for your help," she called after me.

I set the bags down harder than necessary. "You never ask. That's the problem."

When I turned around, she was standing right behind me, close enough that I could smell the hay and horse and something underneath that was just her. Her eyes were flashing with anger, and colour had risen in her cheeks.

"The problem," she said, her voice low and tight, "is that you keep deciding what I need without asking me first."

"Someone has to," I shot back. "You're running yourself into the ground trying to prove you can do everything alone."

"That's my choice to make," she shouted at me.

"It's a stupid choice."

The words came out sharper than I'd intended, and I saw her flinch before her expression went hard.

"Yeah no, we're not doing this. Get out."

"Tessa."

"I mean it. Take your feed and your unwanted opinions and get the hell off my property."

Something hot flared in my chest. "Our property dispute doesn't mean I can't help you when you need it."

"I don't need it," she said, but her voice shook just slightly. "I don't need you swooping in like some kind of saviour every time you decide I can't handle something."

"I never said you couldn't handle it."

"Then why are you here? Why do you keep showing up with feed and advice and that look on your face like you're waiting for me to fall apart so you can catch me?"

Because I want to catch you. Because the thought of you falling and me not being there makes me feel like my chest is being crushed. Because I'm so far past professional boundaries with you that I can't even see the line anymore.

"Because I give a damn," I said roughly. "Is that so terrible?"

"Yes." The word burst out of her like it had been building. "Yes, it's terrible, because I can't." She stopped herself, breathing hard.

"Can't what?" I took a step closer without meaning to.

"I can't let myself need you," she said, and her voice had dropped to something raw. "I can't let myself depend on anyone right now. Don't you understand that?"

"I'm not asking you to depend on me."

"Yes, you are. Every time you show up here, every time you fix something I didn't ask you to fix, you're asking me to need you. And I can't. I won't."

We were standing close now, close enough that I could see the pulse jumping in her throat, close enough that her anger felt like heat against my skin.

"Why not?" I asked, and my voice came out lower than I'd intended.

"Because the last time I let myself need someone, they used

it against me." Her eyes were bright with fury and something that looked dangerously close to tears. "Because I just got out of a relationship where every kindness came with strings attached. Because I'm trying to rebuild my life on my own terms, and you keep, you keep..."

She broke off, her hands clenching into fists at her sides.

"I keep what?" I asked.

"You keep making me want things I can't afford to want right now."

The confession hung between us, raw and honest, and I felt something in my chest crack open.

"Tessa," I said, and I didn't know what I was going to say next because she was looking at me like that, and I could barely think straight.

"No," she said quickly. "Don't." But she hadn't moved away, and neither had I, and the air between us felt charged with everything we weren't saying.

"I'm trying to respect your boundaries," I said roughly. "But you make it damn hard when you look at me like that."

"Like what?"

"Like you want me to cross them."

Her breath hitched, and I saw her pupils dilate slightly. "I don't."

"Yes, you do." I took another half-step closer, and my voice dropped even lower. "You want me to stop being careful. You want me to stop asking permission. But I won't. Not unless you tell me to."

"Wyatt," she whispered.

"Tell me I'm wrong," I challenged. "Tell me you don't feel this thing between us, and I'll walk out of here right now and never bring you feed again."

She stared at me, her chest rising and falling too fast, and I watched her struggle with what to say.

"I can't," she finally whispered.

"Can't tell me I'm wrong, or can't deal with me being right?"

"Both." The word came out broken. "I hate that you're right. I hate that I want..." She stopped herself again.

"What do you want?" I asked, and I couldn't keep the rough edge out of my voice.

"Things I shouldn't." Her hands were shaking now. "Things that complicate everything."

"Maybe complicated isn't always bad."

"It is when I'm still trying to figure out who I am without someone else defining me." She took a shaky breath. "I need to be able to stand on my own before I can, before anything else."

"I'm not trying to define you. I'm just trying to be here."

"But don't you see? That's the problem. You being here, you helping me, you looking at me the way you're looking at me right now, it makes me want to lean on you. And I can't. Not yet. Maybe not ever."

The "not ever" landed like a punch to the gut, but I forced myself to stay still.

"So what do you want me to do? Stay away?"

"I don't know." She pressed her palms to her eyes. "I don't know what I want except for everything to stop being so goddamn complicated."

I reached out without thinking and caught her wrist gently, pulling her hand away from her face. Her skin was warm under my palm, and I felt her pulse racing.

"Look at me," I said quietly.

She did, and the vulnerability in her eyes made my chest ache.

"I'll back off. I'll stop bringing you things you didn't ask for. I'll stop overstepping. But I can't stop caring about whether you're okay. I can't turn that off."

"I'm not asking you to turn it off," she said, her voice

barely above a whisper. "I'm asking you to give me space to figure this out on my own terms."

"Okay." I squeezed her wrist once, then made myself let go. "Okay."

But neither of us moved.

We stood there in the barn with dust motes floating in the air between us and the smell of hay and horses all around, and I could feel every inch of space that separated us like it was a physical thing.

"I should go," I said, but my voice lacked conviction.

"Yeah," she agreed, but she didn't step back.

"Tessa."

"Don't," she said again, but this time it came out softer. "Don't say whatever you're about to say, because I don't think I can handle it right now."

"I was just going to say I'm sorry." My thumb brushed the inside of her wrist before I could stop myself. "For overstepping. For pushing. For making this harder than it already is."

"You're not." She swallowed hard. "It's not just you. I'm the one who can't seem to..."

She didn't finish, but I understood what she meant. She couldn't seem to keep me at a distance, no matter how much she wanted to. I could see it in the way her body angled toward mine, in the way her breathing had gone shallow, in the way she was looking at my mouth like she was thinking about things that would definitely complicate everything.

"This is a bad idea," she whispered.

"Probably," I agreed.

"We're in the middle of a property dispute."

"We are."

"And I'm not ready for anything."

"I know."

"So why are we still standing here?"

That was a damn good question, and I didn't have a good

answer except that walking away from her felt physically impossible.

"Because sometimes bad ideas feel like the only ones worth having," I said roughly.

She laughed, but it came out shaky. "That's a terrible justification."

"It's the only one I've got."

Her hand came up and rested against my chest, right over my heart, and I wondered if she could feel how hard it was beating.

"We can't," she said, but her fingers curled slightly into my shirt.

"I know."

"I mean it, Wyatt. We can't do this."

"I heard you the first time."

But I still didn't move, and neither did she, and the space between crackled with tension that had nowhere to go.

"Tell me to leave," I said, my voice coming out rougher than I'd intended.

"I already did."

"Tell me again."

She stared at me, her lips parted slightly, and I watched her struggle with what to say. Her hand was still fisted in my shirt, holding me there even while her words pushed me away.

I closed the distance between us and cupped her face in my hands, giving her exactly one second to pull away, to tell me to stop, to do anything except look at me like that.

She didn't move.

So I kissed her.

And the world narrowed down to just the two of us, the taste of her and the sound she made low in her throat when I deepened the kiss.

She kissed me back immediately, hungrily, like she'd been starving for this and had finally given herself permission to take it. Her other hand came up and fisted in my shirt, pulling me closer, and I backed her up against the barn wall without breaking contact.

The wood was rough against her back, but she didn't seem to care. She just opened wider and kissed me harder, and I groaned against her lips because this was everything I'd been trying not to think about for weeks.

Her taste. Her heat. The way she fit against me like she was made for it.

I slid one hand into her hair and angled her head back, taking the kiss deeper, and she made a sound that went straight through me. Her leg came up and hooked around my hip, pulling me flush against her, and I had to brace one hand on the wall beside her head to keep from losing all control.

"Wyatt," she gasped against my mouth, and the way she said my name, breathless and desperate and wanting—nearly undid me.

"Tell me to stop," I said roughly, trailing my mouth down her jaw to her throat. "Tell me this is a bad idea."

"It is a bad idea," she panted, but her hands were sliding under my jacket, her fingers hot against my skin through my shirt.

"Then tell me to stop," I repeated, my teeth grazing the sensitive spot where her neck met her shoulder.

"I can't." The admission came out broken. "God, Wyatt, I can't."

I kissed her again, harder this time, pouring weeks of wanting and restraint into it. She met me with equal intensity, her nails digging into my back through my shirt, her body arching into mine.

This was reckless. This was stupid. This was going to complicate everything.

And I didn't care.

Not when she was kissing me like this. Not when her

hands were in my hair, and her leg was wrapped around me, and every soft sound she made went straight to my core.

I broke away from her mouth and kissed down her throat, and she tipped her head back against the wall, breathing hard.

"We should stop," she whispered, but her hands tightened in my hair.

"We should," I agreed, kissing the hollow of her throat.

"This doesn't change anything."

"It changes everything." I lifted my head to look at her, and her eyes were dark and dilated and full of want. "You know it does."

"I don't, I can't." She pulled me down into another kiss instead of finishing, and this time it was even more desperate, even more consuming.

I lost myself in it. In her. In the way she tasted and felt, and the small sounds she made when I kissed just below her ear.

My hand slid down her side to her hip, my thumb brushing the strip of skin where her shirt had ridden up, and she gasped against my mouth.

"Wyatt," she breathed again, and I was starting to think I could live off the sound of my name on her lips.

"I know," I said roughly. "I know we shouldn't. I know it's complicated." She pulled me into another kiss, effectively shutting me up, and I stopped trying to be reasonable.

Her hands were under my shirt now, her palms flat against my stomach, and the feel of her touching me like that made my head spin. I kissed her deeper, harder, until we were both breathing like we'd been running.

When we finally broke apart, both of us gasping for air, I rested my forehead against hers.

"Jesus," I muttered.

"Yeah," she agreed shakily.

We stayed like that for a long moment, just breathing each

other's air, her leg still hooked around my hip, my hand still on her waist.

"That was," she started.

"A mistake," I finished for her, even though it hadn't felt like one.

"The worst idea," she agreed, but her hands were still under my shirt, her thumbs tracing patterns on my skin that were driving me insane.

"We can't do this again," I said.

"Definitely not," she whispered.

But neither of us moved.

I kissed her again, softer this time but no less intense, and she melted into me with a sigh that I felt all the way down to my bones.

This was dangerous. This was exactly what we'd both been trying to avoid.

And I'd do it again in a heartbeat.

The sound of gravel crunching in the driveway shattered the moment like a shard of glass.

We both froze, her hands stilling on my ribs, my lips still hovering just above hers.

Headlights swept across the barn entrance.

"Expecting someone?" I asked, but I already knew from the way her entire body had gone rigid that she wasn't.

"No," she whispered, and I heard real fear creep into her voice.

The car pulled into the yard too confidently, too deliberately, and even before the engine cut, I knew this wasn't going to be good.

Twenty-Nine

Tessa

I was standing too close to Wyatt when I heard the gravel shift in the drive, and I couldn't ignore how the heat of him pressed against me or how the tension from our kiss hadn't burned off yet.

A car rolled into the yard without hesitation and stopped near the barn. The engine hadn't cut like whoever was driving already decided they weren't leaving.

My stomach dropped hard with recognition, and I hadn't needed to see his face to know who it was.

"Tess," Colin called, and his voice hit me like cold water I hadn't braced for.

Every nerve in my body went tight at once, and fear and anger and something far worse tangled together in my chest until I couldn't separate them.

I stayed still and silent, not trusting what would come out if I spoke.

Wyatt moved first, only one step, a smooth, controlled step, but still enough to put himself directly between me and the open space of the yard without making it obvious.

My hand lifted without permission and caught the front

of Wyatt's jacket because I needed the solidness of him to stay upright, even if I wouldn't admit that out loud.

The second I realized what I was doing, I dropped my hand like it burned.

Colin saw it anyway, and I knew it by the way his eyes tracked the movement and by the way something cold and sharp slid into place behind the smile he wore as he walked closer.

He dressed cleanly, and he moved easily, and he still looked like a man who thought he had the right to show up wherever he wanted.

"Well," he said lightly, "this answers a few questions," and I didn't miss the satisfaction curled under his tone.

Wyatt's attention stayed locked on Colin like nothing else in the world existed at that moment.

"You should leave," Wyatt said, and his voice calm in a way that made my skin prickle with warning.

Colin laughed quietly, and I heard the disbelief layered under it.

"That's not your call," Colin said, and I hated how familiar his challenge sounded.

"It is right now," Wyatt replied, and not even a flicker of doubt in him.

I found my voice through the tightness in my throat because I couldn't stand being silent anymore.

"Colin, you need to go." My voice shook, and I hated that it did.

He didn't look at me at first because he'd been too busy studying Wyatt. Like he was measuring a threat.

Then he slid his gaze to me, slow and deliberate, and took in my posture. My nearness to Wyatt and the way our bodies didn't quite separate.

"You look occupied," he said, and I'd heard the nasty edge curling under the words.

"Busy even," he added, and my face heated despite myself.

Wyatt hadn't moved, but I felt the tension in him shift and tighten like a cable taught before snapping.

"I came to check on you," Colin continued, "you didn't answer your phone, which isn't like you."

"That's because I didn't want to talk to you," I said, and my honesty raw and unfiltered.

His mouth curved faintly as if he found that amusing.

"You usually don't cut me off completely unless something's distracting you," he said, and his eyes flicked straight to Wyatt again.

"Or someone," he added.

Wyatt's voice dropped lower, and the warning in it wasn't subtle anymore. "She told you to leave."

"I'm talking to her," Colin snapped, and irritation bled through the calm he was trying to hold.

"Not you," he added, like that settled something.

Then his gaze sharpened on my face as he lined up his next strike.

"So it's true," he said, and his voice turned too sharp to ignore. "You really did sleep with him." The words tore the air right out of my lungs.

My breath hitched despite trying to stop it, and silence stretched tight between the three of us until it'd felt like it might snap.

Wyatt shifted, not forward and not back, but just enough that his presence felt heavier and more deliberate as though he claimed space without claiming me.

"That's none of your business," Wyatt said immediately, and the force behind the words was undeniable.

Colin's smile turned brittle as his eyes flicked between us.

"It became my business the second I saw you two together in that fucking barn," he said, and the venom behind the confession made my stomach drop. "I didn't imagine that hand on his chest, and I didn't imagine the way you were looking at him like you'd already chosen. " My skin flushed hot with exposure.

"You don't own me," I snapped. My voice was louder than expected.

"I never said I did," Colin replied smoothly, "but you don't disappear unless you're tangled up in something you know you shouldn't be."

Wyatt's jaw flexed hard enough that I saw the muscle jump, and the air between them felt charged and dangerous in a way that scared me.

"She told you to go," Wyatt said again, his tone colder than I'd ever heard it.

"I'm speaking to her," Colin replied, and I hated how he pretended he had a right to my answers.

"And I think she has clearly told you she doesn't want to listen," Wyatt told him, and the warning wasn't subtle anymore.

Colin smiled again, and this time it was almost indulgent.

"I'll forgive you," he said to me, "I've had slip-ups." The casual cruelty and the way he shrugged made it even uglier.

"People make mistakes when they're grieving," he said, and the way he framed my body and my choice as weakness made my hands shake.

"You don't get to forgive me for anything." My voice was raw and shaking with fury.

Wyatt moved then in a way that told his restraint shattered.

He took a full step into Colin's space, and his hands came up and fisted into the front of Colin's shirt.

The sound Colin made when Wyatt yanked him forward was sharp and startled, and it sliced through the yard like the crack of a whip.

My heart slammed against my ribs because I'd never seen

Wyatt like that, never known what he was capable of once he stopped holding himself back.

"You don't get to talk about her like that," Wyatt said, his voice low and shaking with contained violence.

"You'll leave now," Wyatt said, and there hadn't been a single ounce of bluff in him this time.

I stepped forward without thinking, and my hand closed around Wyatt's forearm like I could ground him back into control.

"Wyatt, please don't," I whispered, and my voice cracked because I meant it in every way possible.

He hesitated just long enough for me to feel the trembling power under my palm.

Then he shoved Colin back hard enough that he stumbled two full steps before catching himself.

Colin stared at him in shock, and the truth finally landed in his eyes that this wasn't a game he controlled anymore.

"Enjoy it," Colin said to me again, voice been thinner this time. "While it lasts." The threat was brittle instead of confident.

Then he turned and climbed into his car and tore back down the drive in a spray of gravel and fury that echoed long after the engine faded.

The yard fell silent again, and I realized I was shaking so hard I could barely stay upright.

Wyatt didn't turn to me right away, and his shoulders were rising and falling too fast like he was still burning off the violence he barely kept in check.

The heat between us twisted into something darker and sharper now, and my body reacted even while fear crawled under my skin.

"You scared me," I said, and my voice was barely more than a breath.

"I'd do worse to keep him away from you," Wyatt said, and the honesty in it scared me even more.

"You can't," I whispered, my hand still on his arm like I was afraid to let go.

He looked at me, and the intensity in his eyes made my breath hitch all over again.

My pulse stuttered because he'd been right.

The space between our bodies was charged with everything we weren't saying and everything we'd already done.

For one dangerous second, I thought he might kiss me again, and I knew with terrifying clarity that I wouldn't stop him.

Thirty

Tessa

Wyatt hadn't touched me in the night. Not when I hovered too close. Not when the tension crackled so tight it made my teeth ache. Not even when I finally rolled away and pretended I didn't care.

Outside, the ranch was already awake. I could hear a truck door slam. Boots on gravel. The wind ticked the loose clapboard on the porch. Life carried on like it always did. Like nothing in my life tilted on its axis the night before.

Colin had been here.

Wyatt had stayed.

And still, he left space between us that might as well have been a canyon.

I pushed out of bed and dressed quickly. Jeans, a faded long-sleeve, and my boots. I did not give myself time to think about how humiliating it felt to want someone who decided restraint was more powerful than hunger.

When I stepped into the kitchen, Wyatt was already there. Coffee poured. Jaw tight. Shoulders rigid. Every inch of him locked back into control like nothing happened at all.

"I'm taking you to my house until we figure out what that fucker wants."

My spine stiffened. "I'm not running from home."

"You will for a couple days."

"I'm not a child, Wyatt."

"No," he said flatly. "You're a woman an unstable man thinks he owns." His gaze lifted, sharp now. Protective steel running right beside the cold. "You don't stay alone out here until I'm sure he's done circling."

"Circling. Like I'm livestock."

"You're not livestock. You're a target."

The truth of it sat ugly and undeniable between us.

I hated that he was right.

"Pack a bag, Maddy's already waiting to show you around." The sting eased just a fraction at that. Maddy. Some part of the tight knot in my chest loosened at the thought of her.

"I don't need a babysitter."

"I know. You're getting one anyway."

I almost laughed at the phrasing. At the irony of Wyatt Hargrove volunteering himself as my guard while actively pretending we had not almost torn each other apart the night before.

I went back to the bedroom and threw clothes into a bag with more force than necessary.

When I came back out, he took it from me without comment. Our fingers brushed. The contact sparked hard and immediately. He did not pull away, but the control was still there. Tight. Unrelenting.

The drive to his place was silent.

His truck ate up the gravel road with steady confidence. The land rolled wide and green around us, barley fields stretching toward the foothills in the distance. His land. My land. The invisible battle line ran right through the windshield.

His house sat on a low rise overlooking the brewery buildings and the long sweep of fields beyond. It was solid and plain and utterly Wyatt. Stone. Wood. Big windows that let the light in, whether you wanted it or not.

Maddy was on the front step when we pulled up, boots on, backpack at her feet, earbuds hanging around her neck. She spotted the truck and her face lit up in a grin that went straight through my chest.

"Dad."

She ran down the steps and launched herself at him. He caught her easily, arms wrapping tight, his entire posture changing in an instant. The edge drained out of him when he held her. This was the man beneath the armour.

I stood awkwardly to the side, suddenly aware of how strange my presence must look.

Maddy's gaze flicked to me. Her eyes sharpened with recognition. "I can't believe you're here. I've got so much for us to do. Yeah, I know you have to work, but there's still lots of days when you're not at work. And we can gang up on Dad." Maddy talked a mile a minute, and I wasn't sure I caught everything.

Wyatt muttered something under his breath as he took my bag inside.

The ease of her presence melted something in me. The fear retreated a step. I followed them in, feeling for the first time since last night that I could breathe without flinching.

The house smelled like coffee and clean wood and something faintly citrus. Maddy immediately launched into a story about a horse at the barn where she rides in Calgary.

The day flew by, and I settled in as well as I could. Clouds built over the horizon, and the wind picked up. The air smelled like turned earth, and it was a sure sign a storm was coming.

The first crack of thunder rumbled across the prairie when I was halfway to the barn, and I picked up my pace, my boots splashing through puddles that hadn't been there ten minutes ago.

The horses would be fine. They weathered storms worse than this. But something in me needed to check anyway, needed to make sure the barn doors were secure, and the stalls were dry, and everyone was settled.

I pulled open the barn door and stepped inside, shaking water from my hair.

"Jesus," I muttered, looking down at my soaked shirt.

"You too, huh?"

I jumped, my hand flying to my chest as I spun around.

Wyatt stood near the tack room, looking just as wet as I felt. His shirt clung to his shoulders, his hair was plastered to his forehead, and he was holding a hammer like he'd been in the middle of something when the rain hit.

"What are you doing here?" I asked.

"Making sure everything's locked down tight before the real storm hits." He gestured toward the loft. "Had to secure that loose panel up there. Didn't want it ripping off in the wind."

"I was just coming to check on the horses."

"They're good. Fed and settled." He set down the hammer. "Are you planning on running back to the house?"

As if on cue, the sky opened up completely. Rain hammered against the barn roof like machine-gun fire, and through the open door I could see sheets of water coming down so thick I could barely make out the house.

"Guess not," I said.

Wyatt walked over and pulled the barn door shut, latching it against the wind. The sudden dimness made the space feel smaller, more intimate. The only light came from the single bulb hanging near the tack room and the occasional flash of lightning through the windows.

"Could be a while," Wyatt said, leaning back against the door. "The weather report said this system's moving slowly."

"Great." I wrapped my arms around myself. My wet shirt was starting to make me cold.

Wyatt's eyes tracked the movement, then quickly looked away. "There's a blanket in the tack room if you want it."

"I'm fine."

"You're shivering."

"I said I'm fine."

He held up his hands in surrender. "Okay."

We stood there in awkward silence, the rain pounding overhead, and I became acutely aware that we were alone. Just us and a storm that showed no signs of stopping.

"So," Wyatt said eventually. "What do you want to do while we wait this out?"

I looked around the barn. "Not a lot of options."

"We could talk."

"About what?"

"I don't know." He shoved his hands in his pockets. "The weather?"

I snorted. "Thrilling."

"You got a better idea?"

I didn't. At least not one I was willing to voice out loud. Because the ideas I was having involved significantly less talking and significantly more of what we'd done the last time we were alone together.

That kiss had been a mistake. A spectacular, toe-curling, can't-stop-thinking-about-it mistake that I replayed in my head every night since.

Wyatt was watching me with an expression I couldn't

quite read, and I had the uncomfortable feeling he knew exactly where my thoughts had gone.

"Cards," he said abruptly.

I blinked. "What?"

"There's a deck of cards in the tack room. The guys keep them for when they're stuck out here for foaling or a sick horse." He was already moving toward the small room. "We could play cards."

"Sure," I said slowly.

I found the cards on the shelf, next to a bottle of whiskey that was probably older than I was. I grabbed both.

"What game?"

The corner of his mouth quirked up. "Strip poker."

I froze, the bottle halfway to the overturned crate I'd been planning to use as a table. "What?"

"You heard me." He was leaning against the doorframe now, arms crossed, looking far too smug. "Strip poker. Makes it more interesting."

"That's ridiculous," I stopped, because calling it a bad idea would be stating the obvious. "We're not teenagers."

"No. We're two adults stuck in a barn during a storm with nothing else to do. And I'm bored."

"You want to play strip poker because you're bored."

"I want to play strip poker because watching you try to keep a poker face while you're thinking about our kiss will be the most entertainment I've had all week."

I stared at him, my heart hammering. This was a terrible idea. This was reckless and stupid and exactly the kind of thing that would complicate everything we'd been trying to keep simple.

"Fine," I heard myself say.

Wyatt's eyebrows rose. "Yeah?"

"Yeah." I set the bottle down with more force than necessary. "But we're drinking too. If I'm doing this, I'm doing it with whiskey."

His grin was slow and devastating. "Deal."

"Are you ready to lay them down?" Wyatt asked, that damn smirk on his face had me shifting in my seat. But I wasn't going to let him know that he had any effect on me.

I glanced at my cards. At least I had enough clothes on if he was going to beat me this round.

I set my hand face up on the table. "Pair of tens."

He let out a low whistle through his teeth. "And to think, your poker face made me think you had me for a minute there.

He set his hand down, a pair of Jacks.

"What are you taking off first?" he asked, leaning back as he picked up our cards, shuffling them between his hands.

"You're lucky my feet have been killing me all day," I grumbled, kicking off my boots.

He didn't say anything as he dealt out the cards.

Another weak deal, and there was no way I could bluff.

Especially after losing another three hands and taking off my jacket, socks, and hat.

"I think you're cheating," I grumbled, picking up the latest cards he dealt.

"I'd never cheat. Besides, if I wanted you naked, I don't think it would take a game of cards to do it."

I scoffed, waiting for his smirk or a laugh, but his eyes were heated as he looked at me across the table.

"Why are you so eager to get me naked when we hate each other?"

He let out a small breath through his nose as he shook his head. "There's a thin line between love and hate, baby."

Twenty minutes later, I was down to my jeans, bra, and one sock, and I was definitely feeling the whiskey.

Wyatt had lost his shirt and boots, and I was trying very

hard not to stare at his bare chest while he studied his cards with infuriating calm.

"You're bluffing," I said.

"Am I?"

"You do that thing with your jaw when you're bluffing," I said as I watched him.

"What thing?"

"That thing." I gestured vaguely at his face. "The muscle twitches."

He grinned. "Show me yours, and I'll show you mine."

I laid down my cards. Two pair.

Wyatt's grin widened as he revealed a straight.

"Damn it," I muttered, and pulled off my remaining sock.

"That's it?" he asked. "Just the sock?"

I glared at him. "What did you expect?"

"I don't know." His eyes traveled over me slowly, deliberately. "Maybe something more interesting."

"You want interesting? Win another hand."

"Oh, I intend to."

The next hand I won, and Wyatt stood up to undo his belt with maddening slowness, his eyes never leaving mine.

"Enjoying yourself?" he asked.

"Immensely," I lied, trying to ignore how dry my mouth had gone.

He pushed his jeans down and kicked them aside, standing there in just his boxer briefs, and I couldn't look away even though I knew I should.

He was all lean muscle and tan skin and that trail of dark hair that disappeared below his waistband. Every rational thought I ever had evaporated.

"Your deal," he said, and his voice had dropped lower.

I dealt with shaking hands.

I lost the next hand.

"Jeans," Wyatt said, and it wasn't a question.

I stood up, my pulse racing, and unbuttoned my jeans with far less grace than he had. I could feel his eyes on me the entire time, hot and intense, as I pushed the denim down my hips and stepped out of them.

When I looked up, the expression on his face made my stomach flip.

"Tessa," he said, and my name sounded rough in his mouth.

"What?"

"Come here."

It wasn't a command, exactly. More like a request. A plea.

I should've said no. Should've picked up my cards and kept playing. Should've kept the distance between us.

Instead, I walked over to where he sat on the hay bale, and he reached up and pulled me down onto his lap.

"We're not playing anymore," I said, but it came out breathless.

"No," he agreed. "We're not."

He kissed me then, deep and slow and thorough. I melted into him with a sigh. His hands slid up my sides, his thumbs brushing the underside of my breasts through my bra, and I gasped against his mouth.

"Tell me to stop," he murmured against my lips.

"No."

"Tessa," he demanded.

"I don't want you to stop." I pulled back just enough to look at him. "I want you. I've wanted you since that kiss in the barn. Maybe before that. I don't know anymore."

Something fierce flared in his eyes. "You sure?"

"I'm sure." I kissed him again, harder this time. "I'm so sure."

He groaned and stood up, taking me with him, my legs wrapping around his waist automatically. He carried me over to the pile of saddle blankets in the corner and laid me down carefully, following me down to cover my body with his.

"I've thought about this," he said roughly, his mouth trailing down my throat. "Too much. Too often."

"Me too," I admitted, arching into him as his hand slid up my ribs.

He unhooked my bra with practiced ease and tossed it aside. Then his mouth was on my breast, and I stopped thinking entirely.

My hands found his shoulders, his back, sliding down to push at his boxers because I needed less fabric between us, needed more skin and heat and him.

He helped me get them off, then worked my underwear down my hips until we were both finally, completely naked.

For a moment, we just looked at each other, breathing hard, the storm raging outside but forgotten.

"You're so damn beautiful," Wyatt said, his hand cupping my face.

"Stop talking," I whispered, pulling him down. "Just kiss me."

He did, and it was nothing like the careful kiss in the barn before. This was raw and desperate and consuming, all teeth and tongue and the kind of hunger that had been building between us for weeks.

His hand slid between my legs, and I gasped at the contact.

"God, Tessa," he groaned. "You're so wet."

"That's your fault," I managed, my hips rocking into his touch.

He worked me with his fingers, slow and deliberate, watching my face as I came apart. When I was close, trembling on the edge, he pulled his hand away.

I made a sound of protest, but he just kissed me and shifted his weight.

"Condom," he muttered against my mouth. "Please tell me you have one."

"Jeans pocket," I gasped. "Left side."

He grabbed my jeans and fumbled through the pocket, pulling out the condom I'd been carrying since that first kiss, just in case.

"Optimistic," he said with a grin.

"Prepared," I corrected.

He rolled it on then settled between my thighs, the blunt head of him pressing against me.

"Look at me," he said.

I did, and the intensity in his eyes made my breath catch.

"Tell me if I need to stop."

"You won't."

He pushed inside slowly, inch by inch, and I had to close my eyes against the overwhelming sensation of fullness, of rightness, of finally.

"Jesus," he groaned when he was fully seated. "You feel—"

"I know," I breathed. "I know."

He started to move, slow and deep. I wrapped my legs around his waist to pull him deeper.

The storm raged overhead, rain hammered on the roof, thunder rolled across the sky, but all I could focus on was the slide of his body against mine, the sounds he made low in his throat, the way my name sounded when he gasped it.

"Harder," I demanded, my nails digging into his back.

He obliged, his hips snapped against mine with more force, and the pleasure built sharp and fast until I was gasping with every thrust.

"Touch yourself," he said roughly. "I want to feel you come around me."

I slid my hand between us, finding where we were joined, and circled my clit with shaking fingers.

"That's it," Wyatt encouraged, his voice strained. "God, you're so fucking perfect."

The orgasm hit me hard and suddenly, my inner muscles clamping down on him as I cried out. Wyatt groaned and thrust twice more before following me over, my name on his lips as he came.

We stayed like that for a long moment, both of us shaking and gasping for breath, the sweat cooling on our skin.

Finally, Wyatt rolled to the side, pulling me with him so I was tucked against his chest. He grabbed one of the saddle blankets and pulled it over us.

"That was," I started.

"Yeah," he agreed.

"We shouldn't have."

"Probably not."

"This doesn't," I stumbled over my words.

"I know." He kissed the top of my head. "It doesn't change anything. Doesn't solve anything. Doesn't make anything less complicated."

"Right."

But his hand was tracing patterns on my spine, and I was pressed against him like I belonged there, and the storm outside showed no signs of stopping.

"Tessa."

"Hmm?"

"I'm not sorry."

I tilted my head back to look at him. "No?"

"No." His eyes were serious. "I know I should be. But I'm not."

"Me neither."

He smiled then, soft and genuine, and kissed me again.

Outside, thunder rolled, and rain poured down, and somewhere in the back of my mind, I knew this was going to complicate everything.

But right now, wrapped in Wyatt's arms with the taste of him still on my lips, I couldn't bring myself to care.

THIRTY-ONE

TESSA

"This is so boring," Maddy announced, staring at the fermentation tanks with undisguised disinterest. "No offence, Dad, but beer making is not as cool as you think it is."

Wyatt looked mildly offended. "It's a craft. There's science involved."

"There's also yeast," Maddy said. "Which is fungus. Fungus beer. Still boring."

I bit back a smile as Wyatt ran a hand through his hair in exasperation.

"Fine," he said. "There's a public tour starting in ten minutes in the taproom. Go join that one. Maybe their guide will be more entertaining."

"Anything would be more entertaining than listening to you explain hop varieties for twenty minutes," Maddy said, but she was grinning. She looked at me. "You staying with him?"

"Someone has to," I said.

"Good luck." Maddy headed toward the taproom, pulling

out her phone. "Text me when you're done with the fungus lecture."

Wyatt waited until she disappeared around the corner before turning to me. "Fungus beer. My daughter just called my life's work fungus beer."

"She's not wrong," I said, trying to keep a straight face.

"You're not helping."

"I'm not trying to." I walked over to one of the tanks, running my hand along the cool steel. "So. Private tour now that you've lost your other audience member?"

Something shifted in his expression. "You actually want the tour?"

"I'm here, aren't I?"

"You're here because Maddy begged you to come keep her from dying of boredom while I worked today."

That was true. Maddy begged me at breakfast, and since I was technically still a prisoner on the Hargrove ranch because Wyatt hadn't been able to track down Colin, I couldn't say no to big pleading eyes.

But I said yes for other reasons too. After the strip poker and sex in the barn two days ago, I wasn't ready to examine too closely why I couldn't stay away from Wyatt.

"So now you're stuck with me. Might as well make it worth my time."

Wyatt's eyes darkened slightly. "Worth your time."

"Yeah. Impress me, Hargrove. Show me why you spend all your free time making fungus beer."

He moved closer, and the air between us suddenly felt charged. "You want the real tour or the public tour?"

"What's the difference?"

"The public tour stays in the main production areas. The real tour." He gestured toward a hallway I hadn't noticed before. "Goes places most people don't get to see."

My pulse quickened. "Show me."

He led me away from the main brewery floor, down a hallway lined with pipes and gauges. The sound of the public tour starting filtered faintly from the taproom, Maddy's voice audible for a second before fading.

"This is the quality control area," Wyatt said, opening a door. "Where we test batches, check consistency, make sure everything meets standards before it goes to the tanks."

The room was small and warm, filled with equipment I didn't recognize. Wyatt closed the door behind us, and suddenly we were alone in a way we hadn't been all day.

"Is this the impressive part?" I asked, trying to keep my voice steady.

"No." He moved closer. "This is."

He backed me against the stainless steel counter and kissed me.

I should've pushed him away. Should've reminded him that Maddy was just down the hall, that this was his place of business, that we were supposed to be keeping things simple.

Instead, I fisted my hands in his shirt and pulled him closer.

"We can't," I gasped when he moved to my neck. "Maddy."

"Is on a tour that takes forty minutes," Wyatt said against my skin. "And we're on the opposite side of the building."

"Someone could come in."

"No one's going to interrupt." His hands slid under my shirt. "I've been thinking about touching you since you walked out of the barn the other night, and didn't look back. Do you have any idea how fucking hot that was?"

"You've been talking about hops for the last twenty minutes and wanting to get me naked?"

He lifted me onto the counter, stepping between my thighs. "Do you know how hard it is to concentrate on beer when all I can think about is getting you alone?"

My head fell back as his mouth found that spot below my ear. "This is a terrible idea."

"All our best ideas seem to be terrible." His hands were on the button of my jeans now. "Tell me to stop."

I didn't.

I should have. This was reckless even by our standards. But the risk of it, Maddy down the hall, the brewery full of people on tours, anyone could walk past the door, only made my pulse race faster.

"Wyatt," I breathed.

"Tell me what you want." His fingers traced the waistband of my jeans. "Say it."

"You know what I want."

"Say it anyway."

I grabbed his wrist and pulled his hand lower. "Touch me. Now."

His eyes flashed dark and hungry. "Yes, ma'am."

He popped the button of my jeans and slid the zipper down with agonizing slowness. Then his hand was sliding under my underwear, and I had to bite my lip to keep from making a sound.

"Jesus," he groaned. "You're already so wet."

"Your fault," I managed, my hips rocking into his touch.

He kissed me hard as his fingers found exactly the right spot, the right rhythm. I clutched at his shoulders, trying to stay quiet, trying not to think about the fact that his daughter was somewhere in this building.

"That's it," he murmured against my mouth. "Let me feel you."

His thumb circled my clit while two fingers slid inside me, and I had to bury my face in his neck to muffle the sound I made.

"You're so fucking perfect," he said roughly, his free hand sliding into my hair. "So responsive. So desperate for this."

"Shut up," I gasped, but my body was already trembling.

"Make me." He increased the pressure, the speed, and I was gasping his name into his shoulder.

The orgasm hit suddenly and hard, and I bit down on his shirt to keep from crying out. He worked me through it, his touch gentling as I shook apart, pressing kisses to my temple and murmuring things I couldn't quite hear over the rushing in my ears.

When I finally came down, gasping and boneless, he slowly withdrew his hand and helped me fix my clothes with surprising gentleness.

"Okay?" he asked softly.

"Yeah." My voice came out hoarse. "More than okay."

He kissed me again, soft and sweet this time, and I tasted satisfaction in it.

"What about you?" I asked, my hand sliding toward his belt. I could feel how hard he was against my thigh.

He caught my wrist. "Later."

"But."

"This was about you." He kissed my forehead. "And we're running out of time."

As if on cue, I heard voices in the hallway outside. The tour must be moving through.

"Shit," I muttered, scrambling off the counter.

Wyatt steadied me with a hand on my hip, amusement dancing in his eyes. "Easy."

"This is not funny. Your daughter—"

"Is still in the taproom listening to someone talk about barrel aging." He helped me smooth my hair. "We're fine."

"We're insane," I corrected.

"That too." He kissed me one more time, quick and playful. "But you're not bored anymore, are you?"

I glared at him, but I couldn't quite hide my smile. "You're insufferable."

"And you love it."

He wasn't wrong, and that scared me more than getting caught.

We slipped out of the quality control room and back into the main brewery floor, trying to look casual. A group of tourists was examining one of the fermentation tanks while their guide explained the brewing process in enthusiastic detail.

"There you are!" Maddy appeared at my elbow, making me jump. "I thought you guys got lost. The tour is actually pretty interesting. Did you know they use different types of yeast for different..." she trailed off, looking between Wyatt and me. "Why are you both so red?"

"It's warm in here," I said quickly. "From all the equipment."

Maddy's eyes narrowed suspiciously. "Uh huh."

"Did you answer all the questions in the barrel aging section?" Wyatt asked, his voice impressively casual.

"Yeah." Maddy was still looking at us like she knew something was off. "Are we almost done? I want to go riding before it gets too late."

"Yeah," I said, grateful for the excuse to leave. "Let's go."

As we walked toward the exit, I felt Wyatt's hand brush mine for just a second, a brief contact that sent electricity up my arm. "See you both later," he said as Maddy hugged him.

This was getting dangerous. Not just the physical stuff, though that was risky enough. But the way I kept wanting more. The way I couldn't seem to stay away from him, even when I knew I should.

The way "later" felt like a promise I was already desperate to collect on.

Maddy chattered about the tour on the way to the parking lot, but I barely heard her. All I could think about was Wyatt's hands on me, his voice in my ear, the way he looked at me like I was the only thing in the world that mattered.

I was in so much trouble. And the worst part was, I didn't want it to stop.

Thirty-Two
Tessa

Work had been so busy, I hadn't even stopped for lunch. I was back at my house. Colin hadn't been found, but I couldn't stay there any longer. And Dani had come back to stay with me when her meetings wrapped up. I missed Maddy and Wyatt. Missed the touches Wyatt snuck in when Maddy wasn't looking, and the middle of the night sex we'd been having in Wyatt's bed. I felt like a teenager again, sneaking around and trying not to get caught.

As I locked the clinic behind me, town felt wrong the second I stepped onto Main.

Not loud. Not obvious. Just tilted. Like everything shifted a fraction out of place while I wasn't looking, and now the whole street was leaning.

I kept my head down as I crossed the sidewalk toward my truck. I could feel eyes on me from behind glass and doorways. I didn't look back. If I pretended I couldn't feel them, maybe they wouldn't be there.

My hand shook as I unlocked the driver's door.

Cologne hit me first. Too familiar. Too wrong.

"You always forget the back seat," Colin said quietly.

My scream died in my throat before it ever reached the air.

There he was, sitting sideways behind my seat like he belonged there. Calm. Waiting. His phone lay in his palm, screen dark.

I froze with one boot still on the pavement.

"Get in," he said.

"Get out of my truck."

"You can," he replied. "Or you can listen to me and make this easy."

I stayed where I was. My pulse roared in my ears.

He lifted his phone and turned the screen toward me.

Maddy.

On the brewery porch. Backpack slung over one shoulder. Wyatt's truck a soft blur behind her. The timestamp glowed in the corner.

Ten minutes ago.

Everything in me dropped.

"You've been near her," I whispered.

He smiled. "Near is a generous word. Close enough is the truth."

My body went numb. "If you touch her, I'll kill you."

"You won't. You care too much about surviving to try."

My breath came fast and shallow. I could hear my own heartbeat. I could barely feel the ground under my feet.

"Why? Why her?"

"Because you love her," he replied easily. "And because he does. That makes her leverage."

My vision tunnelled. "You leave her alone. I'll do whatever you want."

"That's what I figured."

I slid fully into the seat on instinct alone. The door shut with a soft, terrible finality. The lock clicked down the second it closed.

"I swear to God," I said hoarsely. "If you're lying about this."

He slid the phone into the console and gestured with his chin. "Drive."

I stared at him. "You're out of your mind."

"Probably, but you're the one who's going to take us wherever I tell you."

My hands fumbled the keys. They shook so badly I dropped them once before I managed to start the engine.

"Don't look for him," Colin said. "Don't call anyone. If I see a screen light up, I send a message, and it won't be a picture."

My chest constricted. "You're sick."

"You already told me that," he replied. "Turn left."

I obeyed.

Town slid past like a familiar dream turning wrong. The café. The corner store. The stretch of road that led toward the river bend and then further out into nothing. I didn't speed. I didn't stall. I drove like my body belonged to someone else.

My phone vibrated in the cup holder.

My sob broke loose as I saw Wyatt's name.

"Don't," Colin said softly.

I didn't touch it.

"You're being smart. This is the part where you stop pretending you're in control."

The river disappeared behind us. Fields took over. Then scrub. Then gravel.

My thoughts kept skidding back to the same image. Maddy on the porch. Sun in her hair. A moment of normal I'd never see again the same way.

"You were at his house."

"Briefly."

"You followed a kid."

"I followed your weakness."

Rage flared hot through the terror. "You don't even see what you are, do you?"

He shrugged. "I see what you made me."

That landed cold and empty.

The road narrowed. The sky felt larger. Trees thinned. The sense of being watched replaced itself with the certainty of being alone.

He finally spoke again after several minutes of silence. "You almost had me convinced I couldn't reach you anymore."

"You never owned me."

"I owned your doubt, that was always enough."

The gravel changed under the tires. Deeper. Less traveled. The world grew quieter in a way that felt like being submerged.

I didn't ask where we were going. I already knew the answer wouldn't matter.

My phone vibrated again.

Wyatt.

My vision blurred. "Please," I whispered.

Colin's hand came down on the console between us. Hard. "You're done asking."

I swallowed the sound, trying to claw its way out of me.

The abandoned place came into view like a bruise on the land. A sagging structure set back from the road. Windows dark. The roof was broken in two places. The kind of property people forgot because it hurt to remember it existed.

"Pull in," he said.

I did.

Gravel crunched under the tires as I brought the truck to a stop. The engine clicked and ticked as it cooled.

For a second, neither of us moved.

Then he reached across and shut off the ignition.

My hands slid uselessly in my lap. My muscles stayed locked. My heart felt too big for my chest.

"Get out," he said.

"If you lied about her," I whispered. "If you even scared her."

He opened his door. "You'll behave better if you keep believing she's fine because of you."

That broke what was left of me.

I stepped out onto the gravel. The air smelled like dust and rot and old rain. The sky over the roofline was pale and endless.

The truck door shut behind me.

Colin walked around the hood with lazy confidence and stopped a few feet away.

"Welcome to quiet," he said.

And as the wind moved through the dead grass around my boots, the last thing I saw in my mind was Maddy's face in that impossible slice of normal morning light.

Thirty-Three

Wyatt

The brewery was in that late stretch when nobody came in, and the stragglers were thinking about leaving, when the place belonged to the work and not the customers. The tanks held their steady heat, the lines were purged and ready, the back hallway smelled like grain dust and sanitizer, and the whole building breathed in a low industrial hum that usually calmed the restless part of me. I liked mornings here because the work didn't ask questions. It didn't care about grief or banks or old promises. It only cared whether the mash temp held and whether the schedule got done.

I'd been checking the delivery log with a mug of coffee in my hand, half listening to the rattle of kegs in the cold room while one of my guys stacked empties. No one was arguing. No one was calling. No one needed me to fix anything.

It should've been a relief.

Instead, it felt like the moment right before a storm breaks.

My phone buzzed against the clipboard, and the name on the screen tightened every muscle in my back.

Holt.

He didn't call me at the brewery unless it was an emergency, and Holt didn't spook easily. He'd stared down blizzards, wildfires, a bull with a bad attitude, and a broken gate. He walked into disaster with a calm face more times than I could count.

So when I answered and said, "What's happened," and he didn't immediately say anything, my chest went cold.

"Where are you?" Holt asked.

"At work," I said, already moving toward my office. "Talk."

His breath came through the line like he'd been jogging. "Dani called."

The name hit like a stone. "Why's she calling you?"

"Because she couldn't get you," Holt said sharply. "And she can't get Tessa."

I stopped walking. The back hallway blurred for a second, not because I didn't understand the words but because my body refused to accept them.

"What do you mean she can't get her?" I asked, keeping my voice steady on purpose. Panic was loud. Panic was useless. I needed details.

"I mean, Tessa left for work this morning, and she hasn't come back," Holt said. "No answer. No text. Nothing. Dani's tried. I've tried. I drove by the Callahan place twice, and she wasn't there. The house is locked. The yard's empty. The barn doors are shut."

"Did she take her truck?" I asked.

"Yeah," Holt said. "Ray's old truck. It was gone from the yard."

A thin sliver of relief tried to slide in. Then Holt added, "Wyatt, she's not the kind to disappear without a fight. Not with everything she's up against."

"No," I said quietly. "She's not."

I stood there long enough for the brewery's hum to feel

too distant. I could picture her, jaw set, hands tight on the steering wheel, refusing help because pride felt safer than need. I could picture her doing exactly what she'd said she'd do, finishing errands even when her nerves were raw, just to prove she could still function.

I could also picture a man sitting in the wrong place at the wrong time, watching her like prey, waiting for a moment when her guard dipped.

My hand tightened around my phone. "Where are you?"

"In my truck," Holt said. "Halfway to town."

"Come to the brewery. Call Evan and Travis, I want eyes on every road that leads out, but I want it done smart."

Holt didn't argue. "On it."

I hung up and went into my office, shutting the door behind me. The room was small, the kind of space built for paperwork and quick conversations. I stared at my desk for a second, then grabbed my keys, my wallet, and the charger I kept in the top drawer. My hand hovered over the landline, because part of my brain still believed I could call Ray and ask him what the hell to do.

Ray was gone.

So it was on me.

I called Dani before I could second-guess it. She answered on the first ring, voice too tight, like she'd been holding her breath for an hour.

"Wyatt," she said, and the way she said my name was different now. Less venom, more fear.

"Where are you?" I asked.

"At Tessa's," she said. "I locked the door like you told me. I'm not leaving. I'm not doing the dumb horror movie thing where the best friend goes outside to investigate a noise."

Good. At least one of us was thinking clearly.

"Tell me exactly what happened this morning," I said.

Dani exhaled shakily. "We were up early. She didn't sleep

much. She looked like hell, but she's been looking like hell all week, so I didn't clock it as a red flag. She drank coffee. She stared at a pile of mail like it was going to bite her. Then she left for work."

"I'm going to call Brooke. I've got my men on the roads. And Dani," I added, and my voice came lower without me meaning it to. "If she comes back, you lock the doors, and you call me first. You don't let her talk you into anything."

"I won't," she said, and it sounded like a promise she needed too. "Wyatt, please find her."

"I will," I said, and I meant it with every part of myself.

I ended the call and stood in my office for half a second, letting the fear sharpen into something usable. Then I walked out and found my crew.

"You're in charge," I told the head brewer. "I'm stepping out."

He looked at my face and didn't ask questions.

"Keep the place running anyway."

He nodded once, serious, and I left through the back door like the building was on fire.

Outside, the sun was bright and wrong. The yard looked normal. The world looked like it hadn't shifted.

I climbed into my truck, started it, and pulled onto the road.

Town was only a few minutes away, but the drive felt longer because my mind kept racing ahead, drawing maps of worst-case scenarios over the familiar land. Every ditch looked like a place a vehicle could hide. Every turnout looked like a decision point. Every stretch of trees felt too thick, like it could swallow a person whole.

I kept telling myself it could still be nothing. A dead phone. A forgotten charger. A long conversation with a clerk who wouldn't stop talking.

Then I pictured Colin's smile, too polite and too controlled, and my gut would twist again.

I slowed and drove Main once, scanning the curb, the lots, the usual parking spots. I didn't see Ray's truck. I didn't see her.

I parked near the co-op and went inside.

The bell over the door jingled. A couple of older men by the seed display glanced up, then looked away. The clerk behind the counter nodded at me like this was any other day.

I walked up to the counter and kept my voice calm. "You see Tessa Callahan today?"

The clerk hesitated. "Ray's niece?"

"Yes," I said. "I'm trying to find her."

The clerk's eyes flicked toward the manager's office like he didn't want responsibility. "She came in for mineral blocks for the clinic," he said. "Looked, tense."

"Tense how?" I asked.

He shrugged, uncomfortable. "Like she had a lot going on."

That answer was useless. I didn't let it show on my face.

"Did she leave alone?" I asked.

He glanced down, then back up. "I didn't see anybody with her. I wasn't really watching."

"Who was working the lot?" I asked.

He pointed toward the back. "Jerrod was outside. Loading."

I didn't thank him. I moved.

Out back, the air was thick with feed dust and heat. Jerrod stood near a pallet jack, wiping sweat off his forehead with the hem of his shirt. He looked up when I approached, cautious in the way men got when they sensed trouble.

"Wyatt," he said. "What's up?"

"You see Tessa Callahan today," I asked.

His face tightened. "Yeah." Jerrod nodded toward the lot,

then back at me. "She came out fast. Like she was trying to get gone."

"Was she alone?" I asked.

Jerrod hesitated. "I didn't see anyone walk with her."

My stomach dropped anyway. "But."

Jerrod sighed like he didn't want to be part of this story. "There was a guy," he said. "Not local, I don't think. Clean clothes. Standing by the edge of the lot like he was waiting for someone."

My jaw clenched. "Did he approach her?"

"I didn't see it," Jerrod admitted. "But she stopped when she saw him. Like she froze for a second. Then she kept going. She didn't look around. She just went."

"And the guy," I asked.

"He watched her," Jerrod said, voice low. "Then he got into a dark vehicle and left."

"Did you see a plate?" I asked.

Jerrod shook his head, regretful. "No. Sorry."

"Which direction?" I pressed.

Jerrod pointed toward the road that led out past the last houses, toward fields and gravel and the kind of space that let bad people do bad things.

My pulse hammered.

I forced myself to stay calm, because calm got you answers.

"Thank you," I said. I went back to my truck and pulled my phone out.

Holt, Evan, and Travis were on their way, but I needed more than ranch hands right now. I needed law. I needed an official. I needed somebody to start a paper trail before this turned into a shrug and a prayer.

I called the detachment.

A constable answered, and I gave my name, gave Tessa's name, gave Ray's name, gave the facts in clean sentences that didn't shake. I said the word missing. I said the word suspect. I said the words ex-boyfriend. I said the words not local. I said the words she's vulnerable and being targeted.

The constable said they'd open a file. They said they'd send someone to take a statement. They said if she'd only been gone a few hours, it might be premature to call it an abduction.

I bit down on the rage that flared in my chest like a match.

"It's not premature. She's not the type to vanish. Her best friend is scared. Her phone's dead or off. She's under active pressure from a man with a history of manipulation. If you wait until it's official enough, you'll be too late."

There was a pause, the kind that told me I hit the limit of what this constable could do without permission.

"We'll dispatch a unit to speak with witnesses," he said carefully.

"Do it," I said. "And put a BOLO out for Colin, last name unknown to you, but I can provide it if you need it, and any dark SUV that isn't local. I'm not asking. I'm telling you what's coming."

Another pause. "Sir, I need you not to take matters into your own hands."

I laughed once, sharp and humourless. "You're already too late with that piece of advice." I ended the call and sat in my truck for half a second, hands on the steering wheel, breathing through the heat in my chest.

Then I drove.

Because sitting still while she was out there was a kind of madness I wouldn't survive.

I took the road out of town and forced myself to think like a man who didn't care about comfort, only control. Colin wouldn't stay close to town. He wouldn't risk cameras. He wouldn't risk witnesses. He'd go where the land went quiet, where gravel turned to ruts, where trees hid roofs, where people didn't drive unless they had a reason.

There were too many places like that.

Old hunting shacks. Abandoned cabins. Empty properties people forgot existed. A busted trailer tucked into a bush with a padlock on the door. A stretch of crown land where you could park and disappear for a day, and no one would ask why.

I drove the back roads first, because that's where you moved when you didn't want to be seen. I watched for fresh tire tracks, for disturbed gravel, for a dust plume in the distance that didn't belong.

Half an hour out, Holt's truck and trailer pulled up beside me at a turnout, dust still settling around the wheels. Evan and Travis were behind him, faces tight, posture already braced.

Holt climbed out and came to my window. "What've you got?"

I told him. The co-op. The waiting man. The dark vehicle. No plates. No clear direction beyond the obvious.

Holt's jaw went hard. "Colin."

"Yeah. And we're not waiting for permission to look."

Travis shifted, scanning the horizon. "You got a place in mind?"

"I've got a list," I said, and it wasn't an exaggeration. This land was full of places that could hide a person if someone wanted it to.

Evan rubbed his hands together, restless. "How're we splitting?"

I looked at the three of them and forced myself to stay clear-headed. "We don't scatter and lose each other. We work patterns. We keep phones on. We check in every twenty minutes. You see something, you call. You don't play hero."

Travis's mouth twitched. "We're not the heroic type."

"Good," I said. "Evan, you take the ridge roads and watch for any vehicle that doesn't belong. Travis, you take the south loop past the coulee and the old irrigation sheds. Holt, you're with me. Everyone on horseback, we can cover the ground better than in a vehicle."

Holt expected it because the horses were already saddled as we led them out of the trailer. He climbed onto the back of his horse without a word, and the weight of having him there steadied something in me. Holt was the only one who could pull me back if I stepped too far over a line.

We rode for hours.

The sun climbed, then started its slow lean toward afternoon. The heat built. The dust clung to our clothes. The land stretched out, indifferent and wide, and I hated it for how easily it could hide her.

Every time my phone buzzed, my heart slammed into my ribs.

Each time, it was Evan or Travis reporting that nothing was found.

Once, it was the constable asking where I was and telling me to return to town to give a formal statement.

I lied, and I said I was on my way.

Then we rode deeper into the quiet.

We checked an abandoned equipment shed on an old farm site first, the one that sat half collapsed on a neighbor's back quarter. Holt walked the perimeter while I scanned the ground for fresh tracks. Nothing but old ruts and deer prints.

We checked a hunting shack near the river, the kind of place teenage boys used to sneak beers in when they thought they were grown. The door was padlocked, and the dust on the porch boards was undisturbed.

We checked a broken-down trailer tucked into a stand of poplars, the windows busted, the door hanging loose. It smelled like mice and rot.

Each empty place tightened the fear, not because empty meant safe, but because empty meant we were behind.

Holt didn't talk much; every so often, he'd point at a track, and we'd both lean out to study it, debating whether it was fresh enough to matter.

Late in the afternoon, we stopped at a turnout overlooking a shallow valley. From up there, the land rolled in soft lines, patches of trees breaking the fields, coulees cutting scars into the ground. The kind of view that usually makes people feel small in a good way.

Today, it made me furious.

"She's out there," I said, voice low, and it wasn't a guess. It was a fact that lived in my bones.

Holt's gaze stayed on the horizon. "Yeah."

"I should've pushed harder for her to keep someone with her," I said before I could stop myself. "I should've taken her seriously when she looked like she was about to crack."

Holt finally looked at me. "You can't rewind. You can only move forward."

I nodded, because he was right and because it didn't help. We got back on the horses and kept going.

Dusk started to creep in when Travis called.

"I've got something," he said, and the words hit like a jolt of electricity. "Not her, but something."

"Where?" I demanded.

"Old logging road off the south loop," he said. "There's a set of fresh tracks going in. Deep. Like a heavier vehicle. Looks recent."

My grip tightened on the wheel. "Any sign of her truck?"

"No," Travis said. "Just the tracks and a spot where someone pulled off into the trees."

"Stay there," I said. "Don't go in alone."

"I'm not stupid," Travis replied, but his voice was tight. "Get here."

I kicked the sides of my gelding and took off like a bee stung the horse.

Holt kept pace beside me, silent, braced, eyes scanning everything we passed. The light turned gold, then amber, then thin.

When we reached Travis, he was standing at the edge of the logging road, arms crossed, jaw set. Evan was there too, standing beside him, dust still settling like he'd ridden in fast.

Travis pointed. "There," he said.

I got off and crouched, studying the tracks. They were fresh. The edges were crisp. The gravel was disturbed in a way that hadn't had time to settle.

A vehicle had gone in.

Not long ago.

My pulse hammered. "How far does the road go?"

"Couple kilometers," Travis said. "Then it dead ends near an old line shack. Been empty for years."

Holt's gaze flicked to mine. "We go in together."

I nodded once. "Together."

We moved slowly down the logging road, staying on the grass so we made minimal noise. The trees thickened, the light dimmed, and the world felt like it was closing in, even though the prairie wasn't supposed to close around anything.

The road ended where Travis said it would, at a clearing that held the remains of a small structure. Not a cabin, not really. A shack with a sagging roof and grey boards, the kind of place built for temporary work and then forgotten when the work moved on.

My blood went cold.

I tied the horse to a tree and stood still for a second, listening.

No voices. No movement. No sign of life.

Holt was the first to speak, barely above a whisper. "That could be where he was staying?"

"It could," I said, and I hated how steady my voice sounded, like my body decided terror wasn't useful anymore.

We got out and moved in carefully, boots quiet on the dirt. Evan and Travis flanked, wide, scanning the tree line. Holt stayed close, like he could feel the exact second I might lose control.

I reached the porch first and looked through the window.

Empty. I checked the ground. Fresh footprints.

Two sets, maybe three, hard to tell in the disturbed dirt. One set smaller. One set larger.

My throat tightened. "She was here," I said, and the words felt like a vow and a curse.

Holt swore under his breath.

I moved toward the shack, every muscle in my body braced.

The door was shut, but it wasn't latched properly. It hung slightly open, as if someone had been in a hurry or hadn't cared.

I pushed it with the back of my hand.

It creaked inward.

The smell hit first. Old wood. Dust. Mouse droppings. Stale smoke, faint but real, like a fire had been lit and put out not long ago.

The space inside was small. A table. A broken chair. A pile of old blankets in one corner, mouldy at the edges.

No one was there. Nothing but emptiness and the echo of what could've happened.

I scanned the floor again, and then I saw it.

A single dark strand of hair caught on a splintered board near the doorway. Long. Dark.

My chest seized.

I didn't touch it. I didn't move it. I only stared, because staring was the only thing keeping me from tearing the place apart with my bare hands.

Travis shifted behind me. "What?"

"She was here," I said again, voice rougher now.

Evan's breath came hard. "Where'd they go?"

That was the question that mattered, and it was the one the shack couldn't answer.

Holt moved past me and checked the back corner, then the window, then the ground outside. He came back in with his face set.

"There's another set of tracks leaving on foot," he said quietly. "They went east into the trees."

My pulse slammed. "Why leave the vehicle?"

"Because they didn't want it found on the main roads," Holt said. "Or they swapped vehicles. "

My mind raced, mapping the tree line, the coulee beyond, the faint paths deer used that could lead to a hidden road. It was too much land and not enough time.

I forced myself to breathe. In, out. Control. If we rushed blind, we'd miss what mattered.

"We call this in," Holt said.

My jaw clenched so hard it hurt. "And wait."

"And bring law down on it," Holt corrected. "Wyatt, you want her alive. You want her back. You don't want to stomp through here and wipe out the only tracks we've got."

He was right. And I hated him for it.

I nodded once and pulled my phone out, hands steady only because I didn't have a choice.

I called the detachment and told them where we were. I told them we'd found a likely suspect vehicle, an abandoned structure, recent tracks, and possible hair evidence. I told them we hadn't entered further into the bush beyond the immediate shack area.

I lied about how close I'd come to doing exactly that.

The constable's voice sharpened. They said units were on the way. They said to stay put. They said not to engage.

When I ended the call, the air felt thick. The light outside turned low and bruised, dusk settling into the trees like a lid.

Evan shifted, restless. "We're just going to stand here."

"No," I said, and my voice came out quiet and deadly. Travis looked like he wanted to argue, but Holt's hand landed on his shoulder, firm.

I stepped out of the shack and stared into the trees where the tracks vanished.

Somewhere out there, she was breathing. Somewhere out there, she was alive, because I refused to accept any other possibility.

And somewhere out there, Colin was walking around wearing his sickness like a suit, convinced he could control the world by controlling her.

I stood in the fading light with my hands curled into fists and the taste of metal in my mouth, and I let the promise settle in my chest like a brand.

I hadn't found her yet.

But I'd found a thread.

And I was going to follow it until it became a rope, until it became a noose, until it dragged the truth into daylight, whether Colin liked it or not.

Thirty-Four

Tessa

The cabin looked worse up close, like a carcass rotting in the sun, waiting for someone to put it out of its misery. The weather chewed the boards into a sickly, splintered grey. The porch sagged in the middle, bowed like a snapped spine. One shutter hung by a single rusted hinge, clicking softly in the wind—a rhythmic, patient sound that felt less like a breeze and more like a countdown.

Colin waited while I stood there, rooted to the dirt. He let my eyes rake over the shattered windows and the weeds choking the steps. He let me look at the horizon, where the land stretched out in every direction with nothing to interrupt the emptiness but scrub brush and the skeletal line of distant poplars.

"Go on," he said, his voice a silk-wrapped blade. "It's not going to bite. And if it does, there's nobody that can hear your screams." He laughed like he made a joke, before he glared at me again, eyes cold, jaw clenched.

My mouth was so dry I couldn't swallow. My throat felt scraped raw, the skintight from holding back a scream I refused to give him. Even in the open air, I could smell his cologne—expensive, cloying, and entirely wrong for the wilderness.

"What did you do to her?" I managed. My voice sounded thin, like it belonged to someone else.

He tilted his head, studying me with the clinical interest of a boy watching an insect in a jar. "Who?"

"You know who. Maddy."

He sighed, the sound heavy with performed boredom. "Nothing. I didn't touch her. I didn't talk to her. I didn't even step on her porch."

"That's not the point," I said, my knees beginning to tremble. "You followed her. You were there."

"I watched," he corrected, his eyes bright. "There's a difference, Tessa. Watching is an appreciation. Following is a chore." He smiled—a small, private thing, like he caught me saying something he could use against me later.

"It's fucking creepy." I whispered. "You kidnapped me."

"I brought you somewhere quiet, so you'd finally listen. You've become so loud lately. So distracted. It's not like you," he said as he ran his hand through his hair.

I stared at him, my hands clenching at my sides until my nails bit into my palms. I wanted to lunge and claw the calm right off his face.

"Where are my keys?"

He patted his pocket, a slow, deliberate motion. "Safe."

"My phone."

He patted the other pocket. "Also safe. Don't worry, Tessa. I'm looking after everything now."

My stomach turned. A cold, oily slick of nausea rose in my throat. "Give them back, Colin. Now."

"No."

I took a step forward, a surge of desperate adrenaline overriding my brain. He didn't flinch. He didn't reach for me. He only lifted his eyebrows, his expression chillingly neutral, like a trainer waiting for a dog to test the limits of its shock collar.

"You're not going to hit me. Not yet."

Not yet. The words landed with the weight of a death sentence. My skin prickled with a sudden, frantic heat.

"You're insane," I screamed, and my voice echoed off the mountains.

He stepped closer. I had to fight the urge to stumble back. He didn't crowd me, but he knew how to hold space in a way that felt like a physical weight on my chest. It was a projection of ownership.

"You keep saying that," he murmured, his breath smelling of mint and something metallic. "But you got in the truck. You drove where I told you. You did exactly what I asked. That doesn't sound like I'm the one who's lost my mind. It sounds like you've finally found yours."

"I did it because you threatened a child!"

He made a sound that could've been a laugh if there had been any warmth in it. "You did it because you're predictable. You've always been so easy to move, Tessa. I just needed the right leverage."

The wind shifted, dragging dry grass against the cabin's foundation with a sound like a long, low hiss. Somewhere, a bird called once, then went abruptly silent, as if it realized it wasn't alone.

Colin nodded toward the porch. "Inside. The sun is going down, and the wind is picking up."

My body rebelled. A heavy, sickening resistance settled in my limbs. "No. I'm not going in there."

His gaze sharpened. The mask of gentleness slipped, just an inch, revealing the jagged edge underneath. "Tessa," he growled. I hated the way he said my name.

"I'm not going in," I said, forcing each word into place like a brick. "You want to talk, you can do it out here."

He looked past me, and my heart stuttered. My brain immediately filled the empty space behind me with Maddy's face, sunlight on her hair, backpack on as she walked home.

"I can talk anywhere," he said, his eyes returning to mine. "But I don't think you can. You're going to start shaking soon. Then you'll start begging. Then you'll embarrass yourself in front of the trees. It's better if we're inside."

I held my breath, trying to force my spine to stay straight, trying to hide the tremor in my hands. He watched the struggle with the patient eyes of a predator watching a deer tire itself out. He knew the exact moment my resolve cracked.

"You don't want anyone hurt, right?" he added, his voice dropping to a conspiratorial whisper. "If you think I don't have eyes on that little girl right now, you don't know me as well as you thought."

"You're bluffing." The words felt hollow as I forced them out.

"Can you take that chance? Can you live with being wrong?" He gestured to the door again. "Come inside and talk like an adult. Before things get... complicated."

My jaw clenched so hard my teeth ached. If I ran, he'd hunt me down. If I fought, he'd use it as an excuse to break me. If I screamed, the sound would simply dissolve into the scrub brush.

I went up the steps because my body wanted to live, and because the thought of Maddy paying for my defiance was a terror more potent than the cabin.

The porch boards groaned under my boots like a warning. The door was swollen with age, sticking fast when I tried the handle. Colin reached around me—his chest brushed my shoulder, a brief, horrifying contact—and shoved the door open with a hard shove of his hand.

The smell hit first. It was the scent of a grave. Old smoke, damp wood, and the sharp, acidic tang of mouse droppings.

Something sour and forgotten rotted in the corners. Light slanted through the grime-filmed windows, striping the floor in dusty, sickly gold. A table sat crooked in the center, one leg propped with a flat stone. Two mismatched chairs. A small iron stove with rust blooming along its seams like dried blood.

It was the kind of place designed for things that weren't meant to be found.

I froze in the doorway, my stomach churning. Colin stepped past me as if he were entering a palace. He surveyed the room, a faint, satisfied tilt to his mouth.

"See," he said. "It's fine. Private."

"Why here?" I whispered, my eyes darting toward the shadows.

He shrugged. "It's quiet. Out of the way. It's ours for a while."

Ours. The word made my skin crawl.

He walked to the table and set two items down with exaggerated care. My keys. My phone. He placed them in the center of the wood like a ritual sacrifice. Then he pulled a chair out and sat, folding his hands on the tabletop.

"You're going to stand there all day?" he asked.

"I might."

He sighed, shaking his head. "You'll faint. You're already pale. You haven't been eating, have you?"

"You don't know anything about me," I snapped.

He laughed softly, and the sound made the hair on my arms stand up. "I know you better than you know yourself, Tessa. I know the way your pulse jumps in your neck when you're lying. I know the way you try to look brave when you're seconds away from a breakdown. I know what actually scares you. And it's not me. It's that I can see through you."

He nodded at the other chair. "Sit."

"No."

His tone didn't change, but the air in the room suddenly felt ten degrees colder. "Sit. Down. Tessa."

The room felt smaller with every second. The walls seemed to be leaning inward, pressing the oxygen out of the air. My legs gave a warning tremble. I knew he was right; if I didn't sit, I was going to collapse.

I crossed the room in stiff, robotic steps and sat on the edge of the chair, poised to bolt. The wood was cold and rough against my thighs.

"Thank you. That wasn't so hard, was it?"

"What do you want, Colin?"

He blinked slowly. "I want you back."

The words were so absurd I almost laughed. "Back? You kidnapped me to ask for a second chance? There's nothing to go back for, I don't need you."

His eyes sharpened. "That's melodramatic. I gave you everything, I protected you."

"You caged me! I left because you were the problem. You were the thing I needed protection from."

His jaw tightened, a muscle leaping in his cheek. "You don't get to rewrite our history just because you're embarrassed you left. And now you are wrong about being able to live without me."

Something hot and feral flared under my ribs. I leaned forward. "I was wrong about you being a man. I thought you were a partner. But you're just a parasite with a bad haircut."

The air between us went brittle. Colin's expression went deathly still.

"You always had a talent for cruelty," he said quietly. "It's one of the things I'll have to fix."

"Fix? You don't get to fix anything. I left you; I was free of you. There is nothing to fix."

"You ran back here like a child," he replied, his voice rising.

"Back to this pathetic ranch and your uncle's memory. Don't talk to me about freedom while you're drowning in his debts."

"Don't you dare talk about Ray."

He smiled, a jagged, ugly expression. "Why not? He's gone. He can't help you. Neither can that cowboy you've been sniffing around."

I rose so fast the chair screeched against the floor. "Go to hell."

Colin didn't move. He stayed seated, relaxed, watching my outburst like a parent watching a toddler's tantrum. "Sit down, Tessa. You can scream, you can throw the chair, you can even try to hit me. But when you're done, you're still going to be in this room. And I'm still going to have the keys."

I stood there breathing hard, my chest heaving. I hated the weakness of my own body. I hated that exhaustion made my thoughts slippery. I hated that he was right; I was trapped in a box of his making.

Colin let the silence stretch until my shoulders started to sag. Then he spoke again, his voice dropping back into that terrifying, honeyed softness.

"I didn't come here to hurt you, Tessa. I'm not a monster."

"You're holding me hostage!"

He tilted his head, looking almost sincere. "I'm being desperate. There's a difference. People do strange things for love."

"This isn't love," I whispered.

"You used to think it was." He stood up, and my entire body went rigid. He didn't lunge. He walked to the little counter by the stove and opened a cupboard with a piercing squeak. Inside were old tins and a kettle with a rim of rust. He took his time, acting as if he were in his own kitchen.

He pulled a lighter from his pocket. The click of the flint was loud in the silence. A flame bloomed, dancing in his eyes.

"You planned this," I said, the realization sinking into my gut like lead. "The cabin, the stove... you've been here before."

He flicked the lighter shut. "I like to be prepared. I wanted to talk to you somewhere you couldn't run. Somewhere, the world couldn't interfere."

He crouched, opened the stove door, and lit the tinder he'd clearly placed there earlier. The fire caught, the dry wood popping and hissing. Smoke curled into the room, smelling of ancient dust and burning sap.

He returned to the table and sat, folding his hands. "Now. Tell me the truth."

"What truth?"

"Tell me you didn't mean it when you left."

A cold, hysterical laugh bubbled in my throat. "I meant every second of it. I've never been happier than the day I walked away from you."

His eyes narrowed. "No. You were overly emotional. Which you know is something I don't appreciate."

"Now you're in over your head here. This ranch is rotting, your uncle is a corpse, but I can help you. I can take the weight. The money, the decisions, you won't have to worry your pretty little head about it anymore."

"I'd rather lose the ranch than let you help me."

He sighed, as if I were being a difficult child. Then, he reached into his pocket and pulled out his phone. He tapped the screen and turned it toward me.

It was a picture of Maddy. She was further away this time, walking toward the barn on Wyatt's property. Someone was standing in the shadows of the trees—a blurred figure in a dark jacket.

The timestamp was from twenty minutes ago.

My breath hitched so hard it hurt. The terror, which had been a dull roar, suddenly became a deafening scream in my head.

"I told you," Colin said, his voice a low hum. "I'm close enough to touch everything you love. So, stop fighting me. Stop pretending you have a choice."

I stared at the picture until it burned into my retinas. My hands were shaking so violently I had to hide them under the table. He won. He found the one nerve he could pull to make me move, and he was pulling it with everything he had.

"What do you want me to do?" I whispered, the fight finally draining out of me.

Colin's smile was almost tender. He reached across the table, not for my hand, but for my phone. He turned it off and slipped it into his pocket. Then he took my keys and did the same.

"We're staying the night," he said, his voice final. "It's safer. Nobody is looking for you out here yet."

The word yet hung in the air like a noose.

He stood and walked to the door. He turned the lock with a heavy, metallic clunk. Then, he pocketed the key and looked back at me, the firelight casting long, distorted shadows behind him.

"You can sleep on the cot," he said, pointing to a narrow, rusted frame in the corner. "I'll stay up and keep watch."

The offer was a threat. He was going to watch me sleep. He was going to own my unconsciousness the same way he owned my day.

I didn't move. I stayed in the chair, my spine rigid, watching him. Outside, the wind moved through the dead grass, whispering a warning I couldn't escape. I was alone in the dark with a man who thought possession was a virtue, and the night was only just beginning.

Thirty-Five

Thirty hours of dirt roads that bled into the horizon like bruises. Thirty hours of checking abandoned barns where the only thing waiting was the stench of dry rot and the hollow whistle of the wind through termite-eaten timber. We asked the same questions to the same tired, hollow-eyed faces in three different counties, getting nothing back but shrugs and the kind of quiet fear that settled into a town when people realized a predator was walking among them.

I drove with both hands locked on the wheel, my knuckles white enough to glow in the sickly green light of the dash. Every time the truck jolted over a pothole, my heart spiked against my ribs like a trapped bird. The tension in the cab was thick enough to choke on, tasting of stale coffee and unwashed adrenaline.

"You wanna slow it down," Holt said, his voice a low, jagged rasp. He didn't look at me. He couldn't afford to take his eyes off the black ribbon of road. "The gravel is turning to silt. Road's getting rough."

"I'm not missing anything," I replied. My voice didn't sound like mine. It was a cold, alien vibration in my throat.

He snorted, a sharp, bitter sound. "You're not missing her by driving us into a ditch either. If we flip this rig, she dies out there. Is that what you want?"

I eased off the gas, just a fraction. Gravel popped under the tires like small-caliber fire. The road narrowed into little more than twin ruts cutting through scrub and waist-high dead grass that hissed against the undercarriage. Trees crowded closer, their skeletal branches clawing at the dark sky, reaching for the truck as if trying to pull us into the blackness.

The radio crackled to life, the static sounding like teeth grinding together.

"Nothing on the east ridge," a voice said, sounding small and defeated. "We checked the culvert and the old irrigation shed. No sign. Just some old tire tracks that could be months old. No sign of Tessa."

"Copy," Holt said, his jaw muscles jumping. "Head back toward the main road and keep your lights low. If he's out there, we don't want him seeing you before you see him. Stay sharp."

Every mile we covered without finding her felt like another shovelful of dirt on a casket. I was failing her. I could feel the weight of it stacking up on my chest, making it harder to draw a full breath.

"She should've called," I muttered.

Holt glanced at me sideways, the dash light hollowing out his features until he looked like a corpse. "She's stubborn as hell, Wyatt. You know that."

Earlier, the sun had been a cruel, bright eye in the sky, and we'd been forced to stop at Tessa's place to regroup and trade the horses for trucks. Dani had been pacing the living room like a caged animal, her pink hair pulled up into a messy, frantic knot. She was wrapping her arms around herself so tight I thought she might splinter apart right there on the rug.

Maddy sat curled on the couch, knees drawn up to her chin. She'd pulled her hoodie sleeves over her hands, disappearing into the fabric. She hadn't cried. Not once. No hysterics, no sobbing—just a terrifying, thousand-yard stare that made her look sixty years old instead of fourteen. That quiet scared me more than any scream. It was the silence of a child who already accepted that the world was a dark and hungry place.

"She wouldn't just disappear," Maddy had said when I'd crouched in front of her. Her voice was flat, devoid of the melody of childhood. "She wouldn't do that to me."

I'd swallowed hard, the lump in my throat feeling like a jagged stone. "No, honey. She wouldn't."

"She promised she would let me know if she was leaving town," Dani added sharply, her voice cracking. "She promised. We had a plan. She wouldn't break a plan."

I hadn't said what we were all thinking. Those promises didn't mean shit when someone else decided they had a claim on your life. Those plans were just paper when a man like Colin decided to turn the world into a hunting ground.

Maddy had finally looked up at me then, her eyes too steady, too perceptive. "You're going to find her."

It wasn't a question. It was a command. A debt I was now carrying through the dark.

"I am"

She studied my face for a long second, looking for the lie. She didn't find one, but she didn't find peace either. She just nodded once. "Okay."

That faith sat heavy in my marrow now as I turned us down another unmarked track, the brush scraping against the doors like fingernails.

"You sure about this one?" Holt asked.

"Yeah," I said, my pulse beginning to thrum with a sick, instinctive rhythm. "Ray mentioned an old hunting cabin out this way once. It's off the tax maps, buried in the timber. Nobody uses it anymore."

"Nobody sane," Holt muttered.

The headlights swept over broken fence posts and a rusted gate hanging open on one hinge like a broken jaw. The land dipped into a hollow, then rose again, the road barely visible beneath overgrown, yellowed grass. The air felt different here. It was colder, thicker, smelling of stagnant water and things that died in the shade.

I felt it before I saw it. That wrongness. That prickle along my spine that told me we were no longer alone in the woods. The trees seemed to lean inward, whispering.

Out of nowhere, I hit the brakes, the truck skidding slightly.

"What is it?" Holt asked. I leaned forward without a word, squinting into the void, and killed the lights.

"You serious? We won't see a foot in front of us."

"Good."

The world dropped into a terrifying, absolute darkness, broken only by the faint, ghostly glow of the dash and the cold, uncaring stars overhead. My eyes adjusted slowly. The silhouettes of the trees emerged, jagged and sharp.

"There," I whispered, pointing through the windshield.

Holt followed my gaze. A faint flicker of light glowed ahead, low and unsteady, half-hidden by a screen of dying pines. It wasn't a fire; it was the sickly, orange light of a fire through a grime-covered window.

"Campfire," he murmured.

"No. It's inside," I said. "It's trouble."

I opened the door, and the hinge let out a faint groan that felt like a betrayal. I grabbed my rifle and stepped out, my boots crunching softly on the gravel. The night air was biting, smelling of damp earth and something sour, the scent of a place that had seen too much shadow. I motioned for Holt to stay put, to be my backup in the dark, then I started forward.

Every step felt like walking toward a cliff edge. I kept low, moving with the slow, agonizing precision of a man walking through a minefield. The cabin emerged from the dark like a wound in the land. The boards were warped and grey with age, looking like the skin of a leper.

And there, parked crooked near the tree line, was the vehicle that made my blood turn to ice.

Her truck.

My pulse slammed so hard it felt like it would burst the vessels in my neck. I crouched behind a fallen, moss-covered log, my heart hammering a frantic rhythm against my ribs. I forced myself to breathe. In. Out. Don't let the rage blind you. Think.

Voices drifted through the thin, rotting walls of the cabin.

A man's voice. It was calm. Horrifyingly controlled. It was the voice of a man who believed he was doing something righteous.

And then, hers.

God, her voice. It was raw, stripped of its usual warmth, sounding like it had been shredded by hours of screaming or silence.

I closed my eyes for half a second, praying to a God I hadn't spoken to in years. When I opened them, the cabin was still there. The orange light was still flickering. This wasn't a nightmare I could wake up from. This was the reality I had to survive.

I edged closer through the wet grass, keeping low and slow, through the wet grass, staying in the deep shadows cast by the pines until I was close enough to hear the individual words, their breathing, the creak of a chair.

"You don't get to decide when I eat," Tessa said. It was a

snarl, but I could hear the exhaustion under it, the way her voice wavered on the edges. "I'm not a child, Colin. I'm not your project."

"You are when you don't take care of yourself," Colin replied. His tone was honeyed, dripping with a poisonous kind of concern. "You're pale, Tessa. You're thin. You've let yourself go since you left. Sit down. Eat the soup. I made it just the way you liked."

"I hate you," she whispered.

"You're just tired," he said, and I could hear the scrape of a bowl across the wood. "Sit down, or I'll have to make you sit. And we both know how much you hate it when I have to be firm."

I saw red. A hot, blinding wash of fury that nearly sent me over the threshold right then. I didn't care about the plan. I didn't care about the law. I only cared about the fact that his hands were anywhere near her.

I stood up. I didn't sneak anymore. I stepped into the spill of light from the window.

"Tessa."

Her name left my mouth like a prayer, a promise, and a death threat all at once.

The silence that followed was absolute. Then frantic movement inside. Tessa turned so fast she nearly stumbled, her face appearing in the window for a fleeting second, white as a sheet, eyes sunken and shadowed, before she rushed toward the door.

She burst through the exit, her face flushing, then crumpling into a mask of pure, unadulterated relief. Her eyes locked onto mine as if she were a drowning woman, and I was the only piece of wood in the ocean. She looked like she was afraid I'd vanish into the mist if she dared to blink.

"Wyatt," she breathed. It wasn't a name; it was a prayer.

Colin stepped out behind her, slow and deliberate, a pistol

pointed at her head. Shock flashed across his face, a momentary flicker of human weakness, before it smoothed into something ugly, smug, and deeply amused. He leaned against the doorframe, the lantern light behind him casting his face in shadow.

"Well," he said, his voice smooth as oil. "Look who finally managed to find the trail. I was starting to think you were losing your touch, cowboy."

I didn't look at him. I couldn't. If I looked at him, I'd kill him, and I needed to make sure Tessa was whole first. My eyes stayed on her, cataloging the damage. The bruise on her cheek. The way she was holding her arm.

"Are you hurt?" I asked.

She shook her head, once, a sharp, jagged motion. "No. I'm okay."

"Did he touch you? Tell me the truth, Tessa."

Her jaw tightened, her eyes darting to Colin and back. "No. Not the way you mean. He just, well..." Her chin quivered.

I growled.

Colin laughed softly, a sound that made the hair on my neck stand up. "Always the hero. Always riding in on a white horse. It's a bit cliché, don't you think?"

I took another step forward, my boots heavy on the earth. Holt appeared at my shoulder, his silhouette massive and intimidating, silent as the grave. He had his hand wrapped around the stock of his shotgun.

"Step away from her, Colin," I said. My voice was quiet now. That was the dangerous part.

"This has nothing to do with you. This is between me and my woman," Colin replied, his eyes narrowing. "You're the interloper here. You're the one trespassing on a private conversation. You don't belong in this story."

"I hate to break the news to you, Colin, but she's *my*

woman." I lowered my rifle, knowing that Holt would put him down without question if needed. Shoving my hands in my pockets, I rocked on my heels. "I haven't required anything of her, other than being who she is, and I've become attached to how she looks at me when I make her fall apart."

I knew I was egging him on, but I needed him to mess up. His weakness was Tessa, and the irony of that was that she was mine too. Tessa's eyes were locked on me, and I felt like we were able to almost telepathically talk to one another.

"He's way better than you ever were, Colin. So even if I left with you, it would be Wyatt I dream of. He's who I'd be thinking of all the time." She smirked, and god I wanted to hide away with her for a month after these last few days.

Colin's jaw twitched; he was getting mad, and the gun in his hand was starting to shake. What I needed to figure out was if it was rage or if it was getting too heavy for him to keep holding.

"Tessa's really bad at poker." I laughed, then I caught Holt's eye, and his look asked what the hell I thought I was doing. "Strip poker really isn't her game."

"Wy, you said you wouldn't bring that up again." She pouted.

"Want to play again with me, baby?"

"Oh, I want to play with you." There was no question she meant the innuendo. Colin grimaced and shoved the gun to Tessa's head. Well fuck that wasn't what I'd planned. Her eyes grew round, and she stared at me again; all the lightness was gone.

"Colin, I'm fucking tired of this. You've got about three seconds," I said, moving my hand toward my belt, "to make the smartest decision of your remaining life. Step off that porch with your hands where I can see them."

He glanced at Holt, seeing the barrel of the shotgun Holt was now leveling, then back at me. A flicker of real, sharp fear finally pierced through his arrogance. "You gonna shoot me in cold blood? In front of her?"

"Yep," I said, my voice as cold as the frost on the ground. "Then I'm going to take her home. I'm going to take her back to the people who actually love her."

Tessa swallowed hard, her eyes darting between us. "Wyatt. Please."

I gave her a small nod.

Colin saw the shift in the air. He saw the way the shadows were closing in. In a desperate, pathetic bid for control, he stepped closer to Tessa, his hand reaching out to brush her arm, a claim, a final act of possession.

She flinched as if he'd branded her with a hot iron.

That was the end of my patience.

I moved. I was across the clearing before he could draw a breath. Holt grabbed him, a blur of motion, slamming him against the side of the cabin with enough force to make the old wood scream. I reached Tessa, catching her as her knees finally gave out. I pulled her against my chest, wrapping my arms around her until she was shielded from the sight of him.

She made a sound halfway between a sob and a gasp, a primal release of air, and clutched at my jacket with both hands. She held on so tight I could feel her knuckles grinding against my ribs. She was terrified that if she let go, the world would dissolve back into that orange-lit room.

"I've got you," I murmured into her hair, the scent of her finally drowning out the rot of the cabin. "I've got you, Tess. You're safe. I promise."

Colin was shouting something incoherent as Holt wrestled him to the ground. Colin's voice was high and reedy now, the mask of the sophisticated predator completely shattered, leaving behind nothing but a small, mean man.

Tessa's breath came in sharp, uneven pulls, her whole body vibrating with a tremor that felt like it might shake her bones apart. All the fight, all the adrenaline that kept her upright for hours, was draining out of her, leaving her heavy in my arms.

"You came," she whispered against my chest.

"Always. Every time. I told you I would."

Sirens began to wail faintly in the distance, a low moan that grew into a scream as they tore through the woods, the blue and red lights beginning to strobe against the trees like a fever dream. The law was coming to clean up the mess, but the damage was already done.

Colin laughed, a wild, broken sound from the dirt where Holt had him pinned. "You think this is over, Wyatt? You think you can just take her and fix her? I'm in her head, I'm the thing she sees when she closes her eyes. She can't outrun me!"

I held Tessa tighter, resting my chin against the top of her head, shutting out his voice. I looked at the cabin—the sagging roof, the diseased light, the wound in the land—and I knew he was right about one thing. It wouldn't be easy. She was safe now, but the recovery would take a lifetime.

THIRTY-SIX

TESSA

I didn't remember the drive. My brain folded in on itself the second Wyatt's hands closed around me outside that cabin, and the world finally stopped tilting. Everything after that blurred like someone dragged water across wet ink.

But I remembered Wyatt's hand on my knee. Heavy. Warm. Steady. An anchor in a world that wouldn't stop spinning.

Every bump in the road vibrated through me. Every breath he took seemed to move straight through my skin. I didn't cling to him, but some part of me leaned toward that heat like it was the only thing keeping me upright. My body reacted before my head caught up, curling toward the place his hand rested.

Holt's voice crackled through the radio in low, broken pieces. He sounded controlled, but too controlled. Shaken under the surface. Like one wrong syllable would shatter something he didn't have the strength to pick up tonight.

Headlights carved tunnels through the dark prairie. They flicked across the windows and caught my reflection again and again. My eyes didn't look like mine. They were too wide, too bright, rimmed with the kind of fear that didn't fade just because the danger moved thirty miles behind you.

My breath kept sticking in my throat.

My chest felt hollow and tight at the same time.

The truck slowed. I felt the shift before I heard it. Gravel crunched beneath the tires. Holt said something through the radio. Wyatt answered, but the words blurred before my brain could make sense of them.

A door opened.

Cold air rushed in.

"Easy," Wyatt said. His voice was rough, low, scraped raw at the edges. "Hey. Look at me."

It took a moment before I realized he was talking to me.

My hands were shaking. I didn't even notice until I saw the tremors catching in the passing glow of the porch light. My teeth began to chatter. Not loud. Not frantic. Just enough that the bones in my jaw clicked.

Wyatt saw it instantly. His whole body shifted toward me.

"Hey," he murmured, voice dropping into something gentle. "You're safe. You hear me."

I nodded because speaking felt impossible.

My tongue was thick. My throat refused to open.

He reached in, helping me down from the truck like I was made of blown glass about to shatter. One hand braced at my elbow. One warm palm steady at the curve of my back. His touch made my knees react, not with fear, but with something like collapsing relief.

I hated that I needed him.

I held on anyway.

The house rose ahead of us with every step. Too bright. Too open. Too safe. My home. Mine. Yet the sight of it made my throat clench in a way I didn't understand.

The porch light spilled in a golden pool across the boards.

And then Dani burst out of the doorway.

She didn't shout my name. She didn't waste time asking questions. She ran straight at me with a sound caught between a sob and an exhale.

She crashed into me with enough force to rock me back.

I let myself fold into her. My fists clutched at her shirt like it was a rope, and I was sliding off a cliff. She smelled like lavender soap and fear and the stale coffee she always forgot in the microwave.

"You're here," she kept whispering. Her breath shook against my ear. "You're here, you're here, you're here."

"I'm here," I whispered back. The words cracked. They scraped out of my chest like something breaking loose.

Wyatt stepped back without being asked. I felt it more than saw it, the way his body withdrew to give us space. It hit me somewhere deep that he knew when to move and when not to.

Dani pulled back just far enough to grab my face in her hands. Her palms were warm. Her thumbs brushed under my eyes as if she was checking for bruises.

"Did he hurt you?" she asked, voice sharp as a blade.

"No." The word flew out fast. Too fast. "No. He didn't."

Her jaw clenched. Her eyes flashed. "I don't care. I'm still going to key his face."

A laugh tried to escape. It came out as a shuddering breath that sounded like a sob.

She kept her hand wrapped around my wrist as she pulled me inside, holding me like she thought the wind might steal me again. The house felt wrong. Familiar, but shifted. Or maybe I was the one who shifted. Maybe something inside me had been rearranged without permission.

Wyatt came after us. He closed the door softly and controlled.

The click of the latch echoed inside my ribs.

Final.

Safe.

Contained.

I sagged into the couch. I didn't remember choosing to sit. My body simply dropped.

Dani hovered like a small, furious hawk before disappearing into the kitchen, muttering threats about blankets and homicide and hydration.

Wyatt stood a few feet away. He didn't fold his arms or loom or fidget. His hands slid into his jacket pockets like he didn't trust them. Dirt streaked his jaw. Sweat dried in the collar of his shirt. There was a scrape across his knuckles, swelling, blood dried dark in the cracks of his skin.

His eyes devoured me.

Trying to decide if I was whole.

Trying to decide if he could breathe yet.

"You need anything?" He asked. His voice was rough and tired. "Anything at all."

"I don't know," I said honestly. The truth felt strange on my tongue. Raw and heavy.

"That's okay. You don't have to know right now."

Dani reappeared with a blanket and a glass of water. Both her hands shook as she draped the blanket over my shoulders. She pressed the glass into my palms like she was handing over something sacred.

"Drink," she ordered.

I obeyed.

The water tasted like metal and dust and safety.

She looked at Wyatt then. Really looked. Something wordless passed between them. A silent conversation layered with gratitude and warning of I swear to God if you break her, I'll bury you in the yard.

"I'm going to make a call," she said. "And then I'm not leaving her side."

Wyatt nodded. "I'll be outside."

"No."

The word ripped out of me and hung in the air.

Both of them froze.

My heart slammed against my ribs.

I felt my pulse in my throat, in my fingertips, everywhere.

"I don't want to be alone," I said. Softer. Smaller. "Not yet."

Wyatt didn't move. He just watched me with that look that made my chest ache. He gave me space to take it back. I didn't.

Dani let out a long breath and nodded. "Fine. But if either of you start trauma bonding or spilling your souls or whatever, I'm throwing something at both of you."

Wyatt's mouth twitched. "Fair."

She stomped down the hall, already dialing.

Silence stretched across the room.

Not awkward.

Just full.

Wyatt finally lowered himself into the chair across from me. He didn't crowd me. He didn't talk. He just sat there with the kind of stillness that made my lungs want to work again.

"You don't have to talk," he finally said.

"I know." My fingers tightened around the blanket. "I know."

My hands trembled. The glass shook. I didn't bother hiding it.

"You scared the hell out of me," he said. Not accusing. Not angry. Just truth.

"I know."

"You don't get to do that again."

My gaze snapped up. His eyes were raw. Not watery. Not shining. Just torn open.

"I didn't mean to," I whispered.

"I don't care," he said quietly. "Meaning to or not, doesn't matter."

Something in my chest shifted. Loosened. Tightened. I didn't know how to hold myself upright under that kind of intensity.

"I didn't think you'd find me."

His jaw flexed. His breath left hard and controlled.

"I was always going to find you."

The certainty in his voice hit me somewhere deep and trembling.

My throat burned.

"Why?"

He didn't blink. Didn't breathe. Didn't look away.

"Because you're mine."

The words crashed into me. Hot. Sharp. Terrifying. Alive.

My pulse spiked so fast my vision shimmered at the edges.

I felt it in my ribs. In my stomach.

He saw the effect immediately. His voice dropped to something rougher.

"Not like ownership, or control. Not anything he ever told you it meant. Mine like I couldn't lose you and stay standing."

My breath wavered.

"You don't owe me anything."

"I know." He leaned forward just enough that I felt heat radiate from his body. "That's why it's mine to give."

The room felt too warm.

Too alive.

Like every molecule shifted toward him.

"I keep thinking I should feel relieved. But mostly I just feel hollow."

"That's shock, it'll pass."

"And then what?"

"Then we deal with the rest."

I huffed out something that wasn't a laugh. "You make it sound easy."

"It's not easy. But it's doable. Especially if you let people help you."

I studied him. The man who tracked me across fields. The man whose voice pulled me out of fear like a rope. The man who held me with both arms when my legs refused to work.

"Thank you," I whispered.

He shook his head. "You don't thank someone for doing what they'd do again without hesitation."

My eyes stung. The room swayed slightly.

"I don't know how to be normal after this."

"You don't have to be normal." His voice softened again. "You just have to be here."

The house creaked. The wind tapped against the window. Dani murmured into her phone down the hall.

I breathed in slowly, the movement shaky but real as Wyatt watched me. Not like I was fragile or broken. Like I was alive.

THIRTY-SEVEN

It was quiet, but not the peaceful kind. The kind that felt like it might snap if I breathed too deeply or moved too fast. Every muscle stiff and sore, my throat dry, my head thick and heavy. For a moment, I didn't know where I was. The ceiling looked wrong. The light slanting through the window didn't match my internal map of the house.

Then I felt it. Weight. Warmth. The faint drag of someone else's breath against my skin.

Wyatt was asleep on the floor beside the couch, long legs folded awkwardly, shoulders braced against the cushions like he'd sat down for a second and his body finally quit on him. His hat lay on the coffee table within reach.

His head was tipped back against the couch, turned just enough that his temple pressed into my bent knees.

Like he needed a point of contact with me before he let himself sleep.

I didn't move at first. I couldn't. The sight of him there made something inside me go soft and sharp all at once, like relief had teeth. He looked wrecked in the honest way men only did when they stopped pretending. Dirt streaked his jaw.

There was a scrape on one knuckle, already swelling. His lashes cast faint shadows under his eyes. His mouth was slightly open as he breathed, slow and even, like his body finally decided it was safe enough to let go.

I could feel the heat of him through the blanket and the thin wall of air between us, even though he wasn't touching me anywhere but my knees.

Dani was sprawled on the far cushion of the couch, curled tight, pink hair a bright mess against the throw pillow. Her hand was still on my thigh, fingers slack now, like she anchored herself there in the night and refused to move. On the other side of me, Maddy was curled into my back, knees tucked close, her arm looped around my waist with unconscious possessiveness. Her breathing was deep and steady, the kind kids managed when their bodies finally decided the world could wait.

Three people. All asleep. All close.

My chest hurt.

I stared at the wall and let my body catch up to the fact that I was here. That I was home. That the air smelled like old wood and dust and coffee instead. Like Uncle Ray had been through the room before I woke up.

My fingers curled into the blanket. My hands were still trembling, faintly, like my nervous system hadn't gotten the memo that the immediate danger passed. My heart thudded heavier than it needed to, each beat a reminder that I was still here, whether I felt ready for that or not.

Wyatt shifted in his sleep. The movement was small, almost nothing, but I felt it through my knees. His brow furrowed for a second, like he was chasing something in the dark. His hand tightened on my ankle, then loosened again.

My stomach rolled. Not with fear this time. With something worse. I swallowed, throat dry, and tried not to replay the night in fragments. The cabin. Colin's voice. The way time twisted into something meaningless. The way I held myself together by sheer spite.

Then Wyatt was there. In the split second, my brain refused to believe it. The way the world snapped back into colour when I saw him standing there, real and furious and steady.

The way I'd run into him like I'd been falling for days.

I turned my head slightly, just enough to look down at him again.

His head was still there, heavy against my knees, like my body was a place he'd chosen to rest.

I lay there for a long time, listening to the house breathe around us. The soft tick of cooling pipes. The faint hum of the fridge. The occasional creak of old wood settling. My own pulse beating too loud in my ears.

Eventually, the urge under my skin got too sharp to ignore.

I needed air. Because if I stayed still one more minute, I was going to start shaking hard enough to wake them all, and I didn't want anyone's eyes on me yet. Not Maddy's. Not Dani's.

And not Wyatt's.

I moved carefully. I slid my leg a fraction, testing whether his head would follow. It didn't. It shifted slightly, then settled back against the couch cushion, his jaw relaxing, his breath deepening like he'd fallen right back into it.

My knees ached where his weight had been. The sensation lingered anyway, like my skin remembered him even when he wasn't touching me.

I eased myself upright, bracing one hand against the couch. My back protested, stiff and sore. My body felt like it had been wrung out and left to dry. The blanket slid off my shoulders and pooled at my hips.

For a second, I just sat there, hovering in the quiet, staring at the three of them like I couldn't quite believe they were real.

My bare feet touched the floor, and the cold shot up my legs, sharp enough to make me suck in a breath. I waited, heart hammering, but nobody moved.

I stepped around Wyatt carefully. His boots were off. His socks were dirty at the heels. There was something almost stupidly intimate about that.

I moved to the front door. A restless pull, like if I didn't get outside I might start crawling out of myself. I eased the door open and stepped onto the porch, letting the cool morning air wash over me.

I breathed in slowly, tasting dew and dirt and the faint bite of autumn creeping closer. The sky was pale and wide, the sun still low enough that the world looked gentler than it had any right to.

The ranch stretched out in front of me, bathed in soft light. The grass glistened faintly. The fence line cut a familiar path toward the south pasture, posts leaning here and there, rails weathered and worn. The barn stood solid and patient, like it always had, red paint faded but stubborn.

I stepped down into the yard, bare feet sinking into cool dirt. The ground felt real under me. Solid. I welcomed the sensation, let it anchor me.

Every step felt deliberate. Measured. Like if I moved too quickly, the decision waiting for me might lunge out of the dark and demand an answer I didn't have yet.

I reached the fence and rested my hands on the top rail. The wood was rough under my palms, splintered in places, familiar enough that my hands knew where to settle without thinking.

This land had shaped me. It raised me. It had bruised me. It taught me how to stand back up when everything hurt. It had also taken from me in ways I hadn't been ready for.

Ray. The debts. The silence he left behind. The weight of a legacy I wasn't sure I could carry without breaking.

I could leave.

The thought slid through me smooth and tempting. The city waited with its clean lines and predictable systems. No fences to mend. No machinery held together by stubbornness and hope. No memories lurking in every corner. And Wyatt would buy it.

I didn't let myself dwell on that too long, but the thought lingered anyway. The ease of it. The relief. The constant tightness in my chest might finally loosen if I handed this responsibility over to someone who knew exactly what he was doing.

My hands tightened on the rail until my knuckles ached.

I hated how much sense that made. I hated even more that part of me trusted him with it.

A sound broke the morning quiet behind me. The front door jerked open hard enough that the hinges complained. Footsteps hit the porch, fast. Heavy. Barely controlled.

I flinched instinctively and turned.

Wyatt was in the doorway, shirt rumpled, hair flattened on one side, eyes wide and sharp with the kind of fear that didn't belong on him. He scanned the yard like he expected to find emptiness. Like he expected to find proof, I vanished again.

His gaze locked onto me at the fence. Relief hit his face so hard it almost looked like pain.

He crossed the yard in long strides, his breathing not quite steady yet.

"Jesus," he said when he reached me. His voice was rough, scraped raw. "You vanished."

"I needed air."

"You didn't say anything."

"I didn't want to wake anyone."

His jaw worked as he studied me, eyes flicking over my bare feet, my posture, the way my hands gripped the fence like it was the only thing holding me upright.

"You scared me," he said quietly, as he reached out and pulled me into his embrace.

My throat tightened. "I'm sorry."

He shook his head once. "I'm not angry."

We stood there in silence, our arms wrapped around one another, the morning stretching out wide and uncertain. His presence felt heavy and grounding all at once. I could feel the pull of him even now, the way my body registered him without my permission.

"I don't know what I'm doing," I whispered.

"You don't need to figure it out right now," he said. I glanced at him. His gaze was fixed on the pasture, expression unreadable. The morning light caught in his eyes, turning them a softer blue than usual.

"You're thinking about selling."

I stiffened.

"I'm not asking," he added quickly. "I can just see it on your face."

I exhaled slowly. "I'm thinking about everything."

"That's fair."

"I don't want to lose this place. But I don't know if I can save it."

He didn't answer right away. When he did, his voice was steady. "Whatever you decide, it should be because it's right for you. Not because you're scared. Not because you think you owe anyone anything."

I swallowed. "That's a lot easier to say when you're not the one drowning."

He turned to face me fully then. "I know."

Something about the way he said it made my chest ache.

We stood there, wrapped in one another, the fence creaking softly under our weight, the land stretching out in front of us like it was waiting for something I wasn't ready to say.

Thirty-Eight

The noise drained out of the brewery slowly. The last clink of glass. The scrape of chairs being turned upside down and stacked, employees waving as they left for the night. The hum of the refrigeration system took over, settling into a lower register, like a living thing easing into sleep. By the time I locked the front door and slid the bolt home, the space felt different. Intimate. Watchful. Like it knew something was about to happen and was willing to keep the secret.

She'd come in as the last customer left and stood near the bar. She ordered a drink, her fingers wrapped around a lowball glass she hadn't taken a sip from. Her hair was loose, falling over one shoulder in a way that felt deliberate even if it wasn't. Like she'd dressed for herself and ended up dressed for me anyway.

She looked over her shoulder when she heard me coming behind her.

"You're closed now?" she asked. Her voice was steadier than I expected. Mine wasn't.

"Yeah, just you and me."

She nodded once, like that answered something inside her. "Good."

I set my keys down on the bar slower than necessary. Gave myself a moment to breathe. To remember she'd been through hell and that wanting her didn't give me the right to take anything from her she didn't offer.

She watched me do it. I could see the flicker of awareness cross her face. The way her shoulders dropped a fraction, like she noticed I wasn't going to rush her.

"I wasn't sure you'd still be here."

"I wasn't sure you'd come."

A ghost of a smile touched her mouth. "Guess we were both wrong."

I moved behind the bar on instinct, poured her water without asking, and set it in front of her. She didn't reach for it. Her eyes stayed on me instead, following the movement of my hands like she was grounding herself in something solid.

"How are you?"

She huffed a quiet laugh. "That's a loaded question."

"I know."

She leaned against the bar, glass forgotten. "I'm here."

It wasn't much. It was everything.

I nodded. "That's enough."

Her gaze sharpened at that, something flickering low and hot beneath the exhaustion I knew too well. She pushed away from the bar and moved before stopping close enough that I could feel her heat, the faint tremor running through her like her body hadn't quite decided it was done reacting yet.

"You keep saying things like that," she said softly. "Like you don't need anything from me."

I swallowed. "I don't."

"That's a lie."

I met her eyes. Didn't flinch. "It's not."

She studied my face like she was searching for a crack, a

tell, something she could call out and use as an excuse to pull back. When she didn't find it, her breath shuddered out of her.

"I didn't come to thank you."

"I know."

"I didn't come to talk about what happened."

"I know."

"I came because everything still feels wrong," she said, the words finally roughening. "Because I wake up and it's like my body doesn't belong to me yet. Because I don't know how to be normal again, and I needed something to remind me that I'm still here."

I didn't move. Didn't touch her. Didn't give her anything she hadn't asked for.

She stepped closer anyway.

Her fingers brushed the edge of my shirt, tentative at first, like she was checking whether the ground would hold. When I didn't stop her, didn't lean in or take over, her hand flattened against my chest, warm and steady, and something in her expression shifted.

She kissed me like she'd already made peace with the consequences.

It wasn't frantic. It wasn't desperate. It was slow and deliberate and full of intent, like she was choosing the moment instead of being carried by it. Her mouth was warm, soft, insistent in a way that sent a jolt straight through me, down to a place I hadn't let myself acknowledge since the night I'd found her.

I let her lead. Let her set the pace. When she pulled back, breath uneven, I rested my forehead against hers and forced myself to stay right there.

"You sure?" I asked quietly.

"Yes."

It wasn't hesitation in her eyes. It was hunger. It was

need braided with fear and the fierce determination of someone who decided she was done being afraid of her own body.

I kissed her again, deeper this time, my hands finding her waist, her back, the curve of her spine under my palms. She made a sound low in her throat that felt like it was meant only for me, and the restraint I'd been holding onto tightened, not loosened. Care sharpened it. Focused it.

The brewery disappeared around us.

There was only the press of her body, the way she fit against me like she'd always known where she belonged, the way her fingers slid up my arms and hooked into my shoulders like she was anchoring herself to something solid. The taste of her. The sound of her breathing. The heat that built between us, slow and relentless, until it felt like the only honest thing left.

Moving my hand to the back of her head, she instinctively pulled to the side, letting my lips slide down to her neck and tasting the sweetness of her skin.

I couldn't get enough of her and needed more than just a little taste.

Slowly, I moved her toward the fireplace, the warmth of its flames cutting through the early autumn night. Letting her go, I grabbed a blanket from the cupboard.

"You have everything here," she said as I spread it out on the floor.

"The customers like them in the winter." I held out my hand for her, and I sat on the floor, pulling her down so she was straddling my lap.

I didn't think my cock could get any harder, but it strained against my jeans, begging for release.

My kisses trailed down Tessa's neck to her shirt, where I slowly undid the first button, smiling when I realized it was a pearl snap and came undone easily. She helped me by unbuttoning her shirt the rest of the way, revealing the swell of her beautiful breasts barely encased in a black lace bra.

My mouth watered as I pushed aside the thin material and circled one of her pretty pink buds with my tongue, teasing her other breast with my free hand.

She moaned, her hips instinctively bucking closer to me.

I kissed down her chest and stomach, moving my hands between us to unbuckle her jeans.

I thought she'd protest or give me some kind of smart comment, but instead she leaned back before she stood again, letting me slide off her jeans and revealing her beautiful, bare pussy, already wet and waiting.

I met her heated gaze as I spread her legs before I slowly flattened my tongue against her sensitive flesh.

She shivered, opening her legs wider to feast on her beautiful pussy.

Tessa leaned back against the stone of the fireplace as I pushed my face deeper, burying my tongue in her sweet heat as she gasped in delight, her hips bucking toward my awaiting mouth as if she couldn't wait for more.

Sliding my hand up her leg, I curled a finger inside of her wet pussy, moving it in the same rhythm as my tongue on her clit, just the way she liked it.

Her breathing was labored as her hips pressed toward my face with wild abandon, her whole body shaking as she came hard, and I lapped up every bit of it.

But that wasn't enough. I needed more of Tessa. I loved hearing her moan and the way she felt when she came undone for me.

"Wyatt," she gasped.

"Yes, baby?" I asked, meeting her hooded gaze before sucking long and hard on her clit.

"I need you in me," she moaned, her legs shaking, barely keeping her standing.

"Not until you come on my tongue again. I want to taste you before I fuck you," I murmured into her soft flesh, kissing her mound before diving my tongue back in.

"Wyatt," she breathed hard, her hips moved erratically, chasing her own high.

I added another finger inside her, hooking it toward the spot she liked.

I was rewarded when she gushed, her whole body shaking as she rode out her orgasm on my awaiting lips.

I lapped up every last bit of her, her breathing still ragged as I slowly stood up.

Unbuckling my jeans, I met her heated gaze. Her face flushed from the orgasms, and a lazy smile was on her face. "Lay down," I said as I stood and kissed her hard.

Pulling a foil packet out of my wallet, I tossed the rest of it aside, not caring that my jeans were at my ankles and my shirt still on.

I just needed to fill Tessa. She spread her legs for me to kneel between them as I rolled the rubber over my cock, I slid closer, letting just the head press against her pussy.

She moaned, immediately spreading her legs further for me.

"What if I said it was time to close the bar and I needed to head home?" I asked, stroking the base of my cock as I locked eyes with her.

She bolted upright, sitting up and gripping my shoulders. "Wyatt, if you don't fuck me right now, I may combust."

I laughed, putting one arm around her waist and pulling her flush against me, the head of my cock seeking out her entrance.

"Okay, okay, I guess I can give you what you want."

I sealed my words by kissing her, putting everything into it that I couldn't say out loud.

I wanted to tell her that my time with her had been the best I ever had.

How I loved not just the taste of her and fucking her but being with her.

I filled her slowly, but my girl was always greedy. She gripped my ass, filling her to the hilt as if she couldn't get enough.

Our bodies moved together, the music still streaming around us as our heavy breathing matched its rhythm.

I knew I was close, but couldn't end it without feeling her come on my cock again.

Sliding my hand between us, I found her clit, still continuing my thrusts.

"Fuck, Wyatt," she murmured, gripping onto my shoulders as her body shook around me.

It didn't take long for her to moan, pulsing as we came together, her beautiful pussy milking my cock.

I didn't stop until I knew she released every last drop, and then I slumped down, my legs like gelatine as I leaned on her for support, leaving small kisses along her bare shoulders.

She lay against me, cheek pressed to my chest, listening to my heartbeat like she was memorizing it. My hand traced slow, grounding lines along her back, felt the rise and fall of her breath gradually even out. The quiet settled around us again, deeper now, weighted with something neither of us could pretend wasn't real.

"This doesn't fix anything," she said eventually.

"I know."

"It doesn't make it better."

"I know."

She lifted her head, looked at me like she needed to see whether I'd changed my mind. "Then why does it feel like I can breathe again?"

"Because you let yourself. Not because of me."

She considered that, then nodded like she'd accept it for now.

We dressed slowly. Not awkward. Not rushed. The kind of quiet that didn't need filling. When she finally stepped back, there was something resolved in her posture that hadn't been there before.

"I can't do this again."

I didn't ask what this meant. I already knew.

"I know."

"I'm going to need space. And I don't know what that looks like yet."

"I know."

Her eyes softened, just a little. "You make it hard to walk away."

I held her gaze. "That's not a reason to stay."

She exhaled, long and shaky. "No. It's not."

At the door, she paused, hand on the handle, and looked back at me one last time.

"Thank you," she said, and this time she meant something different.

I nodded once. Let her go.

The door closed behind her with the same quiet finality as the night she'd come home shaken and broken but alive.

I stood there long after she was gone, the brewery breathing around me again, knowing with bone-deep certainty that this wasn't the end.

Thirty-Nine

The house was quiet with no Dani roaming around at all hours. Just the soft settling of old boards and the faint, constant hum of the fridge, like it was trying to pretend life was still normal.

I spread the paperwork across Ray's kitchen table.

It wasn't one stack. It was five. Bank notices with their polite threats. Tax arrears that didn't care about funerals. Statements with numbers that didn't feel real until I read them twice, and my stomach tightened like I swallowed a fist. Equipment loan forms. Letters I hadn't opened until now because I'd been clinging to the lie that if I didn't look, it wouldn't be there.

I sat down hard, the chair scraping against the floor, and stared at the pages in front of me until the words blurred.

My hands didn't shake anymore. That was the scary part. Something in me had gone still, like a lake after a storm when everything sinks to the bottom, and you can't tell what's alive and what's drowned.

I opened one envelope over, then another, then another,

making myself read the dates like they were facts and not accusations.

Past due.

Final notice.

Recovery.

I swallowed, and it scraped.

"Okay," I said out loud, because if I didn't speak, I was going to disappear. "Okay, Ray. Here's where we're at."

My voice sounded wrong in the empty kitchen. Too small for the weight of what I laid out. I pressed my palm flat to the table, feeling the grooves in the wood, the nicks and scratches he'd never bothered sanding down because work mattered more than pretty.

The coffee mug Dani left sat near the sink. Pink lipstick on the rim, proof that someone had been here to hold me together for a couple of days, and then had gone back to a life that didn't revolve around my grief and my ranch falling apart.

I couldn't blame her.

I couldn't even blame myself.

I could blame Ray, though. Just a little. Enough to keep breathing.

"You left me a mess," I said, and my throat tightened, but I didn't let it break.

The air didn't answer. The house didn't creak in response either. So I kept going, because apparently I was the only one who could.

"I've got two choices," I told him, tapping the table twice like it could anchor me. "I fight for this, or I don't. I stay, and I bleed for it, or I cut it loose before it bleeds me dry."

I shifted papers, lined them up, tried to make the chaos look orderly enough that I could stand to look at it. The numbers didn't soften. They didn't care that I'd grown up feeding calves behind this barn or that my first scar had come from this property or that I'd learned to swear in this kitchen when I was too young for it.

The numbers stayed sharp.

My jaw ached from clenching.

"Wyatt's offer would fix it," I whispered, and the words tasted like betrayal even though they were true. "It'd solve the immediate problem. It'd stop the auction and the vultures and the phone calls."

I saw his face in my mind without asking for it.

The way he looked when he found me, like he held his breath for days and only exhaled when I was safe. The scrape on his knuckle. The exhaustion under his calm. His hand on my knee in the truck, heavy and steady, like he was telling my body it was allowed to exist.

It wasn't the time for that memory. It wasn't fair. It made everything tilt. I shoved the thought away and focused on the table.

"But if I sell," I said, firmer now, "I lose it. I lose the land, what you built. I lost what you wanted."

Did I actually know what he'd wanted?

Not the version I'd built in my head. Not the myth of Ray Callahan, stubborn rancher, silent guardian, man who never asked for help and never offered softness.

The real man.

The one who'd written a list that included telling me he was proud, like it was just another chore he'd get to when the weather cleared.

Call Tessa. Ask about her job. Tell her I'm proud.

I stared at the table until my eyes stung.

"You didn't even get to that," I said, and the steadiness in my voice slipped. Just a fraction. "You died before you could do the one thing I needed you to do."

My chest tightened hard enough I had to bend forward,

elbows on the table, forehead hovering above the papers like I might drop into them and vanish.

I breathed through my nose.

In. Out.

In. Out.

The way I used to before a hard case at work, when a dog was snarling, and an owner was crying, and I had to be the calm one because nobody else could.

I was always the calm one and I didn't want to be that one anymore.

"I don't know what you thought you were protecting," I said quietly. "But you didn't protect me. You just left me alone with it."

The silence stayed.

My eyes slid to the far end of the counter, to the corner where Ray kept the mail sorted with a stubborn sort of logic only he understood. A small wooden rack with slots labelled in his uneven scrawl. Feed. Vet. Taxes.

I pushed back from the table and stood. My legs felt heavy, like my bones were filled with sand. I walked to the rack and ran my fingers along the edges, then opened the drawer beneath it.

It stuck, like it always had. Ray had meant to sand it down for years and never bothered.

I yanked harder. The drawer gave with a groan, and the sound made my skin prickle. Inside was the usual chaos. Old receipts. Elastics. A flashlight. A pocketknife. A folded map of the county that looked like it'd been opened and closed a thousand times.

And an envelope.

Not new. Not crisp.

Yellowed slightly at the edges like it'd been handled, then hidden, then handled again.

My name was on the front.

Tessa.

No last name. No address. Just my name, in Ray's handwriting.

My lungs stalled.

For a second, I couldn't move, like my body didn't trust what my eyes were telling it. Heat rose under my skin, then drained away so fast my fingers went cold.

I took the envelope out like it might bite.

It was thick, more than a single sheet. The paper inside pressed against the flap.

I sat down at the table again without remembering the steps between the drawer and the chair. My hands hovered over the envelope, and my heart started doing that awful thing where it beat too hard and too fast like it was trying to escape.

I stared at my own name until the letters swam.

"Of course," I whispered, because what else could I say? "Of course, you wrote a letter."

My fingers trembled as I slid a nail under the flap and tore it open. The rip sounded obscene in the quiet kitchen, too loud, too final, like I was tearing through something that was supposed to stay sealed.

Inside were three pages, folded carefully, and a smaller slip of paper tucked behind them.

I didn't look at the slip yet.

I unfolded the first page.

Ray's handwriting met me like a fist and a hand at the same time. Uneven, slanted, pressure heavy enough to leave grooves.

> Tess,
> If you're reading this, then I didn't get the chance to say this out loud, and I'm sorry for that.

I'm sorry for a lot, but I'm not good at saying it when there's air and eyes and time moving. Paper's easier. Always was.

I swallowed so hard my throat burned.

My vision blurred. I blinked hard and forced myself to keep reading.

I know you're mad at me. You've got every right. I left you too much to carry and not enough warning. I told myself I was sparing you, but the truth is I was sparing myself the look on your face if you knew how bad it'd gotten. Pride's a disease in men like me. It doesn't kill you all at once, it just eats the good parts first.

My chest tightened. I pressed the heel of my palm to my sternum like I could hold my ribs in place.

He kept going.

You've got a choice to make, and I won't pretend you don't. You can sell. You can stay. Either way, I need you to hear this plainly.

None of this was ever supposed to be a chain around your neck.

I breathed in, and it shuddered on the way out.

My fingers gripped the page too hard, the paper bending slightly under the pressure.

I made this place because I didn't know how to

make anything else. I loved it because it gave me work, quiet, and something I could fix with my own two hands. But I never wanted it to be the thing that kept you from having a life.

I never wanted you to feel like you owed me.

My eyes stung, and the sting turned into heat behind them, and then into a sharp wet pressure that made my throat close.

I inhaled through it.

I kept reading.

I didn't tell you everything because I knew you, Tess. I knew you'd come running. You'd have dropped your life and pretended it was your choice, and you'd have called it duty, and you'd have stayed out of stubbornness and guilt. And I couldn't stomach the thought of you living that way.

If I'd told you the truth, you'd have stayed for the wrong reasons.

I went still.

The words didn't look like much on the page. Just ink. Just a sentence.

But something in my body reacted like it'd been struck.

My hands went numb. My scalp prickled. My stomach rolled, slow and sick, like it was trying to decide whether it wanted to empty itself or turn into stone.

The truth.

He'd said it twice now, in two different ways, like he'd been circling it.

I read the sentence again, slower.

If I'd told you the truth, you'd have stayed for the wrong reasons.

My pulse thudded hard against my throat. I tasted metal.

I forced myself to move. I turned the page with fingers that didn't feel like mine.

I don't know what you remember about your mother. I don't know what you remember about coming to me, and it wasn't my story to tell. But I'm telling you now, because you deserve to know and because I don't want you to spend your life thinking you were unwanted.

You were wanted.

You were loved.

You were mine before you ever knew my name.

The kitchen tipped.

Not literally, but it felt like it, like gravity changed its mind and for one hot second the world didn't know which way was down.

My lungs locked.

I tried to breathe and couldn't.

A sound came out of me, small and raw, like a wounded animal. I pressed my hand over my mouth to choke it back, but the tears came anyway, hot and fast, spilling down my cheeks and onto the paper.

I shook my head once, hard, like I could throw the sentence off my skin.

"You're lying," I whispered to the empty house, but my voice sounded thin and terrified, and I already knew he wasn't.

I wiped my face with the back of my wrist and looked again. The words didn't change.

You were mine before you ever knew my name.

My stomach flipped, hard enough that I had to put my head down for a second. The table was cool against my forehead. The paperwork under my arms crinkled. My breath came in sharp pulls, too shallow, too fast.

"No," I whispered. "No, no, no."

Because it didn't make sense.

Because it made too much sense.

Because all the little things I'd filed away as Ray being Ray suddenly shifted into a different shape.

The way he watched me without looking like he was watching. The way he corrected my posture when I was a kid and then pretended he hadn't. The way he showed up to my high school graduation and stood at the back like he didn't deserve a seat, and the way his eyes had been wet when he thought no one could see.

The way he never called me kiddo. Never called me sweetheart. Never used language that might claim me out loud, like he didn't trust himself with it.

My hands started shaking, properly this time. Not the faint tremor from shock. The real kind. The kind that rattled my teeth and made my skin feel too tight.

I forced myself upright again. My eyes locked onto the page like if I stopped reading I might stop existing.

I took you because she wasn't fit. And I did... I did the best I could with what I had, which wasn't much besides land and work and a quiet house.

I didn't tell you because I didn't want you to feel like you had to stay.

I wanted you free.

Free to go to the city and hate the dust and love whatever you loved.

Free to be angry at me if you needed to be.

Free to walk away and not feel like you were leaving your own blood behind.

I swallowed and tasted salt.

My fingers curled around the page so tightly my knuckles ached.

Behind the words, behind the lines, I could hear his voice. Gruff. Matter of fact. Terrible at softness, even when he was trying.

And somehow that made it worse.

You'll have questions I can't answer because I won't be here. I'm sorry for that, too. But here's what I need you to hear, Tess.

You don't owe me anything.

Not the ranch. Not your time. Not your life.

If you stay, stay because it's what you want.

If you go, go knowing I loved you the whole damn time.

I cried then.

Not pretty. Not quiet. Ugly, shaking sobs that bent me over the table until my ribs hurt and my throat went raw.

Because I spent my whole life thinking I'd been left twice.

Left by parents who didn't want me.

Left by a man who kept me at arm's length like I was temporary.

And now I was holding proof that the only person who had stayed, really stayed, had been the one I accused of never choosing me at all.

I dragged in air, and it snagged. My chest felt split open.

I wiped my face again and stared at the bottom of the last page.

There was a final line, pressed hard into the paper.

I'm proud of you. I was proud of you before you could walk.

Love,

Ray

My vision blurred so badly I had to blink repeatedly just to keep the ink in focus.

I sat there for a long time, letter trembling in my hands, breath coming uneven, my body caught between grief and something else I couldn't name. Something that felt like a wound and a balm at the same time.

Eventually, my eyes dropped to the smaller slip of paper tucked behind the pages.

It was folded once.

I opened it with shaking fingers.

A birth certificate. My original one, the one he said was tucked away for safekeeping.

Father: Raymond Callahan.

My stomach dropped again, but this time it didn't take me with it. It settled, heavy and awful and real.

I stared at it until the paper stopped meaning words and started meaning facts.

I didn't speak. I couldn't.

The kitchen clock ticked quietly like it hadn't just watched my whole life rearrange itself.

Somewhere outside, a bird called and then went silent.

My hands finally lowered to the table. The letter and the birth certificate lay in front of me like a final piece to a puzzle that I hadn't known was missing.

I pressed my palms flat on either side of them and closed my eyes.

The grief was still there. The debt was still there. The ranch was still breaking down around the edges. Colin still put me in a cage and made my body learn fear in a new language.

My chest rose and fell slowly, like my body was finally remembering how to breathe without panicking. I opened my eyes.

The paperwork was still spread across the table. The numbers were still sharp.

But the decision inside me shifted, quiet as a hinge turning.

I looked at the letter again.

Then I looked at the stacks of debt.

Then I stared past the window, out toward the yard where the fence line cut across the pasture like a promise that could be repaired if someone stayed long enough to do it.

My throat tightened, but my voice came steady when I finally spoke.

"Okay," I whispered, and the word didn't break this time. "Okay, Dad."

The title felt strange on my tongue. Too late. Too heavy.

But it was true.

"I hear you," I said, staring at the land like he might be standing out there with his thermos, squinting at problems like he could bully them into behaving. "I'll choose."

I rest my hand over the letter, palm pressing gently, like I could hold him in place for another second.

And I didn't say what the choice was out loud.

Not yet.

But my body already knew.

Because for the first time since I'd come home, it didn't feel like the ranch was a trap.

It felt like a place that had been waiting for me to stop running.

I gathered the pages carefully, folded them back into the envelope with hands that still trembled, and held it against my chest.

Then I sat there in the quiet kitchen for a long time, letting the truth settle into my bones, letting it hurt, letting it warm, letting it change the shape of everything.

While outside, the wind moved through the grass.

Reaching for my phone, I sent a text.

> Me: Hey, can you have Jackson watch my animals for a bit?

> Brooke: Sure, it's no problem. Are you okay?

> Me: Yeah, I just have to go to Calgary.

> Brooke: You've got a permanent place here if you want it.

> Me: Thanks.

FORTY

WYATT

The brewery usually settled me. Even on bad days, even when the fermenters ran a degree hot or a delivery showed up late, or a batch didn't taste the way it should, there was a rhythm here I could lean on. Stainless steel. Clean lines. Honest work. If something went sideways, you could trace it back and fix it.

That morning, I'd been chasing that feeling like it was a rope I could grab before I went under.

I started before dawn, walking the floor with a coffee that'd gone lukewarm, checking valves and taps and inventory with the kind of focus that wasn't focus at all. It was avoidance dressed up as responsibility. It was me trying to keep my mind on kegs and numbers instead of the quiet stretch of days where I hadn't heard Tessa's voice.

She asked me not to come around.

She hadn't said it with cruelty, but it still landed like a gate slamming shut. I told myself it was fair. I'd told myself she needed space, and I wasn't the sort of man who took a woman's boundary and treated it like a suggestion. I'd told myself a hundred things, and most of them sounded good until the nights hit and the valley went dark and my phone stayed silent.

By the time the sun climbed high enough to throw light through the big front windows, the place smelled like fresh mash and citrus cleaner and the faint metallic tang that clung to everything in a working brewery. It should've felt like home.

It didn't. Not today.

I was at the bar with a clipboard in front of me, pretending I cared about a delivery schedule, when the front doorbell chimed.

We weren't open yet. Only the staff came through that door before hours.

I didn't look up right away. I heard boots on wood, slow and heavy, and my chest tightened before my brain caught up. Holt didn't walk like he had time to spare. Holt didn't come into town for no reason.

When I lifted my eyes, he was standing just inside the doorway, cap pushed back, jaw set like it was the only way he kept his teeth from grinding through each other. Dust clung to his jeans. His shirt was darkened with sweat at the collar.

He looked like a man carrying news he hated.

"Boss," he said.

I set the clipboard down carefully. Too carefully. Like if I moved too fast, I'd spook whatever was about to happen next.

"What is it?" I asked.

Holt didn't come further in. He stayed by the door as if he needed the exit close, as if he'd driven hard and planned to drive harder.

His gaze met mine and held. No humour. No softness. Just blunt honesty.

"Her truck's gone," he said.

For half a second, I didn't understand the sentence. It didn't attach itself to meaning. It hovered.

Then it landed.

It landed so hard my stomach dropped, and my skin went cold.

"What," I said, and the word came out flat, not because I wasn't feeling anything, but because there was too much, all at once, and my mouth didn't know what to do with it.

Holt swallowed. "I went up the lane. Just like you told me, and I checked the yard first."

I stared at him, unblinking.

He took a breath, slow and controlled, like he was keeping himself steady on purpose for me. "The house was dark. No movement. No smoke. No sound. I waited a minute and called her name a few times."

My hands curled around the edge of the bar without me deciding to. The wood felt solid under my palms. I needed something solid.

"And," I said.

Holt's jaw flexed. "Nothing."

"Did you go inside?"

"No," he said, and there was a bite to it, like he already knew I'd hate that answer. "You've been clear about not crossing her line. I knocked, and nobody answered."

My throat tightened. "The barn."

"I checked it," Holt continued. "Everything looked in order. Water tanks full, the feed bins were closed. No gates swinging open. Everything was normal, except she wasn't there."

Normal. That word didn't belong. Nothing about the last few weeks had been normal.

I forced my fingers to loosen on the bar. "So she could've been out."

"Maybe," Holt said. My pulse thudded hard enough I could hear it. I felt it in my throat. In my wrists. In my teeth.

"Maybe she came to town," I said, though it sounded thin even to me.

Holt's eyes stayed on mine. "Then she'd have left tracks. Yard looked settled. Dust on the step. No fresh tire marks I could see. If she left, it wasn't this morning."

I swallowed again. It didn't help.

"How long?" I asked.

Holt shook his head. "Can't say. A few days, I'd guess."

She asked me not to come around. I listened and gave her space. And now she was gone.

I pushed away from the bar and started walking without thinking, a line behind the counter, then back again, like movement could keep panic from taking root.

Holt tracked me with his gaze. "Wyatt."

I stopped. My boots planted hard. "Did you see any note?"

"No," he said.

My jaw clenched so tight it hurt. I dragged in a breath through my nose, slow, controlled, the way I did when I needed to keep my temper from deciding for me.

"Okay," I said.

Holt's brows pulled together. "Okay."

"Did you call Dani," I asked.

"Went straight to voicemail," Holt said. "Twice."

That didn't settle anything. It made it worse.

My phone vibrated on the bar where I left it. The sound cut through my chest like a hook. I lunged for it before I could talk myself out of it. For a split second, I expected to see her name, to see some message that explained everything, that made it all make sense.

It wasn't her.

It was a number I didn't recognize, but the first three digits were local, and something in my gut tightened.

I answered. "Wyatt Hargrove."

"Mr. Hargrove," a woman said, professional and too bright, like she'd been trained to keep her voice steady no matter what kind of mess she was calling about. "This is Marlene Fisher from the credit union."

My blood cooled again. Different cold this time. The cold of paperwork and signatures and consequences.

"I'm busy," I said bluntly.

"I understand," she replied smoothly, not missing a beat. "It won't take long. I'm calling regarding the Callahan estate."

Holt's head lifted slightly, attention sharpening.

My stomach turned. "What about it?"

"We've received confirmation from the county and from the estate's legal representative," Marlene said, as she shuffled some papers around. "We've been given the green light to proceed with the purchase agreement submitted by Hargrove Brewing." The words didn't make sense together. Green light. Purchase agreement. Hargrove Brewing. Callahan estate.

It took a second for my mind to catch up, and when it did, anger flashed so hard behind my eyes I saw spots.

"What," I said again, rougher this time. "What did you just say?"

There was a pause on the line, a polite recalibration. "We can proceed, Mr. Hargrove. The necessary authorizations are in place, so we can finalize the terms of the sale and begin the transfer process as early as this afternoon."

My grip tightened on the phone until my knuckles ached. "Who authorized it?"

"I can't disclose details over the phone," she said, still polite. "But the estate has provided the required documentation."

The estate. There was only one person who could've done that. Tessa.

My chest went tight, tight enough that breathing took effort.

Holt's voice was low beside me. "What's happening?"

I held up a hand, not looking at him, my eyes fixed on a

spot on the bar top like if I looked away, I'd lose my grip on myself.

"Marlene," I said, keeping my voice even by force, "are you telling me Tessa Callahan signed my letter of offer?"

Another pause. Not uncertainty. Caution.

"I'm telling you the file has been cleared to move forward," she said. "The seller's side has indicated acceptance and provided the documentation we need."

My throat burned. "When."

"Two days ago," she replied.

I dragged my hand down my face, feeling the roughness of my own stubble. "I'll call you back."

"Mr. Hargrove," Marlene said quickly, "there are timing considerations. If you'd like to maintain the current terms, we'll need confirmation from you today."

"Fine," I snapped. I softened it a fraction because she didn't deserve my temper. "Fine. I'll be in touch." I ended the call and stood there with the phone still pressed to my ear like my body hadn't caught up to the fact that the conversation was over.

The brewery suddenly felt too quiet. The hum of refrigeration. The faint drip of a tap line. The distant clink of glass as someone in the back moved a crate.

Holt stared at me. "What?"

I lowered the phone slowly. My voice came out like gravel. "The bank says they've got the green light to accept my offer on Ray's place."

Holt's face hardened. "What, how?"

I didn't answer because answering made it real.

Holt swore under his breath, sharp and vicious. "So she's gone?"

I swallowed. "Looks like it." A tight silence stretched between us.

Something hot rose in my chest, fierce and ugly. It wasn't

just anger. It was grief tangled up in it. Grief because I'd thought after everything, after being dragged out of that cabin, after breathing again on her couch with Dani and Maddy nearby, she'd at least let herself be held for a minute longer.

Instead, she disappeared. She'd chosen a clean cut and made a decision that looked, on paper, like she surrendered.

I wanted to slam my fist into the bar hard enough to crack the wood. I didn't. I kept my hands flat. I kept my voice low.

"I told myself this might happen," I said to Holt, more confession than conversation. "I told myself she'd either dig in and fight, or she'd bolt."

Holt's expression didn't soften. "Don't take it personally."

"It is personal," I said, and the truth came out sharper than I intended. "Because she didn't just accept the offer. She did it without telling me. She didn't even give me the chance to be honest with her about what she means to me."

Holt's gaze held mine. "Maybe she didn't want your honesty."

That hit. It hit because it wasn't impossible.

I exhaled slowly. "No. She wanted control. She wanted to do it on her terms. And she knows if she looks me in the eye, she wouldn't be able to go through with it."

Holt's jaw flexed. "You think she cares that much."

I heard my own heartbeat again, loud and stubborn. "I know she does."

The certainty tasted like arrogance. It also tasted like the only thing keeping me upright.

I looked past Holt to the front windows. Outside, Main Street went on living. People walked by with coffees and dogs and nothing on their faces that suggested the world was tilting.

Tessa had vanished into that normal, and she'd done it quietly, like she was trying not to leave ripples. "Where do you think she went?" Holt asked.

"There's only one place she has to go," I said without hesitation. "Back to Dani. Back to the apartment. Back to a place where she doesn't have to look at Ray's handwriting on every damn label and feel like she's failing him."

Holt nodded once. "So what now?"

I looked down at my phone in my hand. The bank's number still sat on the screen like a dare.

What now?

A version of me wanted to chase her immediately. Drive hard. Show up at her door. Demand explanations. Demand she look at me and tell me to my face she was walking away.

That version of me was angry and hurt and selfish.

The version of me that mattered, the one that had promised Ray, the one that held her when she broke, knew what I actually had to do.

I had to fix the problem she thought she was solving by making this decision. If nothing else, I would make sure she didn't lose her land because she was terrified.

I had to accept the sale and erase the debt without taking what wasn't mine. And I had to do it in a way that left no room for ambiguity, no loopholes, no bank clawing it back later, no developer circling with paper and smiles.

My throat tightened again, but my voice steadied. "Now I go to the credit union."

Holt's brows rose. "You're going to sign today."

"I'm going to control the terms," I said.

Holt stared at me. "You're going to buy her ranch."

"I'm going to pay off Ray's debt," I corrected, each word deliberate. "I'm going to make sure the land doesn't change hands out from under her."

Holt's expression shifted. Surprise, then understanding. "How?"

I swallowed, feeling the burn in my throat. "With lawyers.

With conditions. With paperwork that keeps her name on title while I take care of the debt."

Holt let out a low breath. "She's going to lose her mind." Holt's gaze sharpened. "And you think she'll let you do this."

"No," I admitted. "She won't, but she can't do anything once it's done."

Holt's mouth twitched, humourless. "So you're not asking."

I met his eyes. "No. I'm not."

The statement sat heavily. It tasted like the kind of control I hated. The kind Colin used.

But there was a difference, and I needed Holt to understand it, and maybe I needed myself to hear it out loud too.

"This isn't me taking her choice," I said, forcing the logic into the open so it couldn't rot in the dark. "She chose to sell because she thinks it's the only way to survive. She's choosing survival. I'm just changing what it's going to cost her."

Holt's face tightened. "You're playing a dangerous game."

"I'm not playing," I said quietly. "I'm finishing what Ray couldn't."

Ray had been drowning and never told her. He'd been drowning and still writing to-do lists, still trying to give her something worth coming back for.

He failed at some of it.

I wasn't going to.

I grabbed my keys off the bar and shoved my phone in my pocket. My hands didn't shake. That was the part that scared me. The calm that came after impact, the calm that meant I locked onto a target, and nothing else mattered.

Holt watched me. "You want me with you."

"Yes," I said. "And then after, you're driving back out to the Callahan place. I want eyes on it. If she comes back, if anyone shows up, you call me immediately."

Holt nodded. "What about Maddy?"

The reminder hit like a hand on my chest. My kid. My anchor. The one piece of my life I couldn't afford to shatter with my own choices.

"I'm picking her up after her lesson," I said. "I'll tell her the truth, enough of it anyway. Then she's going back to her mom's tonight like planned."

Holt's eyes narrowed. "And then."

"And then," I said, voice low, "I'm going to get Tessa back."

Holt didn't react. He just stared at me, like he was trying to see if I'd lost my mind.

Forty-One
Tessa

The apartment lights were off, the curtains half open. Late afternoon sun poured in and painted long stripes across the floor. Everything looked exactly the same as the day I left, but it didn't feel like the same place. The couch, the throw blanket, the coffee table with its chipped corner. The little plant on the window ledge that should've been dead but stubbornly wasn't. A stack of library books that Dani never returned.

Time moved without me. That was the strangest part.

Dani came out of her bedroom and froze when she saw me standing in the kitchen. "You're home." She blinked a few times, making sure I was real, and waited.

I tried to breathe, I pulled air in, felt it scrape down my throat, felt it catch in my chest, and then it came out in a shudder that made my knees wobble.

The sound I made wasn't pretty. It wasn't even dignified. It was the kind of noise that came from somewhere deep, the kind you didn't choose. My vision blurred immediately. My skin went hot, then cold.

Dani was on me in a second.

Her arms wrapped around my ribs, tight and fierce, and it should've made me feel held. It did, and it didn't. Because the second she touched me, every single thing I'd been bracing against snapped at once.

I folded into her, face pressed against her shoulder, and my body started shaking so hard my teeth clicked.

"I'm sorry," I heard myself say, the words tumbling out broken. "I'm sorry. I'm sorry. I'm sorry."

"For what?" Dani demanded, voice thick. "For surviving. For coming home. For not being dead. Shut up."

I tried to shut up. I tried to swallow it back down. But my chest heaved, and my hands fisted in her shirt like I needed something solid to keep me from floating away.

"You didn't do anything wrong," she said, and the anger in her voice was aimed at the universe, not me. "You didn't. You did what you had to do."

I wanted to believe her.

The problem was, my body didn't.

My body still remembered the truck, the smell of cologne that didn't belong, the way my stomach had dropped so hard I thought I might throw up. My body remembered the way my own voice had sounded when I tried to bargain like a frightened animal. It remembered the cabin walls breathing in the wind. It remembered the way relief could feel like nausea when it came too fast.

And now, standing in my apartment, I felt the same thing again. Relief, nausea, grief. All tangled together until I couldn't tell one from another.

Dani guided me toward the couch, hands steady on my shoulders. "Sit," she said.

I sat because I didn't trust my legs.

The cushions dipped under me, and it hit wrong, that softness. The ranch had hard edges. Wood and metal and dust. Survival. Out there, everything was sharp enough to cut. Here it was all upholstery and quiet, and my body didn't know what to do with that.

Dani crouched in front of me, elbows on her knees, eyes level with mine. Her eyeliner had smudged a little. She looked tired. She looked older, somehow. Not in a way that made her less Dani, but in a way that said she'd been holding too much too.

"Do you want water?" she asked. "Tea. Food. Do you want me to put you in the shower?"

A wet laugh jerked out of me and turned immediately into a sob. My hand flew to my mouth like I could catch it.

Dani's face cracked. "Oh, babe."

I shook my head. "I don't know what I want."

"That's fine," she said. "I know what you need."

She stood and disappeared into the kitchen. I heard the tap run. A glass clink. Cabinet doors opening and closing. The ordinary sounds of living, the kind that used to comfort me. Now they felt like they belonged to someone else's life.

My gaze drifted to the window. Calgary sprawled beyond it, all glass and steel and traffic sliding along like veins full of light. Somewhere down on the street, a car horn blared. Someone laughed. A siren rose and faded. The city didn't pause to ask if I'd been okay out there. It didn't care that I'd left a piece of myself in a valley.

My phone sat in my pocket like a stone.

I hadn't turned it on yet.

I didn't have the courage to see what was waiting.

Dani returned with a glass of water and two Advil on her palm like an offering. "Drink," she ordered, voice gentle but unarguable.

I took the pills, swallowed them dry because my hands were shaking too hard to lift the glass. Dani held the water to my mouth like I was sick. I hated it. I clung to it.

The water tasted like home and guilt.

When she set the glass down, she sat beside me, close enough that our shoulders touched. Her knee bumped mine lightly, a silent reminder that I wasn't alone even if my brain kept trying to convince me otherwise.

"So," she said softly. "Talk to me."

My throat tightened. I stared at my hands in my lap, at the faint dirt still under my nails that I couldn't quite scrub out. Proof. Residue. A little piece of the place I'd left.

"I left," I whispered. She went quiet. Her hand slid over mine. Warm. Steady.

"I signed the letter of offer Wyatt had given Ray," I admitted. "I didn't tell him. I didn't tell anyone. I just did it."

Dani's fingers tightened around mine. "Tess."

"I couldn't stay," I said, and the words rushed out before I could stop them. "I couldn't breathe there anymore. Every time I opened a drawer, it was Ray. Every time I turned around, it was the debt. Every time I looked up, there was that valley and those fences and that stupid, stubborn land staring back at me like it was daring me to fail. And I kept thinking about the cabin and how small that space felt, and then I'd walk into my own kitchen, and it felt just as small. Like I traded one kind of trap for another."

My voice cracked. I swallowed hard.

Dani's eyes shone. "You're not trapped here."

"I know," I said, but I didn't sound like I believed myself.

My body was still braced for something to happen. For a door to slam. For a voice to rise. For a demand. For control disguised as care.

Instead, there was only Dani, breathing beside me.

I pressed my fingertips into my thigh hard enough to hurt, grounding myself in pain because it was easier than drowning in the soft.

"I keep thinking," I said, and my voice dropped. "I keep

thinking he's going to show up. I keep listening for footsteps in the hall."

Dani's face went pale. "Colin."

I nodded.

"I hate that he's still in my head," I whispered. "I hate that I'm here and I still feel like I'm waiting for the other shoe to drop."

Dani's jaw clenched. "He's not coming back."

"You don't know that," I said, and the fear in my voice embarrassed me immediately. "I don't know where he is."

Dani's hand slid to the back of my neck, fingers threading into my hair. "I know," she said. "I know. But he's been dealt with. You're safe. You're here. You've got me, and you've got locks, and you've got a building full of nosy neighbours who'd love a reason to call the cops."

I tried to smile. It didn't work.

Dani leaned her head against mine. "You're not alone," she murmured.

The words hit a place in me that was still bruised.

I swallowed hard. "I left him there, without a goodbye."

Dani didn't ask who. She didn't need to.

Wyatt.

The name sat between my ribs like a live thing.

I could still feel the weight of his hand on my knee in the truck, the way it steadied me without asking permission. I could still hear his voice when he said easy, like he was talking to a horse spooked by thunder. I could still remember the scrape on his knuckle, the dirt on his jaw, the way he'd sat on my floor like sleep was optional if it meant I kept breathing.

And then, days later, in the brewery, like he'd been starving and trying not to show it. The way my body had lit up, furious and relieved and alive all at once. The way I clung to him because I wanted to feel normal, and the only normal I could find was heat and hands and the illusion that nothing could touch me while he was there.

I told him I needed space.

Not because I'd stopped wanting him.

Because I'd wanted him too much.

Because wanting him felt like losing control, and control was the only thing I had left.

Dani shifted beside me. "You're thinking about him."

I flinched. "Don't."

She sighed softly. "I'm not going to tease you. I'm not going to make a joke. I'm not even going to call him Cowboy Daddy, even though it brings me joy."

A broken laugh escaped me despite everything. It sounded ugly.

Dani smiled faintly, then it fell away just as quickly. "Tess."

I swallowed. "I shouldn't have... done that."

"Had sex," Dani said, blunt but gentle.

My face heated. "Don't say it like that."

"How should I say it?" she asked quietly. "You clung to someone who made you feel safe."

I stared at the window because looking at her felt too intimate. "I didn't want it to mean anything."

"And it did," she said, not cruel, just honest.

My chest tightened. I pressed my palm to my sternum, as if I could hold my heart still.

"I can't," I whispered. "I can't fall apart and also have him. I can't be the woman with a ranch drowning in debt and the woman who wants him."

My throat burned. Tears rose fast, hot and humiliating. "I'm a coward," I whispered.

Dani's hand tightened around mine. "You're a human being."

I sucked in a breath, and my lungs trembled. "I keep seeing his face when he realizes."

Dani's mouth tightened. "He'll be mad."

"He'll hate me," I whispered.

Dani turned fully toward me. "He won't hate you."

I laughed, sharp and raw. "You don't know him."

"I know you," she said. "And nobody can hate you."

That cracked something.

The sob came out of me hard. My shoulders shook. My stomach clenched like it was trying to fold me in half.

Dani pulled me into her arms, and I let her, because I couldn't hold myself together anymore.

"I wanted to stay," I choked out against her shoulder. "I wanted to fight. I wanted to be the woman who could handle it. I wanted to be the one who came home and fixed everything and proved I wasn't just some city girl. I wanted to be strong."

Dani's hand moved up and down my back, slow and steady. "You are strong."

"No," I said, and it came out viciously, because the word felt like a lie people told to make themselves comfortable. "Strong would've been staying and doing the work. I would've faced it and not panicked. Strong would've been calling the lawyer, making a plan, and sitting in that county office until they gave me answers. Strong would've been not letting Colin get under my skin again. Being strong would've been not needing Wyatt like a life raft."

Dani held me tighter. "Stop."

I pulled back just enough to look at her, eyes burning. "I don't want to be someone who needs saving."

Dani's eyes were wet. "Nobody wants that. But sometimes you do, and that doesn't make you weak. It makes you alive."

I shook my head hard, tears flying. "I hate that I left Ray. He was my dad, Dani, and I never knew."

Dani's face softened as the words drained out of me.

My father was gone. His ranch was gone now, too. The

valley was still out there under that huge sky, and I was here in a condo with beige carpet and city noise and a glass of water on a coffee table. It didn't add up. It didn't feel real.

Dani brushed my hair back from my forehead, gently. "Do you want to sleep?"

I swallowed. "I don't think I can."

"You can," she insisted. "I'll be right here. I'm not going anywhere."

The promise hit a place that was still raw from being taken. From being trapped. From having my choices ripped away, and then having to make another choice that felt just as brutal.

"I'm scared," I whispered.

Dani's voice broke. "I know."

"I'm scared that if I close my eyes, I'll hear him," I admitted, shame burning in my cheeks. "I'll hear the cabin. I'll hear the door. I'll hear his voice telling me I'm choosing to stay, like I wanted any of it."

Dani's arms tightened around me until it almost hurt. "Listen to me. You're safe. If you hear anything in this hallway, it'll be Mrs. Bellows from 4B taking her recycling out and judging everyone's life choices."

I managed a wet, ugly laugh.

Dani kissed the side of my head. "That's my girl."

I closed my eyes for a second and tried to breathe.

My phone still sat heavy in my pocket.

I couldn't ignore it forever.

After a minute, I pulled it out and stared at the dark screen.

Dani watched me carefully. "You don't have to turn it on right now."

"I do," I whispered. "If I don't, I'll imagine the worst."

My thumb hovered.

The second the screen lit, notifications stacked like a punch.

Missed calls. Messages. Voicemails. Numbers I recognized. And then the name that made my stomach flip.

Wyatt.

There were too many.

I stared until my vision blurred.

Dani leaned closer, voice soft. "What is it?"

"I can't," I whispered.

Dani's hand covered mine, warm and steady. "You don't have to answer him."

"I should," I said, and the guilt hit so hard it felt like nausea.

Dani didn't argue. She just stayed close.

I opened the most recent message.

It wasn't long.

> Wyatt: Where are you?

> Wyatt: Tessa, answer me.

> Wyatt: Please.

That one hit different. That one didn't sound like anger. It sounded like a man with a fist around his own throat, trying to keep himself from begging.

I pressed my knuckles to my mouth, hard.

"I miss him," I whispered, and the words fell out like a prayer. "I miss him so much I feel sick."

Dani's eyes filled again. "Oh, babe." She wrapped her arms around me again, and this time, I let myself collapse fully. I let the sobs come. I let them tear through my chest and shake my shoulders and leave me raw.

I cried until my throat hurt and my eyes swelled and my skin felt too tight, until I couldn't remember what I'd been holding back anymore. I cried for Ray. I cried for the ranch. I cried for myself, the version of me that went back to that valley and thought she could be brave enough to carry it all. I cried for the fact that the only man who'd made me feel safe in weeks was the same man I'd pushed away.

Dani held me through it all, rocking slightly, murmuring nonsense and comfort and curses at the universe.

When the sobs finally eased into hiccupping breaths, I wiped my face on my sleeve and stared at the ceiling like it might give me answers.

Dani's voice was barely a whisper. "You're going to get through this."

FORTY-TWO

WYATT

Outside, the sun was bright and almost warm. A breeze moved down Main Street carrying the smell of bakery bread and diesel and the faint tang of fall on the edges. The world looked ordinary.

Holt's truck was parked at the curb. He climbed into the driver's side. I got in on the passenger side, because for once I didn't trust my hands to stay calm behind a wheel.

As we pulled away, my phone buzzed again in my pocket.

Another call.

Unknown number, but local.

I answered because I couldn't afford not to. "Hargrove."

"Mr. Hargrove," Marlene said again, still too bright. "I wanted to confirm your availability for today. We have all the documents ready. I also need to advise you that if this isn't done soon, there's interest from another party in all of Mr. Callahan's property. So if you're proceeding, the sooner the better."

My jaw clenched. "I'm proceeding."

"Excellent," she said. "We'll see you shortly." Her voice was too chipper, too excited, and I wanted to scream at her that this was wrong. I ended the call and stared out the windshield.

"Let's go," I said as I dialled another number.

"Hey Wyatt, what's up?" Brooke's chipper voice asked.

"Do you happen to be at the arena still?" I'd seen her there checking the horses that boarded there.

"Yeah, need me to grab Maddy for you?"

"That would be great, I've got a meeting I can't push back." She was Tessa's boss, and I didn't really want to get into the details, but I would if she questioned me.

"No problem, I was heading to your place after I'm done here, so she can hop in." She was silent for a moment, and I heard some rustling in the background. "Wyatt, have you talked to Tessa? I'm worried about her."

"I haven't, but after this meeting I intend to."

"Good. See you later."

"Thanks, Brooke," I said just before I hung up the phone.

At the credit union, Holt parked in the lot and killed the engine. I opened the door and stepped out, the air hitting my face like a slap. I rolled my shoulders once, grounding myself.

Holt got out, too. "Are you sure this is the right thing?"

I looked at him. "Yeah no, I don't think it is at all, but she's not going down without me fighting."

The fluorescent lights buzzed overhead, and I understood, suddenly, why Ray hated this place. It sucked the warmth out of a man. It made you feel like a file number.

Marlene met us near the front, heels clicking on tile. She was all pressed blazer and professional smile, clipboard in her hands like she could hold the world steady with paper.

"Mr. Hargrove," she said. Her smile tightened when she saw Holt, like she didn't like extra witnesses. Good. Let her be uncomfortable. Let her remember this wasn't just ink. It was land. More importantly, it was people.

She led us into a small office with framed photographs of

fields and a poster about "financial wellness" that made my stomach turn. She set a folder on the desk, thick with documents.

"I'll walk you through the terms," she said.

"I already know the terms," I replied. "I'm changing them."

Her eyebrows lifted. "Excuse me."

I leaned forward, palms on the desk, and kept my voice calm even though something vicious beat under my ribs.

"The debt gets paid," I said. "Every outstanding piece of it. Taxes. Operating credit. Any liens attached to the land. All of it."

"Yes," she said cautiously. "That's what this purchase agreement accomplishes."

"No," I corrected. "This purchase agreement transfers title."

She blinked, then smiled like I was being difficult. "That's how purchases work."

"Not this one," I said.

Marlene's smile faltered. "Mr. Hargrove."

"I'm not taking her land," I said, each word slow and clear. "I'm taking her debt."

Silence stretched, thick and tense.

Holt stood behind me, arms crossed, a quiet wall.

Marlene inhaled, then tried again, voice still polite but firmer. "If your intent is to provide financial assistance to Ms. Callahan, there are other mechanisms. Loans. Private arrangements. Gifted funds."

"I'm not gifting anything," I said. "And I'm not loaning her money she can't repay. I'm making this clean."

Marlene's eyes narrowed slightly. "Clean for whom?"

"For her," I said.

Her lips pressed together. "I'm not sure we can facilitate what you're describing."

"You can," I replied. "You just don't want to."

Her cheeks coloured faintly. "This is a financial institution, Mr. Hargrove, not a charity." Marlene's voice softened, which was almost worse. "May I ask why?"

I held her gaze, steady and cold. "She signed those papers two days ago, because she thinks she's out of options, because that's the bull shit you've been feeding her since she got here. She's not going to lose everything, not if I can help it."

Marlene exhaled slowly. "Ms. Callahan accepted the offer."

"She accepted it under pressure," I said. "And she accepted it without understanding that there were other options..."

Marlene's eyes flicked down to the folder, then back to me. "Even if we can structure something, she would need to agree to amended terms."

"She doesn't need to agree to anything, that's between Tessa and me."

"And if she doesn't like the terms you're describing?" The woman leaned back in her chair, like she was preparing for some kind of gotcha moment.

"Then you proceed with the original purchase," I replied, voice hardening. "But you're not doing that without giving me twenty-four hours to speak to her."

Marlene's mouth tightened. "That isn't reasonable."

"It's the only reasonable thing," I said. "If you've really got another party sniffing around, you already showed your hand. I'm in the driver's seat here because I have a signed letter of offer, that land it mine regardless of who's name is on the title."

Holt let out a low breath behind me, almost a sound of approval. Marlene looked at Holt like he might rescue her from this. He didn't.

As we left the office, the credit union's lobby felt too bright, too cold, too full of people who had no idea what it cost to keep land in a family. I wanted to burn the fluorescent lights out with my stare.

Outside, the sun hit my face, and for half a second, I felt like I couldn't breathe.

Holt opened his truck door and paused. "You're going to go after her."

"Yep," I said.

We climbed in.

As Holt started the engine, my phone buzzed again. This time it was Brooke.

I answered. "How's Maddy?"

Brooke's voice was careful. "She's asking questions, and I'm running out of lies."

I swallowed. "I'm on my way."

"Wyatt," Brooke said, and there was steel under the softness, "is Tessa okay?"

I stared out at the road. "I don't know."

Brooke breathed out. "Then you need to be honest with your kid."

"I will," I promised.

I hung up and leaned my head back against the seat, eyes on the ceiling for a second, letting the weight settle.

Holt drove toward the barn.

My mind kept circling one brutal, simple truth.

Tessa hadn't just left the ranch.

She'd left me and Maddy. And I hadn't realized until now how much I'd started thinking about her in my day-to-day life.

When we pulled up the drive, Maddy spotted the truck immediately. She was still in her riding clothes, hair pulled back, cheeks flushed from effort. She looked older than she had a month ago. Like life had been teaching her lessons she didn't ask for.

She walked toward me fast, not running, but close. Brooke followed behind at a slower pace, eyes sharp and worried.

I stepped out of the truck.

Maddy didn't bother with hello. "Where is she?"

My throat tightened. I crouched slightly, bringing myself closer to her height even though she was nearly there already.

"I don't know," I said carefully. "But I'm finding out."

Her eyes filled, fast and furious. "Did she leave?"

I swallowed. "It looks like it."

Maddy's mouth trembled. She pressed her lips together like she was trying not to let the sound out. "Why?"

"I think she's scared," I said, because it was the cleanest truth I had. "And tired. And she thinks leaving is the only way to stop the pressure."

Maddy shook her head hard. "That's stupid."

"It might be," I said gently. "But when people are overwhelmed, they do things that feel like the only way to breathe."

Her eyes flashed. "Did she say goodbye to you?"

The question hit deep. I forced myself to keep my voice steady. "No."

Maddy's face crumpled for a split second, then she straightened, anger sliding into place like amour. "So what are you going to do?"

I stood, slow. "I'm going to make sure the ranch doesn't get taken from her. And then I'm going to go get her."

Maddy's gaze locked on mine. "And you're going to bring her back."

I hesitated, because I couldn't promise what wasn't mine to promise.

Maddy saw it. Her voice went sharp. "Don't do that thing you do when you don't want to tell me the truth."

I exhaled. "I can't force her, sweetheart."

"I know," she said, voice breaking. "But you can try."

I nodded once. "I will."

Brooke stepped forward, touching Maddy's shoulder. "Come on, kiddo. Let's find some feed for your mare."

Maddy didn't move right away. She stared at me, searching my face like she was looking for cracks.

"You're mad," she said.

"Yes," I admitted. I forced my jaw to unclench. "I'm not mad at her for being scared. I'm mad at the situation. I'm mad at the bank, mad at Ray for leaving her buried under paperwork. And I'm mad at myself for giving her space and letting her disappear."

Maddy swallowed, eyes shiny. "Okay."

I reached out and squeezed her shoulder once, quick and steady. "After you feed your mare, get your stuff packed up. I'll take you to your mom's instead of meeting her somewhere."

She nodded, but her face stayed tight. "You're going to see her tonight?"

A ghost of a smile tried to pull at my mouth. It didn't make it. "Yeah, I am."

She stepped forward suddenly and hugged me, hard, arms tight around my waist. She didn't do that much anymore. Not since she'd hit the age where affection turned embarrassing. The fact that she did it now made my throat burn.

I wrapped an arm around her shoulders and held her for a beat. "I've got you," I murmured, and I meant it.

Brooke led her away, glanced over her shoulder, and gave me half a smile.

Holt was watching me like he had something to say and didn't know where to put it.

"What," I asked.

He shook his head once. "Nothing. Just looks like you're about to burn the world down."

"I might," I grumbled as I headed toward the house.

Holt grunted. "Fair."

FORTY-THREE
WYATT

Maddy sat in the passenger seat with her knees pulled up, earbuds looped around her fingers but not in her ears, staring out the windshield. Calgary was an hour out, the prairie stretching wide and pale under a sky that looked scrubbed clean, and I kept both hands on the wheel like I could hold the day steady if I gripped hard enough.

Two weeks.

That was all I'd had, and it hadn't been enough. It never was. She'd filled my house up just by existing in it, by leaving her shoes all over the place and humming to herself while she fed the chickens, by laughing at Holt's terrible jokes and then pretending she hadn't. She'd ridden until her thighs ached and she'd smiled that fierce, hungry smile she got when she was doing something that made her feel capable. She'd made the place feel like a home again.

And now I was bringing her back to the city, back to her mother, back to the life that didn't include me.

Maddy glanced over at me, eyes sharp and too old for her age, then looked away again. She'd been doing that all morning, like she was checking on me in little stolen moments and deciding whether to push.

She finally did.

"Dad," she said quietly.

"Yeah, sweetheart."

"You're doing the jaw thing."

I breathed out through my nose, the sound rougher than I meant it to be. "Am I?"

"You are." She tilted her head, studying me like I was one of her horses about to spook. "Are you mad?"

"No."

She didn't even pretend to believe that. "Are you sad?"

I swallowed. The road shimmered ahead, heat already rising off the pavement even though the sun wasn't fully up. "I'm... thinking."

Maddy made a small sound. "That's worse."

I glanced at her, despite myself. "How's that worse?"

"Because when you think, you go quiet," she said. "And when you go quiet, you decide things without telling anyone."

That one landed clean.

I tightened my grip on the steering wheel until my knuckles ached, then forced my fingers to loosen. "I'm not trying to decide things without telling anyone."

"You kind of are," she said gently, which was infuriating because she was right. "It's about Tessa, isn't it?"

The name hit like a bruise pressed too hard.

My eyes stayed on the road. "Not just her, I'm thinking about you too. You've made the ranch feel like a home again, and I hate that you're leaving."

Maddy's laugh was soft, without humor. "Dad."

I didn't answer, and silence stretched between us for a few miles, the kind that wasn't empty. It was full of words I didn't want to say because saying them made them real.

I swallowed again, jaw working even though I didn't want it to. "I'm alright."

"No, you're not," she said, and her voice was steady, not accusing. Just certain. "You look like you did when I was little and you thought I didn't notice."

My chest went hot, then cold. The road blurred for a second, a white line stretching out like a thread I was holding onto with my teeth.

"You shouldn't have had to notice," I said quietly.

Maddy shrugged a little. "I did anyway."

I nodded once, stiff. "Yeah."

Her shoulders eased, like my admission loosened something in her, too. "Then why are you taking me back first? Let's go get her."

Because you're the one thing I won't drag into this, I thought.

"Because you come first." I looked over at her, and she gave me a crooked smile. "I know you want to see Tessa, and if I knew what was going to happen, I'd take you with me, but kid, she's not in a good place. So as soon as I know what's happening, we'll find you."

Maddy's expression softened, and for a second, she looked younger as she nodded. We drove in silence again, but it wasn't the same silence.

When the city finally rose up on the horizon, glass and steel catching the sun, my stomach knotted. Calgary always made me feel like I was wearing the wrong skin. Too many people. Too many lanes. Too much noise. The world pressed closer here, and it didn't leave room for the kind of quiet you could hear a fence line in.

Maddy's mother lived on the south end, wide streets. Neat yards. Houses that looked like they'd been designed to impress.

I pulled into the driveway and killed the engine. The sudden quiet rang.

Maddy didn't move right away. She stared at the front door, then turned toward me. Her eyes were bright but stubborn, like she refused to cry even when she wanted to.

"Text me," she said.

I smiled faintly. "I always do."

"No," she insisted. "Like, actually text me. Not just thumbs up my messages and pretend that counts as parenting."

A laugh tried to come out of me and caught halfway. "Alright."

She'd always hugged with her whole body, even when she was trying to act cool. I held her carefully at first, then tighter when her shoulders shook once against my chest.

"I love you, Dad," she mumbled into my shirt.

My throat went thick immediately. "Love you too, sweetheart."

She pulled back, blinked fast, and then her voice went quieter. "Be nice."

I stared at her, caught off guard. "Nice?"

"Yes," she said firmly. "To Tessa, give her a reason to come back to us."

My chest tightened. "I promise."

"Dad."

"Yeah."

"If you love her," she said, voice steady but quiet, "you should tell her. Because people don't always stay long enough for you to figure it out later."

My breath caught so sharp it hurt.

Maddy climbed out before I could answer, closed the door carefully, and walked up the path toward her mother's front steps. She didn't look back. She didn't need to.

I sat in the truck and watched until the door opened, and

her mother pulled her into a hug. I watched until Maddy disappeared inside, swallowed by a life that wasn't mine.

Then I put my hands on the steering wheel and let my forehead drop against it.

For a moment, I couldn't breathe.

The thought of turning the truck around and driving away without doing what I'd come to do made my chest feel like it was collapsing. The thought of going to Tessa's building and knocking on that door made my palms sweat. I could feel the memory of the last time too clearly, standing in a hallway that smelled like someone else's cooking, delivering news that didn't belong to me to deliver.

Tessa's face had been so pale then.

Her eyes looked like they were trying to hold the world together by force.

I walked away from that door feeling like the villain.

I started the engine, put the truck in reverse, and backed out of the driveway.

My hands shook on the wheel, not enough to lose control, but enough that I noticed. My chest felt tight, my jaw clenched, my tongue pressed hard against the back of my teeth like I was holding words in.

Traffic picked up as I headed toward the core. I followed directions I memorized on the drive out, the turns, lights, and ramps that led to Tessa's building. My pulse kept kicking hard against my ribs, impatient and angry and afraid all at once.

I shut the truck off and stepped out. The air smelled like exhaust and concrete warming in the sun. My boots hit the sidewalk too hard, each step heavy with intention I couldn't pretend wasn't there.

Inside, the lobby was clean and bright. Someone's dog barked behind a door. A woman in workout gear carried a bag of groceries past me, her eyes sliding over my hat and work jacket with mild curiosity, then away.

I took the elevator up, my reflection staring back at me in the mirrored walls. I looked tired. Older than I felt. My eyes were bloodshot, my jaw unshaven enough to make me look rougher than usual.

When the doors opened on Tessa's floor, the hallway felt too quiet. I stood outside her unit for a long moment with my fist raised, not touching the wood yet.

There were a hundred ways this could go wrong. Dani could tell me to get lost. Tessa could refuse to see me. Tessa could look at me like I was the last person she wanted in her life, and I'd have to swallow it.

Or she could look at me like she looked at me that night, hollow and shaking, and I'd have to resist the instinct to wrap her up and keep her there even if she hated it.

I knocked.

Footsteps sounded inside, quick and purposeful, and then the door swung open.

Dani stood there with her pink hair pulled into a messy knot, no eyeliner, no sharp jokes ready like knives. She wore a soft hoodie and leggings, barefoot, her face drawn tight with a kind of exhaustion I'd never seen on her before.

She looked at me and went still.

For a second, neither of us spoke.

Then Dani's gaze flicked down the hall, like she was checking for someone behind me. Then back to my face. "Oh," she said, and her voice was quiet this time. Flat. "It's you."

The echo of the last time hit me hard, like the hallway itself remembered.

I swallowed. "Morning."

Dani blinked once, slowly. "It's afternoon."

"Yeah," I said, because it was, and because I'd lost track of time somewhere between anger and fear.

She stared at me for a long moment, her expression

unreadable. Then she stepped back half a pace and opened the door wider.

"Come in," she said.

I hesitated. "Is she..."

Dani's jaw tightened. "She's in the bedroom. She's been sleeping since she got here."

My chest tightened. Relief and something heavier moved through me.

"Thank you," I said quietly.

Dani's eyes flashed. "Don't thank me. You don't get points for showing up. You get points for what you do next."

The apartment felt warm, dimmer than the hallway, curtains drawn partway. It smelled like coffee and laundry detergent and something floral that made me think of Dani, not Tessa. There were blankets piled on the couch. A mug on the coffee table. A letter, folded, sitting near the edge like a thing that had been handled too much.

Dani closed the door behind me, and the sound hit the same way it had that night, final and contained.

My pulse kicked harder.

Dani walked ahead of me toward the kitchen, then stopped and turned, arms crossing over her chest.

"Before you see her," she said, voice low, "you need to decide what you're here for."

I held her gaze. "I'm here for her."

Dani's eyes narrowed. "That's not the answer I want to hear."

I exhaled through my nose, fighting the urge to snap back. "I'm here because she left and didn't say goodbye, and I'm in love with her." I shouldn't have told Dani before I told Tessa, but I needed to share it.

Dani's gaze softened a fraction. "Okay."

I swallowed. "Is she okay?"

Dani's laugh was humourless. "Define okay." She rubbed a

hand over her face, then dropped it, her voice losing its edge. "She's breathing. She's eating a bit. She's not... she's not gone, Wyatt. But she's not here either. Not all the way."

Dani stepped closer, her voice steady. "She didn't come back because she stopped caring. She came back because she has to stop hurting."

"I know," I said, and my voice sounded like gravel.

Dani tilted her head, studying me. "Do you?"

I met her eyes. "Yeah. I do."

Silence held for a beat, thick and charged.

Then Dani said quietly, "She signed papers."

My stomach dropped. "I know."

Dani's brows lifted, surprise flickering. "You know?"

"I know," I repeated, and my hands curled at my sides, restrained. "I got the call."

Dani's face hardened. "So you're here to yell."

"No," I said immediately, because the word felt wrong in my mouth. "I'm here to give her her home back."

Dani's eyes narrowed. "What?"

"I was the buyer, and as of this morning, the debt's paid, and Tessa is the sole owner of Callahan Ranch."

After a long moment, she nodded once, sharp. "Okay."

I walked down the hall on legs that felt too heavy. My palms were damp. My heart thudded loudly in my ears. I stopped outside the bedroom door, stared at the wood, and for a second, I was back in that other hallway, the day I told her Ray was dead.

Back then, I'd knocked and changed her life in one sentence.

Now I was about to knock and ask her not to leave mine.

I lifted my hand and I knocked once.

Then a faint shuffle, like someone shifting in bed.

The door opened, and Tessa stood there in an oversized shirt that looked suspiciously like one of mine. Her hair a mess, eyes still heavy with sleep and something deeper. She looked smaller in this space, paler, like she left part of herself under that prairie sky and hadn't found it again yet.

Her gaze hit mine and froze.

I felt it in my chest like a punch.

"Wyatt," she whispered, and my name sounded like a bruise.

I didn't move. I didn't reach for her. I kept my hands at my sides because Dani was right and because Tessa looked like she'd bolt if I breathed wrong.

"I needed to see you," I said quietly.

Her eyes flicked over my face, over my jacket, over the line of my jaw like she was checking for anger, for judgment, for the things she expected.

"What are you doing here?" she asked, and her voice tried to be hard. It wasn't.

"I brought Maddy back," I said. "And then I came here."

Something shifted in her expression at Maddy's name, a flash of guilt, maybe, or tenderness. She swallowed.

"You shouldn't," she murmured. "You shouldn't have come."

I held her gaze. My chest ached. "I'm not good at staying away."

Her breath hitched, just a little.

Tessa's fingers tightened on the edge of the door. "I asked you to stop coming around."

"I know. And I tried."

Her eyes narrowed, hurt and anger flickering. "No, you didn't."

I nodded once, accepting it. "No. I didn't."

The admission hung between us, heavy and honest.

Tessa's throat worked as she swallowed. "You're angry."

"Yes," I said, because lying would only make it worse. "I'm angry."

Her shoulders rose, defensive. "Then yell at me and get it over with."

My jaw tightened. I forced my voice to stay low. "That's not why I came."

Her eyes searched my face, suspicious.

I took a slow breath. "You didn't say goodbye. I've been trying to convince myself you did it because you needed space. But the truth is, Tess, it scared the hell out of me."

The words landed in the small space between us like something fragile.

Tessa's expression cracked, just for a second. Her mouth trembled, and she bit down hard, like she refused to let it show.

"I didn't mean to," she whispered.

"I don't care," I said, and my voice roughened. I softened it immediately. "Meaning to doesn't matter. You were gone."

Her eyes shone, and her breathing went shallow.

"I didn't know how to stay," she said, barely audible. "I didn't know how to keep breathing there."

My chest tightened, sharp and hot. "You could've told me."

Her laugh was small and broken. "Why? So you could talk me out of it."

I held her gaze. "So you wouldn't have to carry it alone. You don't have to do this alone anymore."

Tessa's shoulders sagged a fraction, like the fight drained out of her in a slow leak.

"You signed the letter of offer," I said quietly.

"I thought if you had the land, then maybe Ray wouldn't totally cease to exist." She kept her gaze locked on the floor, but I could see the tears rolling down her cheeks.

"Tessa," I said, voice low. "Look at me."

Her eyes locked on mine, furious and wet.

"I'm not here to take anything from you," I said. "I'm here

because I can't watch you burn your life down out of grief and fear."

Tessa's breath came shaky. She pressed her forehead lightly to the doorframe for a second, eyes squeezed shut, like she was trying to hold herself together with wood and willpower.

"I can't," she whispered. "I can't do the ranch, Wyatt. I can't do the debt. I can't do the valley watching me fail. I can't deal with you looking at me like you think I can. I'm tired."

The last word broke. My chest hurt so badly it felt like my ribs were being pried apart. "I know," I said. "That's why I'm here."

Tessa's eyes snapped up. "What does that mean?"

I took a breath, slow and careful. "It means I'm going to say something you probably won't like, and you can tell me to get out after. But you're going to hear it first."

My heart pounded hard enough that I could feel it in my throat. "I'm not letting that land change hands," I said.

Tessa's face went blank. "What?"

"The debt is gone, I've cleared it all, but the land is in your name," I repeated, voice steady.

Her eyes narrowed, sharp. "You can't do that."

"I can," I said, and I hated how the words sounded, like control.

Tessa's shoulders shook once. She swallowed hard. "I don't understand."

I nodded, because that was fair. "You don't have to understand yet. You just have to listen."

Her gaze held mine, raw and furious and exhausted.

"The land is yours free and clear. You can come back when you're ready, or you can stay here, or you can do whatever you need to do. But the land isn't going to be taken from you."

Tessa went very still.

Then her voice came out small, almost broken. "Why?"

The question hit the center of me.

Because I loved her, I thought. Because she'd gotten under my skin and into my bones. Because the valley felt wrong without her, even when she made it feel like a warzone while she was there. Because I couldn't take the look on her face when she realized she was losing everything, Ray left her. Because I'd rather bleed than watch her drown.

But I didn't say all of that.

I said the truest part, the part I could say without asking her to carry my feelings too.

"Because I love you," I said. "And you deserved better than what was left in your lap."

Tessa's eyes filled completely. A tear slid down her cheek, and she didn't wipe it away.

"I didn't tell you goodbye," she whispered, like she couldn't stop confessing now. "I was going to. I sat in my truck, and I tried. And then I knew if I saw you, I wouldn't leave."

My throat burned.

I held myself still. "I would've let you go."

She gave a tiny shake of her head. "No. You would've looked at me like you look at me, and I would've stayed, and I would've hated you for it."

The honesty gutted me.

I nodded once, slowly. "Maybe."

Tessa's breath came out shaky. "I don't hate you anymore."

The words landed like a hand on my chest.

I swallowed hard. "That's good," I replied with a chuckle.

A ragged laugh escaped her and turned into a sob. She pressed her palm over her mouth, eyes squeezed shut, shoulders trembling.

I didn't move closer. I didn't touch her. I stayed where I was because she needed control more than she needed comfort.

After a long moment, she opened her eyes again and looked at me through tears.

"You shouldn't be here," she whispered.

"I know," I said.

"And you came anyway."

"Yeah," I admitted. "I did."

Tessa's gaze dropped to my boots, then back to my face. Her voice came out rough. "I'll pay you back. All the money you spent to save me."

"No," I said immediately. Firm. "You won't."

Tessa's eyes narrowed again. "That's not how money works."

"It is for me," I said, and my voice softened. "You don't owe me a damn thing."

Her breath caught at that, her cheeks flushing faintly, and I saw it, the memory between us, the night at the brewery that had felt like a match struck in a dark room.

From the kitchen, Dani's voice drifted, careful. "I made coffee."

Tessa blinked hard, like Dani's normalcy reminded her she was in an apartment in Calgary and not in a nightmare.

She looked at me again. "Are you staying?"

"I'll stay as long as you want me here," I said. "And if you want me gone, I'll leave." Tessa nodded and walked out of her room.

Dani set a mug down in front of me, then one in front of Tessa, then sat across from us. Her eyes looked tired, her face stripped of humour.

For a moment, none of us spoke.

Then Dani asked quietly, "Maddy's okay?"

I nodded, my throat thick. "Yeah. She is."

Tessa's fingers curled around her mug. Her voice came out small. "Tell her I'm sorry."

Dani's gaze sharpened. "You can tell her yourself when you're ready. You don't get to carry that alone either."

Tessa flinched, but she didn't argue. She stared into her coffee like it held answers.

I watched her, chest aching, and made myself stay still. Because this wasn't about me storming in and fixing things. It was about being here when she decided whether to let herself be held.

Then I looked at her and said the simplest truth I had left. "I'm not leaving you behind."

FORTY-FOUR

TESSA

I hovered in the doorway between the kitchen and the living room, my mug still in my hands, watching him the way I watched storms on the prairie when I was a kid. Measuring distance. Counting seconds. Trying to decide if it was going to pass by or hit the house full on.

He looked up when he felt me there.

Not startled. Just present.

"Hey," he said softly.

My chest tightened on the word like my body was still bracing for someone to tell me I'd done something wrong.

"Hey," I managed back, and it didn't sound like my own voice.

Wyatt's gaze went over me; he noticed everything, whether I wanted him to or not. The faint tremor in my fingers. The way I kept my weight on the balls of my feet like I might have to run. The way my shoulders stayed up around my ears as if lowering them would invite something bad.

I swallowed. "I slept."

His mouth twitched, not quite a smile. "You passed out."

I took a step forward, then stopped. My body hesitated

even when my mind was trying to move. I hated that about myself, the way fear rewired my muscles. Like I'd lost my right to be impulsive. Like everything had to be measured now, filtered, checked for danger.

Wyatt didn't fill the space. He didn't reach. He just stayed where he was, giving me room to choose.

I took another step.

My bare feet hit the rug, and I felt the fibres under my toes, the small grounding detail that reminded me I was here. I was in the apartment. I wasn't in that cabin. I wasn't in the truck with Colin's voice in my ear. I was here.

Wyatt's gaze dipped to my feet, then rose again, and I saw the flicker of concern he didn't let himself speak.

I swallowed hard and finally let the words that had been sitting like a stone inside me come up. "I've been thinking."

Wyatt's expression didn't change, but his posture shifted, subtle and immediate. Like he'd braced for impact.

"Okay."

I could've laughed at how careful he sounded, like he didn't want to startle me. Like I was a horse with a raw spot under the saddle, and one wrong touch would make me bolt.

I hated that I liked it.

I hated that I needed it.

"I'm going back," I said, and my heart hammered as if saying it out loud might summon consequences.

Wyatt blinked once.

Then he didn't move.

"My father deserves more from his legacy than what I've done so far." The thought still made my stomach twist in a way I couldn't fully explain, because it was grief layered over grief, anger braided into longing. A lifetime of believing my parents left without care, only to find out one of them had been there the whole time, watching from a distance, building a life around me without ever telling me it was his right to.

"We're going to talk about Ray being your father another time," he said, quieter. "When do you want to go?"

"Today," I said, and the decisiveness surprised even me.

Wyatt's breath left him slowly. Relief, maybe, but he kept it leashed. "Alright."

"I'm not going back to be saved," I said, the words sharp because I needed to draw the line before my fear tried to convince me I owed him something I couldn't give.

Wyatt's gaze stayed steady. "I know."

"No," I said, too fast. "You don't. You think you do, but you don't. I need to say it."

He went still. "Okay. Say it." He arched his brow and crossed his arms. Damn it, he was hot when he did that.

I took a breath and felt it catch halfway down, like my lungs still didn't trust air.

"I'm going back because it's mine. Because I can't live in a city and pretend that land isn't calling me. Because I can't leave him there alone, not now that I know. Not now that I know he didn't leave me, not really. He just made a choice he thought would hurt less." My voice cracked on the last word.

I hated that tears came so fast. I hated that my body betrayed me with softness when I was trying to be firm.

Wyatt didn't speak. He didn't interrupt. He let me fall apart in small, controlled pieces.

I wiped my cheek with the back of my hand, angry at myself for needing that much emotion just to be honest.

"And I'm going back because I'm tired of running. I've been running my whole life. From my parents. From Ray. From the truth. From men like Colin, who always made me feel like my choices weren't mine. I'm done."

Wyatt's jaw flexed, something dark flickering there at Colin's name, but he didn't let it take over. He stayed present with me instead of letting his anger get the best of him.

"I'm done," I repeated, quieter. "And I'm not going back to lean on you."

Wyatt's gaze didn't waver. "Okay."

I blinked at him, thrown off by how easily he accepted it.

My chest rose too fast. I forced a slower breath, tried again, sharper. "I'm serious, Wyatt. I'm moving into Ray's house. I'm not moving into yours. I'm not becoming your responsibility."

Wyatt's eyes softened. "Tessa." My name in his mouth was careful, like he knew it could be a wound or a balm, and he didn't want to choose wrong.

I lifted my chin. "I just got out of a relationship. A bad one. And I don't need anything complicated. I don't need a man who wants to fix me. I don't need a man who wants to own me. I don't need to feel like if I take one wrong breath I'm going to owe someone my whole life."

Wyatt's expression tightened, not defensive, just pained. "I don't want to own you."

"I know," I said quickly, and I did know. That was part of what scared me. Colin always wanted something from me, and he called it love. Wyatt wanted nothing from me, and somehow it still felt like I was standing at the edge of something big enough to drown in.

I exhaled, shaky. "If I stay over sometimes, or if you stay at my place sometimes, it doesn't mean it's forever."

The words sat in the air, heavy and raw.

Wyatt's gaze held mine, and I saw something in his eyes that made my stomach flip, something like longing and acceptance braided together.

"It doesn't have to mean forever," he said in agreement.

My throat tightened. I hadn't expected him to agree so easily. I expected a fight. A push. A wounded look. The subtle punishment of silence.

But Wyatt just... accepted it. Like he understood what I

was really saying underneath the boundaries. That I was terrified of losing myself again, and of needing anyone. That I wanted him, and wanting him felt like standing too close to the edge of a cliff.

"That's what you want," he added, carefully. "Right now."

I nodded, grateful for the phrase right now because it gave me room to breathe.

Wyatt's hands unclasped, then clasped again, like he was resisting the urge to reach for me.

"I'm not looking for forever as payment," he said quietly. "I'm looking for you to be safe enough to sleep, and so you don't carry all of it alone."

My chest tightened. "Good, I can't carry it alone." The admission came out before I could stop it.

Wyatt didn't pounce on it. He didn't turn it into a victory.

He just nodded once, like it was a truth he respected. "You can be independent and still let people help you."

My mouth twisted. "That sounds like something you'd say because you're good at helping."

Wyatt's mouth twitched too, a faint echo of humour. "Maybe I am. Listen, Tessa, you don't belong to me, and I don't want you to feel indebted in any way. I meant what I said last night, I love you, and I want you by my side, but I'll wait for you. However long it takes, I'll wait," he said, low and absolute.

My throat worked as I swallowed, my chest tight in a way that felt like pain and relief tangled together.

Wyatt's gaze dipped to my mouth for half a second, then back to my eyes, like he was forcing himself to stay with the words and not the pull.

I stared at him, my body trembling faintly. "I'm scared," I admitted.

Wyatt nodded once, like fear was not a flaw, just information.

"I know."

I exhaled, shaky. "I'm scared that if I go back, I'll fail. And I'm scared that if I don't go back, I'll hate myself forever."

Wyatt's voice was quiet. "You won't fail because you don't know everything on day one. You only fail if you stop showing up."

The words landed deep, not like a pep talk, but like a truth that didn't care if I was ready.

I nodded, swallowing hard. "Okay."

Wyatt's gaze stayed steady. "Do you want to drive with me? I can send the guys back to get Ray's truck."

"No," I said quickly, and the firmness surprised me. "I need to drive."

Wyatt nodded. "Okay."

"And you're going in your truck," I added, because the thought of being trapped in someone else's space still made my skin crawl.

Wyatt didn't blink. "Okay."

I stared at him, my chest aching with the simplicity of his acceptance.

"Why are you being so agreeable?" I asked, and it came out almost angry, because part of me was still waiting for the trap.

Wyatt's mouth twitched faintly. "Because you're not asking for anything unreasonable. You're asking for control. You're telling me you need space and you want your life to stay yours."

My eyes burned. For a second, the apartment felt too small for what was sitting between us, for everything unsaid. The air seemed thicker. Warmer. My skin was too aware of itself, of my pulse, of the way my body kept remembering his arms around me in the dark, the way it had felt to be held without being owned.

I forced a breath in, slow and shaky.

"I need to pack," I said.

Wyatt nodded. "Okay, I can wait outside. Or I can wait in the truck. Whatever feels better."

My chest tightened again, hot and strange.

"I don't want you to leave," I admitted, and the honesty startled me because it wasn't about safety anymore. It was about the quiet inside me that started to recognize his presence as something steady.

Wyatt's eyes darkened, just a fraction, like the words hit him somewhere tender.

"I won't," he said.

I swallowed hard. "But I also don't want you hovering."

Wyatt nodded, like that wasn't a contradiction, like he understood the line I was trying to walk.

"I can be nearby without being on top of you," he said quietly.

"Okay," I whispered.

Wyatt's gaze softened. "Okay."

I went into my room, the small space that had once been mine and now felt like borrowed air, and I started packing on autopilot.

My hands shook as I folded. My stomach churned, empty and unsettled. Every few seconds, my mind flashed with images I didn't ask for. The cabin door. Colin's voice. Wyatt's arms. The crunch of gravel. Holt's shadow moving in the dark.

I breathed through it.

In for four.

Out for six.

Again.

When my suitcase was half full, I stopped and sat on the edge of the bed, staring at my hands. They looked normal. They didn't look like hands that had been trapped. They didn't look like hands that had clutched at Wyatt's jacket like it was the only thing holding me together.

My fingers curled into the blanket.

A sob rose in my throat, and I swallowed it hard.

Not yet.

I stood again and finished packing, moving slower now, more deliberate, like each folded shirt was a decision. Like each zipper pull was me choosing a direction.

When I finally carried my suitcase out into the living room, Wyatt was still there, exactly where I'd left him, sitting on the edge of the chair, hands clasped, gaze lifting the moment I appeared.

He stood immediately.

"Ready," he asked.

I nodded. "Yeah."

Wyatt's gaze flicked to the suitcase, then back to my face. "Dani."

"She's asleep," I said quietly. "Or pretending she is."

Wyatt's mouth twitched. "Probably pretending."

I hesitated, then said, "I'll call her when I'm on the road. I can't do the goodbye thing right now."

Wyatt nodded, no judgment. "Okay."

We moved toward the door.

Outside, the city noise hit me like a wave. Cars. Voices. Concrete. I hated how normal it all was.

Wyatt's truck was parked at the curb, right behind mine. "I'll follow you."

My throat tightened. "Okay."

When we finally pulled into the yard at Ray's, my stomach dropped in a way that hurt. The place looked the same and completely different. The fence line. The barn. The house with its worn boards and familiar windows.

My house.

My father's house.

The truth of that still felt like a bruise.

Wyatt killed the engine and waited, watching me like he didn't want to move too fast.

I stared at the porch, my breath shallow.

"You want me to come in," Wyatt asked quietly, "or you want space."

I swallowed. My voice came out rough. "Come in, please."

Wyatt didn't move, but his voice came low. "Are you alright?"

I nodded, but my throat worked like it was trying to swallow a sob.

"I can't promise anything," I said suddenly, and the words came out rough because they'd been building. "I can't promise I won't change my mind. I can't promise I won't wake up tomorrow and want to run back to Calgary and pretend none of this happened."

Wyatt's gaze held mine. "Okay."

"And I can't promise you anything," I continued, my voice shaking now. "Not forever. Not commitment. Not whatever you might be hoping for. I don't even know what I'm capable of right now."

Wyatt's face softened, but his voice stayed steady. "I'm not asking you for promises."

I swallowed hard. "I need you to hear it anyway."

"I hear you."

The porch boards creaked under my feet as I stepped closer, and Wyatt didn't back away. He stayed where he was, letting me choose the distance, letting me own my own body again.

I stopped an arm's length away.

My skin was buzzing, nerves lit up, my heart beating hard enough I could feel it in my throat. I wanted to touch him, and I was terrified of what touching him would mean, even though I'd just told him it didn't mean forever.

My breath caught.

Wyatt's voice came lower. "Tell me what you need right now."

I stared at him, and the truth sat right there, simple and frightening.

"I need to feel like I'm not broken," I whispered.

Wyatt's eyes softened, something raw flickering under the calm. "You're not broken."

My laugh came out shaky. "I feel like I am."

Wyatt took one slow step closer, stopping again before he touched me, his hands still at his sides. His voice was quiet, steady. "Can I?"

The question hit me in the chest.

I nodded.

Wyatt's hand came up, warm and careful, and he cupped my cheek like I was something precious, like I was a person and not a problem. The contact sent a sharp wave through me, not just emotion, but sensation, like my skin had been waiting for kindness it could trust.

My eyes stung immediately.

Wyatt's thumb moved once, slow, wiping the edge of a tear I hadn't felt fall. His gaze held mine. "You came back."

"I did," I whispered.

I lifted my own hand slowly, hesitant, and touched his wrist. The skin there was warm, the veins under it real. He didn't move. He let me do it, let me set the pace.

My fingers curled lightly around him.

Wyatt's breath hitched, just once.

"Tessa," he said, low.

The way he said my name made my knees go soft. I stepped closer, closing the last inch, and my hand slid up to his jaw. His stubble scraped my palm, rough and grounding. My heart was pounding so hard it felt like it might bruise my ribs from the inside.

Wyatt didn't move.

He waited.

I tipped my face up, my breath catching as his thumb traced my cheekbone again, slow and steady, like he was reminding me I could be gentle and still be strong.

"I'm going to live in this house," I whispered, almost against his mouth now. "And I'm going to fight for this place. For him, for me, and for us."

Wyatt's gaze held mine. "That's all I've ever wanted."

The words hit deep, and I didn't have anything left in me to argue with them.

I rose onto my toes, my hand tightening on his jaw like I needed the anchor, like I needed the reality of him under my palm.

Wyatt stayed still, giving me the choice down to the last breath.

I closed the distance and kissed him.

It wasn't soft at first. It was shaky and hungry and careful all at once, like my body didn't know whether to cling or flee. His mouth was warm, his hand still cradling my cheek, and when he finally kissed me back, slow and steady, it felt like he was answering my fear with something I could hold.

My chest loosened on a broken breath.

I kissed him again, deeper this time, and the world didn't tilt. It didn't crack.

Forty-Five

Tessa

Fourteen days of waking up in Ray's house, my house, and getting shit done. The fence line on the north pasture didn't fix itself, so I fixed it. The gutters didn't clean themselves, so I climbed the damn ladder and did it myself. The paperwork Ray left behind didn't organize itself into something that made sense while I was gone. So I spent three nights at the kitchen table with a six pack of Hargrove beer and a calculator until it did.

I was doing it.

Work at the clinic had become my anchor. My hands were steady when they needed to be—holding a frightened dog still for vaccinations, reading the subtle tension in a horse's shoulder, speaking in that low voice that made animals trust me even when they were hurting. Brooke welcomed me back without fanfare, like she expected I was coming back.

Wyatt kept his word, exactly like I'd known he would.

No hovering. No showing up unannounced with excuses about "just checking in." He answered when I texted. He gave me space when I didn't. Three nights ago, when I asked him over for dinner, he'd shown up with wine and stayed in his lane in my kitchen, letting me lead.

When he left that night, he kissed me at the door, slow and deliberate, his hand firm at the back of my neck, and then he'd driven home without asking to stay.

I wanted him to stay.

But I hadn't been ready to ask.

Tonight was different.

Tonight, standing in my bathroom after a long shift at the clinic, I wasn't second-guessing myself. I knew what I wanted. I spent two weeks rebuilding my life on my own terms, proving to myself that I could stand on my own two feet, and now I wanted Wyatt in my bed. Not because I was lonely or scared or looking for someone to make me feel whole.

Because I wanted him. Because he made me feel like myself, only better. Because choosing him didn't mean losing myself anymore.

I pulled out my phone and typed the message without hesitation.

> Me: Come over tonight.

Not a question. A statement.

His reply came within seconds.

> Wyatt: Everything okay?

I smiled at the screen, shaking my head. Of course, that was his first thought.

> Me: Everything's fine. I want to see you.
> Come over.

Three dots appeared, disappeared, appeared again.

Wyatt: I'll be there in twenty.

I set the phone down and looked at myself in the mirror. Hair still damp from the quick shower I'd taken after washing the smell of antiseptic and animals off my skin. No makeup. Jeans that fit well and a soft flannel shirt, I left unbuttoned enough to be interesting.

I looked like myself. Strong and a little rough around the edges. Exactly how I felt.

When Wyatt's headlights swept across the front windows, my stomach tightened with anticipation, not anxiety.

I met him at the door, pulling it open before he could knock.

He stood on the porch, hands in his pockets, and his gaze did that thing it always did, moving over me, reading me, making sure I was okay. But this time, when his eyes met mine, something shifted in his expression. Like he could see exactly what I was thinking.

"Hey," he said, voice low and a little rough.

"Hey, yourself," I answered, and stepped back to let him in.

Wyatt crossed the threshold, and I caught the scent of him, cedar and cold air, soap and something underneath that was just him. He showered too. Changed into a clean shirt. His jaw was shadowed with stubble, and his hair looked like he'd run his hands through it a few times on the drive over.

God, I wanted him.

He turned to face me, starting to ask if I was okay, but I didn't let him finish.

I stepped into his space, reached up, and pulled his mouth down to mine.

Wyatt made a surprised sound against my lips, his hands moving to grip my hips, but he didn't hesitate. He kissed me back like he'd been thinking about it just as much as I had, his mouth hot and certain, his fingers tightening on my waist.

When I finally pulled back, we were both breathing hard.

"I don't want you to go home tonight," I said, looking him straight in the eye. "I want you to stay. In my bed. With me."

Wyatt's gaze darkened, his pupils blown wide. "Tessa."

"I'm not asking for permission," I interrupted, my voice steady. "I'm telling you what I want. And if you want it too, then stop looking at me like I might break and kiss me again."

Something flashed in his eyes, heat and hunger and something almost like relief.

"I'm not worried you'll break," Wyatt said, his voice dropping lower. "I'm trying to make sure I don't mess this up."

I slid my hands up his chest, feeling the hard muscle beneath the soft cotton, feeling his heart beating fast under my palms. "You won't mess it up. I know what I want, Wyatt. I've known for days. I just needed to be sure I was doing this for the right reasons."

"And are you?" His hands flexed on my hips.

"Yeah." I met his gaze without flinching. "I'm doing this because I want you. Because I've been thinking about your hands on me and your mouth on me and what it would feel like to let myself have something good without overthinking it to death."

Wyatt's breath left him in a rush. "Jesus, Tessa."

"So stop being careful with me," I said, rising up on my toes so my mouth was almost against his. "I'm not fragile. I'm healing, and there's a difference."

His hands slid from my hips to the small of my back, pulling me flush against him, and I could feel every hard line of his body against mine.

"Tell me if you need me to stop," he said against my mouth. "Any time. Any reason?"

"I will," I promised. "But I won't need to."

I kissed him again, harder this time, letting my teeth catch his bottom lip. Wyatt groaned, low in his throat, and his control slipped just enough that I felt it, the want he'd been keeping leashed, the desire he'd been holding back out of respect for my boundaries.

I wanted all of it.

My hands found the buttons of his shirt, and this time they didn't shake. I worked them open with steady fingers, revealing his chest inch by inch. Tan skin. Defined muscle. That scar near his collarbone I'd noticed before and wanted to trace with my tongue.

Wyatt watched me, his breathing rough, his hands still on my back but not moving, letting me set the pace.

I pushed his shirt off his shoulders and let it fall to the floor.

"Your turn," I said, my voice lower now, husky with want.

Wyatt's eyes flashed. His hands came to the buttons of my flannel, and he held my gaze as he undid them, one by one, slow and deliberate. When he pushed the fabric off my shoulders, I wasn't wearing anything underneath, and his sharp inhale was the best sound I'd heard in weeks.

"Tessa." My name was rough in his mouth, almost reverent.

"Bedroom. Now."

I took his hand and led him down the hallway, no hesitation, no second-guessing. My bedroom was exactly as I'd left it this morning, bed made, lamp on the nightstand casting warm light across the quilts Ray's mother stitched decades ago.

I turned to face Wyatt and reached for the button of my jeans.

His hand caught mine. "Let me."

It wasn't a request, not exactly, but it wasn't a demand either. It was an offer, and I took it.

"Okay," I breathed.

Wyatt's fingers made quick work of the button, the zipper, and then he was sliding the denim down my hips, taking my underwear with it, kneeling as he went, his hands warm and sure on my thighs. When the jeans pooled at my feet, I stepped out of them, standing in front of him in nothing.

He looked up at me from his knees, and the expression on his face made the heat pool low in my belly.

"You're so damn beautiful," he said, his voice rough.

I reached down and threaded my fingers through his hair, tugging just hard enough to make him groan. "Get up here. Now."

Wyatt rose, his hands skimming up my sides, and I reached for his belt. This time, he didn't stop me. I got it undone, popped the button of his jeans, and slid the zipper down slowly, my knuckles brushing against the hard length of him straining against his boxers.

His breath hissed out. "Tessa."

"Off," I said, hooking my fingers in his waistband.

He pushed both jeans and boxers down in one motion, kicking them aside, and then we were both naked, standing in my bedroom. My gaze dropped, taking in all of him, broad shoulders, defined chest, the trail of dark hair leading down to where he was hard and ready for me.

The wanting was so sharp it almost hurt. Wyatt's eyes flashed dark, and he moved, backing me up until my legs hit the mattress. I sat, then scooted back, and he followed me down, covering my body with his.

The first full press of skin on skin made us both gasp.

"Christ," Wyatt muttered against my neck. "You feel so good."

His mouth found mine, kissing me deep and hungry while his hand slid down my body. There was nothing between us, and his hand was sliding up the inside of my thigh, slow and deliberate.

"Tell me what you want," he murmured against my lips.

"Touch me," I breathed. "I want your hands on me."

His fingers found me, slick and ready, and I gasped at the contact. Wyatt groaned low in his throat. "God, Tessa. You're so wet."

"For you," I managed, my hips rocking into his hand. "All for you."

He worked me with sure, steady strokes, his thumb circling where I needed it most while his fingers slid inside me. The pleasure built fast and sharp, stealing my breath.

"That's it," Wyatt said roughly, watching my face. "Let me see you."

I gripped his shoulders, my nails digging in as the tension coiled tighter. "Don't stop. Please don't stop."

"Never," he promised, and increased the pressure, the rhythm, until I was gasping his name and arching off the bed.

The orgasm hit me hard, waves of pleasure rolling through me, and Wyatt worked me through it, his mouth on my neck, murmuring words I couldn't quite hear over the rushing in my ears.

When I finally came down, panting and boneless, I opened my eyes to find him watching me with such raw hunger it sent another spike of heat through my core.

"I need you inside me," I said, reaching between us to wrap my hand around his length. He was hot and hard and velvet over steel. "Now, Wyatt."

His hips jerked into my grip, and he groaned. "Condom. Wallet."

I released him reluctantly while he reached for his jeans, fumbling in his back pocket. He came back with a foil packet, tore it open with his teeth, and I took it from him.

"Let me," I said.

I rolled it on slowly, stroking him as I did, watching his jaw clench and his eyes go dark. When I was done, I lay back and pulled him over me.

"Come here," I whispered.

Wyatt settled between my thighs, bracing himself on his forearms, his face inches from mine. The blunt head of him pressed against my entrance, and we both went still.

"You sure?" he asked, his voice strained.

"I've never been more sure of anything." I wrapped my legs around his waist and pulled him down. "I want all of you."

He pushed inside, slow and steady, and the stretch and fullness of him made my eyes roll back. God, it had been so long, and nothing had ever felt like this—like coming home and jumping off a cliff at the same time.

"Fuck," Wyatt groaned when he was fully seated. "Tessa. You feel—" He couldn't finish, just dropped his forehead to mine, breathing hard.

I rolled my hips experimentally, and we both gasped. He pulled out almost all the way, then thrust back in, deep and sure. I cried out, my hands clutching at his back.

"Like that?" he asked roughly.

"Yes. Just like that. Harder."

Wyatt set a rhythm that had me meeting him thrust for thrust, our bodies moving together like we'd been doing this for years instead of the first time in weeks. His mouth found mine, kissing me deep and dirty while he drove into me again and again.

The pleasure built fast, that coiling tension gathering low in my belly.

He slid his hand between us and circled my clit with his thumb while he thrust into me, and the dual sensation had me gasping.

"That's it, baby," Wyatt encouraged, his voice rough.

The orgasm slammed into me without warning, my inner

muscles clamping down on him so hard he cursed. I cried out his name as the pleasure ripped through me, wave after wave.

"Jesus, Tessa." Wyatt's rhythm stuttered, and then he was following me over.

We stayed like that for a long moment, both of us trembling and gasping for air. Finally, Wyatt rolled to the side, taking care of the condom before pulling me against his chest.

"That was—" I started, but couldn't find the words.

"Yeah," Wyatt agreed, his hand stroking down my spine. "It was."

I tilted my head up to look at him, and the expression on his face made my chest tight. "We're definitely doing that again."

His laugh was low and warm. "Give me twenty minutes."

"Deal."

It turned out he only needed fifteen.

The second time, I pushed him onto his back and climbed on top, taking my time as I sank down onto him inch by inch. Wyatt's hands gripped my hips, his eyes locked on where we were joined.

"Look at you," he said roughly. "Riding me like you've made me yours."

"Maybe I have," I said, rolling my hips in a slow circle that made him groan.

"Take what you want," he said. "I'm yours."

I braced my hands on his chest and started to move, finding a rhythm that had pleasure sparking up my spine with every roll of my hips. Wyatt let me control the pace at first, watching me with dark, hungry eyes. But when I started to move faster, chasing my release, his hands tightened on my hips, and he started thrusting up to meet me.

"That's it," I gasped. "Just like that. Don't do anything different."

One of his hands slid up to cup my breast, his thumb circling my nipple, and the added sensation had me crying out.

"You're so fucking perfect," Wyatt growled. "Look at you, take what you need from me. So strong. So beautiful. So fucking sexy bouncing on my cock."

His words pushed me higher, and when he slid his other hand between my legs, the heel of his palm pressed against my clit, and he squeezed his fingers into my pussy. The sensation of his cock and fingers pushed me over the edge, and I shattered. My inner muscles clenched around him as I came with a sharp cry, my body shaking with the force of it.

Wyatt followed moments later with a groan, his hips jerking up as he spilled inside me.

I collapsed onto his chest, both of us breathing hard and slick with sweat.

"Okay," I panted. "Now I'm satisfied."

Wyatt's laugh rumbled beneath my cheek. "Just satisfied? I must be losing my touch."

I lifted my head to glare at him. "Don't fish for compliments."

"Was that what I was doing?" His eyes sparkled with mischief.

"You know exactly what you were doing." I kissed him, slow and deep. "And for the record, you definitely haven't lost your touch."

"Good to know." He rolled us so I was on my back again, his body covering mine. "Because I'm not done with you yet."

Heat flared through me despite the fact that I'd just come twice. "Oh?"

"Third time's the charm," he said, his mouth trailing down my throat. "And this time, I'm taking my time."

He did.

By the time the sky started to darken outside my window,

I was thoroughly satisfied, completely spent, and certain that I just had the best sex of my life.

When Wyatt's breathing finally steadied, his forehead pressed to mine, his body still covering me like a shield I didn't need but wanted anyway, he said my name like it was the only word that mattered.

"Tessa."

I opened my eyes and found him watching me with an expression I couldn't fully name. Something raw and open and almost undone.

"You okay?" I asked, and a smile tugged at my mouth because usually he was the one asking me that.

Wyatt huffed a laugh, breathless. "Yeah. More than okay." He shifted his weight, careful not to crush me, and brushed a strand of hair off my forehead. "You?"

"I'm perfect," I said, and meant it.

His thumb traced my jaw, slow and reverent. "You are."

I rolled my eyes, but the warmth in my chest didn't fade. "I mean, I feel perfect. Good. Really good."

"Good." Wyatt's voice dropped lower.

By the time the sun started creeping through the curtains, we were tangled together under the quilt, slick with sweat and completely spent.

Wyatt's arm was slung across my waist, his face buried in my neck, and I could feel his heartbeat against my back, steady and strong.

"You should stay for breakfast," I murmured, my voice rough from overuse.

Wyatt's lips brushed the curve of my shoulder. "Are you cooking?"

"I was thinking you could cook."

He laughed, low and warm against my skin. "Fair enough. I wore you out, the least I can do is feed you."

I smiled into the pillow, feeling lighter than I had in months. Maybe years.

This, lying here with him, knowing I'd chosen it freely, knowing I could choose it again or not choose it, and either way I'd still be whole, this felt like coming home to myself.

"Wyatt," I said quietly.

"Hmm?"

"Thank you."

He stilled behind me. "For what?"

"For waiting. For not pushing. For letting me come to you when I was ready."

Wyatt's arm tightened around me, pulling me closer. "You don't have to thank me for that."

"I know," I said. "But I'm going to anyway."

He was quiet for a moment, his breath warm against my neck. Then, soft enough, I almost missed it, "I love you."

My heart stuttered.

It wasn't the first time he said it. He told me two weeks ago, standing in my apartment with my whole life in chaos around me. But hearing it now, in the aftermath of this, of choosing him, of choosing us, of choosing myself first and then him second, it landed differently.

It landed true.

I turned in his arms until I was facing him, my hand coming up to cup his jaw.

"I know," I whispered. "And I'm getting there."

Wyatt's eyes softened. "That's all I need."

I kissed him, slow and sweet and unhurried, and for the first time in my life, I understood what it meant to be truly wanted. To be loved without being diminished.

To be my own person and his but still completely whole.

When we finally dragged ourselves out of bed, Wyatt pulled on his jeans and wandered into my kitchen shirtless, rummaging through my fridge like he belonged here.

I watched him from the doorway, wearing nothing but his shirt from last night and a pair of underwear, my hair a disaster, and my body pleasantly sore in all the right places.

"You have eggs," he called over his shoulder. "And bacon. I can work with this."

"There's coffee too," I said, moving to the counter and starting the pot.

Wyatt glanced at me, his gaze tracking over the shirt I was wearing, and something heated in his expression. "You look good in my clothes."

"I look good in everything," I shot back, grinning.

He laughed. "True."

We moved around each other easily, falling into a rhythm that felt natural. He cooked. I poured coffee. We didn't talk much, but the quiet was punctuated only by the sizzle of bacon and the occasional brush of his hand against mine when we passed each other.

When breakfast was ready, we sat at the small kitchen table Ray had built decades ago, and I looked across at Wyatt—at this man who'd been patient when I needed patience, who'd given me space when I needed space, who'd shown up when I asked him to without making me feel weak for asking.

"What?" he asked, catching me staring.

"Nothing," I said. "It's just, this is nice."

His mouth curved. "Yeah. It is."

We ate in comfortable silence, and when we were done, Wyatt helped me clean up without being asked. I went and reluctantly changed out of his shirt into my scrubs.

"I should probably head out," he said eventually, leaning against the counter, doing up the buttons on his shirt. "I need to head to the brewery."

I nodded, even though part of me wanted him to stay. "I've got to get to work too."

Wyatt reached for me, pulling me close, and I went willingly, my arms looping around his neck. "Last night," he said against my hair. "That was—"

"Perfect," I interrupted. "It was perfect."

He pulled back just enough to look at me, his hand coming up to cup my face. "You're perfect."

I rolled my eyes, but I was smiling. "Stop."

"Never."

He kissed me one more time, slow and thorough, and then he pulled away with visible reluctance.

"I'll see you soon," he said.

"Yeah," I agreed. "You will."

I walked him to the door and watched as he climbed into his truck, gave me one last look through the windshield that made my stomach flip, and drove away.

When the dust settled on the driveway, I closed the door and leaned against it, a smile spreading across my face.

I'd done it.

I'd chosen something for myself. Something good. Something that didn't require me to shrink or apologize or explain.

And it felt damn good.

I pushed off the door and headed back to my bedroom, pulling on my socks and boots. I grabbed the truck keys off the hook.

But for a second, I stood in the middle of my house and let myself accept that it was mine.

The strength. The choice. The certainty that I was exactly where I was supposed to be.

And for the first time in a long time, I believed it.

"Thanks, Dad," I whispered before I headed out.

EPILOGUE
TESSA

The late afternoon sun slanted across the kitchen table where I sat with a mug of coffee, reviewing supply orders for the clinic. Outside, I could hear the steady rhythm of Wyatt working in the barn, the clang of metal on metal as he fixed something that had probably been broken for weeks.

It had been a year since I'd come back to this place, to Ray's land—my land—and decided to stop running. A year of early mornings and late nights, of learning how to balance the ranch work with my shifts at the clinic, of figuring out what it meant to build a life that was entirely mine while letting someone else be part of it.

The house had changed. Small things, mostly. New curtains in the living room. A repaired porch railing. The garden plots I started as a kid now yield everything I'd need to get through the winter again. Dad's things were still here—his books, his tools, the photographs I'd finally been brave enough to hang on the walls—but they shared space with mine now. With ours.

Wyatt's truck keys on the hook by the door. His boots by mine. His coffee mug in the dish rack.

He didn't live here. Not officially. He had his place, and his ranch to run, the brewery in town that had become more popular as the days passed. But most nights, he was here. And the nights he wasn't, I drove to his place and fell asleep in his bed.

We'd found our rhythm. Independent but intertwined. Strong on our own, stronger together.

I heard his footsteps on the porch before the screen door opened.

"Hey," Wyatt said, kicking off his boots. "You got a minute?"

I looked up from the supply order and immediately clocked the tension in his shoulders. "What's wrong?"

He ran a hand through his hair, a gesture I learned meant he was working through something complicated. "Just got off the phone with Maddy."

My stomach tightened. "Is she okay?" I asked.

"Yeah. She's—" Wyatt pulled out the chair across from me and sat heavily. "Her mom wants her to move here. With me. Permanently."

I blinked. "What?"

His jaw tightened. "Apparently, her priorities have changed. She wants to focus on her marriage, travel with her husband. Having a teenager around doesn't fit the lifestyle she's after."

The bitterness in his voice was sharp enough to cut.

"Jesus," I said quietly.

"Yeah." Wyatt leaned back in his chair, staring at the ceiling. "So Maddy's moving here. At the end of the month. She'll start school here in the fall."

My mind raced. Maddy here permanently.

"How does Maddy feel about it?" I asked carefully.

Wyatt's laugh was hollow. "She's trying to be tough about it. Says she's fine, that she likes it here better anyway. But I can hear it in her voice—she feels like her mom's choosing her husband over her."

"Because that's exactly what Rena is doing," I said bluntly.

"Yeah." Wyatt scrubbed a hand over his face. "Maddy asked if you were okay with it. With her being here full-time."

My chest tightened. "What did you tell her?"

"That you'd be thrilled. Because you will be, right?" He looked at me, and I saw the vulnerability there. "I know it changes things. We've had it good this past year. This will be different."

I reached across the table and covered his hand with mine. "Maddy's family. She's always been welcome here. This is just making it official."

"She's going to need you," Wyatt said quietly. "More than she has before. She's going to be hurting, even if she won't show it. And I'm going to be figuring out how to be a full-time parent instead of the fun weekend dad."

"We'll figure it out together," I said firmly. "All three of us."

My phone buzzed on the table. I glanced at the screen and felt a smile tug at my lips.

> Maddy: Is it weird that I'm kind of excited? I mean, my mom sucks right now, but at least I get to live with you and Dad full-time. And the horses.

I showed Wyatt the text. Some of the tension left his shoulders as he read it.

"She's going to be okay," I said softly. "She's tougher than you think. Wonder where she gets that from."

Wyatt's laugh was rough but genuine. "Text her back. Tell her we're excited too."

Me: Not weird at all. Your room at your dad's place is going to need decorating it still looks like it belongs to a little girl. I'm thinking we can make a girls' trip out of it, head to the city. What do you say?

Maddy: YES. Can we get those fairy lights? And maybe paint one wall a different colour?

Me: Whatever you want, kiddo.

Maddy: I love you, Tessa.

My throat tightened as I typed back.

Me: Love you too.

Wyatt watched me over the edge of his coffee mug, something soft in his expression. "You're good with her."

"She makes it easy," I said honestly. "She's a great kid."

"Yeah, she is." He set down his mug. "I just hate that Rena's making her feel like she's not wanted."

"Maddy knows she's wanted here," I said firmly. "By both of us. That's what matters."

Wyatt's fingers tightened on mine. "I'm going to need to be at my place more, at least at first. Let her settle in without feeling like she's intruding on what we have here."

"That makes sense," I said, even though the thought of fewer nights with him made my chest ache. "She needs to know your place is her home."

"But I don't want you to feel like I'm pulling away," Wyatt continued. "Or like you're less important. You're not. You're —" He paused, searching for words. "You're it for me, Tessa. You know that, right?"

Heat crept up my neck. Even after a year, hearing him say things like that still did things to my chest. "I know. And I'm not going anywhere. Maddy needs her dad right now, and I support that completely. We'll adjust."

Wyatt stood, pulling me up with him, and wrapped his arms around me. I pressed my face into his chest, breathing in the familiar scent of him—sweat and hay and the faint smell of hops from the brewery.

"What did I do to deserve you?" he murmured.

"You showed up when I needed you," I said simply. "Now I'm returning the favour. For both of you."

He pulled back just enough to kiss me, slow and sweet, and I let myself sink into it. A year ago, I'd been terrified that wanting him meant losing myself. Now I knew better. Wanting him, choosing him, loving him—and loving Maddy too—it had only made me find my true self.

When we finally broke apart, I glanced at the clock on the wall. "I need to get back to the clinic. Brooke's got a surgery scheduled at four, and she'll need help prepping."

Wyatt nodded. "I've got to head to the brewery anyway. Got a meeting with the distributor about expanding to more locations."

"Look at you, business tycoon," I teased.

"Hardly." But he was smiling. "Are you coming back here tonight?"

"Yeah. I'll pick up groceries on the way home. We're out of everything."

"I'll cook," Wyatt offered.

"You always cook."

"That's because you burn water."

I swatted his chest. "I'm getting better."

"You made toast this morning without setting off the smoke alarm. I'm very proud."

"Ass."

He grinned and kissed me again. "See you tonight."

"Wyatt," I said as my heart threatened to beat out of my chest. He turned as he headed for the door. "I love you."

He froze, all emotion fell off his face, before he broke out in a grin. "I know, love you, babe." He winked at that was it. No drums or trombones, just us.

The clinic was quiet when I arrived, the waiting room empty except for Mrs. Patterson's ancient tabby in a carrier, waiting for his yearly checkup. I waved at Susan, the receptionist, and headed back to the exam rooms.

"Tessa, good, you're here," Brooke said, looking up from where she was reviewing charts at the small desk in the corner. "I need you to prep the surgical suite. Mrs. Kowalski's bringing in her Lab for that mass removal."

"On it," I said, already moving toward the supply cabinet.

I was elbow-deep in surgical prep when Brooke joined me, already scrubbing in.

"How's the ranch?" she asked.

"Good. Fixed the fence on the south pasture last week. I still need to get the barn roof patched before winter."

"Are you doing that yourself?"

"Probably. Unless I can convince Wyatt to help."

Brooke smiled faintly. "Well that won't take much convincing. How is Wyatt?"

"Good. Busy with the brewery." I hesitated, then added, "Maddy's moving here. She'll be starting school in the fall."

"She's the same age as Jackson." Brooke's tone was carefully neutral. "That'll be an adjustment."

"Yeah."

We worked in silence for a few minutes, the familiar routine of preparing for surgery. I'd done this enough times that my hands knew the movements without thought—laying out instruments, checking the anesthesia machine, making sure everything was exactly where Brooke would need it.

"Jackson's been hanging out at the fire hall all summer. I wish he'd find a different hobby, I don't like what Bill fills his head with." Brooke said, eventually, with a sigh. I was sure it was hard for her. Her husband had been a firefighter. Grant passed away in a car accident three years ago, so she kept a pretty close watch on Jackson.

"Maybe when Maddy gets here, we can get the two of them in the same place. He can help her settle in. They can hang out at Wyatt's. There's enough people around all the time." I handed her a towel.

"That might be good, thanks, Tessa." Brooke's worry eased from her face

The surgery went smoothly. Mrs. Kowalski's Lab came through without complications, and by the time we'd finished closing and moved him to recovery, it was nearly six.

<hr>

Wyatt

The distributor meeting at the brewery ran longer than I'd planned. By the time Marcus finally signed off on expanding distribution to three more towns, it was nearly five, and I still had evening chores waiting at home.

I was loading equipment into the truck bed when my phone rang. Unknown number with a 403 area code. Calgary.

I almost didn't answer. Then something made me swipe to accept.

"Hello?"

"Wyatt?" The voice was familiar, even after all these years. Deep, with that slight rasp that came from too much smoke inhalation and not enough water.

My hand tightened on the phone. "Cal?"

"Yeah," Cal Mercer laughed, and I could picture him perfectly—leaning against whatever surface was closest, that crooked grin that had gotten us both into and out of trouble more times than I could count. "Been a while."

"Six years," I said, my mind already calculating. Six years since I'd met him in Jasper. "What's going on? Is everything okay?"

"Everything's good. Better than good, actually." There was a pause, and I heard papers rustling in the background. "I got a promotion. Provincial Wildfire Supervisor."

"Cal, that's—" I stopped, processing. "That's huge. Congratulations."

"Thanks. Means I'll be traveling more, overseeing crews across Alberta. But here's the thing—they're stationing me regionally."

Something cold settled in my gut. I knew what he was going to say before he said it.

"They picked home," Cal said quietly. "I'm coming back, Wyatt. End of the month."

I stared at the brewery parking lot, at the mountains in the distance turning purple in the fading light. Cal Mercer. Coming back.

"That's good," I managed. "It'll be good to have you around again."

"Yeah?" Cal's voice carried something I couldn't quite read. Relief, maybe. Or concern. "I wasn't sure how you'd feel about it. We didn't exactly leave things on the best of terms."

That was an understatement. The last time I'd seen Cal, we'd been standing in the parking lot of the Rusty Spur, both of us half-drunk and fully pissed off, saying things that probably should've ended a friendship. I'd told him he was running away. He'd told me I was burying myself alive.

Turned out we'd both been right.

"That was a long time ago," I said. "We were different people."

"Were we?" Cal asked, and there was something in his voice that made me think he'd been wondering the same thing. "I don't know, man. Some things don't change as much as we'd like to think."

I thought about Tessa. About Maddy. About the life I'd built in those six years, piece by careful piece.

"Some things do," I said.

Cal was quiet for a moment. "Are you seeing someone?"

"Yeah. Tessa. She's—" I stopped, not sure how to explain what Tessa was. What she meant. "She's everything I need."

"I'm glad," Cal said, and he sounded like he meant it. "You deserve that."

"What about you?"

"Married to the job," Cal said with a laugh that didn't quite land. "Same as always."

I leaned against the truck, watching the last of the sunlight fade. "When you get back, we should grab a drink."

"I'd like that." Cal paused. "And Wyatt? I know things are probably going to be... complicated. With me being back. But I'm hoping we can put the past behind us."

"Yeah," I said. "Me too."

We said our goodbyes, and I ended the call, staring at my phone for a long moment.

Cal Mercer was coming back.

That meant questions I thought were buried would resurface. History that stayed safely in the past would be present again. And Brooke—

I pocketed my phone and climbed into the truck. Whatever complications Cal's return would bring, I'd deal with them when the time came. Right now, I have a woman waiting for me who made everything else feel manageable.

Even the ghosts of old friendships and complicated histories.

Tessa

I finished cleaning up and was heading toward the front when I nearly ran into Brooke in the hallway. She had her phone in her hand, and her face had gone carefully blank in a way that made me pay attention.

"Everything okay?" I asked.

Brooke looked up, and for just a second, I saw something raw flicker across her expression before she smoothed it away. "Fine. Just got a call from an old friend. Someone I haven't heard from in a long time."

"Good news?"

Her laugh was short, humourless. "Complicated news." She slipped her phone into her pocket.

"Well, if you ever want to talk about it," I offered.

Brooke's smile was tight. "I appreciate that. But some things are better left in the past."

She walked away before I could respond, and I watched her go, wondering what kind of history could put that look on her face.

By the time I got home, the sun was setting, painting the sky in shades of orange and pink. Wyatt's truck was already in the driveway, and when I walked in with bags of groceries, I found him in the kitchen, already pulling out pans and ingredients.

"You weren't kidding about cooking," I said, setting the bags on the counter.

"Figured you'd had a long day." He kissed my temple as he passed by to grab an onion. "How'd the surgery go?"

"Perfect. Brooke's good. Really good."

"That's good." Wyatt started chopping with practiced ease. "You tell her about Maddy?"

"Yeah. She offered to have Jackson show Maddy around school when she starts. They're the same age."

Wyatt's hands stilled. "That's... that's really nice of her."

"Brooke's practical like that. Sees a problem, offers a solution." I hopped up onto the counter, watching him work. "She got a weird text today, too. She seemed pretty rattled by it."

"Yeah?" Wyatt's voice was carefully casual.

"She said it was complicated."

Wyatt's jaw tightened, just slightly. "Lots of complicated histories in a small town."

I studied him. "You know something."

He looked up, meeting my eyes. "Cal Mercer's coming back. He was a wildfire fighter before he moved up to management. Brooke used to be—" He paused. "I don't know exactly what happened, but he just up and left after the fire that she was caught in."

The kitchen fell quiet except for the sizzle of onions hitting the hot pan.

"I remember him, he was a bit older than me," I said finally.

"Aren't we all," Wyatt said flatly as he set down the knife and turned to face me, his hands bracing on either side of my thighs on the counter.

"Yes, you are old, man," I giggled.

"Pretty sure you can't tell I'm older." He winked, and he was right. There wasn't anything slowing this man down. "And right now I'm thinking about you, and me, and the fact that I get to come home to you every night."

I looped my arms around his neck. "Oh, that was sappy."

"True though."

"Can't argue with that."

He kissed me, and I let myself forget about Maddy's

impending arrival, about Cal Mercer coming back to town, about the way Brooke's face had gone carefully blank. Right now, at this moment, it was just us. Just me and Wyatt and the life we'd built together, one choice at a time.

When we finally broke apart, Wyatt rested his forehead against mine.

"Thank you," he said quietly.

"For what?"

"For choosing me."

I cupped his face in my hands. "Best choice I ever made."

And I meant it. A year ago, I'd been terrified coming back here meant giving up my independence, my strength, my sense of self. Instead, I found all of it and more. I found home. I found purpose. found a man who loved me without trying to own me, who gave me space to be strong while offering his strength when I needed it.

I found myself.

"Come on," I said, sliding off the counter. "Let's make dinner. And then you can show me just how much our age difference doesn't matter ."

Wyatt's smile was soft, genuine. "All night, babe."

I laughed and shook my head, because he wasn't lying; it would be all night.

Outside, the sun finished setting, and inside, we made dinner in comfortable silence, side by side. Just like we would tomorrow, and the day after that, and all the days that came after.

Whatever challenges were coming, we'd face them together.

And we'd be just fine.

Sneak Peek of Rough Enough

Brooke

I wiped a bead of sweat from my forehead with the back of my gloved hand, narrowing my eyes against the glare of the sun through the barn window. It bounced off the limestone peaks of the Rockies like a warning, sharp and unforgiving. Up here, where the foothills began their steep, rocky climb toward the clouds, the heat was different. It was dry, a thirsty heat that sucked the moisture out of the grass until it turned to gold-leaf tinder.

I was chest-deep in a stall at the Hargrove ranch, my shoulder pressed against the warm, twitching flank of a mare named Duchess. She was three weeks overdue and remarkably cranky about it. The barn was dim, the air thick with the scent of sweet hay, old manure, and the sharp, medicinal tang of the antiseptic I'd used to scrub in.

"Easy, Duchess," I murmured. My voice was a low, rhythmic rasp, a tool I'd spent nearly two decades perfecting. It was a voice designed to bridge the gap between human anxiety and animal instinct. It had calmed everything from thousand-pound bulls to feral barn cats, and usually, it worked on me, too.

But not today.

Today, the skin along my shoulder blades, the skin that stayed tight, silvered, and forever sensitive beneath my cotton shirt, was prickling. It was a phantom itch, a deep-seated hum in my nervous system that usually preceded a storm. Or a disaster.

Beside me, Tessa Hargrove held the mare's lead rope. She was more than just my vet tech; she was a friend in a town where friendship usually came with a side of heavy-handed judgment. She looked toward the open barn doors, her nose wrinkling as she caught the draft.

"The wind is shifting, Brooke," she said softly. "It's coming from the south now. Smells like the Porcupine Hills are catching it again."

I didn't look up. I couldn't afford to. I was currently navigating the mare's internal anatomy, feeling for the position of a foal that seemed determined to stay put. "As long as it stays on the other side of the ridge," I said, though the words felt hollow. In Alberta, a mountain ridge was a polite suggestion to a wildfire, not a barrier. When the Chinook winds started howling through the passes, fire didn't just crawl; it flew.

I finished my exam and slowly withdrew, stripping off the shoulder-length plastic glove with a wet snap. Duchess let out a long, shuddering sigh, her tail swishing in annoyance.

"She's just stubborn, Tessa. Like her owner." I stepped back, wiping my hands on a clean towel. "The foal is positioned correctly, heart rate is strong. She's just not ready to let go yet. Give her another twenty-four hours. If she hasn't dropped by tomorrow morning, we'll talk about inducing, but I'd rather not force the issue if I don't have to."

"Wyatt's already pacing the brewery floor," Tessa said with a tired, affectionate smile, patting Duchess's neck. "Between the foal and Maddy moving back next week, he's a walking heart attack. He keeps checking the horizon like he can scare the smoke away just by glaring at it."

I headed for the wash station in the corner of the barn, the cold water stinging my cracked knuckles. "Maddy's a good kid. She'll be good for Jackson. He's spent too much time this summer pretending he's a thirty-year-old ranch hand. He needs someone his own age to remind him he's still fifteen."

I thought of my son, Jackson, likely at the fire station right now, hanging on every word Chief Bill Evans said. It was a constant source of friction between us, his idolization of a man I barely tolerated, and his obsession with a profession that had nearly ended my life before it had even begun. To Jackson, fire was a thrill, a legacy. To me, it was the monster that lived in my nightmares.

I was still scrubbing, the water turning a murky brown in the galvanized sink, when the first siren cut through the heavy afternoon air.

It wasn't the high-pitched, frantic yelp of a police cruiser. It was the deep, guttural wail of the River's Edge Fire Department's heavy bush trucks. The sound vibrated in my teeth, a low-frequency hum that made my breath hitch.

"Two trucks," Tessa whispered, stepping out into the light to look toward the main road. "That's more than a ditch fire. If Bill is rolling the heavies, something is crowning."

I dried my hands, my movements stiff and robotic. I followed her to the barn door, the transition from the cool shade to the searing sunlight making my head throb. We watched as a white supervisor's truck crested the hill, kicking up a plume of grey dust that hung in the stagnant air like a shroud.

My heart did a slow, sickening roll in my chest.

It wasn't the truck I recognized. It wasn't Bill Evans's aging, dented Chevy with the faded decals.

This was new. High-clearance, decked out with the latest

comms arrays, and sporting the provincial wildfire insignia on the door. It looked like a predator, sleek, efficient, and out of place in our sleepy, dusty valley.

The truck slowed as it passed the Hargrove driveway. The driver didn't turn his head, but even through the dust and the glare of the windshield, the profile was unmistakable. I'd seen it on the back of my eyelids for nineteen years. The sharp line of the jaw. The set of those broad, immovable shoulders. The way he gripped the wheel at ten and two, like he was trying to choke the life out of it.

Cal Mercer.

The world seemed to go silent, the roar of the sirens fading into a dull roar in my ears. The man who had pulled me from a furnace when I was nineteen, the man who had seen me at my absolute broken worst, and the man who had disappeared before the smoke had even cleared from my lungs.

"Is that?" Tessa started, her voice trailing off as she looked at me. She wasn't just my tech; she knew the town lore. She grew up here but was a bit younger than I was. When Tessa came back to town, and started working for me she put together the "official" version of the night Grant Tanner became a hero and Cal Mercer became a coward who ran.

"He's the new Regional Supervisor," I said. My voice sounded thin, like it was being filtered through a layer of ash. I forced myself to reach for my medical bag, the leather handle familiar and grounding. "I heard he was coming back. I just didn't think it would be today."

"Brooke, you're shaking," Tessa said, reaching out to touch my arm.

I pulled away, not out of unkindness, but because if I let anyone touch me right now, I'd shatter. "I'm fine. It's just the heat. And the wind."

I turned back toward my truck, my boots crunching on the gravel. I needed to move. I needed the routine of the clinic.

I needed to see Jackson and make sure he was nowhere near whatever fire Bill Evans was currently chasing.

"The wind is rising, Tessa," I said, my back to her as I climbed into the driver's seat of my vet rig. The interior of the truck was like an oven, the steering wheel hot enough to blister. "We need to get the portable oxygen units checked and the emergency burn kits restocked at the clinic. If this season is as bad as the forecast says, Duchess won't be the only one struggling to breathe. And if Cal Mercer is back in town, it means the province thinks we're about to burn."

I started the engine, the familiar rumble of the diesel motor a small comfort. As I backed out of the driveway, I saw the dust cloud from Cal's truck lingering on the road like a ghost.

I had spent a decade and a half building a life in the ruins of what happened nineteen years ago. I had a son I adored, a practice I'd fought for, and a husband I'd buried with all the honours this town could muster. I had kept my secrets tucked away beneath my clothes, hidden under the silvered lines of my skin.

But as I drove toward town, the scent of smoke grew stronger, bitter and biting.

Cal Mercer was back. And in a town like River's Edge, you couldn't keep a fire buried forever. Eventually, the wind always shifted.

The drive back to the clinic took me through the heart of River's Edge, or at least the three blocks that qualified as the heart. I passed the brewery, where I could see Wyatt Hargrove through the glass-fronted taproom, phone pressed to his ear and his eyes fixed on the horizon. He caught sight of my truck and gave a brief, tense nod. In a town this small, everyone's business was everyone's business, but the threat of fire was the one thing that superseded the gossip.

I pulled up to the clinic, a converted 1940s farmhouse on

the edge of town. It was a white-shingled building with a wrap-around porch and a sign that read River's Edge Veterinary Services. It was the only place I felt truly in control, the one place where I was Dr. Tanner, the woman with the answers, rather than Brooke, the girl who got burned.

As I stepped out of the truck, the heat hit me again, but there was something else in the air now. A tension. The town felt brittle.

I saw Jackson's bike leaned against the porch railing. My heart eased slightly. He was here, not at the station.

I walked inside, the bell above the door chiming with a cheerful sound that felt entirely wrong for the mood.

"Jackson?" I called out, tossing my keys onto the counter.

He appeared from the back room, a tall, lanky fifteen-year-old who seemed to grow an inch every time I blinked. He had Grant's hair, that thick, dark mahogany, and his restless energy. But he had my eyes.

"Did you see the truck, Mom?" he asked, his voice cracking slightly with excitement. He didn't wait for an answer. "The province sent a Supervisor. A real one. Chief Evans says he's a specialist."

I walked behind the counter, my hands trembling as I started organizing the patient files, anything to keep from looking at him. "I saw the truck, Jax."

"Chief Evans says he used to live here. He said he was a legend before he left." Jackson leaned against the counter, his eyes bright. "Do you remember him? Cal Mercer?"

I froze, a file folder gripped so tightly the cardboard crinkled. Do I remember him?

I remembered the way his laughter sounded in the dark. I remembered the way his hands felt, calloused and steady, on my waist. I remembered the way he looked at me like I was the only thing in the world that mattered, right up until the moment he let the world burn down around us.

"He was older than me, Jackson," I said, my voice remarkably steady despite the riot in my chest. "He left a long time ago. People change."

"Bill says he hasn't changed. Says he's still the best line-boss in the West." Jackson sighed, looking out the window toward the fire station. "I wish I could go out on the line with them. They're going to need help if the wind keeps up."

"No," I said, sharper than I intended. Jackson flinched, and I softened my tone, reaching out to squeeze his shoulder. "No, Jax. You're fifteen. You stay here. You help me with the animals. That's where the real work is during a fire. Not out there chasing smoke."

He shrugged me off, not with malice, but with the typical teenage need for distance. "Whatever, Mom. I'm going to go finish cleaning the kennels."

I watched him walk away, and for a second, I didn't see my son. I saw Grant. I saw the recklessness, the need to be the hero, the desperate urge to be seen.

I turned to the window, looking out toward the mountains. The smoke was thicker now, a bruised purple smudge against the blue sky.

Cal was out there. Somewhere in that smoke. And I knew, with the same certainty that I knew the Foal would eventually come, that he wasn't just here to fight the fire.

About the Author

Bonnie lives in southern Saskatchewan, Canada with her husband "Mr. Farmer", and two kids.

When she's not at her desk writing you will find her in the field helping "Mr. Farmer" with farm work, at the rink for hockey practice and games, or at the hall waiting for dance class to finish.

Also by Bonnie Poirier

Flying Diamond 5 Ranch Series

Rancher's Edge

Rancher's Pride

Rancher's Heart

Rancher's Strength

Flying Diamond 5 "Bedtime Stories"

Rancher's Rescue

Rancher's Healing

Gatlin Bourbon Brides Series

His Borrowed Bride

His Rescued Bride

His Ransomed Bride

The Morton Family Saga

The Arrangement

The Atonement

The Awakening

The Assignment

Heart of a Wounded Hero "Bedtime Story"

A Time to Heal